LOVE &
DEATH
IN
CYPRUS

LOVE & DEATH

IN

CYPRUS

HARRY BLACKLEY

This is a work of fiction. Names, characters, places and incidents are the products of the author's imagination or are used fictitiously, and any resemblance to actual persons, living or dead, business establishments, events or locales is entirely coincidental. Statements based on accounts of the time have been used to create a sense of authenticity

National Library of Australia Cataloguing-in-Publication data:

Blackley, Harry.
    Love and death in Cyprus.

    ISBN 0 646 44758 0.

    I. Title.

    823.4

Project management by Limelight Press Pty Ltd
Unit 15, 6 Thames Street
Balmain NSW 2041
ABN 80 095 617 897

Edited by Susan Rintoul

Designed by Lore Foye

Printed and bound by Griffin Press, South Australia

To all my family and friends

Special thanks to Gina, Hasan, Hilkat, Leyla, Nafia and Serkan for their support; to my editor, Susan Rintoul, and to Helen Bateman of Limelight Press who made the whole thing happen.

LONDON DAILY NEWS 19 SEPTEMBER 1958
Roger Smith, Nicosia, Cyprus

LEDRA STREET, *Nicosia's Murder Mile, has again been the scene of shootings. On a hot autumn day sudden and brutal death has once more come to Cyprus leaving a Greek Cypriot youth dead and a Turkish Cypriot woman in a critical condition. This brings the total number of innocent civilians killed in the past year to 21. The woman, whose name has not been released, was walking in Ledra Street at 3pm this afternoon when she was hit by two shots at close range. She was in the company of a British soldier. Eyewitnesses stated that the soldier, not in uniform, returned fire killing a sixteen-year-old youth. The youth has been identified as Tassos Papadopos. He died instantly after being shot in the head and chest. Police said that a gun was found next to Papadopos' body. Several Greek Cypriot witnesses have claimed that Papadopos did not fire the gun. None of the witnesses claim to have seen who did fire the shots. An Army spokesman stated that a British soldier is being questioned over the incident. Unconfirmed sources say that the soldier is a National Serviceman who has been in Cyprus for over a year and is believed to be involved in anti-terrorist activities. Sources state that his companion is the daughter of a well-known Turkish Cypriot. Her condition, in the Military Hospital, Nicosia, is reported as critical with severe wounds to the chest and lower leg. Her family is at her bedside. Greek Cypriots make up 80 per cent of the population. Archbishop Makarios III joined Colonel George Grivas to begin an armed struggle that commenced in 1955 to remove the British yoke. A secret organisation, EOKA (National Organisation of Cypriot Fighters) was formed and began a*

*terrorist campaign of sabotage and intimidation. The conflict
widened to bombings and murders with the result that British
troops were sent to Cyprus to quell the uprising. At present Britain
maintains close to 40,000 troops on the island but has had little
success in capturing the EOKA leaders. Grivas remains at large
despite massive search operations throughout the island. Sir Hugh
Foot, a diplomat, had replaced Sir John Harding, a military man,
as Governor in the hope that a negotiated settlement could be
reached. Despite his efforts, so far, Foot has had limited success
and this latest killing will only further inflame the situation.*

Cyprus 1958

Ledra Street was crowded with shoppers, Greeks, Turks and
British soldiers enjoying the latest cease-fire on the troubled
island of Cyprus, weary from years of murders, bombings and
curfews. Alexander and Leyla turned into the half-mile-long
street that runs straight until it reaches the Turkish quarter
where it ends in a T-intersection. Its pavements are littered
with bicycles and street vendors pushing carts between the
cars trying to drive through, and traffic grinds along slowly.
The smells of coffee, sweet sugary cakes and aromatic spices
filled the air. Alex Forbes strolled happily with his arm
protectively round the waist of his companion, a young
Turkish Cypriot woman, Leyla Ozkara. They made a
handsome couple, both tall and slim.

"You see, Leyla? Even though there's a truce, there are
several Military Police along the street. It's probably because
so many civilians have been shot here."

"It's terrible to think of women and children being shot in
the back. But let's forget all that, it's such a perfect day."

Couples strolled arm-in-arm, enjoying the warm sunshine
between the shadows cast by the buildings jammed on either
side of the narrow street.

"That's something you don't see in Scotland." He gave Leyla
a nudge.

"What's that?" She followed his look.

"There, those two men walking with their arms around each other."

"It's not unusual here. You must have seen it before."

"Suppose so. Must have done." He shrugged.

Alex wore cream shorts, long white socks and a blue shirt. Leyla was dressed in a long golden caftan style dress, pale green sandals and had a handkerchief pinned on top of her dark, brown hair, piled high.

"There's nothing like this in Dunkeith! Boy it's like a real Eastern bazaar."

"Look, Alexander," Leyla stopped at a shop selling spices, its baskets filled with rich red, yellow and dark brown powders. They meant nothing to Alex, the only flavourings he knew were tomato or HP sauce.

"This one is cardamom," she pointed to a basket filled with a dark rich powder. "And this is garlic," picking up a handful of what appeared to Alex to be flower bulbs like his mother planted in pots each winter.

Pepper, soft white cheese, saffron and tiny red chillies. It was all too much for Alex and, hand on her elbow, he gently moved her on to the next shop. Pots, pans, copper and brass, strange teapots and farm implements hung up on wire, the owner seated on a chair at the door, puffing away on a cigarette.

"This is so different. I could never go back to Dunkeith. It's dull and boring."

August is by far the cruellest month in Nicosia but the heat of summer remains unabated well into September when the days begin to grow shorter. The sun pours down for thirteen hours on the dry, dusty capital.

"It doesn't seem as busy as last time we were here."

"When it's hot like this, many people flee the city for the mountains where they have a small house in one of the cool valleys. Or some go to the beaches at Famagusta." Leyla squeezed his hand as she said Famagusta.

"Kyrenia's nice too. You get the evening sea breeze," Alex enthused.

"Oh, yes," she nodded. "Staying at a friend's house. A siesta between noon and three in the afternoon, then a long evening spent drinking coffee, eating and meeting old friends from distant parts. It's really nice. My father likes doing that."

In the old walled city of Nicosia, the only relief is the shade cast by the white painted houses crammed side by side. Before the first rays appear, shopkeepers are pulling up the metal cage shutters to expose their wares to passers-by.

Loud voices call out to strollers, "Come, Sir, come and see my beautiful gifts, buy something for the lovely lady. Join me inside where it's cool for some tea or cola."

The Armenian, Greek and Lebanese sellers pleaded with supplicant hands. Since the outbreak of violence, business had been bad due to so many blockades and curfews. Young boys and girls peered at the foreign shoppers, unsure if they should smile or grimace at these people who had come to their island. Almost all were Greek Cypriots. The shopkeepers had no such problem. Here was business and who knows when the next curfew would come and leave only locals who had no interest in buying souvenirs and trinkets.

"Look, Alex, aren't they beautiful?" Leyla pulled him by the hand to the window of a small jeweller's shop. It was full of gold chains, bracelets and bangles.

Smiling and putting his arm around her waist, Alex peered at the display. "Well, it's all just gold. There are no diamonds or rubies or pearls."

"Ah, but Alexander, gold is best of all. It is just like money. You can always sell gold for a good value but how can you tell if a diamond is good or bad?" she asked.

"If it's beautiful, why would you want to sell it?"

"When a Turkish girl gets married she receives many gifts of gold chains and bracelets. The Greeks and the Italians too, they pin money on the bride's dress. But we receive gold. Later, if you need to buy something you can sell the gold. Gold is better than money, it goes up in value." Leyla nodded to emphasise her case.

"Well, I think that you are beautiful and you will become better each year we're together." He kissed her on the cheek. "It's hard to believe that I've known you for over a year."

"Please Alex, not in—" the sentence was never finished.

A shot rang out and then another. Leyla fell and Alex dropped to his knees, hand on his pistol. Less than a hundred feet away he saw a young man with a gun. Instinctively, Alex squeezed the trigger and saw the head explode. Blood and grey matter stained the whitewashed wall of a Greek café. He looked down to see blood spreading across Leyla's breast. Colour drained quickly from the lovely face as he bent to touch it.

In an instant two Military Police with their distinctive red caps pushed him to the ground. A third, a burly sergeant leant over Leyla. He shouted, "Get him out of here." The two MPs dragged him down a narrow laneway to a wide street where a Military Police van was parked, a corporal armed with a sten gun leaning on the bonnet. Protesting, Alex was bundled in the back of the van, falling to the floor. The door slammed and with a scream of tyres he was driven away from Ledra Street.

Struggling to sit up in the van, he managed to speak. "My girl, Leyla, my girl! We have to get her to a hospital."

"Don't worry, mate, the Sarge will look after her. She don't look too good. Thank your lucky stars they didn't get you." The bigger of the two MPs spoke in a broad Scottish accent. Then he pushed Alex back down again. "It'll be bloody chaos there. At least you got the bugger. Little shite." He spat out the window.

The van took a violent left-hand turn and Alex was thrown against a steel upright. The pain in his head was sharp but brief. He lost consciousness.

He opened his eyes, the light bright, and groaned as the figure of a tall Military Policeman came into focus. "Just relax, soldier." An immaculately dressed officer with no insignia to mark his regiment or corps spoke the words. Alex sat up and squinted at the officer and the man standing next to him. The tall, distinguished-looking man was dressed in a dark grey suit, blue striped shirt and red tie. He guessed that they must be intelligence people. They sat down opposite him.

"Listen, son," the man in the suit said, quietly, leaning forward. "We have a serious situation here. Your work with Major Pitt has been discovered. That's why you were targeted today. Now we have to get you out of here and back to the UK. We're not going to press any charges."

Alex frowned at the suggestion of charges being laid for what had happened. He looked from one man to the other. "What charges?"

"A young man is dead. You killed him. Serious stuff."

"He shot at me and Leyla," a frightened Alex protested.

"Perhaps. There will have to be an investigation." The officer shook his head.

"There are bound to be ructions from the Greeks," the man in the suit said. "We'll issue a statement saying that you've been taken to the UK for questioning. It'll blow over as soon as the next bomb goes off. Unless they try to take revenge for the boy's death."

"What? Me?" Alex stuttered.

"Either you or the girl's father. Mehmet Ali's involved too. Who knows? You never can tell with Greeks."

"But what about Leyla? My girlfriend. Is she okay? Can I see her? I'm not going anywhere until I see her. Or her father."

The officer held up a hand to stop the flow of words. "Sorry, Sergeant, but that won't be possible. You'll just follow orders."

"If I can't see her, can you tell me how she is? Where is she?"

"Just sit there and I'll see what I can find out," the man in the suit looked compassionately at Alex. He nodded to the MP. "Go and phone the Military Hospital and check on the girl." The room was silent until the MP returned.

"Well?"

"Sir! The Ward Sister was not available but the receptionist said, 'Sorry but Miss Ozkara is no longer with us. She's gone'."

The man in the suit stood motionless for a second, then with a grimace he spat out the word "bugger". Turning to Alex he spoke softly. "She didn't make it. Jesus, I'm sorry."

Alex burst into tears, into uncontrollable sobs. Clenched fists pounded the table. Mouth and throat full of mucus and phlegm, he was unable to speak. Then he began to choke and the man in the suit thumped him on the back. Finally the coughing subsided and Alex sat hunched, head down, water dripping from his nose. Someone handed him a handkerchief.

"This is a tragedy. We understand how you must be feeling but we have to put this incident behind us."

"Incident! Incident! What do you mean—incident? It was bloody murder." Spit flew out of Alex's mouth.

"Yes, I know. But you killed a young Greek boy and they won't forget that. So you are going home and Mehmet Ali will go to a safe refuge, maybe Famagusta. No chance of the Greeks getting at him there."

Feeling dazed, Alex looked around the almost bare room. "Where am I now, Sir? Can I go to the hospital, can I see Leyla?"

"No chance. Your connection with Mehmet Ali has obviously been uncovered so now you are all compromised. You'll have to leave. You're at RAF Nicosia and you will be on your way shortly. You're not going anywhere. Understand?"

The man in the suit nodded to the officer who continued. "That's all for now. You'll get a full briefing once you get to the UK. The troopship *Duneera* is due to sail this evening and you'll be on it. After two weeks in the Med, this thing will blow over."

The man in the suit stood up. "I can't say much, but things are happening. We don't want to jeopardise anything by having you around here. It shouldn't be long before something comes out."

Alex wasn't sure what he was talking about. He sat in glum silence thinking about Leyla, seeing the blood. His confused mind turned to the possibility that he could be in serious trouble for shooting a civilian. He was sure that the young man had had a gun in his hand. His head throbbed and he felt close to tears again.

"We'll just get you checked over by the MO, then you can get on your way," the suited man said in a brisk, commanding voice.

"Will I be going back to Camp Kermia to get my gear?"

"No, we'll arrange all that. We don't want you anywhere near Camp Kermia."

Alex stood up with difficulty, his legs trembling, and then sat down again.

"Take your time Sergeant," the man in the suit said. "Right, I'll see you chaps later. Have a nice trip home and try to put all this behind you." He gave a tentative wave.

Alex stared at his departing figure. A feeling of failure and loneliness brought tears to his eyes again. All he could see in his mind was his beautiful Leyla and how he'd hoped to marry her one day. The officer looked with sympathy at Alex who sat, bent over, head in his hands, moaning and rocking like an animal in pain.

Cyrus 1950

THE DAY BEGAN as usual for Mehmet Ali Ozkara in the little town of Ghazientop not far from the northwest coast on the island of Cyprus. The biggest landowner and *muktar* (or mayor), he lived well. His wife Gulten had been up since first light to bake the dough that she'd prepared the night before. After lighting a fire in the large dome-shaped brick oven in the backyard, she set out dishes of olives, haloumi cheese, cold meat and sliced tomatoes. When the Turkish bread began to puff up, she called her husband and her only child, eleven-year-old Leyla.

Stretching, Mehmet Ali stepped outside to the prepared table. He breathed in the smell of the glowing embers and waited while Gulten put the fresh bread on the table. "Thank you, *Anne*." He called her by the Turkish name for mother.

Gulten nodded and returned to the kitchen to eat her breakfast. He smiled as Leyla appeared. "So, another day of school? Good, good, study hard, my little one. Education is everything."

"Yes, *Baba*," Leyla kissed him on both cheeks," you say the same thing every morning."

"That's because it is important. As the great Ataturk said, the education of our children is the future of the nation."

"But he was speaking about Turkey, not us?"

"No, he was speaking about Turks. For too long we have sat back, doing nothing, believing it is all the will of Allah. We have to change."

"You have a good life, *Baba*, and nothing much has changed here." Leyla's head tilted to one side.

"Not for a hundred years or more. You're right in some ways."

"The men go to work in the fields, dig the potatoes, and they look after the oranges and lemons." Leyla passed him a plate of small Cyprus olives. "The women look after the children and see to all the cooking and cleaning. What can change?"

He looked at his lovely daughter, just beginning to show the first signs of emergence from childhood. She'll be tall and beautiful, he thought. "But the whole world is changing and I must think about your future." He wagged a finger at her.

"You'll still go down to the coffee shop for business during the day. That's where it all happens. Then after dinner you'll be back there again, talking with the men about politics and playing endless games of backgammon or dominoes."

"I must say I like that, but you, my child, a daughter, how will it be for you?"

"What do you mean, *Baba*?" She looked puzzled.

"Well, you are a bright girl. Will you be happy to stay at home and walk through the narrow passageways to visit the other women? I don't think so. With all this wireless and now a new picture thing, life will change."

"You are in a serious mood this morning." Leyla frowned.

"It's this new Archbishop, the one who was Bishop of Kition, near your uncle in Larnaca. He's talking about freedom for Cyprus. Hah." His clenched fist shot up. "What does that matter to us? He wants to stir up all the old trouble. We've been through all this before. First in 1931 and since then. The Greeks keep thinking that they are part of Greece. Cyprus is British and should stay that way or go back to Turkey."

"Turkey?"

"Cyprus has never owned Cyprus." His body tensed.

"What do you think will happen, then?" Leyla knew her father would have the answer.

He waved his hand as if brushing away a fly. "Forget all that. School will be finished soon and I promised that you could come with me to Morphou again. Learn how to do business with my Greek friend Demetrio."

"The mayor? The one with the son, Georgio?" She tilted her head to one side.

"And you can forget all that," he growled in a kindly manner. "We only do business with Greeks, we don't socialise with or meet their sons."

"*Baba!*"

"We'll talk about it later. When school is over. Now, off you go and don't let me hear any more talk about boys. Time enough when you are older," he scolded. "Off you go or you'll be late. Tell *Anne* to bring me some more coffee."

Gulten brought in his coffee and a message from Salih in Velos Street. "He says it's about the passageway at the end of his yard. Can you go see him? When you've finished your breakfast, he said."

"I'll just drink my coffee. He can wait."

He walked down the deserted street and glanced at the more prosperous houses clustered close together on one side of the village. Each house had a kitchen eating area, bedrooms and a sitting room as well as a yard where chickens and other animals were kept. Only a few were fortunate enough to have a special room set aside for visitors. He thought how lucky he was, others in the less well-off area made do without a sitting room and a barn attached to the building for the animals. It was a constant problem, the poor drainage, when there was heavy rain.

"Look, Mehmet Ali," Salih protested. "It's always the same. Osman allows his bit to silt up and then I get flooded." He pointed to the passageway between his house and his neighbour.

"You're not exactly under water, Salih. Anyway," he sighed, "leave it to me. I'll get Osman to fix it up." Why couldn't Salih just speak to Osman, he thought, as he stepped over the muddy patch and headed off for the coffee shop. He stopped and watched as Nico Polites came hurtling down the street from the Greek quarter.

"Why the rush, Nico?"

Panting, Nico asked if Mehmet Ali could come and settle a dispute.

"Is it urgent?"

Nico took a deep breath of air and then noisily exhaled. "Urgent? Urgent? You know my Rose is getting married on Saturday. I have enough to do without John Katos deciding that now he will make some alterations. He'll block the road from the church to the square. It's too much."

Mehmet Ali smiled. A wedding, he thought. That's one thing we have in common. Nico was a Greek Cypriot. About sixty Greek Cypriot families lived in a collection of houses around a small square on the outskirts of town. They had their own coffee shop, a small store and a barber shop. Mehmet Ali was called only when they couldn't settle a dispute. Apart from occasionally sharing celebrations on a feast day, there was little intermingling of the community with the Turks. Over the centuries, Greek customs such as a wedding dowry and a less rigid approach to the rituals of Islam had become common in Ghazientop.

"Let's go, then. We'll sort it out. A wedding is important. Mr Katos can wait till after the weekend."

After settling the conflict, he remembered that he would need his cash account book. He walked slowly back home.

Gulten was surprised to see him. "Back so soon?"

"I forgot something. My cash account book. Can you fetch it for me?" He watched her departing figure. If only she had been given a good education, he thought, how much better our lives would be. Still, Leyla was bright and eager to learn. After dealing with his daily problems, he enjoyed sitting, talking to his daughter, educating her in politics and business. Even if she married a good man, the farm would be hers.

"You forgot to shave again," Gulten scolded him as he kissed her on both cheeks.

Raising his arms in mock surrender, he laughed and ambled down to the coffee shop to see who would be making a payment today.

"You see, Leyla *hanim*. We must be grateful for the revolutionary ideas of Kemal Ataturk, the Father of the Republic of Turkey. He transformed the old Ottoman Empire. Women, he insisted, must be educated."

Leyla nodded. She'd heard her father talk on this subject many times before.

"He banished the veil and then changed the language from Arabic script to a new phonetic western style. We embraced the reforms here in Turkish Cyprus more so than in the remote villages in Turkish Anatolia."

"We're not the same, *Baba*. And not everyone is like you."

"I was only a boy but my father, he was enthusiastic about the new ideas."

"I would have liked him, I think."

"Ah yes. And with you my only child, and a girl, it is even more important that we remain faithful to his dream of a modern Turkish people."

Leyla lowered her head. She knew how much her father had longed to have a son.

"We are Muslims, but we must recognise that the fatalism inherent in the teachings of Islam has in some ways been detrimental to the progress of our people." His thoughts returned again to Leyla and her education.

Mehmet Ali's English was rudimentary. He dealt with Greeks to sell his produce, and he spoke the language fluently, although any writing was beyond him. He was aware that the most successful Turks were those who spoke English and had studied at universities in London and Manchester. Leyla must learn good English, he decided. At twenty-one years of age he had married his second cousin, sixteen-year-old Ferriha. It was several years before she fell pregnant and gave birth to a son. But she had died in childbirth, followed shortly by the child who had lived only a few days. After a long period of mourning, a second wife was chosen from a family which farmed potatoes in Larnaca in the south of Cyprus. Gulten was twenty-four, a plump, short woman with good childbearing hips. Her father had been unable to arrange a marriage for her at an earlier age and was grateful and generous when he accepted the offer from Mehmet Ali's father. Unfortunately, Gulten gave birth to a girl, Leyla, and due to complications was informed that she would be unable to conceive again. Mehmet Ali accepted the will of God. He determined that his only connection to the future, Leyla, would learn the ways of the business world and be able to take his place one day.

"Leyla? Today you can miss school. You will come with me to Morphou. I have business with Demetrio Katos, my Greek friend."

She clapped her hands. "I like going to Morphou. It's so much bigger than here. They have so many more shops."

"We're not going shopping." Mehmet Ali looked stern. "I want to talk to Demetrio about your future. Talk about some thoughts I have for your education. Demetrio is an important man who knows many things."

"But he is not involved in our school, is he?" Leyla looked puzzled.

"I don't mean the school here in Ghazientop. It's all right, but the Greek schools are better, I think."

"Greek schools?" She gave her father a strange look.

"We'll talk about it with Demetrio. Don't worry your pretty head. Nothing is decided."

Leyla listened as the two men discussed the buying and selling of the recent crop. People passing by the coffee shop stared then laughed at this unusual sight. A Turk and a Greek, each with a child, discussing business. They had never seen such a thing before.

"Now, Demetrio, I have something else to discuss with you. Leyla will finish her primary school soon. I thought it would be good for her to attend a Greek school. Mix with different people. I think your schools are very good."

Demetrio shrugged and smiled at the compliment. "Georgio goes to the Pancyprian Gymnasium in Nicosia. It's the best. He stays with my sister during the week. Is that what you are thinking?"

"No, no. Nicosia is no good. It's too far away. For a boy, yes it's fine, but a girl, no." Mehmet Ali shook his head vigorously. "They have a good Turkish school in Nicosia."

"Then what?" Demetrio looked uncertain.

"Children, go and find a *simit* seller. Here's some money." Mehmet Ali handed Leyla a few coins. When they had gone some distance, Mehmet Ali leaned forward. "Demetrio, my friend. You have a very good Greek school for girls here in Morphou. It's not far. The bus comes here every day." Demetrio nodded agreement.

"I should be planning the education of a son but it is not the will of Allah," Mehmet Ali sighed, a disappointed sigh, and then hunched his shoulders. "Now there is only to be one, my Leyla. I want her to have the best education so that one day she makes a good marriage with a man, also with a good education. A lawyer or doctor, maybe."

"You are a wise man, my friend. I am hoping that Georgio too will go on and perhaps study medicine. Education is the future."

"The great Ataturk said so. Now, can I get Leyla into the Greek gymnasium here in Morphou? She can leave home early on the bus and then be home before dark."

"Leave it with me." Demetrio nodded. "I will speak to the school. It will be okay. But are you sure that Leyla will wish to attend a Greek school?"

"Leyla is a bright student. She likes the challenge. Besides, if I say she will come here to school, then she will."

"Children can be difficult." Demetrio turned to see his son and the young Turkish girl coming back, animated and chatting.

"Ah, my friend, the world is moving so fast now." Mehmet Ali murmured. "My wife, my mother, my grandmother, none learned to read and write very well. But first we had the radio and now there are pictures on little screens, pictures that come out of the very air. One day soon those pictures will come to Cyprus. Then where will our culture be?"

"So. Here you are, children." Demetrio winked. "Next week I will have some news for you Mehmet Ali Bey. The school."

A large enthusiastic crowd had greeted Mihail Makarios when he arrived at Nicosia Airport on a hot day in June 1948. He was overwhelmed by the reception. A muscular, bearded man of medium build, he was hoisted high above the cheering crowd. "Makarios! Makarios!", his name was called out by the adoring mob. He was carried triumphantly to the terminal building where he was finally released.

Standing there, arms held high, Makarios made his first political speech. "You want me, you have elected me to be your Bishop. So, I now dedicate myself to the Church and to Cyprus. I will use all my energies to win freedom for Cyprus and break the chains of colonialism."

The inspired crowd carried him off to a waiting car for the drive to Larnaca many miles to the south. Makarios was deeply impressed by the enthusiastic reception. Here I am, he thought, a village boy and beloved by so many. God must have a purpose for me. On 13 June 1948 he had been ordained Bishop in the Cathedral of Larnaca. With boundless energy, he travelled the island, of which he knew very little. His sermons were delivered to packed churches everywhere. His oratory stirred a people desperate for a leader. Following the death of Archbishop Makarios II, on October 18, 1950, Makarios was elected head of the Church and so national leader of the Greek-speaking people of Cyprus. At the age of thirty-seven, he was the youngest ever elected to this office. His Beatitude, Archbishop Makarios III, Ethnarch of Cyprus, had arrived at the first step of where he now believed his destiny lay, the world stage.

Born to peasant parents, he had come a long way from that humble birth. By October 1950, with not a single dissenting vote, he was elected Archbishop of Cyprus, an ecclesiastical and political position of great power in the predominantly Greek-speaking island. He now controlled the richest organisation in the land, the one unifying force that prevailed over all others. Upon his election as Archbishop, Makarios made his intentions clear.

"I take the holy oath that I shall work for the birth of our freedom and shall never waver from our policy of *Enosis*, uniting Cyprus with mother Greece."

In his mind he knew that he would do more than return Cyprus to Mother Greece. By achieving this aim he knew he could become one of the greatest of Greek heroes and perhaps even be rewarded by becoming leader of the Hellenic world. The idea of a Greater Greece encompassing all the land of former empires still burned in the hearts of many Greeks. By uniting Cyprus with Greece, Makarios dreamed that he would be taking the Motherland a giant step towards the dream of reclaiming Constantinople and the lands of Asia Minor.

On Thursday, as usual, Mehmet Ali drove to Morphou for market day. Sipping coffee in front of the Cyprus Garden café in the town square, he listened as Demetrio Katos told him the news.

As Mayor of the town of some fifteen thousand people he knew everyone. A prosperous farmer in the green and thriving Morphou valley, he was an influential man. "There will be no problem. Leyla can attend the girls' department. It is excellent, believe me," a happy Demetrio said. He liked Mehmet Ali. They enjoyed meeting over coffee, although they had never been to each other's homes. Their friendship was based on buying and selling.

"She can start in September?" Mehmet Ali raised his eyebrows.

"Of course. And it's a good idea of yours. We are all here together on this island whatever the future holds. We must live together, respect each other. Appreciate those things we share rather than let old, hateful memories, keep us apart. She will learn to write in Greek and this will be a great help to you in business."

Mehmet Ali nodded in agreement. "English too? That's important."

"They all learn English. The headmaster said that Leyla could have extra tuition in English instead of Greek history."

Mehmet Ali shook his head in wonder. "Can you believe this? My daughter at a Greek school. It's a new world."

"That's progress, I suppose," Demetrio agreed, "I don't think it's a bad thing. Too often we cling to the past. What good does it do?"

"Speaking of the past. What do you think of this new bishop, no, Archbishop, Makarios? Did you see the latest newspaper headlines?" He looked anxiously at his friend.

"The one where he swore on holy oath that he would win freedom and unite Cyprus with Mother Greece?"

"That's the one. That kind of talk can only lead to trouble, my friend. Already I am hearing about some of our people talking about how they will oppose such a thing." The information was spoken in a conspiratorial manner.

"The Church should stay out of politics," Demetrio said with passion. "What do they know of running a country? They don't allow them to interfere in politics in Greece. Why should we let them here in Cyprus?"

"They are opposed to the communists and the communists are the only real political party here." Mehmet Ali looked at his friend knowing that he was more familiar with Greek Cypriot politics than he was.

"I know that. Now, I hear that His Beatitude has been meeting with people in Greece, government people and a retired Greek army colonel, Grivas." He spread his arms wide with an uncertain shrug. "My friend Spiro who buys my oranges and I bring in his lovely olives, he told me when I was in Athens last week. It's all over Athens about Cyprus."

"Grivas? Is that the son of Grivas in Trikomo? The grain merchant?" Mehmet Ali seemed mystified.

"Yes, it's him. He didn't want to be in the business so he went to Greece and joined the army. He was a hero in Anatolia against the Turks. But they lost to Ataturk. It was a bad time for Greeks in Turkey. They were let down by the British and French and never stood a chance against Ataturk and his army." Demetrio was despondent.

"But Demetrio, like you said, it's time to forget the past. Ataturk was only doing his best for the Turks. You can't blame him for that. But this man Grivas, Georgio, I think was his name. I remember meeting his father in Nicosia once. He must have been unhappy to see the boy go." Mehmet Ali's voice was filled with sadness, thinking how heartbreaking it would be to have a son and then lose him.

"Anyway, Spiro says that this George Grivas is a bad egg. He learned all about guerrilla tactics in Anatolia then used this knowledge against the Nazis. But it seems he also used some dubious tactics against any Greeks who didn't give his Resistance fighters food and shelter. He killed a few, Spiro said. Can you imagine, killing your own people?" Demetrio held up his hands in disgust.

"So how come he's a colonel?"

"He's retired. He was pensioned off after the Greek Government said he was a terrorist."

"And Makarios meets with him? Why?" Mehmet Ali's eyebrows shot up.

"I don't know if this is true and please do not repeat it. I think, Spiro thinks, that the Archbishop may use Grivas and his knowledge to form a Resistance group here in Cyprus." Demetrio grimaced as if in pain.

"But surely no-one will support this kind of thing. Does anyone really want to get rid of the British? Things have been good these past few years. We even have Cypriots running departments in the government now. That's a good thing, isn't it?" Mehmet Ali looked for a positive response.

"I think so, but who knows? The Archbishop is calling for a referendum to see what the people, our people, think. The communists wanted to do the same but now Makarios will do it through the Church. You have to put your name to whether you support *Enosis*, joining Greece, or not. The books will be at the Church door for everyone to sign." He gave a wry smile.

"Then everyone will know who is against this *Enosis*. You can't take a vote like that. You must know this." Mehmet Ali rocked back in his chair, shocked at the idea.

"My friend, you are right, but what can I do? I don't want to join Cyprus to Greece. They can't even keep a government for more than a few months. With the British, we have stability. Greece is so poor it can't even feed its people. Who wants to be part of that mess?"

"So you will vote to make Cyprus part of Greece?" With a sad face, Mehmet Ali knew what the answer would be.

With a look of shame at his lack of courage, Demetrio gave a wan smile. "What else can I do? Most of my business is with Greeks or Greece. I say no to *Enosis*, the Church will excommunicate me. That is what I have heard. I can't do it, sorry, my friend."

"Well, I hope it doesn't come to that. Surely the British will never agree to give up Cyprus. They don't have much left of their great Empire. Everyone is leaving." Mehmet Ali rose to his feet. "It's time I was off home. Let's hope there is better news next time I see you."

The two business friends shook hands and vowed that they would remain on good terms no matter what the future brought to their shared homeland.

Scotland 1934

ALICE FORBES HURRIED down a narrow, steep lane on her way to look for work. From the River Abertay every street and lane climbed up the hills of the industrial city of Dunkeith. Famous throughout Scotland for jute, cakes and marmalade, the city of almost 200,000 people was still in the grip of the Great Depression. Alice caught up with Jessie Caird past the rows of tenement houses and the brewery with its sweet smell of malt, hops and dreams. It was just before seven on a cold, dreary April morning.

"Are you goin tae Lachlan's as well?"

"Aye. Eh hope tae a start the day. We thousands oot oh work we'll be lucky." Jessie's breath came out in a white mist.

"Ach, ye never know." Alice tried to sound cheerful then she coughed. "Just thinking about the jute makes me cough. Terrible stuff it is. Gets in yer hair, yer clothes and yer lungs."

"Tae think it comes fae a lovely green plant in India."

"Is that right?" Alice looked at Jessie with respect for her knowledge.

"Eh, it's like hemp and flax. Course, we only get the fibre inside."

"It's no getting any better, is it? England's daen awright but no us."

"Thanks tae that bastard Churchill."

"Whit dae ye mean?"

"You remember. When he lost the election here tae Neddy Scrymegeur. Back in, what? 1922, eh think."

"Oh aye. A good man, that Neddy. He's the ane that wanted to ban the sale of drink. Is that right?"

"Peety it never happened. Ah the women eh ken voted for him. The drink's awfay stuff. It's nae guid for the men."

"Ye're right there, Jessie. Meh man's an awfay man with a drink in him." Alice thought of her husband still lying in a warm bed when she'd left home.

"Well, remember what Churchill said when he lost? He said he'd never come back tae Dunkeith and we'd be the losers. He's never lifted a finger tae help Dunkeith."

"Ach he never lived here. What wid he ken about the likes of us? Just a bloody snob of an Englishman." Jessie coughed and spat out a gob of spittle.

"God, look at the crowd." As they turned a corner they could see a large mob of women outside the mill gate. "Must be over a hundert."

"C'mon. The gaffer wull be oot any meenit." Alice hurried to get to the crowd.

In 1934 Lachlan jute mill was still busy, processing the yarn. A hundred women, some having just produced another mouth to feed, pressed in. They stood there in the cold, dark dawn, damp-smelling clothes filling the open air with a dank fetid odour that only increased the stink of fear and poverty already present.

"Only thirty needed the day. Start at half seven, finish at half five. Half an oor for yer denner." The foreman looked over the huddled gathering. "You, yes, you, Lizzie, you're a good worker." In and out of the crowd went the foreman's finger, choosing those he knew, others he wanted to try and those he knew would work twice as hard as required.

A low moan escaped the lips of those left, and then lips were licked to take away the dryness of failure. Small groups formed in the half-light to share a cigarette, a puff each till it was gone, the glow bringing a cheer in the dark morning, the smoke easing the pangs of hunger.

"Ah wish eh'd gone to Bell's," Alice Forbes whispered, "Ah might have got a start there. Ah ken Eck Wilson, that's if he's still the foreman." But there was no real conviction in her voice.

It was three weeks since she'd worked. Three weeks of cleaning the house and taking the bairns for a walk. If only, she thought, there hadn't been another bairn so soon after the first.

Alexander Forbes had come into the world in a slum dwelling that had been demolished as unfit for human habitation before he was three months old.

"He disnae look very good, does he?" Alice looked anxiously at the midwife.

"Ach, he'll be fine. Just like his big brother." The midwife sounded positive.

"His legs look awfay funny. Will they straighten up, de ye think?" Alice pulled back the thin sheet to show the baby's bent legs.

"Give him plenty of milk and he'll be fine. Dinnae fash yersel," the midwife tried to reassure Alice.

"It'll hey tae be the bottle. I'll need tae get back tae work sane."

"Ach ye'll be fine, lassie. I hear ye're getting a move?"

"Aye, and soon, eh hope. The rats here are something awfy."

The recently elected Labour Council of Dunkeith had started a program of building small apartment blocks to house those living in condemned buildings. Alex moved with his family to a small one-bedroom flat with a sitting room that doubled as a bedroom. After a few years and the addition of a baby girl, the family was given a two-bedroom flat on the third floor of an apartment block.

With an unemployed father and a mother who worked as a spinner in the Lachlan mill when lucky, Alex Forbes learned at an early age that there were two kinds of people, those who had good jobs and a comfortable life, and those who lived in poverty and endured, rather than lived, life.

Regular visits to the health clinic for sunlamp treatment and cod liver oil had cured his rickets. "It's great to be able to keep up with the other lads at runnin, Mum," he panted.

"That's grand, son. Now away and play again. Runnin'll make ye big and strong." Alice gave him a little push on his way.

In a family that was ardently socialist or communist, Alexander grew up believing that people were shaped by their financial position in life rather than the culture of Scotland or religion. For twenty years before the Second World War Scottish people had endured some of the worst of the Depression. It meant no work, little to eat and for men, an escape into alcohol or fights.

"If the workers could get control of production like they do in Russia, we'd all have jobs and money," Big Eck said, looking up from the *Daily Worker*, the communist newspaper.

"There's work doon in England," Alice muttered more to herself than anyone in particular.

"Shut up, woman. Ye ken nothin' aboot it. What would you know, anyway?" Big Eck spat out the derisory words.

"Ah ken that Joe Wilson's got a good job on the railway in Nottingham," she argued.

"Well, eh'm no going tae Nottingham so you can forget that idea," he retorted and ended the conversation by shaking out the newspaper and holding it out in front of his face.

Alice looked out of the window at the trams going by. The trouble with men, she thought, is drinking. It's not as if they're alcoholics like those poor old men who lie in the gutter clutching an empty bottle. The trouble is that come pay day they head for the pub and drink until the money is all gone. Without money, they stay sober till the next Friday. At least that's me and the bairns' experience. He never wanted to get married. But it was him that got me pregnant at nineteen. It's not my fault that he thinks he could have done better. Now he's like the rest. They drink and fight. Years of unemployment have destroyed them as men. But it's not the fault of women. We're just the ones that have to suffer. They've no respect for our rights.

Bitter men hung around street corners or the pub. Many joined the Communist Party. Helpless men took out their frustrations on their womenfolk.

They had called him Alexander after his father. In family

circles his father was known as Big Eck and he was Little Eck. He hated the name and when he started school he let it be known that he was to be called Alexander. Alice hoped that her Alexander would get a better go than his father. Still, she knew, plenty of men who looked for work in England or took any job on offer. But not her Eck. Oh no, not him.

"Eh'm no goin tae England. Leavin' meh hoose. What'll eh dae doon there ah cannie dae here?"

"Ye could work. Or is that against the Communist Party principles?" she cried.

"Shut up, woman. Ye dinna ken whit yer speakin' aboot." He opened a book from the free library to end the conversation.

"It's all right for me, though," Alice muttered to the book, "to run a loom with 140 bobbins that have to be watched every second. Running up and down the 20-foot run, tying on when a thread snaps, changing the bobbins and breathing in that awfay fluff-filled air. Eh never a chance to sit doon and read a book. It's ten hoors a day with half an hour to eat a piece of bread and cheese with a drink of cold tea."

"That's no a man's job. Now leave me in peace."

"That's right," she muttered under her breath. "That would affect the dignity o man. And if I don't do it? We lose the Council house and the bairns starve. Not that they're ever anything else but hungry."

"Eh'm no listening."

Alice shook her head. "Eh'll go and see aboot makin the dinner."

Big Eck went off to war with all the other unemployed men so for five years Alex only saw him on the few occasions his father had leave from the army. After the war Big Eck drifted from job to job, mostly as a labourer. Growing up, Alex never had a real conversation with his father.

In the evenings the family listened to the radio before retiring early, as Alice had to be at work at 7.30am. Before she left home she would get the three children ready for school, prepare food and if Big Eck was willing, make the sofa bed in the sitting room. Every time there was an argument that led to Big Eck giving Alice a slap or a punch.

Alex would plead with his brother Frank, "C'mon, let's go and stop it."

"Forget it," Frankie whispered. "It's nothing to do with you. It's grown-ups. You can't interfere. You'll only make him worse. Just keep quiet and go tae sleep."

Alex lay there feeling helpless. When I grow up I'll take her away from all this, he thought. Alex loved his mother more so because he was her favourite. He always found time to confide in her. Perhaps it was this need that gave her the strength to stay with Big Eck. He hated to hear the arguments and the slaps behind the bedroom door.

"Mum, why don't we find another place to live? We could manage," he pleaded.

"It's no that easy, son," she said. "Maybe when you're all bigger. But for now, just put up wee it and keep up yer study. One day you'll make enough and then you can look efter yer mum."

"Well, one day we'll leave him, just you and me. When I'm bigger."

"Ach, yer a bra laddie. Yer mother's lucky to have you tae look efter her. It's only when he's intae the drink that he's bad." She patted him on the head.

"But why do you let him go to the pub?" Alex couldn't understand why his mother never seemed to object to his father's drinking.

"Ach, a man has tae have a drink on Fridays. Every man should be able to have a drink especially now he's got a job. It's no easy." She shrugged.

"No everyone drinks, though," he said, trying to understand. "Surely he doesn't have to drink so much?"

Big Eck couldn't help himself and the drinking went on. Alice struggled to keep the house going. Every Friday night they waited to see what kind of mood he would be in when he staggered home from the pub. All too often he was violent and Alex would put his head under the blankets hoping his father would tire and fall asleep. From the time he went to school, Alexander was aware of the shame of being poor. For years his mother had put cardboard in his shoes to stop the wet coming in through the holes in the soles. Other kids had a box with a good lunch inside. He and his brother had a jam sandwich. Second-hand clothes, second-hand pens, the cheapest shoes available on tick or credit brought looks of pity from the rest of his classmates.

"When eh git bigger, Mum, eh'll get a good job and make lots of money."

"That's grand, son. And make sure you look efter yer family."

"If I get married, meh wife'll no work. She'll be looking efter the bairns."

Alice put out a hand and patted him on the head. "Ach, ye'll be a grand man. Make sure ye dinnae drink. Save yer money for yer family."

"That's whut eh'll dae. That's a promise. A good hoose and nae fightin'."

"Now, stop yer blethering. Give me those shoes and I'll put a pit of cardboard inside. It might help tae keep the watter oot now that it's getting on for winter."

"Ach Mum, it looks awfay. Everyone can see it when yer sittin doon in class."

"Well, ye'll just have tae put up with it. Eh've nae money fer new anes." She turned away so that he wouldn't see the tears that began to form in her eyes.

Alexander was bright but the cost of a uniform to go to the Catholic academy was too much so he attended a Catholic secondary school where most boys left at fifteen to enter a trade if they were lucky enough to get an apprenticeship. After two years the Catholic priest insisted that he go to the academy. Alexander felt like a fish out of water. Everyone else came from reasonably well-off Catholic homes. Despite this, he was always invited to birthday parties. Having to buy a birthday present was a problem. This would sometimes prove difficult for his mother's budget and the gift would be small, showing once again his lack of money. Kissing games were popular at these parties and Alex was equally good at "Postman's Knock" or "Spin the Bottle". He envied those classmates whose mothers were either teachers or did not work. How nice, he thought, to come home after school and have Mum there to give a hug and make a sandwich. Arriving home from school after a long bus trip, he would take the key, tied to a string, from inside the letterbox and let himself in to a cold, cheerless house. After eating anything he could find that wouldn't be noticed, he would peel potatoes and other vegetables ready for his mother's homecoming about 6pm. Alice appreciated her son's thoughtfulness, which helped increase the special bond between them.

Alex was the middle child. From the time he was fifteen his brother had worked in the coalmines in nearby Fife. His sister, Fiona, had been born a year after Alex. She had left home at sixteen to marry a tall Highlander from north of Inverness. Fiona produced three boys in quick succession. With her husband and kids she moved to Canada to join his relatives who had settled there. They never kept in touch.

Frank was a happy-go-lucky type. Boxing was a popular sport among miners and Frankie Forbes was no exception. By the age of eighteen he was well known in Dunkeith with the assured support of hundreds of miners at his amateur fights. Alex joined the boxing club and trained whenever he could. After a number of bouts Alex decided to concentrate on his studies and lost interest. Frankie was doing well in the amateur ranks until an accident deep underground left him with a broken ankle that never healed properly. His days of weaving and dancing round the ring were over. Frank finally left to work in the mines in Wales and seldom returned to Dunkeith.

By the time he was sixteen, Alex had almost reached his final height of a couple of inches under six feet. At 175 pounds he was more than a match for his father. One Friday evening he was due to meet one of the girls from his class at school. They had arranged to meet at the bus stop across the street to go and see a picture at the nearby Odeon cinema.

His father came home early, only slightly drunk as he'd lost his money betting. Big Eck pushed Alice against the wall, angry that his evening with the lads had ended too soon. Alex saw red and threw a punch. In the narrow hallway, it was street fighting at its best. Close in, punches were hard to land and when Big Eck brought up his knee into Alex's balls, Alex lashed out uncontrollably. Big Eck sank to the ground clutching his ribs.

Alice pushed Alex back, "Away ye go, son. I'll look efter him. You go and meet yer lassie. I'll be all right," she implored.

He put on his old sports coat with the leather patches that hid the holes in the elbows and left to meet the girl, Irene McTavish. He held her hand through the film but he couldn't get the thought of his mother out of his mind. Irene's father met them after the film to take her home on the bus and Alex walked back home.

"Where's Dad?" he popped his head through the open door of his mother's bedroom.

She was lying in bed alone. "He's in the hospital. They're keeping him in overnight. They think he has a broken rib and they're not sure if it's affected his lung. God, ye must have really hit him hard. I hope he'll be all right," she murmured.

"I'll hit him even harder if he touches you again," Alex rasped. He was disappointed with his mother's words of sympathy for his father. At school the priests and nuns had taught him that Jesus forgives all sins but he didn't see why his mother should have any compassion for his old man. She should have been glad that Alex had belted him. Sometimes he wished that his mother stood up for herself more. She always seemed to make excuses for people.

Without the advantage of parents who could help him achieve his goals, he studied and worked hard to be better than his fellow students. This was not difficult as most were content to do little study. He sometimes heard a classmate refer to him in a derogatory voice, as "that Forbes, he's a swot". To overcome his feeling of being an outsider, Alex strove to be the best at everything. Despite his lanky, wiry frame he drove himself hard and made the football team and excelled at athletics. But talent alone is not always enough to ensure success and after completing his schooling he knew that his mother could not afford to send him to university.

"Ah ken yer disappointed," she said. "But yer father says ye'll just have to get a job like he had to do. Eh'm sorry, son, but I need you to bring in some money intae the hoose now."

Pocket money was minuscule and infrequent so at the age of sixteen he had begun stealing money from his father when Big Eck fell into a drunken sleep. It was enough to go dancing at the local Palais de Danse, where he entered another world.

Too old and too well educated to become a tradesman, Alex tried to join the RAF as a pilot but failed because of poor eyesight. One of his teachers put him on to a chemist, Angus MacDonald, so he settled for work with the pharmacist for two years.

"Ye'll do fine laddie. It's no much money but if ye save hard it'll help when you start yer full-time studies at the pharmacy college," a kilted Angus greeted him at the interview.

Angus MacDonald came from a family of Scottish nationalists.

"Thank you, Angus."

"It's Mr MacDonald! At least until yer qualified," came the firm reply. "It's nine till six, Monday to Saturday. We close one till two. Half day Wednesday."

"Thank you, Mr MacDonald."

The pay was poor but he was able to get a scholarship that paid for the books and instruments he would need during his three years' full-time study. He learned to become a good ballroom dancer and was never short of partners. Each night at the Palais de Danse the bandleader would call for someone to sing. Even the worst performer received a free ticket to the Saturday night dance session. On Saturday, several nets full of balloons were suspended from the ballroom ceiling. When the balloons were released there was a mad scramble to collect as many as possible. Inside a few was a free ticket to the Tuesday dance. Alex didn't mind singing a song and always managed to get a balloon with a free ticket. Under the soft lights, only the girls' dresses attracted attention. A man was noticed only if he could dance and Alex could dance. As the evening wore on, the time would come to ask a girl, "Can I see you home?" The question was seldom asked unless the answer had already been made clear by smiles and body language. Dancing cheek to cheek, her arms around a boy's neck was a good indication that a girl fancied him. Bodies pressed so close together that she could feel his swollen groin if she wished. Other girls would dance apart, indicating a lack of interest. No words were spoken. It was communication by body contact. The girl would collect her coat from the cloakroom and link arms and it was off to the bus station or a long walk home. Standing at her back door or on the tenement stairs, it was kissing and cuddling. At times, the groping and rubbing would lead to ejaculation. Despite his best efforts, Alex never managed to get any further.

Cyprus 1952

A WORRIED FAZIL KUCUK waited at his home for young Rauf Denktash to arrive. Dr Kucuk was a specialist physician and the leading figure in the Turkish Cypriot community. A short, balding man of fifty with heavy bags under his eyes, he looked older than his years.

"Ah, Rauf," he stood up as Denktash entered the sitting room. The two men kissed each other on both cheeks.

"Fazil. Always a pleasure to see you," the burly twenty-nine year-old Rauf Denktash responded.

"Rauf, sit down. I want to talk to you about this Archbishop, Makarios. I think he's a dangerous man. For the past few years he's been agitating for Cyprus to become part of Greece."

"It's a worry, no doubt about that. I think the Greeks see him as a kind of messiah. Even those Cypriots who live in London."

"He may be to them, but to us he's trouble. We don't want to go down that path, *Enosis*, do we?"

"And we won't. Whatever he thinks he's going to achieve, it won't be all of Cyprus going to Greece." Denktash glowered, his face dark.

"You've just come back from England. Congratulations on your becoming a barrister by the way. What's the mood there?"

Denktash looked at the fine rug on the floor for several seconds then looked intently at Kucuk. "Frankly, I don't trust the British. Not in the long run. If we are to prevent this handover of Cyprus to Greece then I suggest we start preparing our opposition now. Before it's too late."

"My thoughts exactly. The only problem is, there're not

very many of us compared to them and we're not as united as the Greek Cypriots. We have about a third of the land, but our community is scattered all over the island. So it won't be easy," Kucuk said.

Denktash nodded. "I've been told and I have yet to confirm it, but it appears that this Archbishop is already making plans to confront the British in the United Nations. You would know better than me, is it true that the Greeks are setting up some kind of organisation to—?"

Kucuk interrupted, nodding briskly." That's what I understand. If they don't get the British to leave peacefully then they will use the same tactics employed in other colonies, violent insurrection."

"Then we would be in the firing line too, along with the British. First they get rid of the British then us." Denktash pursed his lips then exhaled noisily.

"That would be the logical conclusion. Either that or turn us into second-class citizens."

"Over my dead body," Denktash snarled. "We may be outnumbered here but forty miles away we have enough people to outnumber them."

Kucuk's eyes narrowed. "Could we count on Turkey? They have enough problems."

"Not as many as the Greeks in Greece. Besides, it's up to us here in Cyprus to show this Archbishop that we will oppose any attempt to turn the island into a Greek state. We'll do it by force if necessary."

"But we're not ready for that, surely?" Kucuk frowned.

"We soon will be. Call a meeting of all the *muktars* and village leaders. I know that many of them see us in Nicosia as some kind of elite but we can and must convince them that we need to unite. It's that or be eliminated."

"It wouldn't come to that. I'll see Makarios and tell him that we will oppose any attempt to make us Greek citizens. He's a man of God. I'm sure that he will be reasonable. We're fine as a British colony. Why change?"

Denktash cleared his throat, a deep rumble. "You do that. While you try to make the priest see reason, I will organise a meeting. We must start thinking about how we can protect our people if trouble starts."

"Let's have some coffee. Then I must spend some time with the family. I'm so busy they see little of me as it is." Kucuk rang a small bell and a tray with coffee and biscuits arrived in seconds.

Leyla Ozkara entered a new phase in her life. Just before her thirteenth birthday, she was enrolled at the Pancyprian Academy of Morphou. As discussed between the school headmaster and Demetrio Katos, she attended studies only in general history and not Greek history. Mehmet Ali insisted that she wear a small, embroidered head square, pinned to the top of her lovely dark brown hair, piled high and pinned by two combs.

"Leyla, as I've told you, we Turks have been backward for too long. Always we sit and stay the same, never changing because we think it is the will of Allah."

"Are you sure, *Baba*?" Leyla beamed, happy to be just like the other girls.

"There is no need to wear a full scarf. Greek girls often wear a small ornament on the head and you will not look different. You will look just like one of them, even if your thoughts are different."

The senior mistress looked at the Turkish Cypriot girl. Such a beautiful young woman, she thought. Already, her figure was developing. "As you know, Leyla, you will not join the others when they learn about our Greek heritage."

Leyla nodded.

"I have arranged for you to receive extra tuition in English. I understand that was agreed? But I think it's a pity that you won't have the opportunity to learn about the glory of Ancient Greece and the Hellenic Empire."

"Yes, Miss." Leyla scuffed the floor with a foot.

"The Church has carried the torch of our past through over

two centuries. This ensures that our students appreciate our history and keeps alive our love of Mother Greece." She smiled.

Leyla made no reply.

"Well, let's get you started. Come, I'll introduce you to your classmates. All very nice girls."

Many of the girls came from well-to-do families. They lived in houses with modern plumbing and cooking facilities even though they still retained a Cyprus oven in the back garden. Greek women led lives not much different to their Turkish sisters. They were under a strong patriarchal rule but they were able to come and go as they pleased. But looking the same did not prevent some of her classmates treating Leyla as an outsider. At the beginning she was called a dirty Turk, an infidel.

"Dirty Turk," the Greek Cypriot girl Melina hurled the insult in the schoolyard, "why don't you go to school with the other black people?"

Leyla stared at her and frowned. Another girl put her arm round Melina. "Yes, we don't need Turkish murderers sitting in our class."

"Turks are the enemies of Greece." Melina spat out the words as she made a face at Leyla.

A nearby group of girls turned and jeered at her. Leyla bore these insults with a patience that finally led to her being accepted by most of her fellow pupils. Quick and eager to learn, she soon became a source of pride to her teachers. Despite their Greek-oriented education in Athens they appreciated the opportunity to assist Leyla overcome what they saw as her unfortunate background as a Muslim.

The English teacher was in fact English, from Surrey near London. A writer, he was extremely popular and Leyla was one of many girls who wrote poems of love that he found on his desk at regular intervals. Her only real friend was a short, swarthy, solid, dark-skinned Greek girl, Angela, an outsider who grasped the chance of a friend, any friend.

"Angela," Leyla asked, "why am I treated so by the other girls? My family has been Cypriot for a hundred years or more. Maybe longer, I don't know. Yet nobody wants to play with me."

Angela was silent for a long time. She smiled a sad smile. "Nobody likes people who are different, don't you see. For us Greeks the Turks are the enemy. You drove us out of our home in Constantinople and Smyrna. Everyone knows that Turks like to kill Greeks. It's in all the history books. We are afraid of Turks. You know that they like to rape Greek girls?" Angela shuddered.

"My father would never do anything like that." Leyla stamped her foot in annoyance. "He respects women. He once told me that many Turks here in Cyprus were Greek to begin with."

"How can that be?" a startled Angela took a step back.

"It was all to do with taxes, I think he said. Years ago, a long time ago, when Cyprus was part of the Ottoman Empire. If you were a Christian, you paid higher taxes. So, many Christians, Greeks, became Muslim so that they would pay less tax."

"My God, so maybe I am a Turk, that's why I'm ugly. Maybe they see that in me. Do you think that's why they don't like me?" Angela's eyes opened in horror.

"Don't be silly. Turks did not become Christian. Anyway, there are beautiful Greeks and some not so beautiful. It's the same with us." She put out a hand to touch her friend.

"Anyway, you are both smart and beautiful," Angela said.

Leyla blushed at the compliment.

"I'm not but who cares? Who cares? I'm used to it. It doesn't bother me." Angela feigned lack of interest.

"But why do they call me a dirty Turk? I'm not dirty. I wash every day and each Friday evening I go with my mother to the hammam for a bath. Is that not okay?" She tugged at her shirt collar to show her clean neck.

"They are just jealous that you are better looking. Soon we will all be finished with this schooling and find a husband. You will have a good man, but I must accept whatever my father can find for me. It will not be easy. Probably someone ugly, like me."

"Oh, Angela, you should not say such things. You'll find a good man who appreciates you for your kind nature. Perhaps I won't marry," Leyla said with a cheeky smile. "Like my aunt, Nafia, who lives in Izmir. She has no man to tell her what she can and cannot do. But my father, he will have other ideas, he will want grandchildren. Who knows?"

"Maybe a handsome Turk will think I'm beautiful and want to marry me?" Angela giggled. "I'm just joking. My father would kill any Turk who wanted to marry me."

"One day I'd like to go to England. They say it's very beautiful. We could go together." Leyla tried to cheer up her friend.

Summer arrived suddenly in May as it often does in Cyprus. The early morning bus travelled through the evergreen olive groves, the silvery leaves flickering in the sunlight as a breeze moved through the upper branches. In the valley a fine cotton mist blanketed the orange orchards as far as the next gentle slopes. The bus travelled across the flat Messiora Plain that even now was losing its cover of green. In June, little dust devils danced across the pale brown land like dancers in nature's ballroom. Each day began early, no later than six. By three in the afternoon Leyla was on her return journey, happy to see again the verdant green of the ubiquitous orange and lemon trees that meant home was near. Homework kept her busy. Reading books by the Brontë sisters was her favourite. The time passed quickly helping her mother with household tasks.

"Your report is very good, my Leyla." Mehmet Ali glanced at his wife. "Look, Gulten, how well our daughter is doing at school."

"She is a clever girl." Gulten looked with pride at her blossoming daughter. "And lucky that her father wishes for her to be educated like a man."

"Yes, I am blessed that I have such a talented child. Not so much a child any more, eh?" He looked at her over his spectacles. He wore glasses to read with but never in public.

Leyla felt embarrassed but happy that her father was pleased with her progress at school. "The headmaster said that I am one of his best students. I like to learn, even if sometimes the other girls don't like me to win a prize."

"Forget what they think or say." Gulten stopped sewing.

"Thank you, *Anne*, I will always do my best for you and *Baba*."

"Well, one day you will be able to help your father with the farm and the business. With a good education, you may even become a *muktar*?" Gulten looked shyly at Mehmet Ali.

"The world is changing, but not that fast. They may have women in the British Parliament, like this Barbara Castle, but I think it will be a long time before we have anything like that in Cyprus." He pursed his lips.

"But it is possible?" an emboldened Gulten asked.

"Anything is possible. With a good husband, she will be able to help him with the running of the farm when I get too old. I have another twenty or so years. There's time enough to think of these things. For now, my Leyla must think only of study. Yes?"

"Of course, *Baba*, " She bowed her head. "You will live to be an old, old man. And still you will be *muktar* and helping everyone."

"Ah ha, *Anne*, see how clever our Leyla is? Maybe she will be the first Barbara Castle here in Cyprus." He gave a hearty belly laugh.

Cyprus lazed under the unrelenting summer sun. Leyla was kept busy helping her mother with the preparation of meals and house cleaning. The weekend was a time for visiting relatives in different parts of Cyprus. She enjoyed visiting her mother's relatives in Larnaca where they were always welcome. She smiled at the fuss they made of her mother who had married such an important man, the *muktar* of Ghazientop, Mehmet Ali. In Larnaca, Gulten's opinion was asked on all kinds of subjects. Leyla was pleased for her mother. In Larnaca, she thought, they see my *Anne* in a different light and she is much more relaxed and happy here.

Eager to make his presence known outside Cyprus, Archbishop Makarios left Cyprus sleeping under the sun and travelled to Athens. Then it was on to London and New York. The British offered a few suggestions of some form of self-government. Makarios refused such overtures. In America, he worked assiduously to present the case for self-determination to the powerful Greek lobby. Although he represented less than half a million people, the strategic military importance of Cyprus opened up many doors in the US administration. As he had experienced elsewhere, he received a sympathetic hearing but that was all. The United States had its hands full with the Korean War. A church leader of a mere half a million people on a small island was of interest to the US only because of its obsession with curtailing the spread of communism.

Athens 1954

IN MARCH 1954, thousands of cheering Greeks greeted His Beatitude Archbishop Makarios III, Ethnarch of Cyprus, when his plane landed at Athens Airport. His latest speech vowing to deliver Cyprus to Greece had aroused great interest in the Greek media. The public, desperate for some sign that the Hellenic dream still lived, hailed him like a king come to lead them to victory. Makarios met with Prime Minister Papagos and his cabinet members. They were all greatly impressed by the enthusiastic young priest who spoke at length with barely a breath. He admonished the government for its tardiness in forcing the British to consider self-determination for Cyprus. "The people wish to be free to decide their future and that future is already decided. Cyprus will return to Greece where she will be part of the great Hellenic world."

All eyes concentrated on Makarios. Papagos leaned forward, finally managing to interrupt the flow of words. "We must proceed slowly. Britain is our ally and we have no wish to offend them, or the Americans. The time is not ripe to press too hard. These things take time and one thing must be balanced against another, you understand?"

"I'm sorry, Prime Minister, but I have given my oath to the people of Cyprus. It is time for us to act rather than talk. I will meet again with Colonel George Grivas while I am here. It may be that we can hurry a decision from the British Government."

"You may do as you wish, Beatitude. While we may, quietly, be able to assist you, I prefer that this is not widely known. We are in a precarious position. Any wrong move and we may lose government."

"I fully understand. Rest assured that nothing we do will find its way back to Greece."

After resting in his room at the Grand Bretagne Hotel overlooking Constitution Square, Makarios was ready to receive Colonel Grivas. His brother, Andreas, met the colonel in the hotel foyer.

"It's a nice hotel. Only the best for a priest." Grivas grinned malevolently.

"My brother, Michael, is Ethnarch of all Cyprus. It is only proper that when he travels, he travels in comfort. He has many journeys to make each week. Everyone wishes to see His Beatitude."

"I'm sure." Grivas ignored the excuse. "I certainly want to see him. Where are we going?"

"Room 124. His Beatitude is waiting. F-f-follow me." Andreas Mouskos spoke with a stammer.

"How kind of you to make time to see me again." The Archbishop remained seated. Grivas approached and, kneeling, he kissed the ring finger of the most powerful man in all Cyprus.

"Beatitude, it is a pleasure to be here and to greet a Greek son of Cyprus who has distinguished himself in the Church." Grivas bowed as he spoke the words. "You have come far from your humble beginnings in Pano Panayia."

Makarios gave a slight nod of approval

"It is much nicer to be staying in a hotel like this?" Grivas smirked.

"Oh, I sometimes long for those peaceful days in Panayia. The cedar and pine forests were so cool and calming on a hot day. The winters were cold, very cold, but the snow covered mountains reminded me of the majesty of God." He put his two hands together as if in prayer.

Grivas sneered at the romantic picture. "Yes, but what about the dirt roads, a poor school and the cattle in the room next to yours?"

"Ah yes. Not the best of schools but a wonderful teacher. A

Deacon from Kykko. Tassos, as I recall. He showed me how to read and write and later introduced me to the monastery. I would still be there but my superiors thought I showed promise for higher things."

"So they paid for you to go to Athens. While you were studying at the University I was fighting the Germans," Grivas boasted, chest expanding.

"I know about your exploits. You are a brave man, a good fighting leader. A hero in Greece." The Archbishop leaned forward in an imperceptible bow.

"Beside you, I am nothing. His Beatitude Archbishop Makarios III, Ethnarch of all Cyprus. A man famous and admired wherever there are Greeks."

"Let's dispense with further compliments. Despite my misgivings about ever returning to Cyprus, my duty is clear. I did so like America, but the people have called me and I am obliged to lead them." He smiled, his lips barely visible under his long dark beard and moustache.

Grivas stirred, uneasily, a little put off by this younger man, a priest not withstanding, being so blunt, almost disrespectful to an elder. "Beatitude," he decided to ignore the rebuke, "I have been most impressed with your publicly stated desire to join Cyprus with Mother Greece. I hope that like me, you see that this extending of the boundary of mainland Greece may lead to...who knows? Maybe even more? Yes?"

"First, let's deal with Cyprus. The people have expressed their desire, their wish. It is now up to me to see that wish become a reality. The United Nations will learn of the wishes of my people. It will come about. The free nations will not allow the British to keep us from our destiny much longer. As for any further expansion? Let's take one step at a time."

"Ah, but they are weak, the United Nations. The British, the Americans, will overrule them. They have made beggars of us. There is only one way to drive the British out. To make life uncomfortable, blow up a few places, show them that we mean business. They have enough problems, one small island is nothing to them now." Grivas pounded his right fist into his left hand.

Makarios held out his hands as if to begin a blessing. Turning, he gazed out the large window, deep in thought. The room was cool, fortified against the late afternoon sun by special glass, thick walls and a tiled floor. He turned and fixed his eyes on Grivas.

"Colonel, I am a peaceful man, I believe in our holy quest to unite Cyprus with Greece but I am not a fanatic. Fanatics frighten me, they cannot be controlled."

"Beatitude, the British will never give up Cyprus unless they are pushed to do so. The British are sick of wars and fighting. I know that an armed insurrection, even on a small scale, is all that would be needed to persuade them that it's time to let the people of Cyprus choose their own future. The tide of history is against colonial rulers, as you know. Now is the time to press home our cause, even if it means some sacrifices."

Nodding, Makarios replied that he knew all these things.

"Beatitude, with just a few hundred men, trained in guerrilla tactics, I can make life so miserable for the British they will be glad to be rid of Cyprus. The whole of Cyprus is with us. They just need leadership." He knew that he must convince the Archbishop to back his plans for action. "Without your support and the power of the Church, victory cannot be achieved."

Makarios sat quietly, looking at this small man, his face lined from years of exposure in the battlefield. Grivas tugged at his moustache, waiting for a response.

"I'm not sure that you understand the nature of Greek Cypriots, Colonel. They are not accustomed to war, to fighting. I doubt that you could find fifty men let alone a hundred to join you in a war against the British."

"Greeks have fought against the odds and won all through our history. The Greeks of Cyprus will do the same. All they need is training and weapons," his voice rising as he spoke.

"Yes, and they kill more of each other than the enemy. That is my worry." Makarios paused. Then with a knowing look he continued, "Oh, they don't mind a little knife attack or a paid killing when they feel aggrieved by a neighbour, but real fighting, no, I think not. The Turks are different. In the last Great War the Cyprus Regiment was mostly Turkish Cypriots even though they are a small minority. This is the reality you must face." He inclined his head.

"I am not suggesting a 'war' against the British, but a guerrilla campaign to bring our cause to the attention of the world. A few well-placed bombs and organised demonstrations will be enough. This is not Korea where a hundred thousand have been killed already. A few may die, who knows?" Grivas shrugged his shoulders.

"Colonel, I am sure that there is some wisdom in what you propose. I have promised my people to fight for *Enosis*, and that is what I will do. But persuasion will be the first method I employ."

"It's a waste of time."

"The British are reasonable people, are they not? They will see that Cyprus cannot be denied the right to decide its future. I will employ all diplomatic means to make them see the justice in our demands. The Charter of the United Nations will be the flag we carry into battle."

"As their spiritual and political leader," Grivas persisted, "it is to you that our people look to lead the fight against the oppressor."

"And lead them I will, I have made that promise to them, as you know. How I achieve the promise to join us with Mother Greece is for me to decide."

"Then, may I ask, Beatitude, that you at least agree that I should begin preparations for an armed struggle? It requires time, secrecy and planning, to be ready to fight the British when the time is right."

"Let me think about that." Makarios leaned back in his chair.

"Will you give me your blessing to start work now on the

preparations that will be needed if you fail to persuade the British or the United Nations of the justice of our cause?"

"Ah, my dear Colonel, I understand your impatience. We have been on this road to exercising our claim to choose our rightful destiny for over one hundred years. The international climate is moving in our favour. But we must marshal our forces. We must engage the support of not only Greece but the allies of Greece."

"Of course, Beatitude, by all means." Grivas eagerly nodded.

"It is in the international arena that we must argue our case."

Grivas scowled. "But it will be through deeds of heroism and self-sacrifice that we will draw the attention of international opinion, especially those allies of Greece, as you so rightly say. I trust you see the Greek need for physical heroes? It is on the soil of Cyprus that we must organise our revolutionary army."

"Yes, yes, I am sure that you are right. But I have no desire to see people killed. A few well-placed bombs should be enough to show the British that we intend to stand up against our colonial rulers. But I wish to avoid any unnecessary deaths." Makarios leaned forward, looking intently at his visitor.

"Of course." Grivas shrugged. "We will start by blowing up some installations, but if need be we must be prepared to fight. Lives may have to be sacrificed in order to force a just result."

Makarios turned his face away.

"It is not possible to defeat the British in a conventional war. However, we also know it is impossible to defeat a defiant guerrilla campaign. The Turks showed us that in Anatolia," Grivas said with clenched teeth.

The Archbishop was aware of Grivas' past exploits, some extremely unsavoury. He had heard that Grivas was not afraid to kill opponents and even intimidate his professed friends. His right-wing band of thugs had alienated the people of Greece, leading to his failure twice to enter parliament.

"No doubt you are right. In this regard you are the more experienced. But the Greeks of Cyprus still remember the uprising in 1931. It was a disaster. They are more interested in business and making money."

"This time will be different, I promise you." Grivas placed his clenched right fist over his heart.

The Archbishop closed his eyes, ignoring the gesture. "I will be in Athens again several times in the next few months. We can meet and perhaps form a committee to ascertain the possibility of financial support from Greece."

"That won't be easy." Grivas shook his head.

"I say that you have my blessing to begin some, I repeat *some*, preparations in the strictest secrecy to reach a level of preparedness should the need arise." He smiled, a tight little smile and signalled the end of the meeting by rising to his feet. Grivas knelt and kissed the ring finger of the Ethnarch of Cyprus, His Beatitude, Archbishop Makarios III.

"You have my undying loyalty and support, Beatitude. Together we will lead Cyprus to its rightful place in the bosom of Mother Greece. When the time comes, we will be ready, prepared for battle. By then it will be useless for the British to try to stop us obtaining arms and ammunition. They will be too late, as usual."

So ended the meeting of the two men who would challenge the might of the United Kingdom of Great Britain and Northern Ireland.

After Grivas had left, Makarios opened the windows to clear the room of the smell of Grivas' cigarette smoke. He ordered tea and his favourite baklava. This is a dangerous path I am walking, he thought. But what can I do? An armed struggle may be the only answer, but can I control this man Grivas? Can he control his gangs of volunteers? Greeks are not noted for cooperating with each other. They would rather quarrel. This man Grivas has a need to find a place in history. This may lead to a solution that is not desirable. Somehow I must ensure that he does nothing without my approval.

I'm not sure that I like this man. But then, life is full of compromises.

The following month in Athens, Makarios set up a secret Revolutionary Committee and outlined his ideas to lobby members of the United Nations. The group of six men seated at the table looked at each other, uncertain in the tense atmosphere, as Makarios explained his diplomatic tactics. Grivas was opposed to this continuing postponement of real action.

"It is foolish to keep going around and around meeting all these foreigners. They will agree with you in private but when it comes to voting? Hah! They will say it's a matter for Britain to decide."

Makarios held up his hand as if stopping traffic. "Colonel, you must not act in haste. By lobbying overseas, especially the recently freed colonies, we will build up goodwill for our cause. Then there will be sympathy and support if we do have to resort to some violent activities."

"I say we join all the other peoples fighting to throw off their colonial masters. Ho Chi Minh is showing the value of guerrilla warfare in Indo-China. The Algerians are beginning to harass the French, the—"

"We are not communists or Muslim anarchists," Makarios interrupted. "We will take our just cause to the United Nations, or at least the Greek Government will. If, and only if, that fails will we seek our freedom by other means. Is that clear?"

Grivas glared at the Archbishop and the other members of the meeting. "I for one will start gathering explosives, guns and ammunition. Then I will prepare separate cells in Cyprus to begin attacking the British establishment as soon as I have everything in place."

"You can prepare, but you will not come openly to Cyprus until I invite you. When I am ready, I will tell you to come. To begin the campaign of insurrection." Makarios slammed his pen on to the table. "Anyo," he turned to a young Greek army officer who had been assigned to assist with secretly obtaining arms, "You will arrange a bank account. You and Colonel Grivas will keep control of all funds received from Cyprus, America and our people in London. Be sure that no deposits can be traced back to the donors."

Grivas looked condescendingly at the young man in question.

Makarios saw the look. "You are not yet ready, Colonel. When you are, contact me. Then I will let you know when to come to Cyprus." He rustled his papers indicating he had nothing more to say.

"The meeting is over. I will do what I have to do. You let me know when the real work is to begin." Grivas stepped forward and kissed the Archbishop's ring finger.

Makarios watched in silence as Grivas stormed out of the room. He smiled at the others. Each man kissed his ring finger and departed, leaving him to wonder how long he could contain the aggressive Grivas.

Scotland 1954

In late May, in Dunkeith, Alex's first year at college was coming to an end. He was called to the Dean's office.

"Ah, Alex, just the man I want to see," he said to a nervous Alex. "Have a seat, lad, there's nothing to worry about. You're my best student."

"Yes, Mr Martin." A relieved Alex sat down.

"I have a letter from one of our former students. He's manager of a chemist shop in Bumford in Staffordshire, in England. He'd like to have a student go there and work over the summer holidays. Interested?" The Dean held up a sheet of paper with a colourful heading.

Alex thought that this might be a stroke of luck. "What does he want me to do?"

"This is what he says," the Dean began reading, "'I want someone who's done the two-year pre-college apprenticeship. Someone who can handle the dispensing, under supervision.'

He'll pay your train fare there and back and he's offering ten pounds a week. He goes on to say that he can arrange lodgings at three pounds a week. It'll be for the whole ten weeks so you won't get a holiday."

Alex sat stunned. That would leave me seven pounds a week, he thought. I could save about fifty pounds. Mum will be pleased.

"I don't mind about holidays, Mr Martin. Last year I worked in the shipyard. But this would be better. Does he say when he'd like me to start?" Alex said eagerly.

"Let's see." The Dean looked again at the letter. "As soon as possible after the end of term. So that's in two weeks. Is that all right with you?"

"You bet, Mr Martin. Can you write and say I accept?"

"Well, I'll give him a phone call. I'll explain that you're well qualified for the job and see what he says. I'll let you know this afternoon, or tomorrow if I can't get hold of him today."

"What's his name, this chemist?"

"Milton Nicol. Unusual name for a Dunkeith boy. It must have been before I took over as Dean. I don't recall the name. I'll look him up in the register."

Next day the Dean informed Alex that Mr Nicol had accepted his recommendation. "A cheque is in the post. It will cover your return train fare to Bumford. You may use the phone and call Mr Nicol if you like." He pushed a black telephone towards Alex.

Alex told Mr Nicol that he would arrive in Bumford on Saturday the 30th of June at 4.40pm. He could tell that Mr Nicol was impressed that he'd already checked out the train timetable.

The train arrived at Bumford on time. A short man wearing rimless glasses met Alex at the station. "Milton Nicol. Nice to meet you. We'll just have time to say hello to the staff at the shop then I'll take you to your digs. You'll like it there. Nice people."

Alex shook his hand. "It's pretty warm here. Is it always like this in summer?"

"We're well away from the sea so it's usually warmer than on the coast. I like it. How's Dunkeith? Still much the same?"

"Aye. Nothing much changes there. How long has it been since you left?"

"Ten years. Can't say I miss it. Went back once. My mother still lives there but she likes to come here to see me and my wife and her two grandchildren."

The pharmacy in the market square was bigger than any pharmacy Alex had ever seen. The whole square was lined with stalls selling fruit, vegetables, flowers and household goods. The pharmacy was full of customers.

"Gee. This is bigger than Boots in Dunkeith." Alex looked around the busy shop.

"We have twenty-four on the staff. No bad, ay? We service all the little villages round here. Mostly coal mining villages. It's a great business."

After being introduced to most of the staff, Alex was driven to meet the people he'd be staying with, a Mr and Mrs Fox. Alex learned very quickly that a Scottish accent was not easily understood in middle England. He also realised that by modifying his speech he helped create a new Alexander, one more step removed from the snotty-nosed kid with cardboard in his shoes.

"Alex?" Milton Nicol turned to him as they stood side by side at the dispensing bench. "You've fitted in really well here. Would you like to consider coming back again next year?"

"I'd love to," Alex stopped mixing up a heavy coal tar ointment. "I've enjoyed it. But it's a bit boring after work. There's no dancing here like in Scotland. But it's okay."

"I'll have a word with one of the directors, see if I can get you another pound a week. How does that sound?"

"That'd be great. Would I be able to stay at the Fox's place again, do you think?"

"I'm sure they'd like to have you. Mrs Fox tells me that you a fine, quiet, young man. They obviously like you and of course Miss what's-her-name is away for the summer." Alex walked happily back to his lodgings. Another fifty quid could be saved next year.

That first summer passed quickly with work six days a week and half a day off on Wednesdays. His lodgings were luxury compared to home and he was easily able to save money for the coming academic year. After the evening meal, sumptuous by his standards, Alex spent the evenings reading or listening to the radio. The elderly couple supplemented Mr Fox's wage from the railway by taking in boarders. Alex felt lucky that the other boarder, a teacher, went back to her home in Newcastle for the summer holidays. He had a beautiful big bedroom. On Sundays he watched the local cricket team play on the common before going to see the latest movie after dinner. His favourite that summer was *Brigadoon*, an unreal film about a lost village in the Scottish Highlands that awakens every hundred years.

When he got back, Dunkeith appeared dirty and dark after Bumford. On Saturdays while at college, he worked in a small pharmacy close to where his grandparents had lived. He knew the owner, as his grandfather had been a regular customer for dressings for a colostomy. He'd been shot during the Boer War and part of his bowel had been destroyed. This modest income was supplemented by the sale of homemade whisky to students in other faculties. Chemistry involves the use of ethyl alcohol to produce many compounds such as ethyl acetate. Alex took more than required for his assignment. He stored the excess in his locker. When the laboratory was not in use he mixed the ethyl alcohol with water, glycerine and burnt sugar. This made a raw whisky that tasted reasonably well when mixed with peppermint or dry ginger. It was cheap and alcoholic. That was all that mattered. A steady trickle of friends from his early youth began departing for two years' National Service in the British armed forces.

Cyprus 1955

BY 1955, Makarios had realised that diplomacy would not succeed. The British were too clever at blocking every move to have the United Nations interfere in an internal dispute. After almost three months away from Cyprus, he returned to a tumultuous welcome and set in train the next stage in his plan. A secret message was sent informing Grivas that he was to return to Cyprus. Makarios decided that it was time to broaden the base of support for the *Enosis* campaign.

Clafcos Clerides was a shining example of the importance placed on education by wealthy Greek Cypriots. He had studied at the same Nicosia Pancyprian Gymnasium as Makarios. After studying law at Kings College at the University of London, he had returned to Cyprus in 1951. Makarios summoned him to the Archbishop's palace.

An imposing building in the Byzantine style, the Palace was grand by Cypriot standards but modest compared to those in Athens or Istanbul. The Archbishop was seated, dressed in long black trousers and a white short-sleeved shirt, open at the neck. Clerides walked quickly to keep up with the servant who showed him into the Archbishop's study. The door closed behind him.

"Clafcos, my young school friend. Welcome. Things are finally beginning to move here in Cyprus. It will be a time when we need men of your ability to help in guiding us through difficult times."

"Thank you for inviting me." Clerides made a little bow.

"To achieve our freedom from the British, there are some who see an armed insurrection as the way to achieve our just ends. I am more inclined to a diplomatic, peaceful approach. Gandhi showed that the British couldn't hold out forever against the free will and desire of a people. Is that not so?" Makarios' dark eyes looked pensive.

Clerides coughed and stroked his already thinning hair. "Beatitude..."

"No, please, Michael, when we are meeting in private like this, I beg you." He went to an ornate cabinet. "Can I offer you a glass of brandy?"

"Thank you, yes."

The Archbishop poured two generous servings and raised his glass to Clerides who did likewise and sipped the pale brown liquid. Good grief, he thought, this must be the cheapest one-star brandy in Cyprus. Watching closely, he noted that Makarios seemed oblivious to its harsh taste.

"Michael," Clerides put down the brandy, "my training leads me to believe that all disputes can be settled by reasoned argument. But, as for the British, they are an unusual people. And very adept at prolonging discussions to such an extent that their opponents weary of the game."

Makarios nodded agreement.

"As a result, this forces you to accept a solution that is an unsatisfactory compromise. That is one of their great skills." Clerides went to pick up his glass then stopped.

"Yes, you've spent a great deal of time with them. I agree with your observation. So would you, if necessary, support some kind of armed uprising?"

"Bea—Michael, the British public is weary of the long struggle of war and the effect it has had on their economy and standard of living. If their government continues to engage in efforts to retain the remains of its empire, well, perhaps some limited, a targeted series of attacks on British property, might sway public opinion in Britain. This could force the British Government to accede to our demands." Clerides opened his hands and shrugged his shoulders.

"You know of course, no doubt, that there are some who

wish to follow this path of confrontational methods?" A serious Makarios paused and sipped some brandy.

"Nothing is secret for long in Cyprus. But then, rumours and intrigue are part of our culture. It is the Byzantine way. Often they come to nothing."

Makarios nodded and smiled. "Yes, we are well known for intrigue, are we not? But, Clafcos, would you support these people who see a violent response as the only way to persuade the British to leave us to determine our own destiny? In your opinion, is this feasible? Can we organise such an offensive without alienating the rest of the world?"

"Michael, our cause is a just one. We have the right as Greeks to choose our future and our future is surely to become part of the greater Hellenic world."

"Naturally," Makarios crooned.

"I can only urge caution on how we use violence. Blowing up buildings, especially important ones, this will be good. The use of guns only leads to unfortunate killings that will alarm the people. Old scores will be settled in the name of *Enosis*. We must avoid that."

"So. If diplomatic means fail to bring about a speedy result to our just claims, we will be forced to adopt more aggressive tactics." Makarios stroked his luxuriant beard.

"There's no other option."

"You've already met Colonel Grivas, Is that right?"

"Several times." Clerides inclined his head. "In Athens, and here. He's kept me up to date with his, your, plans."

"Ah, the Colonel has been busy. So you are ready to assist in every way?"

"*Enosis* is our goal and it is only *Enosis* that we will accept," he said firmly.

"Then I can rely upon you, whatever the cost?"

"Michael, I place myself at your side. One day soon you will bring Cyprus to Mother Greece. It is our destiny."

"Good. I need men like you by my side. We will keep in regular contact."

Clerides rose and shook the hand of Archbishop Makarios III. The educated, articulate Greek Cypriot had committed himself to *EOKA* and the struggle to come.

Makarios held on to his hand. "Before you go. We will all of us meet together. Understand me. I don't trust Grivas to organise the rising properly. He is a guerrilla fighter. People like him are not easy to keep under control. When we meet with him, everything must be set up so that it follows my directions."

"I agree."

"You must help set up the organisation in such a way that the British cannot penetrate it and cut off its head. Can you do that?"

"No-one will have direct contact with you or Grivas," he assured the Archbishop.

"If the British suspect me of involvement then I could well be deported. Then others, less capable, will have control. Not you of course, but less intelligent people." Makarios smiled, lips closed.

"The communists have a system of cells, small groups that only know the members in their particular cell. But not other cells or the names of its members. It works well."

Makarios frowned. "Avoid making connections or comparisons with communists."

Clerides inclined his head. "I have discussed these things with Grivas on several occasions. He proposes to enlist young men, single, ready for action. He says we must avoid married men with families. They will be easy to break if captured by the authorities."

"Excellent. Young men leaving their village or home will not arouse suspicion. A married man will." Makarios nodded.

"Grivas suggested that we set up a kind of legal document. One that binds members by Holy Oath to the aims of *EOKA* and our aim for *Enosis* and only *Enosis*."

"What is it he suggests?" Makarios watched as Clerides pulled an envelope from his briefcase and handed over a single sheet of paper. Makarios read out the words,

"I shall work with all my power for the liberation of Cyprus from the British yoke, sacrificing for this even my life. I shall perform without question all instructions of the organisation that are entrusted to me and I shall not object to any order however difficult and dangerous this might be. I shall not abandon the struggle unless I receive instructions from the leader and only after our aim has been accomplished. I shall never reveal to anyone our secret organisation, neither the names of my chiefs nor those other members of the organisation even if I am caught and tortured. I shall not reveal any of the instructions given to me even to my fellow combatants. If I disobey my oath I shall be worthy of every punishment as a traitor and may eternal contempt cover me."

"This oath will be sworn in the name of the Holy Trinity," Clerides added as Makarios put the paper on the table.

"Splendid. Now it must be understood that these brave young men must know only the instructions they receive and nothing more. If they do fail, then only the few members in their cell will be at risk. These young men are our future, the leaders of the future free Cyprus. Now, is there anything more?" Makarios spoke without taking a breath.

"Beatitude, I sense there is some confusion. I have heard, it has been reported, that you met with the leaders of AKEL, the Communist Party."

"That's quite true, I have."

"The communists say that you agree with their approach to the struggle. No violence. They are opposed to Grivas. He is well known to hate communists."

"We all hate communists. But they can be useful!" Makarios smiled.

"They oppose his claim that insurrection is the only way. They say that violence is not the only way. How can you agree with the communists and with Grivas?" Clerides looked mystified.

"I agree with what you say, my dear Clafcos," the Archbishop's face was inscrutable, and then he smiled. "Now be careful with Grivas when we meet again."

He waited until Clerides had driven off, and then went through a small door that led to a narrow passage. Another door opened into the Church of St John. A woman stood in front of the icon of St Ignatius. He gave a gentle cough and returned to the Archbishopric.

A meeting was scheduled for the following month at Clerides' home in Larnaca. Grivas spoke to his driver and constant companion Alexi on the way from Limassol where he had been staying at a friend's house.

"I'm not unhappy to have Clerides officially on board. He's a good lawyer. He won't be involved in any physical action but he will be invaluable in dealing with reluctant members of the middle class and newspaper people."

"He will," Alexi agreed.

"He won't be in the front line but he will be ideal for passing on information. Park here, a little way from the house."

After a few minutes' observation Grivas walked up to the home of Clerides. The front door opened and a swarthy young man nodded for him to enter. Clerides stepped from a side room.

"Here I am at your service," Grivas said with a slight bow.

Clerides kissed him on both cheeks. "Good to see you again. Come through. And I hope I can be of service to you." He waved him into another room.

"You will be extremely useful, with your ability to influence public opinion. You will make our movement a truly national one," he said confidently to the well-dressed lawyer.

Clerides spoke. "It's important that we have supporters from all classes of society, don't you agree?"

"Exactly my point. If we only have the workers and peasants who think to improve their lot, we have a class struggle, not a national one." Grivas shrugged.

"The goal is to liberate the people, not make things better for a few," Clerides said.

"You enlist the support of the more prosperous Greeks. We'll need their money. They too must make sacrifices." Grivas' reply was a command.

"Naturally. Come, the others are waiting."

Grivas rose to his full height, chest out. "I will begin recruiting the key men, young men who have the stomach for a real fight."

Clerides responded with a stony look. Jumped-up little man, he thought.

"Polycarpos Georgjiadis is my first choice," Grivas announced proudly.

"No more names, please," warned Clerides. "Let's meet the others."

After the usual introductions and kissing of cheeks, Makarios began. "I realise that we may have to resort to a guerrilla war. But I will continue to appeal to the Greek Government and the United Nations for the next month or so."

"No longer," Grivas barked. "The British have their hands full at present. Now is the time to strike."

Clerides nodded agreement. "The British will try their usual delaying tactics. But they are very much occupied with events in Northern Ireland and the situation in Egypt now that King Farouk is gone."

"Yes, yes," Makarios said impatiently. "The Suez Canal will be very much to the forefront of their thinking."

"This will make them more determined than ever to hold on to Cyprus. What's the wishes of less than half a million people to them?" Grivas sat up straight.

"What about the Greek Government?" Clerides looked at Makarios. "Will they help us?"

"Hah," Grivas spluttered, "They're happy to lend moral support. Radio and newspaper propaganda. But weapons? No. Very little and we have to pay."

"About our approach. The British Secret Service? Are they aware of what we are planning?" Clerides looked again at Makarios.

"Asleep as usual. I think the CIA in Athens may be aware but they don't share any information with the British. They don't trust the British Secret Service." An amused Makarios held out his hands.

"So what are we going to do?" Grivas looked edgy.

"To begin, there will be no real names used. Clafcos has proposed code names for everyone. All communications will use these names." Makarios turned to Clerides.

"Right," Clerides began," Colonel Grivas, you will be Dighenis, Polycarpos is Akritas and my code name is Hiperides. You will give code names to your area commanders and so on down the line." He looked at each man in turn.

"And His Beatitude?" Grivas chipped in.

"No need. His Beatitude will not require a code name." Grivas glanced at Polycarpos but said nothing.

"We are agreed then," Makarios said, "Dighenis here will arrange for several explosions in strategic places where no harm will come to anyone."

"Everything is ready. No casualties," Grivas whispered.

Makarios nodded.

"That is important. Then a mass distribution of leaflets to inform the people that the time has come. Hiperides will inform them that we must come together and show the British. We can no longer tolerate being a subject people in our own land." Clerides looked around for approval.

Grivas lit another cigarette. Makarios coughed. To no avail.

"The leaflets are ready, even now," Clerides said.

"My men are ready for action, good men like Markos Drakos." A confident Grivas punched the air with a clenched fist. "The first blast will go off at Wolseley Barracks followed by the Secretariat and then the Cyprus Broadcasting Station. Only the barracks have guards so the bombs will be thrown at the signals area. Just a warning of what we can do. Famagusta is ready and Larnaca too."

"Is the radio station a wise choice? It will be a useful tool for His Beatitude to speak to the people," a concerned Clerides asked with raised eyebrows.

"It's only a small bomb, Clafcos, it isn't going to blow the place to smithereens," Grivas laughed, "just leave the heavy stuff to me. You concentrate on the paperwork."

Fortunately, Clerides didn't hear Grivas mutter *kalamarades*, pen pusher, under his breath. Nevertheless, Clerides felt put out.

"Gentlemen, let's concentrate on what happens after we show our hand. Dighenis, you have everything in place for the students? Demonstrations in a week or so? Is that the strategy?" Makarios quickly moved on, anxious to avoid any personal conflicts.

"Yes, of course, assuming my area commanders are reliable. I have to rely on them, although I would prefer to handle the whole thing myself. Once we get some discipline instilled into them, I think we can move forward more quickly."

"I want all communication to go through Clafcos, Hiperides. Use couriers who are not involved in any active work. If they are intercepted, then it's not a problem. What is the code name for Polycarpos again?" Makarios asked Grivas.

"Akritas, Beatitude, only a clerk but with a heart of steel."

"Fine. Then we will await the response to our first show of strength. You, Dighenis, will be invisible but Clafcos here may contact me in person if the need arises. The British may like to play cricket but I think they will not play like gentlemen when they realise our resolve."

"It won't be cricket balls we throw at them." Grivas smiled but his eyes were full of fire.

"Now, I must put politics aside and attend to more pleasant duties." Makarios stood up as each man kissed his ring finger.

At Larnaca Cathedral where he had been ordained Bishop of Kition, he baptised Maria Theophanous. The packed Cathedral watched as His Beatitude dressed in his splendid purple robes adorned with gold insignia poured holy water over the head of baby Maria. After the baptism he signed the register in red ink, a symbolic rite given to the Ethnarch of Cyprus by the Emperor Zeno during the Byzantium period. Regally, his right hand raised, he walked slowly from the altar, pausing at the tomb of St Lazarus who had moved to Larnaca after his resurrection. On the steps of the Cathedral he spoke for a few minutes. To the applause of the crowd he concluded, "Cyprus is Greece and Greece is Cyprus. One day we will be part of the Hellenic world. Soon we will end our bondage and emerge into the sunlight. Greeks on Greek soil." With an imperial wave he climbed into a Mercedes and was whisked away to Lefkara for another christening. Before leaving Lefkara he received a fine Lefkara lace altar cloth. It was a replica of the one bought from a lady in the village by Leonardo da Vinci. The original is preserved in the Duomo of Milan.

Mehmet Ali attended Friday prayers, the one day when almost every Muslim in Ghazientop attended the mosque. At weekends, Saturday usually, he would drive the family to Kokina or Nicosia, usually somewhere not too far. The ancient harbour town Kyrenia was a favourite place to visit. There they would sit and drink coffee and meet old friends. Leyla watched the English sail their yachts on the sparkling blue Mediterranean against the foreground of Kyrenia Castle. A brown stone, walled castle, it had been built in the 7th century for defence against the Arabs. Many changes had taken place to allow for the arrival of cannon and a small church had been added outside the walls.

"Look, *Baba*," she exclaimed to her father, "you can just see Turkey, far away on the horizon."

Mehmet Ali peered into the distance. "It looks dark and brooding. But it's a comfort to know that it's not far away."

"Maybe one day soon I can visit Aunt Nafia in Izmir." Leyla looked inquisitively at her father.

"When you are older. You have plenty of time to visit my sister. Don't be in such a hurry with wanting everything." He smiled but his eyes were serious.

To Leyla, the distant far-off shadow of Turkey, hinting at its dark, menacing interior and millions of people, sent a shudder down her spine.

Life on Cyprus changed little. The years passed, long hot summers followed by cool winters under languid British rule.

Each morning the bus to Morphou passed the neat rows of orange trees, lightly tipped with wispy early mist rising from the damp soil. Leyla was blissfully unaware of the invisible clouds destined to create storms of human tragedy in this island in the sun. At the age of sixteen, she had blossomed into a beautiful young woman, much admired from afar by Greek and Turkish boys alike. She was happy and grateful to be special, the daughter of Mehmet Ali. She had few close friends but was quite popular. The subject was never mentioned but Leyla knew that one day soon her father would raise the subject of marriage. It was usual for a girl to marry by the age of eighteen and that day was fast approaching. While the thought of marriage made her fearful, she wondered what it would be like to lie with a man. Scary, probably, she thought, but nice too. She knew the touch of silk on her breasts, on her nipples and the wetness of dreams at night. Let him be tall and handsome and not have a moustache or a beard, she thought.

"Angela? Do you ever think about what will happen when you get married?" she asked her closest friend at school.

"All the time." Angela made a face. "I've seen my brother without any clothes. He didn't know I'd seen him."

"What was it like? How old is he?" a wide-eyed Leyla gasped.

"Stylianos is nineteen. I saw everything. He's not very tall but he has broad shoulders."

"Yes, but what about...you know? Did you see his private part?" a frustrated Leyla grabbed her arm.

"Oh, yes. It was hanging down. He's very hairy too."

"What was he doing when you saw him?"

Angela giggled, "He was in the bathroom. The door wasn't closed. He didn't know anyone was home. He rubbed it and held it out. Like it was a baton. I couldn't look any more."

"Oh God. What'll it be like, I wonder? You know, when it's put inside?" Leyla shivered.

"I don't know but I sometimes hear my mother and father. They still do it. You know. Making babies. Except that my mother once told me we wouldn't be having any more babies in the family."

"I sometimes touch myself. Do you? It makes me go all funny."

"Me too. But don't tell anyone. Please?" Angela pleaded, taking Leyla by the hand.

"You too? I get all goose bumps just thinking about it. Oh. Here comes Melina. Don't say anything. She doesn't like me."

"Try not to let her bother you. It'll soon be over. School, I mean."

"No. My father wants me to go on. Maybe I can go to university in Turkey or England. I'd like that."

"Lucky you to have a father like that. I'll finish this year. That's enough for a girl, my father said."

"Once you've left I'll have no real friend. It's getting horrible now. Isn't it? I wish people would just get on with life instead of always wanting to change things on Cyprus." Leyla grimaced at the thought of two more years at the Greek Gymnasium without Angela.

When Angela left, Leyla's obvious unhappiness at the Greek school in Morphou forced Mehmet Ali to reconsider her continuation at the school. Despite his misgivings, Mehmet Ali accepted the fact that Leyla must finish her education in Nicosia and he made arrangements for her to begin the next school year at the English School for Girls. Places for Turkish girls were few, but Leyla's report from Morphou had been so good that the school principal had no hesitation in enrolling her for later that year. This entailed Leyla staying in the section situated next to the boarding section for boys. Every weekend she returned home to help her mother with household duties.

"I like school but this is the best time, *Anne*, helping you. All week I think about feeding the chickens, then making the bread." She stood tall over her mother.

"It's good to have you helping me. You do everything so much faster. Even with all your schooling, you are very good with your hands. Your father says the bread is much lighter when you make the dough."

"He just says that. He likes to tease."

"Well, he says that we may go down to Kokina this Sunday. It's not far so we can spend more time by the sea."

Leyla liked to walk along the water's edge, splashing in the gentle waves with her bare feet and gazing far out to sea. How big the world seemed, endlessly stretching out to some far-off lands that, one day, she dreamed of visiting. Far, far away she thought, lies Europe, London, Paris. How wonderful to see all those famous places that she'd only read about in books. On Sunday evenings, after the evening meal, she played backgammon and chess with her father before he hurried down to the coffee shop to hear the latest gossip.

"You are becoming too good at backgammon for me, Leyla. Soon you will win at chess. This education is making you too clever. I never could understand all those mathematics and calculations, but it seems you are using your knowledge to play the game. It's all about working out the odds, is it not?"

"You are in too much hurry to go and drink coffee with your cronies, *Baba*," she wiggled a finger. "That's why I win sometimes."

"Ah, you know your *Baba* so well. You are growing into a very smart young woman. I must find a man who is just as intelligent, one who appreciates the stimulating company of someone like you." His eyes twinkled as he looked at Leyla.

Leyla lowered her head and murmured, "But not every man is as strong and confident as you, *Baba*. A woman must never try to be as clever as her husband."

He glanced over to where Gulten was working on another cloth. Mehmet Ali spoke softly. "True, true, but there are those who have no need of a servant, educated men who understand that a woman is more than just a person to cook and clean the house. The world is growing up, you know."

How lucky I am, Leyla thought, to have such a father.

Whoever he chooses for me will be a good, kind man. Someone handsome too, I hope.

"Enough of this chatter, you have won again and now I will go and make serious talk with the men at the coffee shop. Don't read too long in bed, you must have your beauty sleep, although maybe you don't need it." He smiled then kissed her on both cheeks. Then he kissed Gulten on both cheeks as she looked up from a tablecloth she was embroidering for Leyla's future home.

Under the cover of darkness, Markos Drakos, leading a team of four men, blew up the transmitters at the Cyprus Broadcasting Station. Another team threw bombs at the Secretariat and the Wolseley Barracks in Nicosia. Some hit the targets but others failed to do any serious damage. In Larnaca, the bombs failed to go off and Modesta Pannelis was electrocuted when he threw a damp wire rope over some high-tension wires as he attempted to scale the fence at the British army base. A leaflet signed by "Dighenis the Leader" was left at each bombed building claiming responsibility.

Athens Radio broadcast the news to a dismayed Greek Cypriot community. Much as they believed in *Enosis*, most preferred a peaceful resolution to their claim and were not keen on normal life and trade being disrupted by actual fighting. They realised that the British would clamp down on the transport of goods, trucks would be searched and homes would be raided. The Cypriot population as a whole was stunned at the outbreak of destruction. Greeks viewed the violence as likely to hinder normal business. Neither Greek nor local newspapers praised the initial acts of sabotage. The story of the man electrocuted was headlined in the Greek and Cypriot newspapers.

Grivas was furious and sent a note to Makarios demanding that he contact the press and insist that all acts of insurrection be described as acts of heroism. This, he said, would boost morale and encourage others to join *EOKA*. Makarios was concerned about the amateur efforts of *EOKA*.

School finished early on Fridays. While Leyla waited to catch the bus back to Ghazientop, she was surprised to see various groups of girls and boys clustered together, all reading sheets of paper. Most were Greek Cypriot students with one or two children of English civil servants working in Nicosia. Although anxious not to miss her bus, Leyla joined a small group of girls.

"What is it? Is it something from the school? Did I miss it?" She looked at each one in turn.

"It's nothing to do with school and it's nothing to do with you. Yet!" came the unsympathetic reply.

"Show me," Leyla pleaded, eager to be part of what seemed so interesting.

One girl shouted, "Read it. Now we will see who is really one of us."

Leyla took the sheet of paper and raced back to the bus stop, just in time. Sitting alone on the bus, fear came over her as she read that all Greeks should now know that a secret organisation had been formed. The National Organisation of Cypriot Fighters pledged to fight a war against the British, to throw them out and return Cyprus to its rightful place in the bosom of Mother Greece. *EOKA* had declared its hand. She rushed home to show her father the leaflet.

He already knew its contents. "The radio has been reporting all kinds of bombings in various parts of the island." He shook his head, bewildered at this turn of events. "Makarios has been on the radio. He says he regrets the acts of violence but says he understands the frustration of many Greek Cypriots. He said that they have the right of all sovereign people to decide their own destiny. He is asking the British to act immediately to end the violence by beginning talks to return Cyprus to its rightful owners, the Greeks." He took the leaflet from Leyla and tore it into pieces.

"But what about us?" Leyla asked in a shaky voice. "Is this not our home too? Can we possibly be part of Greece? We belong here, not as part of Greece."

"I'm sure it won't come to that," Mehmet Ali assured his

daughter. "The British are strong; they will catch these bombers and put an end to this stupidity. Makarios must denounce these acts of terror. He is the head of the Church, a Christian. I'm sure that he will have nothing to do with these hot-headed fanatics."

Gulten sat quietly, saying nothing, as she continued with her embroidery, a new head square for Leyla.

He tried to sound optimistic. "My good friend Dr Kucuk says the British will never give up Cyprus to the Greeks, especially with so much trouble in Egypt. After all, he says, Cyprus has never been part of Greece."

"What does that matter?" a worried Leyla frowned.

"If anything, Cyprus must be returned to Turkey as the successors of the Ottoman Empire. Turkey ruled Cyprus for over four hundred years. I am sure that Dr Kucuk will call a meeting of all *muktars* to evaluate the situation. We will go on as if nothing is happening."

Life at the English School became distressing for Leyla and she wished for the school year's end. She was not alone in being ostracised. The English girls were now treated as unwelcome foreigners when previously they had enjoyed visits to Greek homes. It seemed that everyone had become an enemy. On 19 June, more attacks occurred, including one on the police station at Kyrenia. Now the long summer began in earnest with hot, cloudless days and warm balmy evenings when the wind seldom blew. Leyla was happy to be at home in Ghazientop, away from the turmoil of Nicosia.

Makarios made another public appeal for a cease-fire, thinking that this would enable Grivas to regroup. Back came a note from Grivas denouncing the cease-fire. It was imperative, he said, to keep going and show that *EOKA* was strong and capable. Grivas was able to operate from secret locations in Nicosia, Limassol and Famagusta. The labyrinth of streets, back alleyways and well-disguised cellars made it easy for Grivas to move his headquarters at will as he worked alone.

He was not confident of the organising ability of his men and tried to be involved in every decision. Too many attempts at bombings went wrong. Too many men gave away plans under questioning by the military and not everyone obeyed his orders. It was time to set an example. In a cramped little room in Hermes Street he leaned forward, a cigarette hanging from his lips.

Hunching his shoulders, he stared intently at Akritas. "Polycarpos, this type of campaign relies on the absolute, total cooperation of every Greek on Cyprus. They appear to think that they can stand aside or even resist us. So the moment has come to make an example of these cowards, these traitors to the cause."

"I agree, Dighenis," Polycarpos nodded, eager to follow orders.

"Stelios Karalis works for the British. I am confident that he is passing on information. How, otherwise, would the military know about our cache of guns at Palehori? I want an example made of this man. Then there are the communists. They too must be taught a lesson."

"You want them killed? How many?" His face lit up. "It's time to show them that we mean business. A few deaths and they'll all fall into line. They're weak bastards."

Grivas nodded. "Yes, and kill two or three from AKEL. Paramana is a good place to show them. We will need two squads. Can you do this?" he asked, unblinking despite the smoke drifting up to his eyes.

"Certainly. You know young Nicos? He can be relied on to take out any traitors, so he can do Karalis. For Paramana, I will take twenty men, raid a few houses and, well, we can shoot one or two or more."

"Good, then we will have no more opposition. A little killing soon brings people to their sense of duty." Grivas took the glowing cigarette end from his mouth and used it to light another.

Three days later, the Greeks of Cyprus learned of the

killings. Four members of AKEL had been shot dead in Paramana. The bullet-riddled body of Karalis had been left outside the coffee shop in his village outside Dhekelia. The culprits were never caught. After the funeral in Paramana, four widows, all in black, pleaded for an end to the killing of innocent men. They asked that a message be sent to the Archbishop. How many women would be condemned to wear black before the violence would end, they wanted to know. There was no response.

London 1955

The black Humber staff car pulled up at Number 10 Downing Street at eleven o'clock. The driver jumped out and opened the rear door. Field Marshall Sir John Harding OBE MM , Chief of the Imperial General Staff, stepped out and returned the driver's salute. The door to Number 10 opened at the same moment and he strode briskly inside. The butler accepted his hat and said, "This way Sir, the PM's expecting you. Would you like tea or coffee brought in, Sir?"

"Tea will be fine, thank you," Harding replied as the butler opened the door to the sitting room.

Rising to his feet, the shaggy figure of Harold Macmillan held out his hand. "John, good to see you, you know Allan here?" he indicated lanky Allan Lennox-Boyd, Colonial Secretary.

"Yes, of course, nice to see you again, Allan." Harding nodded as he shook hands with the Colonial Secretary.

The door opened and the butler entered, carrying a large silver tray with cups, saucers, a teapot, coffee-pot, sugar, milk and a plate of biscuits. "Shall I pour, Sir?" he inquired of the Prime Minister.

"No, that's fine, thank you, John, we'll look after ourselves for now." Macmillan waved a hand. "I'll ring if we need anything. Lunch at one, I think."

The three men helped themselves to a drink, sat back and looked intently at each other.

"John," the Prime Minister tilted his head back as he looked at Harding, "I would like you to give up your position as Chief of Staff and take on a pretty important job. Cyprus. Things are getting out of hand and I, we, think that it needs someone like you to knock it back into shape. You're up on the whole business, of course?"

"Well, partly. I've been keeping half an eye on things out there. It's always a bit of a problem with these nationalist uprisings. We haven't had a great deal of success in the past. Still Cyprus is a small island, not bad terrain. But it should be easier than Kenya. Depends on what you chaps want to happen? It's still our best strategic point in the Middle East. We'd hate to lose it. Especially with the way things are going in Egypt."

"All right. I have another meeting next door. It won't take long. Allan can bring you up to date with the latest intelligence. I'll see you for lunch at one," Macmillan said, easing out of his chair with difficulty, "Damn hip."

"Right, John," Lennox-Boyd began. "You know how important Cyprus may be for us in the future. I'll give you some background information on the two main characters we have to deal with."

"This Archbishop, Makarios, and a Greek, who calls himself Colonel Grivas?" Harding said.

"Correct. Makarios is now a powerful man on the island. He's felt to be a cross between the Pope and the Prime Minister. He's very young, the youngest Archbishop ever, so he must have something going for him. He was a peasant shepherd boy in a little place in the Troodos Mountains. The rest of his family, mother and father, brother and sister, are pretty well uneducated."

"So he's come a long way then." Harding stated the obvious as he made some notes on paper.

"I'll say. Apparently he decided to become a monk and went to the biggest monastery in Cyprus, Kykko. It's not far from where he lived. It seems he was a bright lad and the Abbott sent him to the Greek school in Nicosia. Did very well there. So they sent him to the university in Athens. Did law and was good enough to win a scholarship to Boston University. Studied theology, so he was obviously earmarked for promotion."

"So how old is he now?" Harding asked.

"Forty-four, I think from memory."

"Married?"

"No, never married. But he's had a few lady friends from what I'm told. Once you become a bishop in the Greek Orthodox Church you're not allowed to marry. We haven't any concrete proof but we think he has a couple of women that he sees from time to time. Just hearsay, mind, but our chaps in the field pick up all sorts of information."

"Interesting!"

"Now, it appears that he was not too keen to leave Boston and go back to Cyprus when he was invited to be Bishop of Larnaca. Can't say I blame him as he's spent most of his adult life out of Cyprus. Apart from the village, the school and Kykko, he probably didn't know much about the island or the people. Boston's rather a nice place. No shortage of Greeks in America. I daresay he could have done well there too."

"So if he was reluctant to return to Cyprus, why did he accept?" Harding asked with raised eyebrows.

Lennox-Boyd laughed and spluttered out, "Seems the poor fellow had been elected so couldn't do much about it."

"I see, so he went back to Larnaca and became their bishop. When did he start involving himself in politics?"

"Here's a newspaper story from when he arrived back in '48." He passed Harding a newspaper. The front page showed a bearded man in the black robes of a Greek priest held high above a group of about a hundred men. Beneath the photo the words in bold read:

"You want me, you have elected me your bishop. So, I now dedicate myself to the Church and to Cyprus. I will use my energies to win freedom for Cyprus and break the chains of colonialism."

Harding put down the newspaper and frowned. "Bit odd, isn't it? Here's a chap, a priest, who knows nothing about his country, doesn't really want to live there and then comes out with what is virtually a political war-cry."

"Must have had a Paul-like conversion, wouldn't you say?" Lennox-Boyd smirked.

"Appears so."

"Of course, that was just the beginning. A couple of years later he was elected the head of the whole Church in Cyprus. Now he's His Beatitude Archbishop Makarios III, Ethnarch of Cyprus. And he was only thirty-seven. It's an amazing story. You can see that this chap is no fool. He must have something." Lennox-Boyd nodded. "That's the fellow we're up against."

"And he's done a pretty good job of it so far, hasn't he? How many men do we have tied up there, ten thousand I think." Harding responded with a grim look.

"You'd know better than me, but if we have to we'll double that to put an end to this conflict, and the PM says we will do whatever it takes!"

"Trouble with these converts is that they're often more fanatical and fundamentalist than the originator," Harding grunted.

"Thing is, the other chap is even worse." Lennox-Boyd threw up his hands.

"Grivas?"

"Colonel Grivas. Now there's a chap with a past. Like Makarios, born in Cyprus, but left when he was seventeen and became a Greek citizen. Joined the army and fought in the Greco-Turkish War."

"So he's seen some action. Was that against Kemal Ataturk? The Greeks took a hammering as I recall," Harding added.

"Correct. It was a bloody disaster for the Greeks. Appears this Grivas was a bit of a hero in Greece. He learned a lot apparently from the guerrilla tactics used by Ataturk. Been putting it to good use too in Cyprus. It's hard to fight on their terms." Lennox-Boyd grimaced.

"Regular officer, was he?"

"I'll say, and a bit more. He actually led a band of Resistance fighters in the mountains against the Germans in the Second World War. Turned out to be a bit of an unsavoury character. Didn't mind shooting a few people he thought were not supportive of his group. We think the Greek Government disowned him after the war. Pensioned him off."

"So did he have a conversion on the road to Cyprus too?" Harding's tone was derisive.

"The man's an opportunist. Couldn't get into the Greek Parliament. Tried twice but failed to get the nod. That's when he turned his attention to Cyprus. Not sure when exactly. Maybe after Makarios made his famous speech when he was elected Archbishop." Lennox-Boyd said dryly.

"What was that?" Harding continued making notes.

Lennox-Boyd shuffled more newspapers and put one in front of Harding. Beneath a picture of the imposing figure of Makarios in full regalia with a golden rod in front of his breast the words in bold read:

"I take the holy oath that I shall work for the birth of our freedom and shall never waver from our policy of uniting Cyprus with mother Greece."

"Powerful words," Harding said, putting down the paper, "so you think that spurred Grivas to think that he might join the action?"

"Can't be sure. He might have been looking for something to do before that. He was out of our sight for quite a while. May have been thinking about his old country for years. Sees himself as a bit of a leader apparently. Nothing to lead in Greece so why not take up the Cyprus thing? You never know with people like that. Old soldiers never die but some don't like to just fade away. No offence," Lennox-Boyd apologised.

"None taken. I know it's hard for some, but I'll be quite happy to go quietly when the time comes," Harding chuckled.

"So, as I understand it, Makarios and Grivas are in this together. Makarios travels around the world, welcomed by

Nehru, Tito and the like, gathering support for his aim of independence. The non-aligned countries love him."

"I can imagine. Anyone who embarrasses the dreaded colonials, what?"

"Yes. Makarios stirs up the people from his position as head of the Church, a pretty powerful Church, while Grivas does the dirty work."

"So my job is to get Grivas while putting the government's proposals to the Archbishop?"

"That pretty well sums it up, John. We know that they work hand in hand. We think that the Archbishop controls Grivas, that he gives the orders, but we'd rather leave him be. Could be that all hell would be let loose if we arrested him. If you can knock out Grivas, we think that Makarios would be prepared to negotiate a settlement of the situation that would be favourable to us. We need to keep control of Cyprus, as you have so rightly pointed out."

"Right, probably right. So, when I get out there, I'll have a chat with Makarios, but if he doesn't see sense, then I go all out against Grivas? Will the government back me? No good half measures in a case like this. It's the Greek Cypriots against us and that makes it more difficult. It's very difficult to win against a popular uprising. You know that. Still, if the Cypriots are like most of the Greeks they don't have much stomach for a fight. Too interested in making money," Harding said disapprovingly.

"Unfortunately Grivas is obviously of the same opinion, so he's had a few Greek Cypriots bumped off just so they know to toe the line. Brutal business, really. He has the Greek population so terrified that they're afraid to refuse to help. Standard terrorist tactics, what?"

"Afraid so. That's what makes it so difficult for the troops. Every single man in the street is a potential threat. You can't trust anyone. The Turkish Cypriots seem to be on our side, though?" Harding looked questioningly at Lennox-Boyd.

"Well, they're between a rock and a hard place. I gather from reports that most are happy if we keep Cyprus as a colony. That way they just go on as usual, British subjects under the protection of the Crown. If the Cyps, the Greeks that is, get independence and control of the island, well, who knows? There's so much bad blood between the Turks and Greeks, the Turks could be forced out. One way or another."

"What about Turkey? What's their view on the whole thing?" Harding glanced up from his note-taking.

"Good question. We've had lots of discussions. Unofficial. They won't have Cyprus as part of Greece, not in a fit. Can't say I blame them. They're both in NATO and friendly at the moment, but, well, you never know. They're always squabbling about one thing or another. Neither has what you'd call stable governments so anything could happen." His face twisted in a sneer.

"I see Turkey's point. It would be like uniting Cuba with Russia," Harding said jokingly.

"Actually, that's another of our worries. Makarios is sometimes called the red priest. He doesn't mind courting the Russians or the Yugoslavs. Of course they're happy to go along. Think how nice it would be for them if they had a friendly ally controlling the eastern Mediterranean. They'd be in there like a shot. Just imagine, we'd lose our bases and the Russians would take them over. It wouldn't matter what it cost them, they'd back Makarios to the hilt." Lennox-Boyd grimaced as if in pain.

Harding changed tack. "I'm glad that it's you and not me who has to deal with those kinds of issues. The Ghana thing still coming along?"

"As well as can be expected. It's all too rushed. Same with Nigeria. These people aren't ready yet. It'll all be a shambles in a few years. You get a few educated chaps and they think they can run a country. All these different tribes and religions. Well, we'll try to keep Cyprus on the right track." Lennox-Boyd looked hopefully at Harding.

"And what about Cyprus in the future?"

"Much the same, John. After all, there are only half a million of them. It's not even Birmingham. Without massive support from us they'd be hopeless. Maybe, at some stage we could give them self-government. Give them a bit of control of internal matters, but independence? Never. They haven't the resources. It's just a big farm with sunshine." Lennox-Boyd laughed.

There was a knock at the door and Lennox-Boyd called out to enter. The butler appeared. "The Prime Minister hopes that you are now able to join him and his guests in the dining room."

"Righto, John, we're ready now," said Lennox-Boyd and both men followed the butler out of the room. The luncheon meeting lasted just over an hour and Macmillan saw the Field Marshall to the front door of Number 10.

"I'm looking forward to hearing good news from you, John. Andrew Wright's done a good job out there."

"I agree."

"He has a first-class team so I'm sure they will bring you up to date on the latest developments. I know the winds of change are sweeping through Africa and we can't help that. But Cyprus is, I think, vital to our role in the Middle East. Sort it out, there's a good chap." Macmillan put a hand on his back as the staff car pulled up.

With a brief salute, Harding left to begin preparations for his move to Cyprus. Poor Mindy, he thought of his wife, another house, and another set of staff. Still, a few more years and we can get off down to Dorset and leave all this military business behind.

Cyprus 1955

Field Marshall Sir John Harding, Governor of Cyprus, met with the military intelligence, police chiefs and public relations staff at his residence in Nicosia.

"Right, gentlemen," he began, "bring me up to date with what's been happening the last few months. I have some idea but I want details."

"Governor," Major Phillips was the first to speak. "After the bombings and other incidents, we rounded up dozens of suspected *EOKA* members."

Harding raised an eyebrow. "Anything positive come out of that?"

"Best get the bad news out of the way, I suppose. We've been using Kyrenia Castle as a temporary prison. For questioning."

"Understood," Harding grunted.

"Unfortunately, sixteen of them escaped. Didn't go down too well with the public. A bit embarrassing, really."

"Not good for morale, that's certainly true." Harding gave a slight nod, busy making notes on a pad of writing paper.

"No, Sir. Especially as one of them was Polycarpos Georgjiadis. We suspect him to be one of the top men."

"I see." Harding looked disappointed.

"Next day, the British Institute in Metaxas Square was burned to the ground. We suspected Georgjiadis. He was picked up the following day following a house raid in Nicosia."

"Good! Then?"

"He was taken to a police station where apparently he had some help from a Greek Cypriot policeman. He escaped again and drove through Metaxas Square on his way out of town. Waving a Greek flag."

"Pretty poor show, what?" Harding sat back in his chair.

"Of course it was all over the newspapers and now he's called the Cyprus Houdini."

"So all this bungling has created a hero in the eyes of the Greek community. That won't help us."

"No, Sir."

"Tell me some good news. Do we know the whereabouts of the fellow Grivas? He's the one we want to catch. The whole thing would collapse if we can get rid of him."

"No, Sir," a police commander spoke up. "He's never in the same place twice. You have to understand that most Greeks are willing to give him shelter and food. Even those who oppose the violence are afraid to deny him help."

"Surely there must be some who would inform on him?"

"And risk death or the destruction of their home? Sorry, Sir, but after *EOKA* made an example of one or two people opposed to them, well, what would you do?"

"We can give them protection, surely?" Harding persisted.

"Not on Cyprus, Sir. And they are not keen to go to a safe place in England."

"So we can't count on any support there." He turned to Lawrence Purcell, a well-known writer in charge of public relations, and said, "Give me a short summary of the situation between the Greeks and Turks?"

Purcell shuffled some notes and began reading. "For centuries Cyprus has been, and still is, a peasant agricultural society. When the Ottomans took over, they applied their *millet* system of government."

"What's that?" Harding interrupted.

"Basically, the Ottomans were fairly lazy when it came to running the various parts of their Empire so they let the local chiefs do the work of collecting taxes and running the show. So long as they were paid, they were happy."

"Who was in charge here?" Harding's eyebrows shot up.

"The Greek Orthodox Church. The bishops and priests were the only really educated people. Nothing unusual there. Broadly speaking, this was the case all over Europe five hundred years ago. Priests and monks. So the Church here collected the taxes on behalf of the Sultan and became wealthy. The Church ran the schools and basically controlled the lives of its members."

"What about the Turks?" Harding asked.

"There were few Turks here at the beginning. Then they were sent from the mainland and bought or were given land. By now they occupy about 34 per cent or thereabouts."

"Why didn't they take over control?"

Purcell glanced at his notes. "Not enough of them, Sir. A few of them became tax collectors and moneylenders like the rich Greeks but they didn't have a leader like the Archbishop of the Church. They've always been disorganised. Little *muktars* running their own modest patch."

"So the Greek Church was the only real power on the island? They did quite well out of it considering they were a subject race?"

"To some extent, yes. The Ottomans were great conquerors but hopeless really in economic and commercial affairs. Brought about their own downfall in the end. It might have been different here if they'd sent a few hundred thousand Turks over from Anatolia."

Major Phillips joined in. "It wasn't all beer and skittles, Sir. The island was stripped of its forests and mineral deposits. It was a basket case by the time we took over."

"That was in 1878?" Harding swivelled round to look at him.

"Right. The Ottomans were fighting the Russians. Again. The Sultan needed the help of Britain. To get it, he leased Cyprus to us. Then we annexed it when the Ottoman Empire joined the Germans against us in the Great War."

"So for sixty or seventy years it's been under Britain. How would you say we've done?" Harding fixed his eyes on Phillips then Purcell.

"To be honest, Sir," Purcell said with an embarrassed look, "not too well. The Greek Church controls everything to do with education. Most teachers come from Greek universities. There isn't one here. So the kids learn all about Greece and its glorious past and almost nothing about our history."

"So that explains why they see themselves as Greeks and not British. Unlike the people of Gibraltar?"

"Correct. But not all of them want to join Greece. It's only a couple of years since the end of the Civil War in Greece. There are millions destitute there, the drachma is worthless and they can't seem to form a stable government."

"So much for the birthplace of democracy," Major Phillips interjected.

"I don't think that sort of comment helps." The Governor looked disapprovingly at Major Phillips. "Then we have to show the people that their best hope for a peaceful future with an improving standard of living rests with Britain, not Greece."

"That won't be easy," Purcell shook his head," The Church, through the Archbishop, really controls how the Greeks think or are allowed to think. It won't be easy."

Harding looked up. "I'll be meeting with Archbishop Makarios shortly. I'll see if I can persuade him to see sense. If we have to, we'd rather lose the rest of the Empire peacefully than in pieces."

Purcell leaned forward, intent on convincing the Governor. "The Archbishop is an educated and clever man. He still has the cunning nature of a peasant. He is a Christian but that won't stop him doing whatever it takes to leave his mark on the history of this beautiful island."

"Right. I think I have sufficient information. Thank you all for your contribution. I'll call you all together again after I meet with His Beatitude." Harding stood up and shook hands with each of the men.

Cyprus 1955–1956

PUFFING ON A CIGARETTE, Grivas faced Georgjiadis with a mournful look. "We haven't enough explosives or guns. Nothing is getting through from Greece. We lost four good men at Ayios Neos when the British captured the caique with a shipment of arms."

"So how do we keep up the pressure?" Georgjiadis asked.

"We use tactics that worked in the past. We eliminate a few soldiers, maybe civilians. The British press will love that."

"Yes, I can just see the headlines."

"Nothing works better than a few civilian casualties. You can lose millions of soldiers in a war but nothing makes a better story than a single brutal death on a peaceful street."

"So how will we do it?" Georgjiadis face contorted into an evil smile.

"Nicos Sampson. He's always happy to kill. See him and say we want him to shoot a few people, even off-duty soldiers. Then the press will jump on the story and the British people will say enough is enough to the politicians." Grivas waved the cigarette smoke away from his eyes.

"More than one? How many?"

"Leave that to Sampson. He works for a newspaper. He knows how to make an impact."

"I'll get in touch with him at once. I don't like this inactivity. The people seem to be losing interest in our struggle."

Grivas lit another cigarette. "The people are like sheep. You know, I'm disgusted at the poor quality of recruits we are bringing in. Get the area commanders to step up training. No more fiascos."

"There are plenty of young firebrands out there. Do we bring them in? They like to have their own little gang."

"Yes, then they do what they like. They fail to obey my orders. I can't be everywhere. But I need to be." An angry Grivas flicked the ash from his cigarette.

"Be patient, Dighenis, they are slow to learn. We'll keep the numbers small. It doesn't take many to create havoc."

"Well, get on to it. It's time for some havoc. Wake them up."

Over the next few weeks, twenty-five people were gunned down in Nicosia, Larnaca, Famagusta and Lefka. After each shooting, Nicos Sampson reported the information in his newspaper only hours after the killings. Graphic pictures showed the bodies of two off-duty airmen killed while walking in Famagusta. The bullet-riddled body of a Turkish policeman killed in Lefka was a clear message to Turkish Cypriots. The murders that caused the greatest outrage were the shooting of the wife of a soldier and her four year-old daughter while they were shopping in Ledra St, Nicosia. Pictures of the slain woman and child, each shot in the back of the head, was splashed all over the British newspapers. This set off a wave of reprisals by British military personnel. Greek Cypriots were beaten up and hundreds more added to crowded Camp K where suspected terrorists were held in abject conditions. The converted football stadium now housed over two thousand detainees who were denied any visits. There was uproar in the British Parliament.

The Member for Ormsby jumped to his feet. "This is a bloody disgrace."

"Language," the Speaker of the House interjected.

"I will not alter a word. We have sent the former Supreme Commander of our armed forces to Cyprus and what has happened? More killings."

The Labour Member for Islington stood up, waving a copy of the *Daily News*. "It's time for Governor Harding to hit back at these murderous thugs."

"I ask the Minister for Colonial Affairs, how many have been killed since this terrorist campaign began?" the Member for Ormsby shouted across the Chamber.

Lennox-Boyd stood at the dispatch box. "The latest figures I have are sixty-five British servicemen, twelve British civilians, about a dozen Cypriot police, over a hundred Greek Cypriot civilians and maybe half a dozen Turkish Cypriot civilians."

"Disgraceful. Time you did something positive." The Member for Ormsby shook his fist at the Minister. Lennox-Boyd gave a grim smile and sat down.

Pandemonium continued as Member after Member urged the government to take some action.

Later that night, Harding received a telex communication from London. Looking stern and tired he faced the Commander-in-Chief of Middle East Land Forces, and muttered, "It looks like we'll have to show that we are taking these matters more seriously."

"What's the best option, Sir? More troops? Curfews? Send home all families?"

"Possibly. First, I propose to introduce martial law. Then anyone caught with explosives or a gun will face the death penalty. Time to show these cowards, catch them."

"Murder gets the death penalty. Now you say that the carrying of a gun will too?" the C-in-C looked pensive.

"It's the only way. If a man has a gun then he intends to use it to kill. So he will suffer the consequences. Get my secretary. I'll sign it into law immediately." Harding wiped his brow. "And get me Makarios!"

"*Baba*," a distressed Leyla turned to her father, "why is all this happening? Everywhere people look at each other in funny ways."

"Everyone is afraid. *EOKA* has terrorised us all."

"All I see is suspicion and even the girls I know at school are going about in groups. But they always walk away when I come near."

"You must carry on at school, for now, maybe if things get worse you will have to leave."

"No-one likes me or the other two Turkish girls. The Greek girls, not the English girls, treat us like lepers. It's not very nice."

"Ah, my lovely, it's the stupidity of all these nationalist zealots. Everyone thinks that they and only they own Cyprus."

"I get frightened. Everyone seems so angry, so on edge."

"These people are turning Greeks against Turks and Turks against Greeks. Why do we have to have this foolishness again and again?" Mehmet Ali shrugged his shoulders in a hopeless gesture.

"But most of the people killed are Greeks. It's not us killing them, is it?"

"No. But it is time for the British to show some real force and stop all this *Enosis* business once and for all. Greeks are killing Greeks. It is out of control."

The Turkish leader, Dr Fazil Kucuk, called an emergency meeting of his community leaders. Twenty men crowded into the main room of his modest home in Nicosia. "I am, we all are, distressed at this attempt to force the British to abandon Cyprus. First, I propose that we change the name of our party to 'Cyprus is Turkey Party'. This will give a clear indication to Britain and the Archbishop that any attempt to end British rule will lead to our determination that Cyprus be returned to Turkey. Agreed?" There was no dissent so he carried on speaking. "If the Greeks want armed conflict then we shall give them armed conflict. Rauf," he said looking at Denktash, "you have men ready to defend our homes and our right to live as we always have? The Turkish Defence Organisation, TMT, is progressing?"

Rauf Denktash stood up. Despite his training as a lawyer, used to winning cases by evidence and argument, he was convinced that there was only one path to follow. "As far as I know, TMT has been preparing for some time. Our stock of weapons is small, mainly shotguns with some Enfield rifles. More will be coming from mainland Turkey. We have a place on the Karpas to bring in small craft, only small boats so they are not easily detected. It's only a few cases at a time, but slowly we will build up an arsenal."

Several voices muttered out, "Let's attack now."

Kucuk raised a hand. "I will keep the lines of communication open with Turkey." Kucuk tried to cool the situation. "Zorlu appreciates the danger of the situation. If we do nothing then the Greeks will get what they want. It's not only our people but also Turkey that will be at risk. He is determined not to give an inch."

"Fazil, it's important that you go to Turkey, London and New York. Foreign Minister Zorlu is a tough man. Keep repeating the notion of our right to be masters in our own community. Partition is the only answer. The alternative is a Greek Cyprus," Denktash gesticulated with a clenched fist.

Ozer Ugur, from the mixed village of Kondera stood up. "Everywhere there are secret meetings, angry talk at the coffee shops. Hot days and youths free from study are roaming the streets in gangs. They are looking for trouble. And creating it."

"Tensions are mounting all the time," Denktash added.

After the meeting, Kucuk sat drinking coffee. He thought how easily passions were stirred in people who inhabited the countries of the Mediterranean, especially Greeks.

Grivas organised gang leaders among students with instructions to punish those who failed to rise in support of the holy cause. Old grievances were settled and families became suspicious even of neighbours. Finally, on 2 August, rioting began in Nicosia. School was abandoned as youths roamed the streets shouting *EOKA* slogans. When the British Institute in Metaxas Square, Nicosia, was burned to the ground the next day, several students were arrested and sentenced to caning for their riotous behaviour. They were taken to Caraolas Camp where they were forced to bend over and receive up to six strokes of the cane. Once again the schools were closed as students protested the canings and letters of protest were sent to the Governor and newspapers in Britain.

Harding stood up as the Archbishop, resplendent in his pink cassock and black robe, entered the room at the Governor's mansion. The black mitre hat made Makarios appear much taller than his five feet eight. Having being been briefed on the background of his adversary, Harding knew that this man could not be taken lightly. Unlike the present-day Pope, Makarios was the most complete combination of temporal and spiritual power and he was aware of his unique position.

"Beatitude, welcome. I appreciate you offering to meet with me. These killings must stop. I trust that we can resolve the difficulties that have led to this most unfortunate situation here in Cyprus," Harding indicated that Makarios should be seated.

"You are most kind to think me worthy of the invitation," Makarios responded with a thin smile and sat down opposite Harding.

"As you know, Beatitude, I have been appointed as Governor to end the current unrest on Cyprus and I am confident that with your patronage we can achieve a positive outcome. As a man of God, you must know that violence only begets violence and leads to nothing but misery for everyone concerned." Harding leant forward in a conciliatory gesture.

"Ah, my dear Field Marshall, of course we can resolve the present crisis. The British Government must see the futility of trying to impose its will on a sovereign people. You have tried this in the past and always this ends in failure. The sun has set on the British Empire, has it not?"

"Beatitude, we are not here to discuss the past but how to deal with the present, are we not?" Harding responded in a calm, steady voice. "My government is not inclined to relinquish its control of the island. Cyprus is seen as vital to British interests in the Middle East, as you are no doubt aware. We are prepared to examine any solution that maintains our control while acceding some form of autonomy to the people of Cyprus."

Makarios sat quietly, hands resting in his lap. This is a military man, he thought. He is used to instant obedience to his commands but he is not a negotiator and will tire of the game of politics. He adopted a placating tone, "Governor, we are both reasonable men. Despite your instructions, you and I know that a people cannot be made subjects against their will."

Harding grunted.

Makarios continued. "The world has seen the decline of the British Empire. It is better to have an honourable withdrawal than to face defeat from a small but determined people. Is this not so?"

"Beatitude, I suggest that you put your proposals to me. By all means, we see the inevitability of some kind of self-government for the people of Cyprus. Right?"

A negative shake of the head was the response.

"But under the protective wing of Great Britain," Harding continued. "Cyprus is no India. It will need the financial support of the United Kingdom and our protection against any possible outside threat or interference."

Makarios nodded, fingers pressed together. "But what about Mother Greece? When we are one with Greece we will be happy and secure."

"That is a dream, as you must be aware. Greece is still struggling to overcome its own internal problems and there are of course the Turks," Harding went on with a knowing look.

"Ah, the Turks. Well, we will look after the Turks. Do we not care for them in Western Thrace? They are welcome in our homeland." Makarios was enjoying this mental game of chess.

"What if the government was to give Cyprus a million pounds on the condition that you abandon the idea of *Enosis* and agree to some form of self-government?"

Makarios smiled and said nothing.

"What about my offer?"

"I appreciate that you are only following orders, but would you have me sell our freedom for some pieces of silver?" Makarios stroked his beard, his lips barely visible.

"Well, Beatitude, I am inviting you to put your proposals, your demands, before me and I will take the matter up with the government. But I want you to make a proclamation that you deplore the acts of terror being perpetrated on British property. Denounce *EOKA* and its leaders."

Makarios remained silent.

"Will you do that?" Harding persisted.

Makarios did not respond.

"I see. Then I ask you to go away, to consider my offer, to discuss it with your colleagues and to let me have an answer soon."

Makarios stood up to indicate the meeting was at an end. Harding waited until he had left the room then slammed a fist down on the table. Makarios heard the sound and smiled as he walked serenely down the stairs and out to his waiting car.

The following Sunday, Makarios addressed the congregation at the Church of Saint Barnabas in Nicosia. His words rang out to a fervent crowd. "The struggle for *Enosis* is our only aim. We shall continue the struggle, not only abroad, but we shall give battle here in our own country. If blood must be shed, we shall shed it for our right to return to the bosom of Mother Greece. Hellenism will be triumphant!"

The congregation rose as one and applause followed Makarios as he moved serenely out of the church into the bright midday sun of a Cyprus autumn day.

The build-up of British troops continued as units departed from their bases along the Suez Canal, until over fifteen thousand soldiers settled in tent camps all over Cyprus. Violence escalated with more Greek Cypriots murdered. Two British soldiers, in civilian clothes, out for a stroll along Ledra Street, were shot in the back of the head. Clashes between Greek Cypriots and the British troops worsened. Arrests were made and a number of militants were sentenced to death. Fear and distrust were everywhere. When two more "traitors" were executed for not assisting *EOKA* and the struggle for *Enosis*, the whole Greek Cypriot population was convinced. Any thought of remaining aloof from the conflict vanished. Opposition to or failure to assist *EOKA* was eliminated.

Governor Harding waved Lawrence Purcell to be seated. "Lawrence, this situation is deteriorating. The government is inviting Greece and Turkey to a conference in London."

"What about the leaders of the Greek and Turkish communities here?" Purcell looked puzzled. "Surely it is they who should be involved?"

"No. The idea is to get Greece and Turkey involved. If both countries champion the rights of their Greek and Turkish communities here in Cyprus, we'll get a stalemate. Neither country will back off. It may be the way to end this nonsense of self-determination."

"It certainly has possibilities. Neither will wish to go to war over Cyprus. I suppose their involvement could force Makarios to abandon *Enosis*?"

"Let's see what happens, shall we? Meanwhile, keep the foreign press on side."

As the conference in London was in progress, violent riots broke out in Istanbul, the former Constantinople so desired by the Greeks. The riots followed a bomb attack on the house in Thessalonika where the great Turkish leader, Kemal Ataturk, had been born. Beginning as a demonstration encouraged by the Turkish Government, it soon got out of hand with great destruction of Greek property. The Greek Cypriots read the reports and were alarmed, for now Turkey seemed to be joining the conflict.

Following the collapse of the Plastiras-Venizelos Government in Greece, Marshall Papagos came to power with an overwhelming majority in parliament.

Archbishop Makarios immediately flew to Athens to try to win greater support for *Enosis*. The King and Queen met him at the airport and crowds lined the street as they drove in an open car to Constitution Square. High above the crowd, his robes billowing out in the breeze, Makarios raised his arms wide and through loudspeakers called out, "In the name of our holy struggle, I demand the support of Greece. Together we will bring Cyprus back to the bosom of the Motherland. Cyprus is Greece and Greece is Cyprus."

The enthusiastic, patriotic crowd chanted his name over and over.

On his return to Cyprus, Governor Harding sent for Makarios again. The atmosphere was tense as Makarios entered the room. He showed no emotion, maintaining his usual calm, priestly manner.

"Archbishop, I am asking you, now, this very day, to go on the radio and denounce once and for all these brutal, inhuman acts being perpetrated by murderous thugs who will never achieve a political solution by these means. Do you understand?" Harding shouted as he banged his fist on the table.

"I am not the cause of any acts of violence, Governor Harding. But you must understand the frustrations of my people, who ask only what is their right and heritage." Makarios spoke softly and with great deliberation.

"Archbishop, we have first-class intelligence that you are closely associated with *EOKA*. You are in regular contact with this man Grivas and you fund the activities of *EOKA*."

Makarios remained silent.

"Do you deny that you are *EOKA* and will you deny it publicly and restore some sanity here?" an angry Harding demanded.

Makarios remained impassive. "All of Cyprus is *EOKA*, Governor."

"Then, I will report to my government that your continued presence on Cyprus is an ongoing threat to peace and stability and that I recommend that you be deported to a place where your involvement and influence is ended. Will you denounce *EOKA* and its activities?" he asked one more time.

"Governor, Sir, you are a military man, you must do your duty as you see fit. I must be faithful to my people and my country. Whatever you do with me, all of Cyprus and all of Greece will be with me." Makarios made a little bow.

"So be it," Harding rasped, "just be glad that you are dealing with the British. Elsewhere, with other people, you would be in prison or dead."

"Ah, yes, you British are civilised people, are you not? But you have tried prisons before and you do not hesitate to hang people, a barbaric act. Yet you judge me who only carries out his duty to free his people," he said with a sardonic laugh, thinking how foolish were the British and their notions of fair play.

The following day, Makarios was arrested at Nicosia airport on his way to Athens. The official statement accused Makarios of being deeply implicated in the campaign of terrorism launched by *EOKA* and stated that he would this day, the 9th of March, be deported to the Seychelles Islands in the Indian Ocean.

In London the British Government released the "Grivas Diaries". The British press splashed the documents over pages of print. Makarios was accused by journalists of being a priestly hypocrite, a man who preached peace but practised bloodshed and killings. Harding smiled when the *London Daily News* and *The Times* landed on his desk the next day. But no-one in the British Government was smiling when President Nasser of Egypt nationalised the Suez Canal in July 1956 and by the end of the year had ended Britain and France's reign of power in the Middle East.

Makarios and Bishop Kyprianos of Kyrenia together with two young priests were housed in San Souci Lodge, the summer residence of the Governor of the Seychelles. The idyllic setting on the hills overlooking Victoria Harbour on the island of Mahe was destined to be their home for the next year.

EOKA hit harder and harder at the British troops and vital installations. Harding responded by dismissing most Greek

Cypriots in the employ of Army and RAF compounds and replacing them with Turkish Cypriots who were considered no threat to the safety of the military. In fact, the Turks were the eyes and ears of the military, responsible for the detection of many terrorists and aborting several bombings. So a new alliance began. A new Turkish Auxiliary Police Force was formed under British officers to assist in the fight against *EOKA*. Many of these police were also members of Denktash's clandestine Turkish Cypriot organisation, first named Volkan, then TMT. Despite British protests, the organisation began to organise attacks against Greek Cypriot property and suspected *EOKA* members. This only led to reprisals from the Greek side and misery for all sections of the population. Now, all trust was gone and anyone from the opposing side was an enemy.

The number of British servicemen on Cyprus now approached 40,000 and a curfew was imposed, further angering the Greek Cypriots. Harding was locked into a military solution and operations began in the mountains, villages and towns to try and track down and capture Grivas. Harding believed that cutting off the head of *EOKA* would bring about its death.

Crookham, England, January 1957

"MY NAME IS Corporal Anderson. I am your instructor for the next ten weeks. You will address me as Sir. Do not speak unless you are asked a question. When I speak, you will stand at attention. You are now in the army. We have our own laws, Queen's Regulations. Officers are addressed as 'Sir'. While you are in my squad you will address me as 'Sir'. You will obey your senior officers at all times. Do you understand?"

The recruits stared glumly ahead, silent.

"Do you understand?" Corporal Anderson shouted into the face of a skinny man in a baggy uniform.

"Yes, Sir," he squeaked out and then the rest of the squad shouted the same.

"Do not question any lawful order. A lawful order is covered in Queen's Regulations. If an officer orders you to drop your trousers so that he can give you a prick with his dick, that is not a lawful order. You can refuse. Unless you are a nancy boy. Any nancy boys here?"

The squad remained silent.

"Any nancy boys here?" the corporal screamed.

"No, Sir," the men shouted back, not quite in unison.

"Good," he screamed. "'Cause we have enough nancy boys in the medics. Horrible little boys. It gives the Corps a bad name. Now, we're going to get along fine so long as you jump when I say jump. I don't want any of you to fail passing out. It doesn't look good on my record. If one of you slacks, then the whole squad will do extra drills until the slacker is up to scratch."

So began eight weeks of marching, arms drill, cross-country

running, climbing up ropes and crawling under barbed wire. Having shared a bed with his brother for sixteen or more years, Alex considered it no great problem to share a barracks with nineteen other young men. At least he had his own bed and a locker.

"It's not too bad, really," he confided to Josh Elliot who had the bed next to his. "Could be worse. At least we're not too far from the pot-bellied stove. It's nice and warm."

Each recruit was issued with two pairs of boots, two uniforms, four sets of underwear, two sets of pyjamas and two berets. Other items included webbing, puttees, badges and Corps insignia that had to be sewn on the uniforms. After dinner, small groups sat together polishing boots and blancoing webbing. The toecaps of the boots were polished to a japan-like finish by alternately adding boot polish then Brasso and spit. This pair of boots was wrapped in an old soft cloth and carefully stored in a locker. These boots were taken out and worn only on parade. The second pair was worn the rest of the time for marching, running or climbing.

"Fuckin' army. Waste of time, all this bull," a voice muttered.

"Just do it. It's only for a couple of months. Then you'll be on the wards."

"Aye, and then you'll wish you were back here," a Scottish voice called out.

Josh laughed. "If I wanted to see my face, I'd buy a mirror, not make one out of spit and polish."

Alex held up his gleaming boot. "It's just to train you to do what you're told."

After lights out at ten, the barrack room was quiet for a while. Then Alex heard the sound of someone crying. Next there was some giggling and whispering, followed by the sound of someone masturbating. Finally, only the sound of snoring broke the silence.

Alex enjoyed the physical aspect of basic training. He was much fitter than most of the squad, and he coped with the strenuous exercise without any problems. The lectures on biology, first aid and basic nursing were boring. The standard was even less than first year at Pharmacy College. Since he expected a posting to a hospital dispensary, Alex made no great effort to score high marks. Alex was older than any other man in the squad. He was also older than Corporal Anderson, who treated him with more respect than he did the others. Alex was the only one with a college education and the fact that he would be a sergeant at the end of training made him a leader who could be relied on to help out with letter writing and other problems. Wilf Marking, a farm boy, eighteen years old, had never been away from home before. Round-shouldered and weedy, for him, life in the barracks was a misery. After a few days he began to wet his bed. Clean sheets were issued only every Friday and Wilf's pyjamas and bed began to smell.

"Fuckin' hell, Wilf," Jack, in the next bed cried out, "you bloody stink, you scrag."

A crowd soon gathered round Wilf's bed. "Get the bastard!" someone shouted and before Alex could stop them, Wilf, with his sheets, was carried down to the showers where he was dumped. The cold water poured down on him as he sat huddled, crying and begging for help.

Corporal Anderson heard the commotion and appeared in his pyjamas. "Break it up, lads, break it up. What the fuck's going on?" He burst through the rabble. "Shite, what's going on?"

Alex explained the situation. Wilf was sent to the medical officer, who passed him on to a psychiatrist at the military hospital in Aldershot. Wilf was discharged from the army as medically unfit for service.

One thing Alex brought to the army from his upbringing was the ability to fight. Scotland loves a hard man, a man who is good with his fists and does not shirk a fight. Boxing and football were tickets to a better life for many young Scotsmen who aspired to fame and fortune. While he had never been an enthusiastic participant, Alex had played his part and was reasonably proficient at the art of boxing. The fear of losing at anything gave him the courage to stand up and fight when needed.

Corporal Anderson slept in a room at the end of the barracks. It was a comfortable little room with a radio, pictures of bathing beauties on the wall and a small wooden chest of drawers with an electric kettle and toaster. In one corner was a sofa-like chair and next to the bed was a bentwood chair with an alarm clock.

Alex knocked on the Corporal's door.

"Enter," came the response in a loud military voice.

"Permission to speak, Sir," Alex said in an equally loud voice as he brought his boots down hard and stood to attention.

"Shut the door and relax. Move that clock and sit down," Corporal Anderson nodded to the wooden chair. "What's on your mind, Forbes?"

Alex carefully moved the clock and pulled the wooden chair away from the bed. With the door closed he could forget the formalities and speak to Anderson like a normal person. "Corp, I've been thinking about the notice on the board. It's asking for volunteers for the boxing team. I thought I might give it a go."

"Yeh, I know from your records that you did a little bit before coming here. Do any good?"

"Well, I only fought a few times, six, actually. I didn't have a lot of time with study and everything. But I did okay, I only lost one. Knocked out. In Greenock. A tough bugger from Glasgow."

"Well, it would certainly be a feather in my cap if you made the team. Leave it with me. I'll speak to Taffy, Sergeant Jones, he's in charge of the boxing team. He's always looking for new recruits. You know you get special privileges if you make the team?" Anderson winked.

"Yes, I'd heard that. Anyway, that doesn't matter. I quite like all the running, the push-ups and the marching. I'd rather be outside than sitting in the stupid lectures."

"Wish I could say the same for some of these other buggers. Bloody unfit lot. They must spend all their time wanking.

Hate to think how we'd go if there was a war on," he said with a derisory laugh.

Corporal Anderson's prediction about privileges was true. A member of the boxing squad was excused not only lectures but also the monotonous drill marching. The down side was skipping, medicine-ball exercises, heavy punch bag work and sparring. As it happened, the first tournament was an inter-Corps night when various boxers from medical units all over Britain came to Aldershot to try to win a place in the Royal Army Medical Corps team. Alex was matched against a young private from a unit in Plymouth. The eighteen-year-old was keen but totally inexperienced and spent three rounds of three minutes each backing away from Alex's straight left-hands. It was a unanimous points decision.

The Company Commander at the Corps Headquarters sent for Alex. The staff sergeant in the front office was quite casual, unusually so, thought Alex. "Just go in," he said, looking up from some paperwork.

"Ah, Forbes!" Major Humble was hatless and waved a response to the salute. "Stand easy. How would you like to stay on here after basic training? I would make you up to sergeant and you could be part of the Corps boxing team. Help out Sergeant Jones, maybe give some lectures on the use of medicines and so on. Good posting. Near London. Lots of time off. Sound good?"

Alex hesitated. "I haven't given it much thought, Sir."

"Well, it's a jolly good offer. Better to spend the rest of your two years here than in some isolated posting where you are not likely to make sergeant. Too many of you chemist chaps already. You've all come in at once."

"I'd still like to give it some thought, Sir, but thanks for the chance to stay here. Can I let you know later?" Alex inclined his head.

"Certainly. Wouldn't want you to stay unless you wanted to. Not our style. Well, off you go and good luck for next week." Humble dismissed Alex with a wave of the hand.

Taffy Jones wanted to make sure that the contest between the RAMC national team and the 4th Parachute Regiment in Aldershot would not be the whitewash of the previous year. Alex was matched against a redheaded corporal, Frank Duffy, who was slightly shorter in height and reach but had arms like legs. As soon as the bell sounded Duffy came out like a whirlwind, his arms flaying like a threshing machine. Alex danced away, back-pedalling with the occasional straight left to Duffy's head. He took quite a number of heavy blows to the arms and one or two to his head. Duffy swung a right hand that caught Alex on the left-hand side at the base of his ribs. He felt a stabbing pain but managed to survive the round only slightly out of breath.

The crowded gymnasium was noisy with rival cheer squads.

"What are you doin', boyo?" Taffy shouted in his ear while taking out Alex's gum shield and passing him a water bottle. "Give him as good as you get. Mix it up with him. He won't hurt you with that round-arm action."

"I'll wait a bit," Alex said, breathing in as much air as he could, "his arms will get tired. He can't keep this up for three rounds."

"Well, start throwing a few more punches, I reckon he took the first round," Taffy coughed.

The second round followed the same pattern but Alex could sense there was less force in the blows and he managed to land some good lefts and a right-hand that shook Duffy and stopped him for a few seconds.

"Listen, boyo," Taffy exhorted, "that was better but you just finished even that round. Step up the pace in the last or we're done for."

The bell went for the third and final round. Alex jumped off his stool and before Duffy could get his hands up Alex shot out a right-hand punch without leading with the left. Down went Duffy who landed right on his bottom. He looked up at Alex and then on the count of six he forced himself to his feet. The referee wiped his gloves and called them to box on. Duffy moved in for a clinch and Alex drove a left into his solar plexus then a right uppercut. Duffy went down and was counted out. Taffy Jones raced across the ring and held up Alex's hand while the RAMC supporters rose to their feet, cheering and making rude gestures to the opposition. Towel wrapped around his head, Alex made his way down the aisle accompanied by many backslaps. Under the shower, he gave his ribs a rub but soon forget the ache in the euphoria of victory. Later that night after a couple of celebratory beers, Alex lay in bed in agony until finally reporting to the sick bay for treatment. Breathing out, he was strapped with tape to stop him breathing in too deeply. While this solved one problem it created another. After two weeks the tape was removed. The tape was cut at the back and then one orderly on each side ripped off the tape together with most of the hair on his chest.

That decided Alex and the invitation to remain at Corps HQ was declined.

Major Humble expressed his disappointment, "Right, Private, if that's your decision. You can go to York, there's a Military Hospital there. You may be lucky to get three stripes, but I wouldn't hold out much hope. Anyway, good luck. Dismissed." Humble ignored the salute.

Three days later, Alex received a train voucher to take him to York in the north-east of England. As luck would have it, there was no vacancy for a Dispenser Class One at the hospital at York.

"How the hell did we manage to get so many pharmacists in at the start of the year?" Alex asked a corporal, a pharmacist, Martin Edwards.

"Don't know." A bored Edwards shook his head. "I suppose some guys got a deferment. How come you're only starting now?"

"I failed one of the exams and had to re-sit it in November." Alex explained what had happened. "Anyway, how long have you been here?"

"Six months. With a bit of luck I might get made up to

sergeant by the end of the year. The two sergeant dispensers finish their National Service about then."

Alex was marched in for his interview. "Sorry about this." The CO put on his cap and returned the salute. "It's a bit rough for you fellows but there's not much I can do. I'll make you an acting-corporal. I can do that. It's a bloody shame that a pharmacist doesn't get a commission."

"Thank you, Sir" Alex winced. "It's not much fun being a National Service corporal, is it?"

"'Fraid not. You'll be in the barracks with the other men. At least you're older than most of them. I know they can be a bit difficult, taking orders from a corporal who's one of them, so to speak."

Alex collected his two stripes from the clothing store. Martin Edwards had warned him to avoid giving too many orders to the other National Servicemen.

"They think all us Nashos should stick together. I try to keep out of everyone's way. I have a cushy job in the dispensary but I don't think there's room for any more there."

Alex was put in charge of the cleaning detail. A short, broad-shouldered labourer from Middlesbrough, Jake Tarrant, told Alex to fuck off when ordered to clean up a mess around the recreation hall. When the possibility of being charged with insubordination was pointed out, Jake spat out. "Take off those bloody stripes and we'll see who's the boss around here."

It was like an incident when Alex had been sixteen. An argument with a big Scot of Italian extract had led to a fight in the schoolyard. Heavily outweighed, Alex had taken a beating.

Alex knew that striking another rank was a serious offence in the British Army and that he was taking a risk if he took off his tunic. But the whole rotten, unfair situation made him angry and slowly he took off his jacket. Within seconds, a mob gathered round and crowded the combatants inside a small circle. This was fine for a street fight but no good if you wanted to use boxing skills. Lashing into each other, hemmed in by a cheering, jeering crowd, it was a typical street fight with no

Queensbury Rules. His greater fitness saw Alex stop Jake with a punch that re-shaped Jake's nose. Nothing beats a punch right on the bridge of the nose. As is the way, sporting and physical prowess meant more to the squad than brains or intelligence and Alex had earned their respect and obedience.

Next morning he was called to the CO's office.

"Left right, left right, left right," the Sergeant Major's staccato voice drummed out. "Halt, salute." Alex stood rigidly at attention for what seemed an age. It was a tactic used to create fear and uncertainty.

Finally, the C.O. looked up. "Forbes, we do not run this unit by force. We have a structure whereby officers command, NCOs carry out the orders of officers and men do as NCOs instruct them. Do you understand?"

"Yes, Sir." Alex offered no further comment.

"Physical violence is used against the enemy, not one's subordinates. Do you understand?"

Alex gave the standard reply. "Yes, Sir."

"I could put you on a charge. That's not good for a man like you. I think it best if we say nothing about the incident. Private Tarrant claims that he walked into a door. Is that correct?"

"Yes, Sir."

"However, I suggest that you put in for an immediate transfer. Do you have anywhere in mind? It's unlikely that you will get a pharmacist posting, unless, of course, you would like to volunteer for Cyprus." He rustled some papers. "I'm pretty sure you would get your sergeant's stripes there." He peered over his glasses. "If you decide to take that chance, you can have a week's embarkation leave."

Packing his gear into his kitbag, Alex chatted with Martin Edwards.

"So you're off to Cyprus." Martin was despondent. "It's not too good out there. Blokes getting killed. Rather you than me."

"Well, it's better than hanging around England. I can get three stripes there. Anyway, the weather should be good. It's in the Mediterranean."

"Well, good luck, Alex. Thank God I only have 450 days to go. Roll on."

Alex collected his train voucher to Dunkeith and one for the week after to Southampton where he would board a ship for Cyprus. Six hours later, he was back home.

"Are ye sure it'll be all right oot there?" Pouring a cup of tea, Alice looked concerned.

"Course it will. Look, Mum, it's a boat trip on the Med then, what, maybe eighteen months in Cyprus. It's better than being stuck in England."

"But what about getting seek. These Arab countries are full o diseases. There's always millions dying." Alice shuddered.

"We've had all our jabs, typhoid, cholera, tetanus, you know," Alex reassured his mother.

"Well, make sure ye bile the waater," Alice persevered. "Ah dinna want to lose my laddie."

"Stop worrying, Mum. There are thousands of troops there. It's not as if it's a real war."

"I'll worry if I want to," she snapped back.

Alex changed the subject. "So you're not at the mill now?"

"No. It got tae be too much. I do some hooses. Cleaning. It's good. Nice hooses and I get to make a cup o tea. Course, the pay's not as good."

"That's great. As long as you enjoy it. If I get made up to sergeant I'll send you some money out of my pay."

After dinner, or teatime, as it was called in Dunkeith, Alex went dancing every night. At the Palais de Danse, to the songs of Jo Stafford and Guy Mitchell, he lived in a world of perfumed girls with eyes closed as they drifted round the floor. His army haircut marked him out as a temporary visitor, a National Serviceman on leave. Girls might like to dance with him but saw no future in walking home with a man who would be gone in a matter of days.

It was time to leave. Alex waved goodbye to his mother as he stepped on to the bus that would take him to the railway station. The sad figure at the apartment window with a long, unsmiling face broke his resolve not to show any emotion. Seeing his tears, the conductor waved him inside without asking for the fare.

England and Cyprus 1957

The *Flying Scotsman* from Aberdeen to London stopped at Dunkeith on time and Alex settled back for the long overnight journey to Kings Cross Station. The carriage was full and he was forced to sit upright for the ten-hour journey. He dozed off for a few minutes at a time. Alex blinked as the train stopped at Edinburgh then Newcastle where he hopped out and bought a tasteless, dry sandwich and a cup of steaming hot tea. Back on the train, passengers huddled into heavy coats and dozed before the next stop at Grantham, still in darkness, then the final leg into Kings Cross Station in London. Stiff and tired, Alex hoisted his kit bag on to his shoulder and headed for the Tube station. Having been to London several times during his army training, he had no trouble crossing the city to Waterloo Station to meet the train that would take several hundred men to Southampton. After an interminable wait, the soldiers boarded the troopship *Devonshire*. Everything was a new and exciting experience.

A National Service sergeant, Jock Kemmet from Edinburgh, was in charge of the ship's dispensary. With Alex and two other pharmacists en route to Cyprus the four formed a little team that did what little work there was to do. The fact that three pharmacist privates were heading for Cyprus did not inspire much confidence in any of them obtaining the rank of sergeant. Below deck, some three hundred men slept in hammocks. The Bay of Biscay lived up to its reputation and the combined smell of sweaty feet and vomit was overpowering. Once the ship reached Gibraltar, the weather improved and everyone spent as much time as possible on deck in the warm sunshine. Alex considered it a Mediterranean cruise. As the temperature rose, Alex joined those who preferred to sleep on the hard deck where at least the air was fresh. The dispensary was well stocked with ethyl alcohol and mixed with orange juice it made a palatable and potent drink that made sleeping a little easier. About twenty QARANCs, Queen Alexandra Royal Army Nursing Corps, were on board heading for Cyprus. As they had officer status, Alex and his fellow pharmacists were able to mix with them only on duty and fantasise like all normal young men. The ship stopped briefly at Gibraltar and again at Algiers where it lay at anchor overnight. Everyone was up on deck to watch the spectacular flashes of guns way off to the south. Next stop was Malta and a few hours ashore. To most on board it was another world, foreign, yet slightly British.

After two weeks the *Devonshire* arrived at its destination. For most on board this was to be home for at least the next eighteen months. Summer had yet to arrive but already it was hot, a dry heat. Crowded in the back of a three-tonne truck, the drive along the south coast and up through the heart of the island to Nicosia was not the best introduction to the beauty of Cyprus. The road was dusty and made worse by the steady stream of trucks and Landrovers moving south. At various places along the way Alex saw tented camps behind barbed wire with soldiers in shorts and doing what he learned was khaki drill. Even with his limited view he could see men and women working along the roadside. They were dressed in the strangest garb, like something out of the *Arabian Nights* without the colour. The women appeared to be doing the hardest work, squatting down and digging with short-handled picks. The men wore a kind of turban and the women some kind of shawl with only the face showing. It was a foreign land indeed.

"Who are those people?" he shouted above the noisy engine.

The truck driver glanced out the side window. "They could be Turks," he shouted back, "or maybe Greeks too. They all look the bloody same to me."

"I thought they didn't like each other."

"Listen, mush, they're the poor people here. We need someone to help build the roads."

"They're working for us?" Alex shook his head in disbelief.

"If you're poor, you'll work for anyone. Our money is as good as anyone's."

"The women look like nuns."

"Nah, they're the Muslims, they follow Mohammed."

Alex sat back, thinking of the name Mohammed. He remembered reading *Ivanhoe* and *The Talisman* by Sir Walter Scot. He recalled that Saladin had been a great warrior leader and found it hard to reconcile this image with the short, dark peasants working by the roadside.

Finally, the long bumpy trip ended and the truck arrived at the British Military Hospital in Nicosia. Armed guards opened the security boom gate. The truck slowly rolled into a wide-open space surrounded by a mixture of old and new buildings.

"Right, lads, home sweet home. More like a prison, you poor sods," the driver laughed as he jumped down and dropped the tailgate.

Alex blinked in the glare from the sun reflecting up from the white sandy ground. Looking around, he could see that the buildings consisted mainly of corrugated tin sheds with some elongated huts. Standing apart was an impressive stone building that was obviously from a colonial past. This was the hospital, a converted government building from the start of the century. Inside, the high ceilings and overhead fans barely kept the wards cool. In typical army style there was not a blade of grass or a tree to be seen and the only decorations consisted of the Union Jack flag and white painted stones outside each hut. After being assigned to a barrack hut, Alex and the other pharmacists met the adjutant, who gave the now-familiar bad news. The hospital dispensary had vacancies for two pharmacists and already three were on staff so they would remain as privates and be assigned the normal duties of RAMC personnel. In a military hospital this meant ward duties, taking temperatures, emptying bedpans, cleaning and any other task that would occupy time. Female nurses, commissioned officers from the QARANCs, acted as ward sisters. They gave the orders.

The barrack for the male orderlies was a featureless long room, painted white with a bed, bedside locker and steel cabinet to house uniforms. It was like being back in basic training. Frustrated, Alex lasted a week before asking for an interview with the adjutant. The Sergeant Major marched him in and he stood to attention.

"Yes, Private, what can I do for you?" the adjutant asked with the emphasis on *you*.

"Sir, I would like to apply to join the paratroopers. Go back to England and do the training." Alex nervously clenched his hands at his side.

"The paratroopers?" he spluttered. "But, man, you've only just arrived here. What's brought this on?"

"Sir," Alex decided that honesty was the best policy, "there's no chance of me getting a pharmacist's position here so I'd like to do something worthwhile. I'd prefer to be a noncommissioned officer in the Paras than stay a Private here. I don't suppose there're too many pharmacists in the Paratroop Regiment."

The adjutant pursed his lips and looked at Alex with a sympathetic eye. "Look, son, I can put forward your request, but I don't give you much hope. However, I understand your thinking. Leave it with me, okay?"

Alex saluted, did an about-turn and left with a sinking heart. But he thought he must have impressed the adjutant as next day he was called to his office. It wasn't the paratroopers but finally he was given some positive news.

"Look, laddie, I've given some thought to your predicament and here's what I have come up with. The 24 Field Ambulance has a sergeant pharmacist due for demob in about a month. I can have a word with Colonel Barry the CO. He might interview you as a possible replacement for Sergeant Mulholland. I can't promise anything, mind, but what can you lose?"

"That sounds fine to me, Sir." After the usual salute, Alex left the office with a spring in his step. So, without a second thought, Alex forgot about the paratroopers and waited for the call to be interviewed by Lt Col P Barry MD. It came the next day. A Landrover arrived to pick him up at 10am. The driver was a private in the Royal Army Service Corps. In the rear was a Medical Corps private armed with a sten gun. That was a surprise. Although he had undergone rifle training, he had assumed that medical personnel did not carry arms. The drive from the Military Hospital headed north from Nicosia through some pleasant little villages. His first real glimpse of Cyprus came as a shock to Alex. Few women were to be seen in the villages. Everywhere were men, seated at tables set out at the edge of the dirt road.

"Why do all the houses have bits of wire sticking up on the roof?" Alex squinted in the bright sunlight.

"See how they're all flat roofs?" the driver removed a hand from the steering wheel and waved out to the right.

"Yeh. So?"

"Well, when they save up enough money they can put on a second level. The wire makes it easy to do that. It's all just bloody concrete. No brick jobs here," he cackled.

"What a funny way to build a house," Alex murmured.

The driver slowed to avoid hitting anyone in the narrow village street. There in the front of a shop with no windows or door, a man was carving pieces off a beef carcass. At such a short distance, Alex could see hundreds of flies swarming all over the meat. "My God, how can they eat meat like that?" he shuddered.

The driver snorted. "Wait till you see what we have to eat. Give that stuff a good wash and it's as good as new."

"I'll stick to tinned bully beef," Alex shook his head in disgust.

"If you hadn't seen that you wouldn't know what you were eating. Wait till you get your knees brown, pal, you'll be surprised what you'll eat. And drink."

"What's it like, this unit?"

"Great. None of the bullshit they have at the hospital. You'll be a regular little brownie in no time."

After a 20-minute drive they arrived at Kermia Camp. It looked like another bare, grassless, tented camp surrounded by barbed wire. An armed RAMC guard opened the now-familiar boom gate. A bitumen road with a dusty, dirt parade ground to one side led to a two storey-house. It was a typical two-storey Greek-Cypriot house, it had been compulsorily acquisitioned for use as a medical centre and officers' mess.

A tall, laconic Staff Sergeant met Alex at a tent alongside the house and shook his hand. "Hi, I'm Staff Archie Campbell, come on in and meet the chief."

Alex was somewhat heartened to hear a broad Scottish accent and marched in, stamped his feet together and saluted a half-naked man slouched in a chair. As far as he could see, the officer wore only a pair of shorts and some kind of wrist-band, which he later found out was his rank. This was Lt Col Barry, an Irish-born medical doctor known to one and all as "Pig".

"Well now, so you're the man they've sent down, "he spoke in a slurred Irish accent. "A pharmacist are ye? Are ye any good? Relax, at ease. Take off your beret, it's too hot for hats."

"I think I'm pretty good Sir," Alex replied, feeling a little strange to be treated in this way.

"Now then, what are ye good at? I know ye can hand out medicine and I see you like to box, but are ye good at anything else?" He lurched forward as he spoke.

Alex was at a loss to think what to say.

"Speak up man, what are ye good at? I've already got a pharmacist, Mulholland. He's 70 per cent, he doesn't drink and he's hardly seen. I could have transferred him but they might have sent me someone who's only 50 per cent. Ye see what I mean?" He winked.

Staff stood there with his arms folded and with a nod and tilt of the head indicated to Alex to get on with it.

"I'm sure I can fit in, I don't mind a drink and I can do most things."

"What do ye think, Staff? He's another one of your lot. Will we take a chance?" He looked at the Staff and Alex looked at the Staff, totally confused at this un-army-like interview. Staff stood there, twirling a bunch of keys on a long chain.

Looking Alex up and down, he said, "We'll need someone to replace Sergeant Mulholland. Private Forbes looks okay to me. We could do worse."

Col Barry leaned back in his chair and his eyes narrowed. "Well, I can't have you in the tents with the other ranks so I'll make you a sergeant, temporary, without extra pay until Mulholland goes. There's no vacancy for another pharmacist sergeant, ye see." He nodded and glanced at Staff.

"He could be made up for the vacancy we have for a clothing store NCO," said Staff and Lt Col Barry pursed his lips by way of reply.

"Can we do that?"

"It's in the Regulations." The answer was quick and confident.

Pig gave Staff a thumbs-up sign. "That's settled then. Get back in the wheels and fetch yer stuff."

Alex was driven back to the Military Hospital to collect his gear and that night ended up drunk as a lord with his master, Lt Col Barry. He had joined Pig's Battalion.

"This is Sergeant Tom Harper, RASC," Staff introduced Alex to the shaven-headed, thickset man whose tent he would share. "Tom and his men look after the maintenance of all the ambulances, trucks and Landrovers."

Alex shook hands. The grip was firm. "You're a regular, I suppose?"

Tom stuttered slightly. "Been in since I was fifteen. Started as a b-boy soldier. Never knew my parents so I left the orphanage as soon as I could. Can't complain. The army's a g-good life."

"Tom's a romantic," Staff laughed, "keeps looking for true love. How's the latest romance going, Tom?"

"C'mon, Staff. You know h-how it's going. You check the b-bloody mail every day."

"Tom waits every day for a letter from Miss Wonderful, or is it Tammy you call her?" Staff grinned.

"Sh-she's a lovely girl. I m-met her on my last leave in UK. Here's a picture of her." He handed a small black-and-white photo to Alex. "Can't keep her away from the dance hall though. She likes to go d-dancing."

"That's tough," Alex sympathised.

"C'mon, Alex, I'll show you my tent." Archie indicated it was time to leave with a sideways movement of his head.

The Staff Sergeant had a tent all to himself. "You'll get used to Tom. Poor bastard. Always looking for love. Sends Miss Wonderful a letter every week. Gets one back every month."

They went in search of Sergeant John Mulholland, the pharmacist. Staff stopped at a large tin shed. The door was locked but opened when Archie Campbell shouted, "Open up, Mulholland. I know you're in there."

A thin, worried face appeared. "Oh, it's you, Staff." He looked at Alex, "Is this my replacement?"

Staff made the introductions and left Alex to get acquainted and learn how the medical store operated.

"All these panniers contain a full set of medicines, injections, scissors, scalpels and so on. We hardly ever use them. Once a month an officer, a doctor, does a check. To make sure everything is in order. If the job was done properly it would take a whole day."

"What do you mean?" Alex began to sweat in the hot shed.

"It's all a joke, really. We check one pannier then sit and chat for an hour. The officer signs to say that everything is okay and that gets passed on to Staff Campbell who tells the CO, if he feels like it. It's Staff that runs the show here. You'll find out."

"The CO said that you're hardly ever seen. Are you kept real busy?"

"No way. I just keep out of the way of Pig. Did Staff mention that I'm leaving earlier than he thought? I've got this shocking tinea so I'm being transferred back to Crookham to let it clear up before demob."

"That's okay. Suits me fine. I'll get my rank as a Dispenser then." Alex gave a cheery grin.

"Well, I've only got a week to show you how it all works. Here's the ledger. Everything is accounted for here. These are the forms to write off any items used, lost or broken. If you have any problems, Staff will show you what to do."

Acting Sergeant Alexander Forbes was welcomed into his new home with a hangover. At least he shared a large tent with only one other sergeant and compared to a barracks it was home away from home.

Next day, Staff Sergeant Archie Campbell brought him up to date with the situation in Cyprus. "We've got the big man, the Archbishop, tucked away in exile. He's a right two-faced bugger but at least he was a tempering influence on the real extremists."

"So things are getting worse are they?" Alex tried not to sound too worried.

"Grivas is the real hard man. Elusive bugger. We just can't seem to catch him. He's really stepped up the attacks since Makarios was whipped off to the Seychelles."

"How does he manage to be so dangerous?"

"Half the lads he has doing the killings are just young thugs looking for excitement. They're just like the gangs in Glasgow. Any excuse for a barney. Three police were shot dead two days ago. Bloody Ledra Street, we should close it down forever."

"Did they catch anybody?" Alex began to wonder if Cyprus had been a good choice.

"They never catch anybody. There's a little Greek shite, Nicos Sampson. He always seems to be right on the spot when there's a murder."

"Who's he? What does he do?" Alex asked.

"He's a photojournalist correspondent for the *Times* of Cyprus. Always there as usual. It's no coincidence if you ask me. It's time the authorities realised that it's no accident he's always at the murder scene."

A few days later, Sampson was arrested and charged with

the murder of one of the policemen. Crowds gathered as he was brought to the court for his trial. Banners were held high proclaiming, "British are the murderers" and "Nicos is innocent". The packed courthouse was stunned when the prosecutor, Rauf Denktash, presented a statement signed by Sampson admitting to the murder. All hell broke loose with people screaming, wailing and shouting abuse. The defence, led by the *EOKA* member, Greek Cypriot lawyer, Glafcos Clerides, alleged that the confession had been made under torture. Eventually, the judge was forced to dismiss the charge on lack of evidence. Denktash was furious. The next month, June 1957, Sampson was stopped at a police roadblock. He jumped out of the passenger seat of the car and pointed a sten gun at the police and threatened to open fire if he was not allowed to pass. Under the strict, almost draconian Emergency Regulations that prohibited the possession of firearms, this was a crime punishable by hanging. Sampson was convicted and sentenced to death. Grivas immediately unleashed his guerrillas against British installations all over Cyprus.

Governor Harding called in his advisors. "Get this man Sampson on a plane and out of here."

"What are you proposing, Sir?" his aide asked.

"I've decided to commute his sentence to life imprisonment. He can serve his time in the UK. If we hang the bastard we'll only create another martyr. The Greeks would love that."

"But, Sir, we know for a fact that he's responsible for several murders. Everyone knows that. We have to make an example of him. For the sake of troop morale."

"It can't be helped. His death would only boost the morale of the enemy. Get him out. That's my decision." Harding was aware of the unhappiness of his commanders as they departed with much muttering.

The decision of Governor Harding to spare Nicos Sampson was all the talk of the camp. While he was a hero to many Greek Cypriots, to some he aroused feelings of shame and loathing for the killing of innocent civilians, including, it was believed, a woman and her daughter. The decision led to disgust among the troops and over a beer the talk was to shoot the bastards first and then claim they had tried to resist arrest.

Archie Campbell was a regular, who had signed on for 22 years. He had served in Germany, Vienna, Palestine, Egypt, Malta and now he was in Cyprus. He was arguably the most intelligent man in the unit. Almost all officers were National Servicemen, doctors who had gone from school to university and were now in the army for two years' National Service. Archie was a voracious reader and had studied the people and history of every posting he'd been to. He sensed that Alex was a kindred spirit and tried to enlighten him about Cyprus.

"You have to understand, son," he said, "these people are not like you and me. They don't mind killing each other over a stolen goat or a sheep. If you offend them by making advances to their daughter, you're likely to find a knife in your back. It's just the way they are."

"I didn't know that," Alex confessed.

"The Turks and Greeks are all the same, it's all about honour. I'll lend you *The Seven Pillars of Wisdom*, you've heard of Lawrence of Arabia?"

"No, sorry, Staff," Alex murmured.

"Shite, man, what have you read?" Campbell looked disappointed.

"Well, I've read Neville Shute and A J Cronin," Alex hesitated, unsure if his response was acceptable.

"Romantic shite," Archie bellowed, "I thought you were intelligent."

"We didn't do Middle East history at school," Alex protested.

"Listen, it's time you learned something other than how to dish out pills. Here's what we have here, right? The Gypos have kicked us out of Egypt so we need Cyprus as our Middle East base. The Greeks want us out so they can join up with Greece, God only knows why. The Turks want us to stay so the Greeks don't knock them off."

Alex nodded as if he understood.

Staff continued. "We're the colonials and that's a dirty word these days. The *EOKA* boys are smart. There are not many of them but they have every Greek helping them so we run around like a dog chasing a butterfly. They're fighting this war on their terms and we have politicians saying we can't do this and we can't do that. Forty thousand bloody soldiers and all we catch are a few kids."

"So what's the point of it all?"

"The point of it all is that we do our time here and then leave it to some other poor sod to do the same. Leave them to it, I say. The Greeks and Turks hate each other so we should let them get on with killing each other. Christ, there're only half a million here. It's not even as many as Glasgow. There're probably more Cyps in London than there are here. Anyway, keep your nose clean and enjoy the cheep booze and fags."

"How long have you been in, Staff?" Alex wanted to learn more about this lanky Scot.

"Since 1946. Couldn't stand Glasgow. Joined up to get oot o the place."

"What did you do before that?"

"Left school at fifteen and started as a draughtsman at the shipyard. Hated it. So I joined up. Did the clerk's course so I could get off the wards."

"Don't blame you. How long have you been a Staff Sergeant?"

"Six years. I've been asked to do more courses and get Sergeant Major but, ach, I like it like this. Nobody bothers me as Company Clerk."

"What about a non-medical commission? Do you not fancy that? Like the Adjutant?"

"Who'd want to be like him? I like my job. I deal with the CO and he's always a doctor. Knows nothing about the army, the regulations. So they always rely on me to keep them on the straight and narrow." Archie looked pleased with himself.

"Well, I'll read that book you mentioned."

"Just come and ask me if there's anything you need to know. The army's a doddle if you work things right."

The men of Pig's Battalion were easily recognised by the fact that they wore shorts, boots with socks rolled over the top, a beret and a wrist band indicating rank. Pig wanted to show that his men were not to be regarded as soft, poofter medicos. The men responded to his attitude by doing their best to show that he was right.

"So what do we actually do in a Field Unit?" Alex looked at Archie Campbell.

"It works like this. You have the base hospital, right? Like the one you were lucky to escape from." Alex nodded happily. "That's a permanent building where serious cases, or at least they're supposed to be serious, are handled. Operations and the like or infections. Then there're us. We're attached to a Brigade. That's several units all under a Brigadier. The infantry and light artillery units are all near here, out in the field, ye ken?"

"Right," Alex began to get the picture.

"So we act as a mobile hospital. You'll soon see. The men learn how to erect a big tent. Takes about eighty men. That's the hospital. You have all the equipment for operations and the like, same as a permanent hospital. Company medics deal with any minor things but every day we have sick parade for the Brigade. On operations, casualties in the infantry units, the serious ones, are brought to us. We get them fixed up so that they can travel, then we send them to the base hospital. Got it?"

"I see." Alex tried to imagine a big tent as a hospital. "So if a soldier wants to be excused duties he has to come on sick parade and get a doctor's line?"

"Right! Now, as soon as Mulholland leaves you'll be in charge of all the medicines and equipment. So when we move, you'll move. I'll stay here. Somebody has to look after the pay and things." Archie smiled contentedly.

"How often do we move?"

"Not often, especially here. It's not far from anywhere to Nicosia. But the lads will put up the hospital tent at least once a week. On the parade ground. Practice for the real thing." Archie tapped a finger to his head. "That's usually first thing in the morning before the heat gets up. Then the tent poles get bloody hot."

"Sounds better and better." Alex smiled at the idea of physical work. The day after Mulholland left, the Brigade went out on an operation to try to catch some terrorists assumed to be hiding in caves in the Troodos Mountains. Pig called on Alex in his tin shed.

"We're just taking ten men, Forbes. I want to take just a few things with me. Let me have a bag with some dressings and a few morphine syrettes. You'll get them back if I don't use them. No need for any paperwork, ye see," he winked and stuck a thumb in the air.

An Acting Sergeant could be reduced to private at the whim of the Commanding Officer. A Substantive NCO could be demoted only as a result of a court martial for a serious offence. Alex decided to keep in Pig's good books.

"Don't ever argue the point with him," Staff Campbell said, taking Alex aside. "Give the silly bugger what he wants. He likes to play doctor sometimes. God help anyone he treats."

Alex filled a canvas bag with a selection of dressings, surgical implements and five morphine syrettes. A syrette was a soft metal tube with a needle attached. After removing the needle cover, it was inserted under the skin and the collapsible tube squeezed to inject the morphine. The heat inside the shed caused many syrettes to leak and they would be written off as faulty. Alex quickly learned to write off a few good items as faulty so that he always had a few spares.

"There you are, Sir." He handed the bag to Pig.

"Tanks, Forbes. See you in a few days." Pig slung the canvas bag over his shoulder and called out for his "four wheels".

Three days after the Troodos Operation, Captain Tom MacGowan conducted the routine check of the medical store. The signed report was duly delivered to the office. Alex was called to Staff's tent to find Pig lounging in his usual chair.

"Ah, Forbes," Pig said, his Irish brogue accentuated by his slight speech impediment. "Captain MacGowan has signed the form to say that all medical supplies are present and correct, right?"

"Yes, Sir. We checked everything," Alex lied, knowing that Pig knew he had lied as the inspection had lasted less than an hour.

"Then," Pig produced the canvas bag, "how do you account for these?" as he put the five morphine syrettes on the table.

"They were spares, Sir, so you can keep them," Alex responded, not with any great confidence.

"What do ye mean, spares? How do we get to have spares?"

"Sir, if I find some things not quite right, I write them off. But I sometimes keep them in case we get an inspection from Brigade. If they want to check the ledger. You know?"

"Ah, so I can keep these?" he squinted at Alex then turned to Staff Campbell. "Is that right, Staff? Can he do that?" Pig relied on Staff Campbell for all military matters.

"Well," Staff hesitated," it's not strictly according to Regs but it's handy if we get a snap inspection from Brigade. We wouldn't want an adverse report from Brigade, would we?" Staff knew that Pig feared nothing more than a bad report from Brigade HQ.

"I see," Pig nodded. "Very clever, Forbes. I see ye know how it works. I tell you what. You can take charge of the Clothing Store as well. Ye seem to be getting the hang of tings."

All other ranks besides officers were supplied with free replacements for worn-out boots, shorts, underwear, tunics and shorts. Once a month Alex took the old, worn-out clothing to the Ordinance Depot at Famagusta. A voucher was issued so that he could indent for new gear. Alex soon worked out that nobody at the Ordinance Depot gave a toss what was thrown on to the pile of old boots, tunics and underwear. He stood on the back of the truck and threw out one boot and called out "one pair". He repeated this until the load was emptied. At the end he would be issued with a voucher for 20 pairs of boots although he had thrown only ten pairs. He went up again in Pig's estimation when Alex presented Pig with a new pair of boots, free.

The Sergeants' Mess consisted of a tin shed with a fridge and a "kitchen" out the back where food was rendered inedible by a private who had never cooked anything in his life. Outside the mess was a large bucket urinal and some distance away the showers and deep-trench latrines. Medical dressings such as strapping tape, bandages and plasters were easily written off as "expendable items" without the signature of an officer. The Sergeants' Mess had a levy that was used to buy non-army food to improve the quality of the meals. Alex bartered around Cyprus, visiting different units. Every unit had a football team that required strapping, elastoplast, antiseptic, bandages and cotton wool. Alex would pay a visit to the British Military Hospital in Nicosia and help himself to whatever he wanted. None of the pharmacists there cared so long as it was "expendable" items. Alex then did a deal with the sports officer, usually a Sergeant, at a unit somewhere on the island. In return for the first-aid dressings he was able to obtain extra food items such as ham off the bone and tinned foods that were not supplied by the Army Catering Corps. When items such as cutlery were lost or stolen, Alex would barter for a new set. Each unit always had something that he wanted or could use to barter at another unit. Thanks to the small size of Cyprus, he visited most parts of the island.

By late July, Alex was well and truly accepted by everyone at 24 Field Ambulance including Pig who regularly included him in his little conferences with Staff Campbell. So he was not surprised when Private Taffy Jones popped into the tin shed and said Alex was to report to the CO. Normally Staff's tent was open at the front so that he and Pig had a view of the other ranks' lines.

That day, the flaps were closed so Alex coughed. "Sir, you wanted to see me?"

Pig was not only a big man; he had a voice to match so it was a surprise to have him reply in a soft voice, "Ah, come away in, Forbes."

Inside the tent, Pig was in his usual seat, Staff stood beside him and a man in a suit was seated in a chair with his back to the entrance. "Ah, sit down, Forbes and meet Major Pitt, he's from the War Office. He wants to talk to you." Pig pointed his swagger stick to a seat.

Pitt was a stocky man, possibly 50 years old, with a pale face and a large moustache. "Hello, Sergeant. I understand that you are a pharmacist with some experience. I want you to listen carefully to me and nothing I say must be repeated to anyone outside this tent. Is that understood?" He spoke with a cultured yet unmistakable London accent.

"Yes, Sir, " Alex replied, wondering what the hell this was all about, fearing that his trading activities might have led to trouble.

"Right," he said, "here's the drill. As you know, we have had very little success in locating and capturing any *EOKA* leaders. They have too many places to hide, too many villages with hidden cellars, too many caves and tunnels. They're always well and truly warned by the locals when we mount an operation. Right?"

"Yes, Sir," Alex gave a slight nod.

"Well, here's what I want to do and I need a chemist to help me. I need someone who can be trusted to do the job quietly, no fuss, no talking about it to his mates. Know what I mean?" he said, watching Alex intently as he spoke.

"Yes, Sir. Part of my training is not to divulge a customer's medication or problems."

"Good," he nodded, "Well, I have developed a chemical that has no smell that can be detected by humans, but can be detected by specially trained tracker dogs. Here's where you come in. This is a medical unit so terrorists and their spies don't watch you and you don't have any locals working inside the compound."

"That's right," Pig interrupted.

Pitt looked at Alex. "I understand that you get around the island quite a bit so no-one will think it odd when you drive around in a truck. Right?"

Alex realised that Pitt had obviously been told about his extra-curricular activities and merely nodded.

"Now, I need someone to dissolve my chemical in pretty large quantities of a soap-like solution. I understand that you did something like that in your last job." He pursed his lips, a regular gesture.

Alex agreed again, wondering if there was anything Pitt did not know about him.

"Right, here's what you will do if you volunteer to help. You will be provided with the crystals, ten ten-gallon carboys, and soft soap. Following my formula, you will, in your shed, make the solution and, when notified, you will load the carboys onto a truck. Then Col Barry here will tell you where to go." He nodded in Pig's direction. Pig put up a thumb.

"You will not know the location until you are ready to leave. That's for security purposes. At your destination a helicopter with special tanks will land and you will transfer the contents of the carboys into these tanks. Okay so far?"

"Yes, Sir," Alex decided not to ask the dozen questions in his mind.

"The helicopter will spray the solution in a circle around a village or cave area where we suspect terrorists are hiding. The idea is that these chaps are always on the move. So when they leave their hiding place to move on, they will pick up some of the chemical, like a scent, as they go through the grass, shrubs or whatever. That's where the dogs come in. They will pick up anyone who has broken through the circle and hopefully we'll get some *EOKA* men among those picked up by the dogs."

"What about me, and the driver? He'll have to help me with the carboys and we'll both get some of this scent on us." Alex tried to picture the two of them lifting the carboys and pouring the solution into tanks without spilling some.

"Good thinking, Forbes. You'll have protective clothing, rubber suits and headgear with plastic visors. After the transfer you will drive to RAF Nicosia and wait for the helicopter to arrive. You and the driver, the truck, the tanks and the carboys will be washed down with pressure hoses to remove all trace of the solution. Or at least to dilute it enough to make it undetectable by the dogs if you happen to be near any, not that you will. Okay?" Pitt nodded constantly as if to emphasise each point.

"Sounds fine so far, Sir." Alex didn't know what else to say.

"Right. Now, we have to ensure that no-one knows where we spray the solution and on an island this small that's not easy. So, you will be sent to locations that are isolated." Alex waited while Pitt took a sip from a glass of water. "Still, even that's not easy so we will use places where mainly Turkish Cypriot villages are near these spots. There are several where we have friendly leaders. They won't know anything about what we're doing but they will ensure that the sound of a regular helicopter is seen by the villagers as nothing to be inquisitive about." He placed a finger against his temple.

"There're always plenty of helicopters and the roads are full of trucks." Alex said.

Pitt went on in the same steady voice. "Most times you will operate just before first light but your truck will have to go through the odd Turkish village so we'll meet with the *muktar* who will let it be known in his town that you are just a medical team checking up on a possible accident." Pitt sipped more water. "You would be surprised how quickly that explanation will get around and be accepted."

"*Muktar*, Sir?" Alex wrinkled his forehead.

"Head man, like the local chief. Every Greek and Turkish village has one. He represents the village and handles any disputes. We have one in a little town, a good man. He's the only one outside our group who will know what we're really up to."

Since the only Cypriots Alex had met were Armenian or

Greek shopkeepers where he had bought souvenirs and tasty items for the sergeants, he knew nothing of *muktars* or Turks for that matter.

"What about if we do some medical treatments in the villages? People with ankle sprains, lice or skin problems? That way we could visit on a regular basis." Alex looked at Pig then Major Pitt. Pig stuck up a thumb and Pitt nodded approval.

"Right, then, it's all systems go, starting in a few weeks. But tomorrow you and I will visit our friendly *muktar*, RAF Nicosia and your contact there. Thanks, Colonel Barry, it's been a good result. I think Sergeant Forbes will do just fine." He rose to his feet and shook hands with Pig then glanced at the quietly watching Staff. "I'll pick you up tomorrow at ten. Okay, Colonel?" Pitt looked down at the lounging Pig. Pig grunted agreement.

After he had left, Pig turned to Staff Campbell. "I was hoping that I might go along with them. There's nothing doing here. Tell you what, we'll have a tent inspection."

There was a touch of Captain Queeg in Pig. Minute, petty things assumed matters of great importance. The other ranks had a corrugated shed that was referred to as the NAAFI although it was run entirely by the corporals. There were the usual metal tables and chairs, a jukebox and a large fridge stocked with Coca-Cola and other drinks. The men were meant to consume the drinks in the NAAFI but often took a bottle back to their tents. When the Coca Cola truck arrived each week, full bottles replaced empty ones. The Greek Cypriot driver would bring the stock up to his level of 20 dozen. But he needed empty bottles to cover the full ones he had left. Off he'd trot to Pig and, waving his arms and touching his head, he would demand his empty bottles. Pig would assure him that he'd be able to get them in a week's time. Then without warning he would hold a tent inspection. All the men were ordered to return to their tents and stand-by. NCOs would be dispatched to make sure that no-one cleaned out his locker. Tapping his swagger stick against his thigh, Pig moved from tent to tent. Each man stood to attention beside his bed.

"Open yer locker, boyo," he commanded and sure enough he found a few empty bottles. The soldier was charged on the spot and ordered to do kitchen duty for a week. Pig entered Geordie Smith's tent. Alex ordered Smith to open his locker. There was not a single empty Coke bottle. In a flash, Pig pointed his stick at the top shelf. Sitting there was a can of self-heating soup. When the unit went out on operations each man was issued with a pack containing soup, chocolate, hard biscuits and so on. Anything not eaten was returned to the Quartermaster. It was against Queen's Regulations to keep anything.

With a triumphant hah, Pig thundered, "Smith, that soup belongs to the Queen."

Standing rigidly at attention, Smith, quick as a flash, cried out in his high-pitched voice, "She's welcome to it, Sir!"

It was just the kind of answer Pig liked from his men. "Make sure ye send it to her," he said, and that was the end of the inspection. Pig was eccentric and slightly mad but the men loved him. Most of them were not the best of physical specimens, and for this reason were assigned to the Medical Corps, much to their chagrin. A Medical Orderly was not exactly on a par with an Infantryman. Pig appreciated this and preferred them to appear scruffy and most un-medical orderly like. Every time they went to the Military Hospital in Nicosia the poor lads who worked on the wards looked at them with envy and awe.

The next day, Major Pitt arrived in an unmarked staff car, no less. On his instructions Alex wore his one and only suit. The first stop was RAF Nicosia. Alex had been there before to attend a dance at the Sergeants' Mess and had actually danced with a young girl, in fact, a fourteen-year-old. Jenny was the daughter of a Flight Sergeant and was in heaven being one of very few women or girls that soldiers could meet socially. Just to touch a girl was enough for a hormonally charged young man.

"Pilot Officer Crooks," Pitt shook the hand of a slim man with a handlebar moustache. "This is Sergeant Alex Forbes. He's the chemist. This is his driver, Mike."

Alex saluted. Crooks waved away the salute and put out a hand. "Right, chaps, let's have a look at the set-up we've organised." Crooks walked over to a helicopter. The heat out on the runway was stifling, the hot sun baking the tarmac. The smell of diesel and oil only added to the sense of the exotic, far removed from the cold, misty air of Scotland. In the distance the heat shimmered up, the hot air rising to create a blurred mirage of undulating trees and flickering buildings ready to dance and vanish into the ether.

"The helicopter has these tanks fitted on each side. The top opens up like so," he climbed up and pushed open the lid, "it should be easy with that size to pour in the solution?"

"All right, Sergeant?" Pitt looked at Alex.

Alex glanced up at the tanks. "We'll need a step."

"All organised," Crooks answered. "Like to have a spin?"

"No time," Pitt said briskly.

"Maybe some other time, eh," Crooks gave a disappointed shrug.

"Kermia Camp is just north of Nicosia," Pitt spoke hurriedly. "We've decided to use sites to the west, within a reasonable distance from camp. We'll go out to the village of Ghazientop."

After a less than an hour's drive, passing through mile after mile of beautiful orange groves, they arrived at a village past Morphou. For Alex, the word village conjured up images of English villages with a pub, thatched cottages, hedges, and nice country lanes. The village of Ghazientop was not like that. There was a kind of open square with a gravel road forking to each side. A hotel or coffee shop faced onto this square with tables and chairs out front. Various shops lined the square, fruit shops, a car repair shop and a general store with goods piled up outside. Old men with grizzled, unshaven faces were playing some kind of board game with dice. Pitt drove on past the coffee shop and turned down a dirt lane that led to a nice looking house with several peppercorn and carob trees in the front garden. After the bareness of the village square it was a pleasant sight. Major Pitt knocked, the door opened and there stood a young woman.

Alex would never forget that first time he saw Leyla. His heart welled up into his throat and eyes. She was the most beautiful girl he had ever seen. She smiled at Pitt and looked straight at Alex with a slight tilt of the head. It was gesture Leyla typically made when she was inquisitive about something or someone. Alex felt an immediate attraction to the dark-eyed young woman in a soft blue ankle-length dress. Their eyes met again and only a cough from Pitt broke the spell.

"Good morning, we've come to see *Muktar* Mehmet Ali."

Bowing, Leyla invited them to enter the house. As he passed, Alex inhaled her very essence. With the merest of motions she briefly touched his arm. Passing Pitt, she led the way into a sunny, well-lit room. A man in shirtsleeves was seated.

"Father, I think these are the men you are expecting?" her voice was soft, the words unintelligible to Alex.

The man rose from the divan. Alex was surprised. The man was tall. Most Turks he had seen were short.

"Mehmet Ali Ozkara," he shook hands with Pitt and then Alex before gesturing them to be seated on a divan covered with a colourful rug. The walls of the room were draped with colourful rugs and everywhere Alex could see copper, brass and ceramic pots and plates. Leyla stood there with an attentive, submissive manner until her father spoke, in poor, halting English.

"Gentlemen, welcome to my home. You meet my daughter Leyla. I offer you some coffee or *cay*, tea? I'm afraid is Turkish coffee but *cay* is Ceylon," he spoke with a distinct accent, a singsong voice. Alex liked the sound.

Pitt asked for Turkish coffee while Alex opted for tea. Leyla made a bowing gesture and left the room. It was with some effort that Alex took his eyes away from the departing girl.

"Mehmet Ali Bey, we are honoured that you have invited us into your home. May I introduce Sergeant Forbes, my assistant?" Mehmet Ali shook hands with Alex. "Your cooperation in assisting us is much appreciated. All of us must cooperate to defeat those who would destroy this lovely island." Pitt sat forward. The divan was comfortable but more appropriate for lounging than a serious meeting.

"Major, my wife, Gulten, speaks no English, is not good she be here. My daughter, Leyla, speak excellent English. She has been to good school, Greek school and English school. She tell you better words what I mean to say," he bent forward apologetically. As if on cue, Leyla entered the room carrying a silver tray with funny flute-shaped glasses on saucers and small cups. The cups were filled with thick, dark-brown coffee. A spoon stood upright in the glass of tea. A glass of water accompanied each cup of coffee. As she passed the tray round, Alex managed to catch her eye and she blinked as if in recognition. There was a pause while they sipped the hot drinks. The fluted glass was hot. Nervously, Alex lifted it to his lips, holding the saucer in both hands. It was sweet but without milk. Pitt's coffee looked like dark-brown sludge. Both he and Mehmet Ali sipped some coffee then drank some water. Alex thought this was a funny way to drink coffee but decided that the water was probably needed to help down the brown mud. Mehmet Ali looked at Leyla and spoke rapidly in Turkish.

Nodding, she nervously translated his words. "Ah, Major, you know well the problems we have here in Cyprus. It is not easy for us who are Turks. We are few, the Greeks are many. Me, I like the British to stay forever, but I know this will not happen. Everyone wants freedom, even if it means they imprison others." He smiled, eyebrows raised, dark eyes open wide. Pitt indicated his agreement. Placing his cup on the brass table he put his hands together, prayer-like.

"As you know from the visit you had from Captain Bryce of the Intelligence Corps, we need the cooperation of you and some other *muktars* with this important operation. There is some danger to you and your village if our plans become known. But I'm sure that you appreciate that."

"Major, we are all well aware of the possibilities. But we are absolutely sure of the certainty if our island should become part of Greece," he smiled but his eyes were serious, "better the uncertainty of what may happen to the certainty of what will happen. We are Cypriots, this is our country. It is not Greek, it is not Turkish. If it is not to be British...?" he shrugged his shoulders.

"Mehmet Ali Bey, the British will always be here if we can defeat these fanatics who do not have the best interests of Cyprus at heart. That is why I am here, to help defeat these extremists." Pitt glanced at Leyla then her father.

Mehmet Ali turned his attention to Alex. "So, Sergeant, I know at times you will pass through my village and the people must just think, 'Oh, there goes a Red Cross truck, must be accident someplace'? Is what we must do?"

"Sir, this is all new to me. I'm just a National Serviceman till my two years are up. It's the army. I do what I'm told. I've only been here a few months. I really don't understand why we have all these problems. I think Cyprus is a beautiful place. Better than Scotland." Alex stammered out the words. He looked at Leyla, feeling foolish at his lack of knowledge. Watching her face intently, he continued. "I understand that the Greek Cypriots want to get rid of the British and join Greece and you, the Turkish Cypriots, would like us to stay. Is that right?"

"Exactly," she translated Mehmet Ali's reply in a single word.

"We've had a slight change of plans." Pitt made a gesture of apology.

"How so?"

"Sergeant Forbes will be operating in this general area. I

suggest that he make Kokina the end of his run. That's about ten miles further, on the coast."

"Why Kokina?"

"That's to make it look as if he is visiting a couple of villages. But he will be stopping somewhere in between."

"I think I understand." Leyla translated. She produced a small stool and sat down next to her father. Listening to her soft undulating voice, Alex found it hard to concentrate on the three-way conversation. Mehmet Ali spoke at length in Turkish and by some miracle Leyla translated his words in a sentence. As the conversation continued, her English began to improve. "You know, Major, it seems that my island is destined to be forever a land of tents and barbed wire camps." His face looked sorrowful.

"How so, Sir?" Pitt looked puzzled.

"It's not so long ago that we had 50,000 Jews here, in camps, concentration camps. They wished to go to Palestine but the British said no and put them here."

"These things happen. Difficult problem." Pitt tried to move on."

"Such a pity. They were nice people. We Muslims have always welcomed Jews but the Greeks, they were afraid."

"Afraid? Of what, Sir?" An open-mouthed Alex asked, turning then to Leyla.

"Ah, young man, like so many of those Jews, you are young. The Greeks are many here in Cyprus. Fifty thousand Jews, all young, there would have been hundreds of thousands in twenty years."

"Crikey!" Alex exclaimed.

"And then the Greeks would no longer be the biggest number in this land. It would be a Jewish homeland instead of Israel."

"Before my time, I'm afraid, Sir." Alex blushed as he felt Leyla's eyes on him.

"Like the young everywhere, you must learn to look ahead to the future, is it not so?" He looked at Pitt with a twinkle in his eyes.

"Still, they've all gone now, right?" Alex frowned.

"Ah, yes, but they will not forget Cyprus. From the camps of Germany and Poland to the camps of Cyprus. It was very hard. With no money to buy food, life was not easy. You live in a tent, Sergeant? It is cold in winter?" The question was a statement.

"I haven't been here in winter."

Pit spoke hurriedly, anxious to get away from the image of British concentration camps. "Right, Sir, well, let's forget all about the Jews and get down to business."

Mehmet Ali spread out his hands, understanding his motive.

"The Sergeant here has suggested that he visit Ghazientop and Kokina on a kind of humanitarian mission, bringing some medical supplies to assist the local nurse. Her name is Hilkat, I believe?" Pitt looked from Alex to Mehmet Ali.

"She knows no English, it will be difficult."

"Blow. Captain Bryce didn't mention that."

Mehmet Ali smiled. "My daughter, Leyla, she speaks perfect English. Perhaps she can assist."

"Wonderful. Then she can act as an interpreter. Excellent. Thank you again." A relieved Pitt clapped his hands together.

"Leyla can discuss with the sergeant how best to arrange this little hospital visit." Mehmet Ali's body shook with laughter. Leyla inclined her head and glanced at a smiling Alex.

The meeting ended with bows from Leyla and handshakes between the men. Pitt then drove down the coast and up a hill to some old ruins. The view was magnificent, powerful and commanding. This was the remains of a palace, he told Alex, which had been built about 500 BC by Phoenicians and later captured by Greeks. Although Alex had read schoolboy potted versions about some Greek gods and kings and the like, he had never heard of Phoenicians.

"There are several good spots around here for you to rendezvous with Crooks," Pitt shouted against a sudden gust of wind. "This won't be a problem down below. It's always windy up here."

"The only wind I've experienced is a hot dusty wind. This is great. I like it," Alex shouted back.

"That's the ancient city of Soli down there," Pitt pointed way down below to the shoreline. Alex nodded. The name meant nothing to him. It was all very strange. His thoughts were still on the girl and how he would handle his next meeting with her. On the drive back to Camp Kermia Alex barely listened to Pitt as he spoke about his work back in London. The lovely garden and cool house kept intruding into Alex's thoughts. Although it was a poor, run-down village, Mehmet Ali's house was a mansion compared to the little flat back in Dunkeith. He could think only of how he might impress the lovely girl. That night, dinner in the Mess was some kind of meat stew so Alex opened a tin of pilchards in tomato sauce. He'd lost a few pounds since arriving at Camp Kermia. Next day, after reveille at 7am and a breakfast of corn flakes and watery milk made from powder, Alex showered and sat in his tin shed thinking about how he would organise supplies for the next visit to Ghazientop. The following day he raided the dispensary at the military hospital in Nicosia. It was left-over stew for dinner so he opened tins of corned beef and baked beans. Pig arrived that night just after seven, catching everyone unawares as this was earlier than his usual visit.

"Hello, lads," he slurred in his Irish accent, "I saw the light on and thought there might be time for an ale." This was his normal greeting when he wanted to have a night of drinking. It wasn't unknown for him to fall asleep on the floor of the Mess. Anyone going for a pee would be told, "Where are ye goin', lad? Make sure ye come back. The night's early yet."

"Nobody would believe this," Alex thought, "only in the army is it possible."

While several non-medical officers and some senior NCOs lived in married quarters off camp and left the base each night, Pig controlled the nightlife of those less fortunate. Beer and brandy were very cheap and no-one was allowed to leave the after-dinner drinking until Pig had finished. He did not arrive at the Mess every night and on those occasions the time was passed playing cards, drinking a few beers then retiring to bed. There was little else to do. When Pig arrived, the cards were put away and serious drinking began. The lucky ones were those still in their tents writing letters. On hearing Pig's blaring voice, they would quickly retire for the night, with lights out. Thanks to his high opinion of Alex, Alex's presence was always demanded. There was no refusing the CO's command. Now, sitting in his tin shed nursing a hangover from the previous night's visit by Pig to the Sergeants' Mess, Alex waited impatiently for the arrival of Pitt's chemical.

A scrawny little private opened the door. "Staff says the CO wants to see you pronto."

Alex found Pig in Staff's tent. He looked very much the worse for wear, his eyes bloodshot and his face a bright red. "Forbes. See that bloody queue?" he pointed to a long line of over thirty men waiting to see a doctor. "They're giving me a headache. Noisy buggers."

"Must be a lot of sickies." Alex wondered what was on his mind.

"Nuthin wrong with most of them. Have we any castor oil?"

"I think there's a half gallon in the shed. It's on the books but I haven't seen it since I took over."

"Well, get it." His voice was raised, hand on forehead, "Get it now, quick as sticks."

It took Alex seven or eight minutes to locate the castor oil. Pig bent a finger indicating that Alex follow him. He strode into the medical room and jerked a thumb at Tom MacGowan who scurried out.

The "patient" looked up dumbfounded. "Right, lad," Pig glared at the soldier. "What's yer complaint?"

"It's me feet, Sir. They hurt something awful. All red and sore. The MO said he thought it was—"

"I don't think. I know. Understand?"

The soldier sank further into his seat.

"Sergeant Forbes here is a chemist. He has just the ting to fix it. Right, Forbes?"

Alex swallowed hard and moved his head in the direction of the Winchester bottle. "How much?"

"An ounce or two should do the trick."

Alex measured out an ounce and a half and handed it to the startled soldier.

"Get it down ye, lad. Ye want to be fixed? Then ye won't need to come back," Pig snorted.

The soldier downed the oil, put on his beret, saluted and left the room. Every soldier on sick parade was given the same treatment. Coughs, sprained wrists, boils, dermatitis, it made no difference. Next day, three men turned up on sick parade. Pig opened the door of the tin shed and gave Alex a thumb's up sign. "I tink the lads are too busy to turn up t'day."

"You fixed that lot up, Sir." Alex returned the gesture.

Unless he was otherwise engaged, Alex opened the clothing store for an hour from 4pm. Singlets, socks and shorts were traded in regularly. He enjoyed this little activity. Then Pig decided that Alex could take on another role, that of Sports Officer. Cyprus was regularly under a curfew with no people out on the streets after 7pm. On a few occasions a truce had been declared and Cypriots and soldiers could move about as if the world were normal. Camp Kermia lay out of Nicosia just off the road leading to Kyrenia on the coast of North Cyprus. Instead of a siesta or rest period, two truckloads, of about 40 men with armed guards would head off for a swim at Five Mile Beach to the east of Kyrenia. It was the job of the Sports Officer to organise this and often join the men for a swim. The road ran through a flat plain then up a winding road through the Five Finger Mountains. Coming round a final bend, Kyrenia and the blue Mediterranean lay way down on the flat coastal fringe.

"What's that Sarge?" the pimply-faced driver asked, pointing to the left.

"Just a minute," Alex began turning the pages of a guidebook he'd picked up in town. "That's St Hilarion castle. It says here that Cyprus has been ruled by Egyptians, Assyrians, Persians and Romans. Castles were important."

"We've got plenty at home, too."

"Yeh, well these are pretty old. It says that the Roman Empire split in two and the island came under the influence of Constantinople and the Byzantine Greek Orthodox Church."

"Shit, that's Makarios' mob."

"Yeh, well then, Richard the Lionheart conquered Cyprus and sold it to the Frankish nobleman, Guy de Lusignan, and began a period of Frankish influence lasting 300 years. The next to come were the Venetians, then the Ottoman Turks. They were the rulers from 1571 to 1878."

"That must explain all the Turks," the driver's head bobbed up and down.

"Anyway, we took over following the Russo-Turkish War. We leased the island from the Ottomans. Then we annexed it. After the war, the 1914 one."

"Here we go, Sarge. This is the best bit."

There at the top of the pass the road snaked down to a flat, green coastal fringe, with Kyrenia and the blue Mediterranean far below. A beautiful sandy beach, Five Mile Beach was a small cove guarded by surrounding hills. Lots were drawn to see who would be positioned on the hills as guards. All weapons were stacked on the beach, watched over by a separate guard. Then it was off with the shorts and boots and into the warm sea. Nothing in Alex's life would ever compare to the joy of that first swim in the Mediterranean Sea.

"This is great. Magic," he shouted to Mike as they splashed about in the water. "It's worth the drive, isn't it?"

"I've never seen water so clear, so warm," Mike swam away and then dived under a wave.

At Five Mile Beach, Alex tasted his first watermelon. Strange land, strange fruit, strange feelings so far from home.

Pig told Alex to organise a football match for the men.

Nearby was a Greek village soccer pitch, now unused. In his usual, inimitable way he insisted that as many as possible play. Sixty men volunteered. Before beginning this Irish version of soccer, Alex lined the men up right across the pitch. The line walked slowly down the length of the pitch looking for any possible booby trap. About halfway down, the call came that something suspicious had been seen.

"Quick, Sarge! What's this?" Geordie Smith called out as the men near him all backed away.

A wire was sticking out of the hard, bare ground. Not wishing to appear panicked, Alex moved everyone back. Looking down, he saw what appeared to be a piece of rusty wire sticking up about three inches above the ground. He pulled it out. Nothing happened. It was just an old piece of wire. After lots of backslapping for his "bravery" the game began. Pig loved the chaos of sixty men charging after the ball. Few goals were scored as twenty men blocked any chance of a shot at goal. It was typical of Pig's desire to belittle any normal rules of organisation. The word of this shambles spread throughout the island and further enhanced the reputation of Pig's Battalion as a most un-medico like outfit. The men loved it.

A truck arrived with the chemical crystals, the soft soap, carboys and two rubber suits and headgear. Alex moved several panniers to make room for the carboys.

"Right. Sign here," the truck driver held out a clipboard with a sheet of paper listing everything that had been unloaded.

"Forbes," Pig sat sprawled in his chair, "better start visitin' that place ye have to visit. Looks like tings might be happening soon."

Alex's heart jumped as he thought about making his cover-story visits to Ghazientop. He had not been able to get the image of Leyla out of his mind. With a good supply of expendable dressings, disinfectants and some skin creams he set off with Mike Tomlinson as his driver. This time they had no accompanying armed guard. The driver's sten gun lay across his knees and Alex had his pistol. The shops in the village all opened on to the street with no front window, and no door. At closing, a metal grille came down to secure the premises.

The Landrover was parked at the rear of Mehmet Ali's house. Leaving the driver to stand guard, Alex was about to go round to the front door when Leyla appeared. At eighteen she had reached her full height of a little over five and a half feet. Girls matured early around the Mediterranean and her shapely figure could be glimpsed as she moved gracefully in an ankle-length pale-golden caftan. Pinned on her dark, auburn hair was a handkerchief and on her bare feet were pale green sandals. She smiled, Alex smiled and so it began, a picture forever in his memory. Mehmet Ali was a Muslim but he had quite a liberal approach to his religion. It was his normal practice to go to Friday prayers. During the holy month of Ramadan he fasted but not always for the whole day. Alex asked Leyla why she did not wear the long headdress commonly worn by Turkish women.

"My father says that it's what is in the heart that counts not what is on the head."

"That's really profound."

For the next two hours they worked together with the nurse, Hilkat, strapping a young boy's swollen ankle, applying cream to a girl with eczema and diluting disinfectant to wash ugly sores. Hilkat was not a trained nurse, just a woman who'd done a course in first-aid. Leyla's head would bend forward to help and her fragrance filled his head. It was like no other perfume he had known. Alex breathed her in like a man desperate for air. At noon, she said it was time to finish, as the village would now rest until later in the afternoon. At the height of summer, the land and buildings never cooled down. The breeze, if any, was warmed crossing the Messier Plain. After a light lunch of olives, cheese and some flat bread, Leyla asked if he would like to visit Vaunt where the air would be cooler.

"Are you sure that your father would not object?" He was apprehensive. All the soldiers had been warned that Greek and Turkish Cypriots jealously guarded their daughters.

"No, no," she sounded confident. "My father says that you are a good man, like a son, helping us. He said that I would come to no harm if I show you our Turkish hospitality. We can take the donkey and cart. It's not far on the little tracks."

Taking only a carafe of water they set off for Vouni. Alex had heard someone say that Cyprus is a "heaven where the mountains meet the sea". High up among the ruins of Vouni Palace, he was in heaven. Breathing in a lungful of air, he exhaled and gasped, "This air is so nice."

Leyla smiled, "It's said to be the cleanest air in all the world. Not that I have breathed any air outside Cyprus."

"Well it's better than any air I have every breathed."

After standing to enjoy the cooling breeze and gazing out to the blue sea below, they sat down on what appeared to be a worn ancient bench. Sitting quietly, shoulders touching, he turned to look at Leyla. She tilted her head to one side and he lightly kissed her lips. Alex had kissed many girls before and held and caressed them. Simulated sex was the nearest he had come to intimacy. Caressing and rubbing against a girl frequently led to ejaculation. Although she must have recognised the telltale stains, his mother, collecting the dirty washing, never made any comment. But this time, a simple kiss, over in an instant, set his heart pumping like nothing he had known before. Leyla smiled and he kissed her again. This time it was a deeper, more intense kiss and they embraced like two lovers. Although he had an immediate erection, strangely, he felt no desire to press it against Leyla. He knew that the moment was too precious to be spoiled by any further advance.

"I'm sorry, I shouldn't have done that," he puffed out. "Please don't tell your father, he mustn't think badly of me."

"Oh, Alexander, you must not blame yourself. I wanted you to kiss me. I have never kissed anyone before, except on the cheek. That's what we do with friends." She said his name as Alezander, a sound pleasing to his ear.

Slowly, they wound back down the track to Ghazientop, Leyla holding the reins, his hand resting on hers. No words were spoken, the bumping of the cart, riding over the rough ground forcing their bodies to come together then move apart. Mike was dozing peacefully in the garden and Alex left him there while he and Leyla returned to the village to treat the remaining patients. "Thank you for your hospitality," Alex said when he told Mehmet Ali that it was time to return to camp.

"You are welcome. Come any time even if just for a visit." Leyla smiled as her father issued the invitation.

For most of the men the camp was a prison. Enclosed in a camp surrounded by barbed wire, with two hundred men and only letters and photos to remind them of the joy of female company, Alex was lucky. His various duties allowed him to get out of camp several times a week. Except during a truce, or out on operations, the men were confined behind the barbed-wire perimeter fence. For some, particularly cooks and office staff, this meant being incarcerated for months on end. Pig turned a blind eye to another practice that was against regulations. One of the RASC drivers, a London cockney, organised the services of a prostitute. A taxi rolled up at the camp entrance with the prostitute inside. Ducking under the boom gate, a customer would quickly get into the taxi. It made a slow circuit of the camp, and then the soldier jumped out and was replaced by the next customer. The prostitute serviced as many as six or seven men and, well rewarded, drove back to Nicosia. Everything was fine until several cases of gonorrhea turned up at morning sick parade. The usual treatment was an injection of penicillin. The particular brand used was a milky suspension of Bistabillin, a nasty concoction that frequently jammed in the fine needle just as it was being injected into the poor patient's buttock. Trying to force it only led to an outbreak of sweat on the forehead. So a new syringe would be filled, hopefully with better results. Pig became impatient with this business.

"Bugger this bloody rubbish," an exasperated Pig muttered. Taking the needle off the syringe, he blew hard in an attempt to unblock it. Then he put the needle back on and tried again. "How's that, lad? Now you won't be running like a sailor's dick," he said to the prone patient.

The circulating taxi was banned forthwith. Pig hated those jamming needles.

One morning he sent for Alex. "Right, Forbes. Get tings ready."

"Is this it, Sir?" Alex felt excited.

"Get the truck loaded up. Ye'll be off in the morning."

Alex worked all day in the stifling heat of the tin shed making the solution. Then the full carboys were capped and later that evening loaded onto the truck. He was exhausted. It was backbreaking work lifting the heavy carboys on to the truck, although the wicker cover made grasping the globular-shaped bottles a little easier. When all was in readiness, he reported for instructions.

"You'll get to bed early and have the Sergeant of the Guard wake you at oh three thirty."

"Where do we meet the helicopter, Sir?"

"Here's your route." He handed Alex a sheet of paper. "The rendezvous time is oh six hundred. Now then, wait no more than half an hour for the chopper."

"What if he doesn't show?" He looked anxiously at Pig.

"If he doesn't show, come back here. Maybe the weather's not right or some other ting these fellas find out. Watch out for booby traps."

The sketch showed the helicopter would come in just past Ghazientop, near Xeros. As they drove slowly along in the dark, down to Nicosia and then headed west to the coast, Alex felt the familiar fear arise in his mind. It was a fear of failure and having to front up before Pig if the mission was unsuccessful. But the fear he felt as the truck rolled through the darkness was a different kind of fear. The air was cool. Perspiration began trickling, running down his back. "This rubber suit doesn't help, does it, Mike? I'm sweating like a pig and it's not the heat."

"Shit, this is real spooky," Mike whispered. "Do you actually think this is dangerous?"

"Hope not. I don't think anyone could know about us. But you never know. Pitt said that a Greek cleaner or office worker at RAF Nicosia might pick up some information."

"They'd all be cleared, wouldn't they?" a worried Mike muttered.

"Maybe at the start. Then who knows? They get a visit from Grivas and it's cough up the info or your son has a nasty accident."

"Yeh," Mike agreed, "they kill each other at the drop of a hat."

Twice they stopped and Alex walked ahead to check that the mound on the road was not recent. The possibility of a mine under the dirt road was ever on his mind after Pig's warning. "Nothing, just a pile of dirt," he said to a relieved Mike. With only the sidelights turned on, Alex pressed forward against the windshield fearing every lump was a booby trap. Through Ghazientop, still asleep and deserted, they pressed on. Because of this slower than expected journey, they arrived at the small jutted plateau just in time to hear the helicopter high above. It swung out over the sea and came in against the still blackness of the western sky.

"Shit, I'm glad I'm not a pilot." Mike watched in wonder. To the east the sun was rising, a golden glow of fire peculiar to the eastern Mediterranean. With a graceful pirouette, the helicopter hovered then landed about 60 feet from the truck.

"Headgear on, Mike, let's go," Alex shouted above the noise of the propeller blades. The helicopter's engine died and in the stillness Alex whispered, "Okay, Mike?"

"Fooking hell," was the tense reply.

Crooks hopped out of the helicopter and waved. "I'll let you fellows get on with it. I don't want much of that stuff on me. Quick as you can."

They heaved the heavy carboys up and emptied them into the tanks. It exerted great strain on their backs. Alex's back was aching and sore by the time he and Mike had heaved the second carboy up to the left tank.

"Fooking hell," came again from Mike "It's a fooking joke, this." Panting, sweating, hurrying as fast as they could, the final carboy was at last emptied into the right tank. The sun was climbing in the sky as they completed their task and Alex paused to capture the majestic beauty of nature quietly going about its day's work.

"Thanks lads, see you later. I'll be back before you so look for me at the gate. Then follow me out to the chopper, it'll be on the far side of the field," the pilot waved and climbed into the helicopter. There was something amazing, almost unreal, about watching a helicopter rev up and then just lift off the ground and whirl away. Standing there in the early dawn, Alex felt part of something powerful. He would never again watch a war movie without being in awe of their power and the unnatural way those machines worked. The empty carboys were put back in the truck and it was time for the return journey.

"God, I hate driving into the early morning sun. Can't see a thing," Mike grumbled.

"Just go slowly," Alex whispered.

"Are you sweating Sarge? I'm sweating like a pig."

Following instructions, they did not remove their protective clothing and headgear. The sweat trickled down and then rose to mist up their visors. This brought the standard response from Mike. "Fooking hell, fooking hell," he muttered constantly. With a limited education, his reading consisted mainly of comic books and magazines. Teaching him how to drive and making him attend lessons given by the resident "schoolie" from the Education Corps, the army had provided him with the chance of getting a reasonable job at the end of his National Service.

Normally, Alex would try to make conversation but this time he sat silent, unable to think of anything to say. Both were emotionally drained with only one thought in mind, to get back to RAF Nicosia as quickly as possible.

"Cat got yer tongue, Sarge?"

"No. Just thinking." Alex fell silent again. Ghazientop was awake and there was the usual small group of men sitting at the coffee shop.

"Funny-looking buggers, aren't they?" Mike glanced at the men outside the coffee shop. "Could be out of the Middle Ages, couldn't it? They love their coffee," he laughed.

Alex nodded. "And talking. Notice there's never any women there."

"Nah. They're all the same, Greeks and Turks. Keep their women under lock and key," Mike sneered.

Alex waved to the men. Some were farm labourers enjoying a coffee before starting work while others were casual workers waiting to be called by a farmer. Alex looked hard, desperately hoping to see Leyla as they drove through the village. A wave as they passed through would have been sufficient but he knew in his heart there was little chance that Leyla would be anywhere other than at home. In the street, the only people out were the usual collection of men in their baggy pants and black shirts together with vendors of fruit, nuts and *simit*, the sesame-coated bread ring. Funny stuff, *simit*, Alex thought. Turks love it.

Crooks was waiting at the gate to RAF Nicosia as promised. Mike followed his Landrover way out past all the buildings to a wide-open space next to a little-used runway. A fire-fighting hose fitted with a high-pressure nozzle was already connected and Alex and Mike washed out the carboys, helicopter tanks, the back of the truck, the cabin and finally each other. They stripped off the suits, headgear and rubber boots.

Wearing arm length rubber gloves, Crooks put all of it into large plastic bags. "I'll get these steam-cleaned and have them sent to Camp Kermia. Ready for next time."

"Thanks, chief," Alex gave a half salute.

"Off you go then, till next time," Crooks gave an American salute as he continued hosing down the ground surrounding the helicopter.

Alex and Mike climbed back into the truck and headed for the entrance gate and the drive back to Kermia Camp. It was almost noon.

"Just in time for some grub," Mike chortled, "not too bad, was it?" Alex realised that they both shared a sense of utter relief that it was over. At least till next time, he thought.

Thanks to his unsanctioned bartering activities all over the island, he was able to make detours on his many trips and visit Ghazientop. It was through these visits to Leyla and Mehmet Ali that he gained an understanding of the reasons behind *EOKA*'s activities and something of the hatred and distrust that existed between the Greek and Turkish communities. He found it very strange that an Archbishop was the leader in every sense of the Greek Cypriots.

"You don't find Church people in politics in Britain." He sat in Mehmet Ali's garden. "They might lead a 'Ban the Bomb' march, but that's it."

"The Greek Church has always been political. Wherever there are Greeks." A serious Mehmet Ali shrugged.

"That's what they do here." Leyla looked at Alex as she spoke. "This man Makarios wants to make us part of Greece. He keeps saying so."

"Sadly, that's true, my lovely." Mehmet Ali nodded, his eyes cold. She reported her father's words. "That's when my father says he began to fear for the safety of our people. He says that what happened in Crete will happen here if we belong to Greece. They will destroy us."

"Crete? That's a Greek island, isn't it?"

"It is now but maybe fifty years ago it was Turkish. Then all the Turks were eliminated or forced out when it was given to Greece." She shivered.

Alex reached out to touch Leyla but stopped abruptly as her eyes opened wide in a warning sign. While she sat patiently, listening, Mehmet Ali spoke at great length with much gesticulation.

He was obviously agitated and passionate. "My father says that even though he is exiled, out of the country, Makarios still organises the money and guns to help Grivas."

As always, she looked serene to Alex. He was constantly surprised at how she could condense a long diatribe into a few words. "Cyprus has never been part of Greece. It has been many things but never part of Greece."

He never took his eyes off her face for a moment even when Mehmet Ali was speaking. He was sure that her father was aware of his attraction to Leyla but he never attempted to stop their meetings.

"My father says that the only hope we have to survive is to hope that our leader, Dr Kucuk, will persuade the British to give part of the island to Turkey so that we may live in peace."

"Is that possible? Would that solve the problem?"

"Oh yes. Greeks and Turks have shared the island for hundreds of years but we have always been separate."

"But aren't there Greeks here in Ghazientop?"

"Here, yes, and in other villages and especially in the big cities. But they do not socialise, is that the word? Each community keeps to itself."

"It's all a mystery to me." He shook his head. "What about school? Are they mixed or separate?"

"Separate. I was educated at the Greek school in Morphou. My father considered it better than our school," she bowed to Mehmet Ali.

"Is that usual?" Alex asked, thinking that Catholics never went to Protestant schools.

"No, this is not a common occurrence. Nearly all Turkish students go to the Turkish Academy in Nicosia. But as a girl with no brother to look out for me, I was not allowed to stay in Nicosia during the week."

"But you said that you went to the English school in Nicosia? How come?"

"I was not happy at the Greek school. My father was reluctant at first but then he saw the wisdom of finishing my education in Nicosia."

"I can't understand why you two groups can't just be Cypriots and all get on together. I mean, this is a great little country."

"Is everyone the same in your country? Scotland? Do you never fight?"

"Not really, well we don't go around shooting each other. Sometimes Catholics and Protestants fight. Bloody...sorry, stupid when you think about it."

"Greeks look down on Turks," Leyla translated her father's comment. "They say we are barbaric, cruel and uncivilised. They mourn the loss of Constantinople, they dream of winning it back one day. Never, says my father."

"I think you are intelligent and beau—" Alex stopped. He realised that Mehmet Ali had been listening intently to the conversation, perhaps even understanding some of the English.

"A big problem here in Cyprus is that Turks are mainly peasants," he intruded, "we have not so many good schools, or teachers, so we do not give our children the possibility to be successful like the Greeks. They own all business and keep it to themselves."

"That's true, unfortunately," Leyla was becoming more agitated and more beautiful in his eyes. She was usually so quiet and polite, but Alex began to see a fire in her eyes. "If the British leave us our fate will not be good. The killings of those innocent British women will be our fate too." A look of horror crossed her face.

Alex followed her to the front door where he stole a kiss and Leyla hugged him. Back at camp he went to Archie Campbell's tent. He was lying on his bed reading.

"I can't understand it, Staff," his face showing frustration.

"How come these two people can't get on together? This is a fabulous place. It's got everything."

"They're Muslims and Christians, sonny. They'll never get on." Archie put down his book. "Anyway, here's the latest. There's a rumour that Harding is being recalled. Seems the powers that be are beginning to think that the hard-line approach isn't working. Shite, we have over 30,000 troops here. It must be costing a fortune. And for what?"

"Surely we wouldn't pull out? The Greeks would massacre the Turks. They're really nice people, the Turks. Religion's a load of baloney, don't you think?"

"Getting to like them, are ye? Or is it just the bonny wee lassie?" Staff's eyes twinkled with amusement.

"Cut it out. She's just a nice girl." Alex turned away so that his feelings wouldn't show.

A month later Harding was gone and Sir Hugh Foot was made Governor with the express purpose of negotiating with Grivas in order to end the violence. Foot was a civil servant, unlike Harding the soldier. He was known as a man with liberal views. The hope was that he would use his diplomatic skills to persuade Grivas and Makarios that a settlement of the problem could be handled better round a table than by armed conflict.

Alex was in a little dream world when Corporal Dick Allen popped his head through the door of the medical store. "CO wants to see you, pronto," he called out in his lilting Devonshire accent.

"Righto!" Alex wondered what Pig wanted now. With nothing on his head, he didn't bother to salute as he ducked his head under the flap on Staff's office tent.

"Ah, Forbes, thur you are," Pig slurred the words, "cab's outside, get your emergency stuff and go with Captain MacGowan, and Smith and Adams with you. Some trouble out there," he said, waving his hand in the direction of the camp entrance. "Could be a bit of shootin' or something. Brigade wants some medics. Look after MacGowan, he's a hopeless bugger. At least you can understand his bloody accent. Take two sets of wheels, just in case."

Captain Thomas MacGowan was from Glasgow. For an educated doctor, he had a very broad accent. Alex often wondered how he communicated with his patients. They were probably all Glaswegians. That would make it easy, he decided.

The trouble, they were told, had begun in the village of Ayios Trimli. Alexi Stanos had been sent there by Grivas to train the local members in laying booby traps. Shortly after, a platoon of the Lancashire Regiment, arriving on a tip, had cordoned off the village. Alexi, his brother from the village, Paul, and three others tried to run the blockade by car but failed. They returned to the village and hid in the barn of an *EOKA* sympathiser. Alexi ordered his brother to slip out and return home. While he was changing into some clean clothes, several soldiers burst into the house and he was arrested, leaving his crying wife and bewildered three young children. Handcuffed, he was bundled into the back of a Landrover and quickly taken to Larnaca for interrogation.

"Right, son, we know there's more than you so let's make life easy for everyone? Just tell us where they're hiding and we'll get them out, no hassles. Okay?" the Intelligence Corps captain gripped the back of Paul's neck.

"Never, I never tell anything." He spat out the words.

"Look, we can do this the easy way or we can do this the hard way. You have a wife and three kids, right?"

"Yes," Paul whispered, suddenly afraid for his wife and children.

"So you won't mind if you don't have any more kids? We can put a little pressure in the right place and pop your balls out like grapes in the hot sun. Want that?" The captain gave him a knowing look.

Paul frowned at the captain's words. "I can't betray my brother and my friends, is not possible."

"Well, we are going to stay in Ayios Trimli until Alexi and

his men come out. If they're not armed, it's just a matter of a few questions."

Paul looked away.

"So they are armed? What have they got? Rifles, sten guns? What?"

"Sten, I think." They will find out anyway, Paul thought.

"Right, so they're armed and if we find them and they don't surrender they are likely to be shot, maybe killed. Is that what you want? A dead brother?" the Captain said.

The thought of damage to his balls and having to visit his mother with the news that she'd lost a son was enough for Paul. "If I tell you where they are hidden, will you offer them the chance to surrender? No shooting?"

"That's a promise, Paul. We don't want anyone shooting. The less shooting the better. We don't want any of ours killed and you don't want any of yours either." The captain patted him on the back.

Paul was placed in a cell at the base at Dhekelia for safe-keeping until the situation at Ayios Trimli was resolved. Most of the soldiers knew the Greek word for halt and surrender. The call was made to the men in the barn adjacent to the house. The response was a burst of gunfire. "Fuck," the Lancashire Regiment Captain, Alistair Dunstan, shouted, "looks like they mean business. Get a bit closer and give them another call, Franklin, ask them to come out, hands up, no-one will shoot."

Crouching down, Fusilier Franklin edged forward and was halfway through calling out the order when another burst of gunfire poured out of the barn. "Fucking shit," he fell flat on the ground clutching his left thigh.

"Bastards," the captain shouted, "open fire. You two get him back." He pointed to two fusiliers. They pulled Franklin back to safety and the captain ordered a message be sent through for reinforcements. Alex and Tom MacGowan arrived to find the barn surrounded by fifty fusiliers. Franklin was in pain but not seriously wounded. Captain Dunstan ordered some men to go into the house and find a way up onto the roof. "Take some petrol, get it down into the barn and set it alight. We'll smoke them out."

Fusilier Peter March was the first man to clamber through the attic of the house onto the barn roof. He was shot and fell to the ground, dead. The other two soldiers quickly poured some petrol through a hole in the barn roof and dropped a lighted tight bundle of straw through the opening. In minutes, the men burst out of the barn. The three escaping terrorists managed to hit another soldier. All three were killed in a burst of gunfire from at least twenty rifles and sten guns.

"Get the fuckin' MO, quick. Scouse is bad," a corporal called out. Alex crouched down with Tom McGowan and scuttled over to the first of the wounded men. He kept out of the way as much as possible as Tom McGowan worked feverishly for almost an hour.

The two heavily bandaged wounded men were placed on stretchers in the back of the Landrover. Alex and Captain MacGowan dropped them off at BMH Nicosia on the way back to Camp Kermia.

Paul Stanos was devastated when he heard the news of the death of his comrades. He knew that he would be suspected of betraying the hideout. He asked the guard for some paper and a pen. He wrote in a long letter to his area commander that he had been tortured and made to confess the whereabouts of his brother and friends. "I held out as long as I could", he wrote, "hoping that Alexi and the others would be gone. I know the penalty for betraying my comrades but for the sake of my wife and children I pray I might be allowed to leave my home, my village and go somewhere, maybe England. They say that I will be released very soon. If I have to die to pay for my sin, then I ask you to look after my children as if they were yours. If I am spared, I will be happy to die fighting for the cause." The letter was passed to Grivas as the supreme commander. Without a second's hesitation he ordered Paul's execution.

The military released Paul from detention and sent him on

his way. The bus pulled up as three men waved it down. They dragged a struggling Paul out, and one of the men shot him in the back of the head in view of everyone on the bus. Paul Stanos, aged twenty-six, did not get to see his wife and children.

A Royal Air Force plane took the body of Peter March back to his family in Liverpool for a private burial service.

"We need time to re-group, step up training and get some more guns and ammunition." Grivas puffed away on a cigarette as he addressed six of his closest men.

"We'll need some more men too," Polycarpos added. "New faces. Too many are being detained. The British are getting to know our best men."

"Well, get on with it. You can't expect me to be everywhere," Grivas snarled.

"I'll do that. Will you take care of the weapons?"

"Who else do you think is capable? Not our pen-pushing friends. I'll get Clerides to try to arrange a cease-fire. Give us some breathing space."

Alex's relationship with Mehmet Ali continued to develop. Even the normally shy and reticent villagers greeted him with smiles and offers of coffee. Mrs Ozkara entreated him to try Turkish coffee. Alex was able to drink if not enjoy the thick, dark, bitter brew. Thanks to his tent-mate, Tom, he quickly learned how to drive and received an army-driving licence. With regular practice, Alex became quite proficient with his army revolver. Winter, such as it was on Cyprus, arrived and after discussions between Foot and Clerides a cease-fire was agreed. All spraying operations were put on hold. For a whole month the troops were able to move about Cyprus without armed guards. Alex asked Mehmet Ali if he might hire a car and asked permission for Leyla to show him those parts of the island noted for their antiquity and beauty.

"Of course you may. I will arrange for a car from my friend

Tashkan, he won't overcharge you. You must be careful. The car is recognised as a Turkish Cypriot car, the plate shows this. Even today you must be vigilant." Mehmet Ali was bestowing a great honour on Alex, even if he did not fully appreciate it. A wise and tolerant man, Mehmet Ali was fond of quoting pearls of wisdom. Alex knew one and said it to please him.

"It is said 'when you have a Turk for friend, you have a friend for ever'." The words slipped from his lips as he looked at Leyla. She blushed and made the little bow of her head, a movement that he'd come to love so much.

Staff Campbell was to be married. His long-time girlfriend, now fiancée, was on her way from England for the marriage ceremony. Sandra was a trained midwife. Staff organised a two-bedroom flat in Nicosia through the married personnel department.

"Come and help me get some better furniture. Sandra will have a fit if she sees that army shite." Archie screwed up his face in disgust.

"Can you do that, Staff? Change the furniture?"

"Do anything you like as long as it doesn't cost the army anything. Let's go. We'll find some decent second-hand stuff that looks as if it belongs in a Cypriot house." Alex was pleased to be invited. He and Staff were now good friends. He decided to confide in him. After all, he thought, he's taking the plunge into matrimony. He'll understand.

"Arch?" he began, hesitating, "Arch, what are the chances of marrying a local girl?"

"Less than zero. Is this the wee lass from Ghazientop? Obviously it is. Look, laddie, you still have what, eight or nine months to go. On what you Nashoes get, you can't afford it for a start. Second, if you asked, you'd be shipped home straight away, bang. You can shag the women but the army won't let you marry them. Are you shagging her?"

"Christ, no," Alex stuttered out, "how can you ask, Jesus, what do you think I am? I wouldn't even think about it. Shite, she's a good girl."

"Look son, they're all good girls. Until you get into their knickers. How many have you shagged? Any?"

Alex shook his head. "None."

"Well, I've shagged plenty. Nurses, German frauleins, wee Scottish lassies, lots. You don't get married just for shag. How do you think she'll go back in the UK?"

"Well, I was hoping that maybe I could get my demob here, in Cyprus. Leyla could stay with her father till then. My qualification is recognised here so I could get a job. Mehmet Ali would make sure I got a job."

"Ye daft thing, you wouldn't last five minutes here. Things like that just don't work out." He shook his head in disbelief.

"Okay, okay," Alex spat out the words, "leave it go. I just thought that you getting married you'd understand."

"I understand okay, ye daft bugger. But you're not getting married. Leave it go till you're demobbed in the UK. Then go home and then see how you feel." He gave Alex a soft punch on the shoulder.

The following Sunday, Alex and Leyla set off in an old Austin for Paphos. They travelled through the Troodos Mountains and stopped at Kykko Monastery where Makarios had been a novice. The mountain air was cool and this helped save the struggling Austin from overheating on the steep, twisting climb. The people at the monastery were very polite even though they recognised Leyla as Turkish. Alex spoke with one of the monks.

"If you are going to Paphos, may I suggest the back road? Here, I will show you." The monk drew a map that was on a par with those drawn by Pig.

For Alex, the word monastery meant a group of monks praying in silence and eating one meal a day. But all the monks at Kykko were chatty and looked extremely well fed. The monk spoke in halting English, sometimes switching to Greek. Leyla told Alex that the priest said that there was a nice drive down through the cedar forest to Paphos. "Very scenic," he said, "and much shorter than the main road."

The road was poor, a little too much for the old Austin. After a while the road forked and as Paphos lay somewhere to the south-west, Alex chose the left-hand road. The hard dirt road gave way to a stony road, with stones the size of tennis balls. He was forced to drive with the nearside wheel on the hard edge.

"Alexander, it's beautiful." Leyla called out, clutching his arm.

"Let go or we'll be over the edge," he cried out in panic. Slowing down, he gave her a look that said sorry for shouting at her. He looked down into the precipitous valley and felt dizzy. The journey was a nerve-racking experience, forcing him to drive very slowly. Alex had no time to look at the magnificent trees that covered the hillsides. Leyla, used to cart tracks, seemed oblivious to the danger. After what seemed a lifetime the little car limped into Paphos at two in the afternoon.

Paphos had been founded in 1400 BC. The most magnificent coastline of coves and rocky outcrops surrounded it, but it had a run down air, as if it had been asleep for centuries. Despite his Catholic education, Alex found that he knew little about the actual history of Christianity.

"I can't believe all this happened here," he shook his head. "The nuns concentrated on the catechism, the infallibility of the Pope and the dire penalties of sin. I don't remember being taught anything about the story of Christianity after the death of Jesus."

"But that is an important part of the story," Leyla gazed up at his face.

"As far as we were taught, Christianity all took place in the Holy Land and Rome, home of the Pope. How strange it is then to discover that St Paul brought Christianity to Paphos when it was the capital of a Roman province. Amazing."

With his arm around her waist, he stood on a sandy beach and looked out at the rocks supposed to mark the place where Aphrodite had risen from the sea in spume of foam. Alex felt something special, almost mystical, to be holding his love, gazing out to the birthplace of the Goddess of Love. At Nea Paphos there was just time for a stroll over some of the most beautiful mosaics he'd ever seen.

Leyla remarked that it was not right that such precious objects should be walked upon. "One day they will disappear," she looked dejectedly at the site, "the tiles will crack and break away until there is nothing left, like the entire ancient ruins in our land. People will steal them because they wish to have them, but they belong to everyone forever. It makes me sad."

Tilting her face toward him, Alex looked into her eyes. "I want you and me to last forever." They stood high above the sea, kissing until finally she broke away.

"We must leave now, my father..." Leyla panted with the little breath she had left.

"God, I've been in another world. I forgot the time. I told your father that I'd have you home by seven. We'd better get moving or he may not let us have another trip away."

Alex made it back to Ghazientop with minutes to spare, and explained how the drive from Kykko to Paphos had taken so much of the day. Mehmet Ali laughed affectionately. "Next time don't go so far. There is much to see here in the north of the island. Have you been to Salamis? It's maybe two hours' drive and you can see more of our ancient history. It is a fascinating place, so old, even older than the Greeks."

Alex's heart jumped at the words "next time". Leyla smiled, her eyes fixed on his. It was arranged that he would hire the little Austin for the following Saturday. He arrived early, at eight in the morning, so that they could have a long day together. Leyla packed a picnic lunch of Turkish bread, olives, a paste of beans, tomatoes, thin slices of pastirma-bastiruma, a spicy cooked meat, cucumber and sweet halva. Most of this was new to Alex but he was learning to enjoy this kind of food. It was simple and easy to prepare. Compared to army food, it was a veritable feast. All roads in Cyprus led through Nicosia. Leyla explained that before the British, Cyprus had only one proper road, the one from Larnaca to Nicosia. Everything else had been tracks suitable only for carts and donkeys. The early part of the journey was through the now familiar orange groves, laden with bright-coloured fruit, on the road between Ghazientop and Nicosia. Leyla suggested that they drive as far as Kantara Castle then travel south to Famagusta.

"We can see Turkey and Famagusta from Kantara." She bit her lip at the thought of Turkey.

Like any ordinary couple finding out about each other, they chattered all the way, embracing all kinds of subjects including religion, both Christian and Muslim. He told her about his upbringing and his fierce desire never to be poor. She tried to imagine this different picture of a world she'd only read about in books. Alex was curious about Islam and she answered his questions in her quiet, calm way.

"You see, Alexander, my father says that there is only one God. You were taught to believe that Jesus is the Son of God, so his father is your God. We believe that Mohammed was only the prophet of God, not God himself. And that is our God. But no-one can truly know God, for we are just human beings. We can know each other but not God. We can only believe."

"But you see," he tried to make her understand, "I haven't been inside a church for more than five years. I'm not sure that I believe in Christ and all the other saints and what have you. Why, if Jesus was poor and said 'blessed are the poor', do we have a Church with lots of money?"

"Father says that God may take many forms and we are not able to see that they are all one and the same. We are just blind, because we are only humans."

"I don't see how they can all be the same."

"Alexander, my father says that we have water, we have ice and we have the steam that comes from the boiling pot. They take different forms but they are all the same, is that not so?" She touched his hand. "Ice becomes water then steam and as the weather changes it goes back to ice." He smiled at this simple explanation of how God can be different yet the same.

"Alexander, we Turkish Cypriots have been isolated, not

part of the great world of Islam. We have been close to Christianity for centuries. As my father told you, it is not necessary to wear the veil or go to pray in the mosque to believe in Mohammed who teaches only that we must all answer before the one God when we die."

Alex experienced a sense of relief that their different religions need not force them apart. He was happy to believe in a God who did not require him to go to church. All a man needed was to live a good life, not killing or harming other people. Leyla looked so lovely and so innocent sitting there beside him. At that moment he decided that he would ask Mehmet Ali if one day he might be able to marry Leyla. At the thought, his face broke into a big, beaming smile. As if reading his mind, she put her arm through his and leant her head against his shoulder.

They turned off at Trikomo, drove across the narrow peninsula on a winding dirt road, and reached their first destination. Kantara Castle was set high up on the Kyrenia range of mountains that tapered off into the Karpas Peninsula or panhandle as the British sometimes call it. Built in the Byzantine period, Kantara castle, like St Hilarion, had been besieged and captured by Richard the Lionheart. Alex parked the car under a solitary tree on some flat ground and together they began to climb the jagged mountain to the peak and the ruins of the castle. Leyla let go of his hand and let out a cry of delight.

"Look, Alex, aren't they pretty?" She knelt down on a grassy slope covered in small flowers.

"Not as pretty as you."

"Have you heard of tulips?"

"Of course I have. My mother used to grow them in a pot. They come from Holland, I think." He brushed his hand over her hair.

"These are tulips." She smiled up at him.

"Bit small for tulips."

"Oh, they are, really. This is the original. They taught us at school that Cyprus is the birthplace of tulips. Somehow, I forget how, they ended up in Holland and they changed them into bigger flowers." She picked one.

"They're cute, anyway, these little ones. Do they grow wild?"

"All over the hills here in the north. You know that one day, long ago, tulips were used as money?" She stood up and held the flower under Alex's chin.

"You never cease to amaze me. How come you know so much?" He smiled at the beautiful girl with the tiny flower.

"It's all from school or in books. *Baba*, my father says that everything we need to know is written in books."

"So it seems." He gave her a gentle push so that she toppled to the ground.

"Come on," she shouted as she jumped up, "I'll race you to the top."

He managed to catch her just before the castle entrance and together they stood, sucking in air, arms around each other, laughing and kissing. The view from one of the chambers was spectacular.

"Look, Alex, see? Away down there? It's Famagusta."

Far away to the south the walled city could clearly be seen. They walked round to the other side and could just make out the dark outline of the Turkish coast.

"No wonder they built a castle here. It covers the coast and the plains to the south."

"Let's find a place to put our picnic." Leyla pulled him by the hand. They sat close together in the warm sunshine and ate some lunch. They leaned back against the remains of a wall and held hands and sat quietly lost in their own thoughts.

"Alexander?" Leyla broke the comfortable silence. "I think we have not enough time to do justice to a visit to Salamis. We should go on to the church of Saint Andreas. You would like that. It is very famous among Christians."

"Whatever is my lady's pleasure." He stood up and made a sweeping bow.

The road was not good but since it was flat it was not as

difficult as the Kykko–Paphos road. They drove through the sparsely populated region and glimpsed an occasional man herding fat-tailed sheep. Alex was surprised at the gently sloping hills and the almost bleak atmosphere that pervaded the dry plain.

"It must have looked like this when the Crusaders came here. All those centuries ago." Alex glanced out of the car window. "The beaches look magnificent. Yet there's no-one here?"

"It's not very good for farming. Not enough rain and no mountain streams." She put her head against his shoulder.

The Monastery of the Apostle Andrew was situated at the very eastern tip of the Karpas Peninsula. At the left-hand side was an enormous square lined with low buildings to house the monks. Alex parked the car next to the church. The sea lapped gently against its protective wall as he looked far out to sea. He could just make out a ship on the horizon.

"There's no electricity here," Leyla whispered at the entrance to the Church. "We must take a candle. Can you pay?"

They ducked low to enter the dark interior lit only by a myriad of candles and were greeted by an old lady enveloped in a long black garment. Leyla held on tight as the old lady put out a gnarled, arthritic hand for a contribution to cover the cost of a candle and a small leaflet. She brought her lips to his ear. "It's quite scary, isn't it?"

"Hold on to me. I'll look after you. Scaredy cat." He laughed quietly, tucking her arm under his.

The walls of the Greek Orthodox church were lined with gloomy icons of saints long forgotten except by the truly devout. He needed no pull on his hand to escape with Leyla into the now overcast but bright day. The leaflet explained the legend of St Andrew and a spring that he had uncovered. The water, the leaflet claimed, was able to cure all kinds of ailments. Apart from the original miracle there were no testimonials from other satisfied imbibers of the holy water. The return journey began along the coast road that led eventually to Kyrenia. The deserted beaches looked forlorn in the fading afternoon light.

"One day," Alex slowed down so that they could look more closely at the shoreline. "I'd like to build a house along this stretch of coastline."

"You would not find much work to do here." She felt warmed by the words he'd spoken.

He stopped the car. "It would be a weekend retreat from the city. That's where I'd be able to get work. Look there! Someone has begun to build a house."

"That's not new. It's old and abandoned," she corrected him. "Why?"

"Probably they ran out of money. People sometimes start something then abandon it."

"I'll never abandon you." He pulled Leyla close and kissed her lips, his hands caressing her neck and shoulders. In the cramped space she pushed her breasts against his chest as he nibbled her ear lobe. And the endless sea rolled in. They pulled apart and looked into each other's eyes.

"I love you so much." Alex kissed the tip of her nose.

"I love you too, my handsome soldier prince."

Her whispered response brought a lump to his throat. "We'd better keep going. Once late is enough." He started the engine and moved off very slowly, unwilling to break the spell. Turning off before Kyrenia, he drove up the hill to Bellapais.

"This where a famous English writer lived." She pointed out a small white painted house up on the hill overlooking the village. "My father says that he was a good man even though he preferred Greeks."

"Look, there're some seats under that tree. We can have a drink there."

"This is called 'the tree of idleness'. It's a mulberry." Taking him by the hand, she led him to the gnarled old tree. "It's supposed to cast a spell over those who sit under its branches."

"Let's hope it's a good spell." A superstitious Alex made a sign of the cross. Bellapais Abbey, perched rather precariously on a natural ledge, was indeed a wonderful setting. They gazed right out over the plains below to the sparkling, blue Mediterranean, as they stood inside the remains of the church. Leyla leaned back against his chest, his arms round her slim waist. They looked through the refectory window at the peaceful vista below, lost in their thoughts, together in their hearts, in the stillness of the empty space.

She turned to face him. "Alezander, whoever God is, you can feel his presence in this place."

They were alone in the refectory. He put a hand under her chin and kissed her softly on the lips. "Leyla, one day I would like you to be my wife. Do you think it would be proper to speak to your father, to ask if it's possible? I love you. I don't ever want to leave you," his eyes never wavered from her gaze.

"Oh, Alexander, I can say yes, please, but my father, it is for him to decide. It is our custom that a suitable husband is chosen for a girl. Although my father is more tolerant than many, as far as his daughter is concerned, I think he will not be different. It is not possible for me to marry a man who is not chosen or approved of by my father."

"Surely your father would not force you to marry someone you didn't love." His face filled with revulsion.

She smiled, a sad smile. "Alezander, please understand. You come from a different world. My mother and grandmother did not meet their husbands until their wedding night. Love grows if there is respect and caring. The family is what is important."

"What if they don't like each other?" He gripped her arms firmly.

"They must learn to like each other and carry out their duties. But that custom is not so common today except among peasants. Now, the two sets of parents meet and if they find each other agreeable, they allow the boy and girl to see each other at a family dinner."

"What if she docsn't like him?" He couldn't get the picture of Leyla with a stranger out of his mind.

"Although the parents have agreed, the girl may decline.

She may agree but only with her father's permission. That is how it is. Forgive me."

"I love you and would forgive you anything. It's all a mess here just now, but one day it will be all right. I can work here. Lots of British people work here." His deep voice resonated in the empty shell of the refectory. Embracing her, he gave no thought to Scotland or his family. Only later did he feel a sense of guilt that he had forgotten his mother and how she would feel about him living so far away.

"Alex, you are not a Muslim. My father would insist that I marry a Muslim man." The words were whispered.

"Could I become a Muslim?"

"Oh, Alex, it is not so easy just to say you will be a Muslim. Perhaps one day you can speak to my father." She did not sound confident.

He wanted to rush back to Ghazientop to speak to Mehmet Ali. By the time they reached there, he could hardly swallow thanks to a lump as big as a lemon in his throat. He dreaded the thought of rejection, of not being good enough for her, of being a soldier, a Christian. Leyla remained calm, only the squeezing of his hand giving any indication of her anxiety.

"Ah, back early. No problems with the car?" Mehmet Ali inquired in his quiet manner as he met them at the door. "Please, come inside, would you like coffee, maybe?"

As soon as they were seated, Alex stood and glanced at a sombre Leyla. "Mr Ozkara, please forgive me, I mean no disrespect."

Mehmet Ali gave him a questioning look. He turned to Leyla and spoke in Turkish. She put her hands together in a prayer-like fashion and nodded to Alex.

"Mr Ozkara, you have made me welcome in your home, I respect you, I respect Leyla, I love her." The words rushed out so quickly that they seemed to lose their importance and dignity.

"Ah, Alexander," Mehmet Ali sighed and turning to Leyla he spoke again in Turkish. She looked at Alex and in a soft voice told him that she would explain her father's words very carefully. "My father says that you are a young man, far away from home. You have not many of your own kind here and so you find my daughter very beautiful." She blushed as she spoke. "It is not possible for you to marry my daughter. You are army and army does not like you to marry foreign women. Apothecary is an honourable profession and one day you will have a good home, a wife and children. But my daughter will marry a suitable man from among our people when the time comes." She lowered her head as Alex struggled with his thoughts. "Mr Ozkara, when I finish with the army at the end of this year, I will stay in Cyprus and find a good position. I am able to work as an apothecary here. Many British people work and live here, many have married Cypriots. I have heard this."

Leyla listened as her father spoke again. "My father says that you will soon complete your time here in Cyprus. You will return to England. What happens then is the will of Allah."

Alex stuttered out thanks for Mehmet Ali's understanding and Leyla was dispatched to bring *cay*. Mehmet Ali spoke a little English but understood it quite well. He used the tactic of speaking through his daughter as a barrier to a deep and meaningful conversation. After the tea and some sweet honey-like cake, Mehmet Ali excused himself. "I have someone to see. It will only be minutes. Please wait. Your mother is preparing the evening meal. You require more *cay*?" And he left them alone, two grave young people.

Alex collapsed on the divan and she knelt at his feet and forced a tentative smile. "That was very good," she said, "more than I expected. We will show my father that we respect his wishes. You must be patient. Please, Alexander, do not run away."

"Your father is a good man, a clever man. He once told me that the world is always changing. He said that Turkey is no longer the Ottoman Empire. He said that we must be open to new ideas so maybe he will change his mind about me?" He stole the smallest of kisses before Mehmet Ali returned.

In a subtle way, Alex was given a kind of recognition as Leyla's suitor and invited to join the family for evening meals when he was able to visit Ghazientop on semi-official business. Unfortunately, Sir Hugh Foot was no more successful in his efforts to bring peace to Cyprus and the killings and bombings began again. There were fifty explosions in a short time.

Alex and Mike resumed their deliveries of chemical solution.

"You know I go home in a couple of weeks?" Mike said as he turned off before Ghazientop.

"Shite. That means I have to get a new driver," a disappointed Alex muttered.

"This may be your last one too. It's not as if this stuff seems to work, does it?"

"If it does, nobody's told me. God, this is the worst road yet. Bloody boulders everywhere. Slow down. It's hard to see if there's anything on the road." Alex peered ahead.

"Just be my luck, wouldn't it?" Mike said anxiously "A booby trap on my last trip."

The rendezvous was a desolate little spot right on the coast. Alex's back ached as they headed back to camp.

"Roll on demob," Mike chortled as the boom gate opened and they were safely back at Camp Kermia.

Then a new situation unfolded. Civil unrest broke out in Lebanon and the unit was put on 48-hour standby. It was rumoured that 24 Field Ambulance would be part of a British landing in Lebanon. The unit would assist with casualties prior to the restoration of law and order.

"Will you be coming with us?" Alex asked Archie Campbell. "Will you still be able to get married?"

"Don't panic, son. I've been through this kind of thing before. It may never happen."

"They've got heaps of that awful penicillin injection at the Military Hospital. It's just about out of date. What say I get a load and take it with us if we go?"

"What for, ye daft thing?" Staff Campbell frowned.

"I could always sell it. On the black market, you know?"

"Think of being another Harry Lime, are ye? Get it if ye want. Ye've always got some scheme in mind." He shook his head in admiration.

"We'd come back here, wouldn't we?" a concerned Alex watched as Staff calmly twirled his long chain and keys. "I need some extra money for all this car hire. It's not cheap, even with Mehmet Ali's help."

"The things lovers will dae. Awa ye go, ye daft bugger. So long as there's no record of it."

With Tom Harper's help, Alex collected ten large cartons of the dreaded penicillin. The standby was increased to 72 hours then five days before finally being cancelled. The US marines made a landing on the beaches at Beirut. The cartons of penicillin injections were buried in a field belonging to Mehmet Ali. Alex was both happy and sad at this turn of events.

Governor Foot arranged a meeting with Clafcos Clerides. Although he was known to have a strong connection with *EOKA*, Clafcos Clerides was allowed to continue his work unhindered, as he was useful to the British as a contact with Grivas and other *EOKA* leaders.

"Ah, Clafcos, good of you to take the time to meet with me. I do hope that you and your charming wife are both well?" He indicated to Clafcos to join him on a heavily brocaded divan behind a large brass table with a coffee pot, cups and an assortment of small biscuits.

"Sir Hugh, it's always a pleasure to meet with you. You are trying so hard to make for a good resolution here. It is not easy, I know, but, well, we can but keep trying." Clerides paused while a footman poured out two cups of coffee then retired, closing the massive ornate door. The stillness of the room with its high ceiling descended on the two men, the only people present. Foot sipped his black coffee and thought how pleasant it was to deal with an educated man who understood protocol and the importance of dialogue.

"Clafcos, this recent spate of bombings, over fifty, is hurting all of our efforts to realise a just solution to the problem here. I am sure that Mr Grivas hopes that this latest series of attacks on government and military establishments will force the government in London to back down. I am not of this view." Governor Foot looked at him, one eyebrow raised.

Clerides avoided his look. "We, all of us, deplore the need to use force to achieve political solutions, do we not, Governor? But the people of Cyprus have waited long enough. You and I know that one day the British will leave Cyprus. The tide of history will carry them away from these shores. So why do we wait for more people to die before the inevitable comes to pass?" He picked up his cup and drank some coffee.

"Of course, you are correct. The government knows it too. But Britain does not like to be pushed, to be forced to concede the inevitable. So, what we, you and I, must do is find a way to end the destruction and arrange a settlement that allows everyone, including Turkey, to keep face. It is here that we must first achieve something. Do you agree?" He gave Clerides a solemn, serious look.

"It is up to you, as Governor, to lead the way out of this stalemate. Do you have something in mind?"

"What I would like is a face-to-face meeting with Colonel Grivas. A place of his choosing. I will be alone and unarmed. Even though this would mean my breaking the law and the military would be unhappy, it's a chance I feel I have to take."

"Well, I appreciate your courageous decision, Sir Hugh, but I can't see how such a meeting could be." There was a moment's silence.

"Clafcos, I am confident that by some means or other you are able to communicate my hopes for a meeting. My wish is to discuss with Grivas how we can end the violence. With his cooperation I am sure that we can work out an arrangement that will satisfy most of the wishes of the Archbishop and *EOKA*. You have defended so many of these young men who have committed offences that—"

Before he could finish, Clerides held up a hand. "Well, Sir Hugh, of course I applaud your plan but I have no way of knowing the whereabouts of Colonel Grivas, or even how he may be contacted. I can, of course, put out the idea and see what happens. Often, without my knowing, I am speaking to a person involved with *EOKA*. So many are, these days."

"Let me say, Clafcos, that I have here," Foot produced an envelope and opened it, "a letter which may by chance fall into the hands of Colonel Grivas. It outlines Prime Minister Macmillan's proposal for self-government for five or six years before any final decision is made on the future of Cyprus. It is an excellent proposal. The PM has also included at my insistence the need to end this infernal State of Emergency, and the need for Archbishop Makarios to be allowed to resume his work. Now, I think that all of us can then join with Dr Kucuk and your friend Denktash to work out the best system, given the circumstances. What do think? Will Grivas agree to meet?"

Clerides picked up the letter from the table. "Well, you certainly have been busy. Who knows? Give me the letter. It may reach Colonel Grivas, I can't promise, you understand?"

"I'm thinking of advising the government to release Archbishop Makarios from exile in the Seychelles. How does that strike you?"

"Would he be able to return to Cyprus?"

Foot shook his head. "Definitely not. Well, not at this stage, anyway. I thought Athens would be fine. Letting him back here at this time might lead to demonstrations. We have enough problems as it is."

"I'm sure His Beatitude will be pleased with your decision. He is the only person who can bring about a resolution to this needless conflict. You have made a wise decision."

"It's only a recommendation at this stage but I am confident that the government will agree. Then, when you get the chance to speak with the Archbishop I hope you will stress the need for an end to this pointless violence. It leads nowhere."

Foot looked hopefully at Clerides.

"I will travel to Athens to greet our leader as soon as his release is confirmed." Clerides stood up and shook hands with the Governor of Cyprus.

Foot's fears of demonstrations were confirmed when Makarios arrived in Athens. Over 100,000 people greeted him on his drive from the airport to his hotel in Athens.

Grivas laughed when the letter from the Governor was put into his hands. The British, he thought, are beginning to understand that the more harshly they treat the people, the more they will resist and in the end win. The first steps in the retreat have begun. So, I will show them that I am not an unreasonable man. "Clafcos?" Grivas spoke into the phone. "Tell the Governor that there will be an end to sabotage and destruction." After a pause, he added, "For now."

Mehmet Ali was appointed regional area commander of Volkan or TMT (Turkish Defence Organisation). "It's not something I wish, but there is no alternative," he informed his wife.

"You'll do a good job as usual." Gulten looked at him with admiration.

"I think that we may have to fight, but it's not my way. The situation is getting really desperate, don't you think?"

"I'm sure that Dr Kucuk knows what he's doing." She continued to knead the dough for some new bread.

Mehmet Ali sighed. His wife Gulten was a great comfort to him with her cooking skills and in bed. But it was to his young daughter that he turned, to discuss political matters. Leyla, he thought was not only a beautiful young woman but well read and eager to be involved in the struggle to survive against the Greeks.

"Ah, my Leyla, these are indeed difficult times. We are so few against the Greeks that we need cooperate with the British at all times, even when they are stupid and so terribly British."

"Don't say that, *Baba*."

"Sometimes, they think that this is like a game of cricket where the rules of gentlemen apply. They do not understand the Byzantine mind," he folded his arms and rocked back on the divan.

"But *Baba*, if the British lose, as they always seem to do these days and we are left to the mercy of the Greeks, will we, and *Anne*, not be worse off?"

"Don't be afraid, my lovely. We will not surrender without a fight. We must do what we have to do." He wiped a hand across his forehead.

Leyla fixed her eyes on the man she most respected in the world. "There are no secrets in this land. The Greeks know you. They know you are a leader who must be involved in whatever it is that you do. Will we not be at risk? Will we ever be safe to live our lives?"

"This is a new and terrible kind of war that we fight. We must do everything possible to help the British defeat these terrorists. They will! These Greek people are thugs, bullies who need something to make them feel important. What are they doing, the heartless murderers? They cannot win, or if they do there is no hope for us." He rocked back and forth.

"But *Baba...Baba*." A troubled Leyla shook her head.

Before she could continue her father sounded more confident. "We will cooperate with the British and they will win. Alexander's work is good. You'll see. They will keep Cyprus as a land for Greeks and Turks. When these fanatics die, *inshallah*, then we will still be British and live again in peace." He paused to catch his breath as the heated words poured out. "The Greeks are not all bad, just their fanatical leaders. Demetrio is also with me. He agrees that business is more important than who is our ruler. Who cares, he told me, the British, the Greeks or the Americans? We need to do business to feed our families, to celebrate weddings, to drink coffee and argue with our friends. He is right."

He pointed a finger at Leyla. "Do the American Negroes care who is in power? No, all they want is a job and to make some money to live like other Americans. This I know to be true." His words gushed out in an impassioned plea as if addressing a crowd. "Whatever is to happen, we must support the British, they must defeat these hooligans, these murderers. We must pray that they will."

"Everywhere, all I see is hate, suspicion, everyone looking scared. Even here in our village," Leyla interrupted.

"Yes, already the Greeks have set up defensive positions in many of the mixed villages. They fear us, the TMT. Even the Greeks here in Ghazientop no longer say hello. I haven't been invited to their coffee shop for months. At least they haven't closed their road."

"It's strange that the Greeks fight each other too, isn't it?" Leyla shook her head. "Only yesterday I read that Grivas or his men are attacking members of AKEL. They say they are communists. Now Greeks are afraid of Greeks."

On his usual visit to Morphou, Mehmet Ali wept openly on seeing his friend Demetrio tied to the door of the church with the word "traitor" on a piece of cardboard pinned to his chest. His heart broke at the sight but he drove past and returned at once to Ghazientop. Women wailed and protested when husbands were murdered for being left-wing trade unionists. The trade union was the only organisation capable of mounting a political challenge to the power of the Church. By attacking the communist-leaning AKEL, Grivas knew he would have the support of the United States with their paranoid fear of communism. As various plans for the setting up of a self-governing Cyprus were discussed, Turkey flexed its muscles. The government of Menderes realised that self-government would eventually lead to self-determination and then union with Greece. So it began to put pressure on the British Government for partition of the island with two separate and independent states, one Greek and the other Turkish. Turkish Cypriots were in strong positions in the police and auxiliary forces. Dr Kucuk asked for a meeting with Governor Sir Hugh Foot.

"So Grivas has offered another cease-fire. You know why, don't you?" he began.

"I think he realises that violence is alienating his own people. That's my opinion." Foot tried to sound convincing.

"You still don't understand the Greek mind, do you?" Kucuk shook his head. "He wants more time to build up his stockpile of arms. And while he does that he has ordered a boycott of all British goods. And no Greek is allowed to do business with Turks. We will be starved into submission."

"At least it gives me time to try to find a political solution." Foot held out his hands in supplication.

"I can't hold my people back any longer. They are taking matters into their own hands. You know that there have been demonstrations in favour of partition?"

Governor Foot shook his head in disappointment. "I regret that. It will only serve to stir up more hatred and fear. The Greeks will never submit to a divided island, you must know that."

"Every day, somewhere, they, the Greeks, conduct rallies in favour of *Enosis*. Why don't you stop these demonstrations? Ban all public demonstrations. We will be happy to accept that."

"It's not that easy. I have to deal with the fact that there are Turks attacking Greeks, Greeks attacking Turks and splinter groups attacking anyone for the sake of what they can loot. This dance of death just goes on and on. We need all parties to come together and work out an amicable solution." He shrugged his shoulders in despair.

"Well, I can tell you that I met with Prime Minister Menderes in Ankara and Turkey will be involved. Menderes is pressing Britain for two separate states in Cyprus." He shook his finger at the Governor.

"That will never work. Too much disruption of the populace. Two small states unable to function. How many would there be in the Turkish Cypriot state? Two hundred thousand? Surely you agree that this would be a ridiculous outcome?" Foot's eyes narrowed as he squinted at the Turkish Cypriot leader.

"I'll leave you to think over Turkey's intentions. Mark my words, Grivas will unleash more attacks as soon as he has enough ammunition. It's the way he works. Neither you nor Governor Harding have realised how he operates."

Foot watched as Dr Kucuk walked slowly from the room. It doesn't get any easier he thought.

It wasn't Grivas but undisciplined members of *EOKA* who broke the cease-fire. In Famagusta they had shot and killed the young wife of an Air Force officer. The British soldiers joined in the dance of violence. This one killing led to an orgy of beatings in the darkened streets of Nicosia, Famagusta, Larnaca and Limassol. Ordinary and usually disciplined British soldiers acted like vigilantes. The Greek Cypriot prisoners in Camp K suffered badly. Alex worried about his Leyla and visited Ghazientop at every opportunity. The meetings were brief and filled with tension and longing.

Feral dogs were an increasing problem in Cyprus. With so many army camps, bins everywhere overflowed with discarded food. It was common for a pack of ten or more dogs to enter the compounds at night in search of food. 24 Field Ambulance was "blessed" with several members of the Catering Corps, men who had undergone a 4-week cooking course after basic training. Much of the food was inedible and left uneaten. The full bins were easily knocked over. Two of the cooks were homosexuals. They shared a tent and no doubt a bed according to many ribald, but basically good-humoured comments from the tough medicos. One day they caught a brown, shorthaired dog and hid it in their tent. It was kept tied up and well fed. At night they would take it out for a short walk round the perimeter. On a surprise tent inspection just before breakfast, Pig found the dog. The cooks were busy preparing the meal and had no time to hide it. The cooks were forced to bring it to Staff's office tent. The sun rose in the sky.

It was hot and the poor creature, tied to Pig's Landrover, had just enough rope to crawl under into some shade. It cringed there for an hour or more while Pig became more and more agitated. Eventually, he sent for his driver and slowly drove off, the dog trying desperately to keep up. In a nearby field, Pig took out his revolver and shot it. The driver dug a shallow hole and covered the body over with soil. For many days, the Pig so beloved of his men was treated like a leper.

Cyprus 1958

IT WAS HIGH SUMMER in Cyprus, in 1958. The release of Makarios led to another truce while talks went on in Athens, London and New York. Grivas announced another cease-fire while he awaited developments. Alex jumped at the chance to spend the day with Leyla. She suggested that they make their long delayed visit to the walled city of Famagusta where she had some relatives.

"I have not been to Famagusta for a long time, not since I was a child. They will like to see me. And you," she smiled as she spoke.

While Alex was not keen to share their limited time with any relatives, he agreed. "They tell me that the beach at Famagusta is the best in all of Cyprus. Can we go there and have a swim?"

"Oh, that is not possible, not for me. But you may swim. I can watch you," she said with that familiar tilt of her head.

The Messiora Plain was rich, golden brown with ripening corn. Alex and Leyla drove along, windows open to catch a breeze, hot though it was. "Better a hot breeze than this stifling air inside," he cried out above the noise of the wind.

"This is a good road, isn't it?" Leyla leaned towards him as she spoke.

"Obviously they need it for the trucks going to and from the port at Famagusta."

"That's why there're so many trucks and buses. It's a popular place, Famagusta. "We're nearly there. Once we get past these villages." He glanced quickly at Leyla.

"I think I can just see the walls of the old city." She leaned forward and peered out through the windscreen. "Yes, there they are, look."

"They're really something. Every time I see them. How old are they?"

"The first walls were built by the Luisignans." She responded automatically. "A long time ago. Then the Venetians came and made the walls higher and much thicker. They had to because of the invention of cannons. When the Ottomans came to Cyprus they found the walls too much and it took a long time to capture the city. Many, many people died and now only Turks live in the old city."

"You constantly amaze me! You know so much about the place. At school we learned about Culloden, Robert the Bruce, Bonnie Prince Charlie and the hated English."

"I know nothing about that. You see?"

"In history class I studied the Thirty Years' War, the American War of Independence, Wolfe in Canada and so much more that most of it was soon forgotten."

"So many places. No wonder you forget. Or maybe one day you will remember it when you read about those times?"

"You're lucky. This is a small island. And I suppose its history is important to you."

"I learned a little about Greece at the Greek school, but my father has told me all about the Turkish history in Cyprus. He knows a lot about that."

"I seem to remember hearing the name Famagusta from my studies at school." He wrinkled his forehead. "I'm not sure where, I don't think it was history because Cyprus wasn't part of our studies."

"I only know a little about it, but I think that somewhere Famagusta is mentioned in a play by Shakespeare, the famous English writer. Maybe we can ask someone? I'm sure that my father will know."

He shook his head in wonder at so much knowledge in a girl so young.

Alex parked the car in a small square. Old Famagusta was

made up of many laneways too narrow for a motorcar. They went up narrow streets, round sharp corners, down a maze of criss-crossing laneways, and finally arrived at the home of her aunt. Leyla referred to her as aunt but explained that she was a distant aunt, her mother's aunt's daughter. Repeated knocking on the dark, solid-timber door of the tiny, whitewashed house brought no response.

"Perhaps my aunt did not receive the message that we were coming today," she fretted. "I'm sure that my mother said that we would visit today."

Alex was not unhappy. Now he had her all to himself. Back through the laneways they wandered, past colourful little shops and open little workshops. They stopped at one where an old woman was making Turkish delight, a delicious sweet much loved by Turks and Greeks alike. Leyla bought some and it was handed over in a sheet of paper rolled up into a conical shape, much like an ice-cream cone. A leisurely walk took them to the beach with its beautiful promenade. People were strolling along the wide esplanade, happy to be out walking as if it was a normal day in a normal place. The beach, stretching for miles, was only crowded on a small area of sand, most people preferring to stay close to the collection of ice carts and food vendors. Here and there, groups of soldiers enjoyed a noisy game of cricket. Alex observed that some of the soldiers, fielding, paid more attention to the young women than the match. Hand in hand they walked along the shoreline, avoiding each little wave with skipping jumps. After a mile they were out of sight of the bathers. They walked up the sand and found a sheltered, sandy drift fringed by stunted shrubs and thick spiky reeds.

"This is nice here. Our own little hideaway." Alex put down the two towels he'd brought from camp.

"No-one can see us. It's just you and me in our own little world." She kissed him on both cheeks.

He pulled off his shirt, dropped his shorts, and kicked off his sandals. "I need to cool off. It's so hot and I need to cool off.

And it's not just the sun," he laughed as he ran down to the sea. Alex splashed about in the water, hoping that Leyla would stand up and see him. She didn't. Panting after a dash up over the hot sand, he grabbed a towel and watched as Leyla removed her sandals and pulled her dress up above her knees.

"It's so hot." She shook her head from side to side, her long hair billowing out. She had unpinned her small square handkerchief to allow cool air to flow at the back of her head. Alex had never seen above her ankles before. Her slim, pale brown legs aroused him even more. Sinking to his knees, he placed a hand just below the inside of her knee. Leyla pulled down her dress and Alex lay beside her, his hand caressing and moving even higher. He stroked the smooth inside of her leg above her knee.

Leyla murmured. "No, Alex, no," but he found it so pleasurable that he couldn't stop. He murmured her name softly and his hand moved higher until he could feel the silky texture of her loose-fitting panties.

"Oh Alex, oh Alex," she whispered moving to the rhythm of his ever-probing hand.

"Leyla," the word came out choked, urgent. "You feel so good."

Leyla gasped as she uttered some more words in Turkish. His arm became stiff and he stopped.

"Don't stop, Alezander, it's so beautiful," she panted. "I can't believe how beautiful it feels when you touch me."

He wanted to keep giving her pleasure. She lay there, eyes closed, moaning between kisses. The sensation, the feeling of joy, filled her mind and body. "I've never felt like this before. I should say stop but I can't. Every time you touch me. Oh, oh," the words came out one at a time.

He lay on top of Leyla. His hands pushed her dress up further so that he could reach and touch her breasts. Her hands ran up and down his back with increasing urgency. She moaned softly as he leaned over again.

He looked into her eyes. "God, I want you." His hands stroked every part of her body.

"Alezander." His name came out in a whisper. Leyla cried out something in Turkish and gripped his shoulders, kissing, sucking, making animal-like sounds. He entered her. Head back, Leyla cried out to stop. Alex pulled back then went in again. She screamed with pleasure. They moved together, kissing then gasping for air. Leyla held his head in both hands, holding on tight. They moved together as one until he felt a pressure that finally gave way. Leyla cried out in ecstasy. Sucking in air, he lay there, on top of her with a feeling of joy that slowly, ever so slowly, subsided. He kissed her lips, her nose, her forehead and neck.

Leyla, in a tiny voice repeated, "Alex, Alex, Alex," as she moved her hands over his bare back and shoulders. Rolling on to his back, he took her hand and held it to his lips. Leyla turned and lay by his side. Caressing each other, they lay quietly together until their breathing returned to normal. They moved slightly apart and looked into each other's eyes with trance-like smiles, faces moist and glowing.

She rolled on to her back to adjust her dress. "Oh no, oh, Alezander. No!" she cried in a small voice as if afraid of being overheard. "Alezander, look."

He looked at her panties, smeared with some blood that had trickled to the inside of her dress. "My God," Alex groaned, realising that he had broken her hymen, that he had taken her virginity. All feelings of joy evaporated and he pulled down her dress as if that would make the blood disappear. With a cry she clung to him, kissing his cheeks over and over, then finally his lips.

She whimpered some words first in Turkish, then English. "Help me, help me. We must clean this dress. I must not return home like this. I will be shamed before my mother. My father must not know. What can I do? A woman's body must not be seen except by her husband."

For a moment Alex was paralysed with fear. Struggling,

shielded by both towels, she removed her dress. She crouched with her knees up to her chin, and watched as Alex carried the dress down to the water. He carefully washed away the blood, trying to wet only the part that was stained. He placed the dress over some of the spiky reeds to dry. They sat, huddled together, whispering words of love, touching each other's faces with gentle fingers. They were reluctant to move, afraid to leave the little shelter, their little shelter. Fear rose up again in Alex, the fear that comes with failure. Leyla sensed his shivers and kissed him gently on the lips.

"Please don't be afraid, Alexander. I will wait some days then I will get out of bed and cut myself. I will put the blood on my pyjamas and show them to my mother. I think it sometimes happens like that. Even if she doesn't believe it, my mother will let my father think that it's so. No-one will ever know."

Alex shuddered. He knew Turks were the kindest, friendliest of people but it was well known that they were fierce protectors of their daughters. Revenge killing for insults was common to both Greeks and Turks.

"Check my dress. Is it dry? Then we must return home and you must not look at me like a puppy trying to please. Raise some topic that will engage my father. Ask him how his people came to Cyprus after the fall of Famagusta." A forlorn Leyla held his hand to her hot cheek.

She sat as close as possible in the little Austin, only moving apart when they passed through a village and Alex had to change gear.

"What a pity your aunt wasn't home." Mehmet Ali lowered his head as he looked at Leyla.

"We waited, *Baba*, but she must have made a mistake with the day."

"It's a fascinating place, Famagusta." Alex desperately changed the subject. "Leyla told me that the Turks came to Cyprus after it was conquered. Did your family come then?"

Mehmet Ali did not appear to notice anything unusual.

"Some time after. I can't be sure. Gulten, we can eat now," he called out to his wife in the kitchen. "I only know that at some time my family, the first to come, were given land here in Ghazientop. My family has been here ever since."

Alex managed to stumble through the evening meal. Leyla kept up a steady stream of questions to her father. Gulten, eyes downcast, said nothing as she saw the desperate looks that passed between her daughter and the young soldier. On the way back to camp he cursed himself for feeling relieved to be away from Ghazientop. Then his thoughts returned to Leyla and the time on the beach. He felt himself stiffen. You're a bloody hypocrite, he thought.

The cease-fire was broken late on Sunday and the news came through that Makarios would not be allowed to return to Cyprus.

Pig called the officers and NCOs to Staff's tent. "It looks like we're going out on an operation. Brigade wants to catch some buggers before things blow up again."

Staff Campbell twirled his keys on the long chain. "Ye're going up the Karpas, the Panhandle. Brigade has intelligence that there's a pack of terrorists hiding there. I thought the Turks had that area covered. Then, I'm not in the Intelligence Corps," Staff chortled. "Colonel Barry has the location. It's pretty wild, isolated, so there won't be too many signs." He gave Pig a withering look.

"Right," said Pig, sticking a smallish map up on a blackboard. "That's where we're going." He jabbed his swagger stick in the general direction of the Karpas region. Everyone leaned forward, peering at the map of the area. "That's where we're going. That's the field where we'll set up the first-aid tents and kitchens." He tapped a spot on the map with his stick. Everyone looked intently at the little map. "If we stay out more than one night we'll get a new team to come out. It's too much work to set up bivouacs. I'll lead off, just follow me, lights on low," he sniffed in deeply, leaving no-one any wiser as to the map reference.

This was not uncommon, so everyone trooped off to the already waiting loaded vehicles. It was just getting dark as the convoy set off, Pig as bold as brass, one leg dangling outside his Landrover. Alex assumed that the Infantry Brigade had gone on ahead because he saw no signs of other trucks. "I hope he knows where he's going," he said quietly.

"It's starting to get really dark," the worried driver replied. As usual, they were expected to set up camp about a mile back from where the operation was to take place, since they were purely a support unit in case of casualties. After about an hour, the convoy slowed to a halt. Pig stepped out of his Landrover, shone a torch at his map, then climbing back in, he moved on. This happened several times and the driver chuckled. "I bet the bugger's lost. Silly bugger." The tone was affectionate.

After another half an hour of stop-starting Pig finally pulled into a field of corn. There was no fence. This was not unusual, as in much of Cyprus goatherds wandered all over the place and a shepherd always tended sheep or goats. Nobody said a word as the men set up a first-aid tent and a small tent for medical supplies.

"Get the kitchen gear out and get cracking on some grub." Pig shouted while everyone else tried to be as quiet as possible. It was after eight and everyone was hungry. It might have been the tension of being out on an operation that seemed to get the gastric juices flowing. The men were ready for a meal. Lighting was kept to a minimum making for a few sore thumbs. The food was all tinned and the cooks hurried to open tins of stew, corned beef and beans, all mixed in the big long, wide gutter-like pans. In the darkness, the cooks opened tins of marmalade as well with the result that the evening meal was greeted with some rude comments.

"Funny bloody stew this," a voice came out of the darkness.

"It's got funny little bits in it. It's like orange peel," a response came. The cause was discovered and it was all eaten, main and dessert courses in one.

"Might as well eat the bread with the stew," Alex chuckled. "There's nothing left to put on it anyway."

It was a long wasted night with nothing happening, at least in the 24 Field Ambulance camp. At first light an angry Greek farmer arrived. It wasn't necessary to understand the language to know that the camp had been set up in the wrong field. Pig did not back off; he just waved his stick and told the farmer to fuck off. Alex should have been laughing like the other men but his mind was with Leyla and how she would manage to fool her mother that her hymen had broken in her sleep.

About ten in the morning, a Landrover and truck rolled up. Several Military Police jumped out and pulled some men from the back of the truck. "We need your tent, Colonel," one of the officers addressed Pig in a commanding voice.

"This one." Pig pointed to the first-aid tent. Some handcuffed prisoners were dragged inside. The other soldiers were Intelligence Corps officers, obvious from the fact that they wore no insignia. Staff had told Alex that this meant any complaints couldn't be followed up, as the complainant couldn't say which regiment the men belonged to. Pig joined them in the tent and the flap was closed. Alex assumed that the men were injured when Pig called out for some first-aid bags. Inside, one man was lying on the ground with one of the officer's boots stamping up and down on the side of his head. Pig grabbed the bag.

"Get the fuck out!" he bellowed.

After about twenty minutes the men were dragged out and driven back the way they had come. Alex never mentioned what he had seen and Pig never referred to it at any time. The operation was called off after lunch and after packing up it was back to camp, the men happy to have been out for the night. Alex was just worried. The next day passed and he was too busy to get to Ghazientop.

Then Pig announced that there was to be a mock amphibious landing at Orga at the far west tip of the northern shore of Cyprus. Another three days went by. Alex had little to do. Orderlies treated a few sprained ankles and burns before it was back to camp once again. By this time he was really in the doldrums and his depression deepened when he was ordered by Brigade HQ to report to Mehmet Ali at Ghazientop. It had been weeks since the last spray job. Alex could not imagine that Brigade would get involved in a personal matter. That was not the army way. Then again, Mehmet Ali had been very cooperative so perhaps they felt the need to keep him on side if he had a family problem. For days Alex had experienced difficulty swallowing. It was as if he had an obstruction or a lump in his throat. He decided to have a word with Captain Tom MacGowan.

"Let's have a look. Nothing there," he said removing the tongue depressor. "Anything worrying you?"

"Not really," Alex replied, glad that it wasn't cancer or the like.

"It's just that ye sometimes get that response if ye're anxious aboot something. It's quite common. It's called *globus histericus*. Just a fancy name for the body's reaction to an emotional state. Ye sure ye're no worried aboot something?"

"It's okay, Tom. So long as it's not physical. Thanks, anyway." He didn't want to go any further with the discussion.

When Leyla opened the door, and greeted him with a smile, a sense of relief flooded his whole body. Looking serene, she led Alex through to the sitting room where her father and mother were seated.

"Ah, Alexander, so good to see you. We have missed you. Have we not, Leyla?" he turned to her with a beaming face.

"Thank you, Sir," He looked at Leyla. "We have been very busy. Many things going on."

"So, you know why we meet?" Mehmet Ali asked with raised eyebrows.

"No," Alex stuttered, lost for words.

"Ah, you see! Leyla, tell Alexander what I want to say." She looked at Alex with those lovely wide, brown eyes and smiled again. He rocked back on his heels.

"My father says that he must visit his mother who is old and his sister. They live in Turkey, a big city called Izmir. It is a long way away."

"Oh," Alex couldn't think what else to say. "His mother, my grandmother lives with his sister who is a teacher at the university. His sister, my Aunt Nafia, is very famous, I think."

Gulten sat quietly looking glum.

"Now his mother is not well and my father must see her if she is going to die." Leyla nodded in her father's direction. "So, you see, he will not be able to help you until his return, in maybe two weeks or more."

"Ah. Ah. That's okay, there's nothing planned as far as I know." He breathed out.

"My father says that his mother has often been sick and dying, but always she recovers. But who knows? One day it will happen so he must go once again."

"Ohh," Alex let out the longest of sighs, "Ohh, well, that's not a problem; I think we have finished with the other business, you know, for the time being." After seven trips to the helicopter he had not heard a word for almost a month. He assumed that the exercise had been a failure. To his knowledge, not a single terrorist had been captured. There had been nothing on the radio or in the Greek Cypriot newspaper. Any success would surely have been hailed as a triumph for the army and a cause for dismay by the Greek press.

Mehmet Ali looked at Leyla and spoke quickly. By now Alex understood a few works of Turkish but Mehmet Ali spoke too fast so he looked at her for the translation. "My father says that you are welcome to visit us when you can, even if he is not here. He says that he now knows several Turks who have married English women. He did not know any before. It is good, he says."

Alex now felt much better and for the rest of the visit he was quite relaxed. Fear had come and gone so easily .His new driver, Terry, was dozing in the Landrover. As Alex prepared to leave, Leyla touched his cheek briefly. "My aunt in Famagusta says that she is sorry not to meet you. There is to be a wedding in her family. She invites me and my mother and also you if you are able to come. She told me that it is fascinating that many Turks marry English women but no Turkish women marry Englishmen." She kissed her finger and put it to his lips.

"I can't promise, but I'll be there if I have to make a special trip to the Ordinance Depot," Alex was happy just to be alive.

"Everything is good," she whispered, "the bleeding was not at the usual time of the month. My mother said it sometimes happens. Especially after riding a donkey."

A much-relieved Alex chattered away to Terry on the drive back to camp. The lump in his throat had gone. Terry sensed a change in Alex. "You're going on like a man who's just been released form solitary. I take it you had good news?"

"Couldn't be better mate, couldn't be better," a cheerful Alex looked up to the heavens.

That night it was his turn to be Sergeant of the Guard. Each evening six men were assigned to guard duty. Two at a time, they walked the perimeter fence keeping a lookout for any intruders, or watchful for a nearby sniper who might fire at a soldier going about his business. The dentist, "Fangs", was a regular soldier. The son of a high-ranking officer in the Fusiliers, Captain Trevor Shulton had signed on for eight years in the army. Automatically an officer because of his qualifications, he received much higher pay than a National Service officer. With very small expenses he could save quite a bit of money and there was the likelihood of promotion to Major and even better pay. Fangs had a dental assistant, Dennis, a nice, well-educated young Corporal who, good as he was at his trade, hated being in the Dental Corps and detested being a Corporal. He crossed off every day on a calendar towards his release. He was hopeless at giving orders and was easily bullied by some of the tougher elements in the unit. One of the worst was a Liverpool thug by the name of Tate.

Dennis plied his trade of making dentures and bridgework in a tiny room at the rear of the main house, close to the medical store. He regularly confided in Alex the problems he encountered when Duty Corporal. "I'm supposed to say who does what shift but people like Tate tell me what shift they'll do. I'm just a joke."

"Next time we're on together, leave it to me." He patted Dennis on the back. The guard roster worked to a set routine from 6pm to 6am the next day. Two men at a time patrolled the camp perimeter on a two-hour shift. Normally most men in the lines would have lights out just after 11pm as reveille was at six in the morning. The first shift was the most prized as it meant an uninterrupted four-hour sleep from 0200 hours until reveille. The Duty Corporal was expected to stay awake all night then go to bed and have the rest of the day off. The Duty Corporal chose pairs for the different shifts. He remained in the guard tent the whole night and would call the Sergeant of the Guard only if there was a problem. Tate threatened to punch up Dennis if he wasn't given the 6 to 8pm shift.

"When you live in the same tent line as thugs, it's not easy to be brave," Dennis complained.

This night he and Dennis were both on duty together and Tate was part of the guard. After inspecting the guard Alex said, "Right, here's the roster."

Turning his head to look at Alex, Tate bleated out something about 'that's the Corporal of the Guard's job'.

"Shut up!" Alex said in a voice that brooked no argument. Standing in front of Tate, Alex looked him square in the eyes. "Shut up or you'll be on a charge in the morning." Then he moved down the line. Tate followed him with a glare.

"Eyes front," Alex shouted a command used to stop a soldier being an individual as eye contact was impossible. "Right, here's the order of duty. Smith and Oliphant, first shift, Tate and Peterson second shift, Green and Davidson 10pm to midnight. Guard dismissed!" He shouted in his best military voice.

As Duty Sergeant, Alex usually stayed awake till near midnight before getting some sleep. That particular night he wrote a letter to his mother then dozed off at ten. Waking up at three in the morning he decided to walk up to the guard tent at the camp entrance to see how Dennis was handling things. He was reading a book.

"Everything okay?" Alex spoke quietly so as not to wake the rest of the sleeping guard.

"Yes, thanks, Sarge," he replied in a whisper. "Tate was absolutely ropeable. He said he's going to fix me for what you did. I can't seem to win, can I?"

Alex decided to confront Tate. He headed off under a star-filled sky to walk the camp perimeter, making as little noise as possible. He came across Peterson doing some stretching exercises on his half of the barbed-wire perimeter. They gave each other a thumbs-up sign.

"Carry on," Alex whispered and moved on. He found Tate seated on an empty oil drum next to a post. He was asleep. Alex gave him a kick on the shins and Tate woke with a start and fell to the ground.

"Wha—? You fucking bastard, I'll have you for that. You can't fucking kick me. I'll have you, mate."

"Shut up, and keep your voice down," Alex commanded. "You were asleep on guard duty. That's a court martial offence. I'll see you on CO's orders this morning."

"You do and I'll have you, don't worry about that, you fucking National Service Sergeant, you can't strike a soldier and get away with it."

"Pick up your rifle and start walking. I'll see you later." Alex spat out the words, knowing that he could be in trouble if Pig decided to believe Tate.

At ten in the morning Alex was marched into Staff Campbell's tent office by Sergeant Major Ernie Stamp. Tate was standing rigidly to attention in front of Pig, hat on head, sitting bolt upright.

"Private Tate," Pig was wearing a proper uniform, "Sergeant

Forbes here has charged you with a serious offence, asleep while on duty. Sergeant Major says that you claim to have been kicked by Sergeant Forbes. That's a serious offence too. Now, you can have this matter dealt with by me and I will set any punishment or you can ask to have this matter tried by Court Martial at Brigade. Have you explained the consequences, Sergeant Major?"

"Yes, Sir," Ernie shouted.

"So, what do you want to do?" Pig glared at Tate.

Staring straight ahead, Tate shouted. "Have it dealt with by you, Sir!"

He'd been told by the Sergeant Major that a court martial is costly and time-consuming with the result that penalties tended to be much higher than any sentence handed out by a Unit Commander.

"Well, Tate," Pig paused, "You see, the Sergeant here doesn't usually make false charges, so I find you guilty and you can have ten days' detention at the Military Prison in Nicosia. Okay?"

Swallowing hard, Tate nodded. The Sergeant Major stepped forward and removed Tate's belt, untied and removed his bootlaces and then marched him out on the double. As luck would have it, Alex was detailed to take him to the Military Prison. The Staff-Sergeant at Reception was a wiry, stiff little man with a pencil moustache. To Alex he looked about forty, but he could have been younger. His face was tanned with deep lines on either side of his mouth.

"Staff Wallace," he gave his name, lips barely moving, in a staccato voice. "Right, sign here. It says that you have delivered Private Tate to Trakia Military Correction Establishment for a period of not less than ten days. Correct?"

"Correct." Alex signed the sheet of paper on a clipboard.

"Right!" Staff Wallace shouted out, "Corporal, take Tate to his cell."

As if from nowhere a Corporal MP appeared and, with the usual abrupt command, marched him off on the double to his home for the next ten days. As they departed, Staff Wallace relaxed his rigid posture and smiled a thin, yet friendly smile. "National Service?"

"Yes, Staff. I charged the silly bugger. He's a bully boy, but I feel a bit sorry for him now."

"Don't worry, son, when we get through with your man, he'll be putty in your hands. C'mon, I'll show you how we do things here." Staff Wallace showed him an empty cell, about ten feet by six. It had a bed and a bucket. The floor was polished timber.

"Here's roughly what happens," Staff Wallace removed his red cap and stroked his close-cropped hair. "Reveille is at 5am. Each day the prisoner scrapes the polish from the floor with a single edge razor blade. Then it's a shower and breakfast. When this is completed the prisoner must dress in full kit for two hours of exercise in the prison yard. This entails running up a hill, crawling under barbed wire and constantly marching at the double."

"In this heat?" Alex wondered if he had been too hasty in trying to teach Tate a lesson.

Staff continued. "After a short break for a meal, the prisoner then spends time polishing the floor of his cell until it gleams like a mirror. Then he gets dressed again in full kit and, standing at attention for an hour, he is given a lecture on the Queen's Regulations."

"God!"

"We don't get many back after they've done their sentence." His face crinkled with obvious glee.

"Do they get any time off? To relax?"

"After an evening meal it's lights out at 7pm until reveille the next morning. They can rest in their cell until the next day. Then, it's the same routine. Works like a charm."

Tate returned to Camp Kermia after his sentence was completed and as predicted by Staff Wallace, he was a model soldier until the day he left Cyprus. Alex was never sure if his spirit had been broken or if he just wanted to make sure that he never returned to Trakia Correction Centre. The men regarded the "new" Tate with some awe, as he was the only member of Pig's Battalion ever to do "time".

Unable to get a car, Alex arranged to meet Leyla in Nicosia at the Ledra Palace Hotel. Terry drove him into town. Leyla looked radiant as she stepped off the bus. He took both her hands and pulled her into a shady corner. After several passionate kisses he asked if she would like to go shopping.

"Of course. But the only decent place to shop is Ledra Street. Is it safe to go there?"

"I think so. There's been nothing the last few weeks. I'm sure it will be fine."

"Did I tell you how much I missed you?" With a tilt of her head Leyla looked at him lovingly.

"Me too. I can't wait for the next hundred days to pass."

"What do you mean?"

"I'll finish my National Service. Then I can see you every day." Alex beamed. "Let's go and look at the shops. It's a beautiful day now that I'm here with you."

Hand in hand they set off for Ledra Street.

Cyprus, September 29, 1958

Seated beside the Military Police sergeant driving the Landrover, Alex glanced back at the two armed MPs in the rear. The sun was just past its zenith as they drove out the gates at RAF Nicosia. As they drove south he watched the landscape pass before his eyes. Feeling totally drained, his eyes misted over as a whirligig moved erratically across the plain, dust spiralling up and fading away into the clear blue sky. It all seemed so strange and so familiar at the same time. I'll never come this way again, he thought. Noticing the wan, tear-stained face, the MP driver nattered away, "Cheer up, Sarge. You'll soon be on the ship back home. Back to some decent grub."

"I'm going to miss this place," Alex said, head on his chest, the tearful words coming out.

"Nah, you'll forget it in a week. A few pints and a pork pie, you'll be in heaven."

"Don't think so. You know I killed a young boy? And I lost my girl, a lovely girl. She never harmed anyone."

"Yeh, I think I heard. Sorry."

"I was going to come back, you know. Live here. It's a beautiful country, great people. Would've been a great life."

"Never mind. I understand you did good work. Got a commendation didn't you?"

"For what? As far as I know nothing ever came of that, that stuff. They never got a single important man from *EOKA*."

"Still, you only followed orders?"

"No, I actually volunteered. Never volunteer. How true," Alex leaned back and closed his eyes for a moment then looked out at the dark outline of the Troodos Mountains. "What a fucking mess," he muttered. Closing his eyes again, his mind drifted off to Dunkeith. All he'd ever wanted was to escape the poverty that had brought such unhappiness to his mother. Since high school he'd dreamed of living in a nice bungalow with a loving wife looking after their children. A real family life, that was all.

The dockside at Limassol was a hive of activity as truckloads of soldiers arrived for embarkation. The Landrover was waved through by the guards at the boom gate and at the gangway a Sergeant Major from the Ordinance Corps stepped forward with a kit bag and a case. "Here's your stuff, mate. Check it's all there then I can get off. Just sign here."

It was all his gear, including all the extra clothing Alex had acquired in his unofficial trading. Shite, he thought, they must have been quick to organise everything and he wondered how the news of his sudden departure was going down back at camp. As a Sergeant he was put in a cabin with three Sergeants from the Ulster regiment.

"Anyone want some singlets, shorts or shirts?" He looked around the cabin.

"Sure thing," said one and he and the others soon grabbed

every bit of extra gear. Alex was happy. The thought that he might be stopped at customs with more army issue than regulations allowed could have spelled more trouble. As dusk fell, he stood on the deck and watched Cyprus slip away. Was it only fifteen months since he'd arrived with such high hopes? The *Duneera* slowly headed south and then west, towards Malta. Despite his high level of anxiety, Alex managed to eat part of the meal served in the area reserved for NCOs. Then it was back on deck for a long look at the star-filled sky before going below deck to sleep. He stripped off naked and lay under a single sheet. With the loud snoring of his fellow Sergeants and his mind going over and over past events, he was unable to sleep. Visions of blood kept appearing as he tossed and turned, thinking about the noise of his gun going off, the head exploding. How can you kill someone, he thought, yet feel no remorse? He thought of the lovely Leyla lying there on the ground, covered in blood, a young life ended because of him. Bloody army, he sighed, they never even let me go to her funeral. Struggling into his shorts, he made his way to the ship's hospital to see if he could get a sleeping pill. The night sister, a QARANC Lieutenant, was a tall, buxom girl about his age, he guessed. As it was the first night out there were no cases of seasickness or diarrhoea so she was glad of company.

"I love this job, its like being on a permanent Mediterranean cruise," she enthused. "I'm Rachel, by the way, pop in any time if you can't sleep. I hate this shift. We can cheer each other up. Once I qualified as a sister, I thought, hell, I'm not going to stick around Bolton so I applied for a commission in the army and here I am."

"Cushy job." Alex couldn't think what else to say.

"At least I only have to look after people who are not really sick, well, nothing serious. The pay is better than in hospital and I'm an officer, me, a lass from Lancashire," she said with a laugh, parodying the Gracie Fields song. Rachel rattled on how she had spent a year in Germany at Munchingladbach before the chance came to join the *Duneera*. "I grabbed it with both hands. Who wouldn't?" she danced from one foot to the other. "Pity you pharmacists don't get a commission like doctors. Must be a bit disappointing?"

"You get used to it." Alex was too depressed to argue. "Anyway, I'll soon be out of it and get back to making some money. Two bloody years on peanuts."

"Where will you be working?

"I'll probably go to Glasgow. The job in charge of the injectable section is there if I want it, I think. It's a pretty good job. Or I could go back to England, they always said there was a place for me where I used to work. I don't know. I'll just wait and see."

"You should have signed on for an extra year. The money's really good and you could have sat for officer training. It's a great life. You meet so many really nice people. Not like the lads back in Bolton. What a dump." She pulled a face.

"You can't get a commission in the Medical Corps. Only doctors or long-term Regulars who've come up through the ranks. It's not like a Regiment. I should have asked for the Black Watch or something."

"Well, you're nearly finished. I hope I get a posting to Hong Kong or Malaya next. They must be exciting places. The mysterious Far East, eh?"

"Look, it's been a tough couple of days. Can you give me a sleeping pill?"

"Surely someone like you doesn't need a sleeping pill?" Rachel looked disappointed.

"Listen, I killed a man yesterday. A girl I was seeing was shot and killed," his eyes began to fill with tears again. "I need something. Can you give me a pill?"

"Ye poor man. Of course I can. Tell me what happened." A concerned looking Rachel held his hand. He explained briefly about his spraying job and Leyla. He didn't mention anything about wanting to get married.

"My goodness. You do need something." Rachel opened a

cupboard and took out a small jar. "Here, take one of these. It's a phenobarb. That'll do the job. Not that I need to tell you."

"Thanks," he took the pill. "You don't know how lucky you are to have this job."

"You can't expect to keep this posting forever. But I intend to enjoy it while I can. Off you go. Come in again if you want."

He woke up the next day, groggy from the barbiturate and still depressed, so Alex kept to himself, walking the decks and reading the daily news bulletin. At meal times he chatted with a few people about the news heralding an end to the conflict in Cyprus. Too fucking late for Leyla, he muttered under his breath. Mealtimes forced him to engage in useless conversations about what everyone was going to do back home. Mostly it was about getting it off with some "bird". Always the talk was about breasts, sex and lots of lovely pints of good English beer. That night, lying in his bunk, unable to sleep, he thought he might as well chat with Rachel rather than lie turning over and over the thoughts in his mind. He slipped on a pair of shorts and padded in bare feet to the Medical Centre. Tapping on her door, he said, "It's me, Alex, Sergeant Forbes. Can I come in?"

The door was opened with a whoosh and Rachel pulled him inside. "Do you need something to help you sleep again?" she asked eagerly.

"No, thanks, not those phenobarb, they're worse than a hangover."

"I had a good sleep. Didn't hear a thing, just the engine noise. Don't know how I'll go when I'm back on day duty." She shrugged.

"God, I can't wait to get home. I want to see my Mum. She's always been there for me. This is all like a dream."

"Here, I'll give you a treat." She rummaged in a cupboard and produced a bottle of whisky. "Nice tan," she said admiring his lean body. In his bare feet she was just slightly taller than him.

Alex smiled and accepted a liberal tot with a dash of water.

Rachel chattered on about her nursing at a hospital in Bolton, how boring it had been, what a lousy town it was. Every now and then she took the glass from Alex and, with a giggle, had a little sip. Alex explained that he'd been a top student at high school but failed to pass the French exam and been forced to wait another three months before going to St Andrews to sit the university entrance French exam. Then he'd made one mistake in the finals of the pharmacy exam and been forced to re-sit six months later.

"Gosh, you've been a bit unlucky." Her big eyes were full of sympathy behind her glasses. Alex leaned back against the examination table. After a second large glass of whisky, he couldn't help himself. He found himself staring at Rachel and her generous bosom. He wanted to bury his head in those breasts, to be held and comforted.

"God, I just feel drained." He groaned.

"Come here," Rachel put her arms round Alex and pulled him close. He breathed in her safe clean smell. Without thinking, he put his arms round her neck. Smiling, she undid the top button of his shorts and slipped her hand down, and held his penis and scrotum.

"I can't," he began, but Rachel pressed against him and kissed him. With difficulty, he managed to put the glass down. He kissed her back hard, tongue in her mouth, and felt his shorts slowly slide down to his feet. Alex was surprised, to find, as he probed with his tongue, that she had a dental plate. Under her stroking, his penis swelled. Rachel pulled up her skirt and wriggled out of her underpants. Alex slipped inside easily. He thought of Leyla as Rachel banged away as if there were no tomorrow. He gasped as his buttocks were pressed again and again into the top of the table.

"Shite!" He ejaculated with a shuddering explosion.

Rachel held on and pushed and pushed until she gave out a stifled cry. "God, that was right great," she panted.

Alex felt weak and clung on to Rachel for support. But she pulled back and adjusted her underwear and skirt.

Overwhelming guilt quickly followed Alex's feeling of physical relief. God, he thought, what am I doing? Leyla, Leyla, was all he could think. Rachel gave him a quick kiss on his cheek.

"There now, you won't need a sleeping pill, will you, you lovely man. Now off you go. You'll sleep well tonight."

In spite of the whisky, he was unable to sleep. All that he could think was how he had let Leyla down. He was ashamed that he could have let lust push her out of his thoughts. But over the next six days, he followed the same routine. Sleep wouldn't come. Rachel was there and she did help ease his agitated state of mind. Twice it was very quick, as a sick patient lay in the next room. It was as if he wished to purge his mind of Leyla and Cyprus. Then Rachel was off night-duty and there was no opportunity for a non-commissioned officer to fraternise with a commissioned officer. They passed a few words to each other walking on deck but that was the end of the affair. At Southampton while waiting to disembark, Rachel came up to Alex on the upper deck. "Maybe if you sign on as a regular you can get a commission. It's worth it. Think about it. I'll think about you." She kissed him briefly on the cheek. A miserable Alex nodded. As Rachel turned away he looked at her retreating figure, thinking that the only thing he wanted was to forget the army forever.

During the cold train journey back through the bleak, winter English countryside from Southampton to London and then on to Corps HQ at Crookham, he thought of the warm sunshine of Cyprus. If peace had come to Cyprus and if Leyla hadn't died, that's where I'd be, he thought, not in this miserable country. After reporting to the Adjutant, he was given an empty room at the end of one of the barracks. For three days he wandered around, ate meals in the Sergeants' Mess and waited for someone to contact him about the shooting on Ledra Street. Finally, he was called into the Company office and given a train voucher to travel to London with instructions to be at Admiralty House at 11am sharp. From St Pancreas

Station, Alex took the Tube to Pall Mall. He emerged from the station and gazed up at the impressive building with its ornate columns. Breathing in deeply, he crossed the busy road and showed the doorman the letter with his appointment details.

Next he showed the letter to a grim receptionist who looked as daunting as the austere interior of the building. "Sit over there," she pointed to a bench, "and someone will come and fetch you."

Despite his uniform, Alex shivered in the coolness of the huge cavernous foyer. It was some time before a tall man in a herring-bone suit approached. "Sergeant Forbes?" he looked down at Alex who immediately jumped to his feet.

"Sir!" Alex's voice echoed in the space.

"Follow me." The man set off at a fast pace, leaving Alex to hurry after him in an unsoldierly manner. He went up a long, curved flight of stairs wide enough for ten men to walk shoulder-to-shoulder and trotted along until they reached a room on the first floor. The man opened a massive door and ushered Alex in and closed the door, leaving Alex standing in an office with only a large desk, a few chairs and filing cabinets. An immense fireplace dominated one wall. A man in shirtsleeves sat at the desk, head down, writing on a large notepad. Looking up, he smiled without opening his lips and indicated that Alex sit down.

"So, Forbes, had a good trip back home? Bit of a change from Cyprus, what. Jolly cold, here. Bit of a shock to the system?"

"Yes Sir, it's all right, though," Alex sat glum-faced.

"Right, well, let's get down to business. I'm Colonel Bird, retired actually. Look after paperwork and various reports here at the War Office."

Alex nodded.

"Sorry about all that unfortunate business in Nicosia, but you are not held responsible in any way. Did what a soldier had to do, right?" Alex nodded again. "Well," he said, tapping his pen on the notepad, "we've looked at the whole picture and decided that the least said the better. Agreed?"

Alex looked blank.

"Not much success with Pitt's solution, eh, but it was worth a try. So, I want you to put all this behind you and get on with your life in civvy street. Can you do that?" he asked, shaggy eyebrows raised.

"Yes, Sir." Alex wondered why he'd come all the way to London to get this information. "About the Greek Cypriot that I shot then? There won't be a charge?"

"None at all. Just one of those unfortunate things that happen. No-one to blame. Fellow took his chances and paid the consequences. Silly, stupid young buggers. Won't change a thing."

"Is there any chance of me contacting Mr Ozkara, Leyla's father?"

"Don't know anything about that. What I'm telling you, young fellow, is to forget all about Cyprus and get on with your career. I understand you have a bright future, a chemist, right?" His look stopped any further questions.

"Yes, Sir, Colonel. Well, that's it, then, is it?" He gave a helpless shrug.

"All done. Finished. Good luck and all that. Can you find your way out?"

Alex saluted and walked out of the room, down the magnificent stairway and out into a misty rain. The sky cleared and a watery sun appeared. It was still early. He began to wander around London, looking in the shop windows crammed with expensive clothes, down to Piccadilly Circus among the hurrying crowds. Although it was still early afternoon, the light was fading fast and all the neon lights sputtered into life as he wandered along, looking up at all the advertising like any tourist. Smoking in the street while in uniform was frowned upon but Alex guessed that the chances of running into an MP or an officer were pretty small so he lit up a cigarette. He ambled along in a shuffling manner, came to Leicester Square and watched a movie trailer up on the big screen at the Odeon Cinema. A rumbling stomach reminded him that he'd eaten little at breakfast. The Aberdeen Steak House looked inviting, but a glance at the menu prices dispelled any thought of a steak and chips. Nearby was a Lyons Corner café with sausage and baked beans for three shillings. That'll have to do, he thought, fingering the one-pound note is his pocket. The warm, steamy interior was a welcome relief from the chilly afternoon. The meal and mug of tea was just what he needed. Then it was on to Trafalgar Square, where he watched the pigeons being fed by tourists rugged up against the chilly wind. Wherever he looked there were young women, pink-cheeked and very attractive. He knew that he looked conspicuous in his army uniform and the three stripes on his sleeve didn't really make him feel much better. Without money, he might as well be invisible. On the train back to camp he sat deep in thought. Pitt's perfume. Useless stuff. Why had they bothered with him if it was no good? Leyla had been the one to pay the price. It should have been me. He closed his eyes and tried to think some good thoughts. He needed a good job and some decent money. By the time the train reached Crookham it was half-past four and almost dark. Head down, depressed, he walked back to camp. The evening meal was roast beef with three overcooked vegetables. Dessert looked like some kind of tapioca pudding so he passed on that and headed for the Sergeants' Mess. After a pint of warm beer, bored and lonely, he went to bed and dreamed of blood and Leyla.

Cyprus, October 1958

Mehmet Ali and Gulten moved to Famagusta for a short time. He was allowed to visit the hospital at infrequent intervals. Leyla's wounds had proven to be less serious than first thought. The leg wound was superficial and the upper body wound had cut a small artery. "That's the reason for so much blood," a dark-skinned doctor explained.

"What about Alexander? Why hasn't he been to see me?" a pale, worried Leyla asked.

"He's gone. Back to England. The army has its ways. They didn't want him to stay in case there was more trouble. I understand from Dr Kucuk that soon all this business will be over anyway. Some kind of agreement?" Mehmet Ali looked away as he spoke.

Leyla struggled to understand. "Will he be coming back?"

"No. Even when this is over, the Greeks will never forget."

Tears trickled down her soft cheeks.

"But you must forget him. It was good that you met him but we will find a good man here for you. This is your home." He looked at his weeping daughter.

Leyla lay silent, her eyes closed.

"Now you must get well and one day soon we will all be happy again. Your mother is anxious to have you home." He kissed her on the forehead and looked down at his lovely daughter and hoped that life would soon return to normal. Two months after the shooting, Mehmet Ali was overjoyed when he was informed by Nicosia Hospital that Leyla had fully recovered from her wounds and could return home to complete her convalescence. Arriving at the hospital, he was met by the discharging doctor, surgeon Dr Ali Atun and Matron Ilhan.

Dr Atun took him to one side. "Mehmet Ali Bey. I am not sure how to approach this matter, but you may rest assured that what I am about to say is not general knowledge. It is for your ears only and when I tell you, then I have forgotten, understand?" Dr Atun held Mehmet Ali's elbow as he guided him away from the front desk. "Leyla has made a good recovery from the cowardly bullets and, and, well...the pregnancy has not been affected."

"Pregnancy? My Leyla! Surely there is a mistake?" An agitated Mehmet Ali swung round to face the surgeon.

"Ah, my friend, I see that you are not aware of this situation. I'm sorry but I have to say that there is no mistake. The girl is possibly three months with child. I am sorry to be the one to inform you. But rest assured, I have not made this fact known to any of the staff."

Mehmet Ali nodded slowly, pursed his lips and turned away so that the surgeon would not see the tears form a mist over his eyes. He regained his composure and turned back to the doctor. "Thank you for your kindness and discretion."

With a sombre face he collected Leyla from the hospital ward and drove home in silence. It is my fault, he thought. I allowed Leyla to mix with a young man who was not one of us. He would not know how to respect a young woman. His kind have different standards. It's in all the books they read. How foolish of me to put Leyla in a position where she could be led astray. But what's done cannot be undone.

Seated in the sitting room, he called for Gulten to join them. "The good doctor has told me that Leyla is to have a child."

Gulten looked stunned. She looked at Leyla then down at the ground.

"Ah, my only child," he said, "this is a sad time indeed for our family. You have shamed us and soon you will leave us. You cannot remain here to show the world that Mehmet Ali has no control over his family."

Leyla, sat, head bowed as he continued. "I have telephoned my sister in Izmir. Even with my mother to look after she says she will be happy to care for you and prepare you for the birth of this child."

"What about the boy?" an unhappy Gulten asked.

"He has nothing to do with this. It is my responsibility for what happened. Leyla will now do as I say." He looked at Leyla who nodded acceptance of her father's decision.

"What will I tell our friends at home?" Gulten began wringing her hands.

"Say that Leyla is going to study in Turkey. In Izmir."

"What about holidays? If Leyla can't come home, people will wonder." Gulten turned a nervous face to her husband. "What will I say?"

"I'll think about that later. Maybe I can find a husband. I don't know, woman. Let's do one thing at a time," he said in a raised voice. He glared at his wife. Leyla's head sank even lower.

In November 1959, Leyla Ozkara, accompanied by her mother, sailed from Famagusta to Turkey. They arrived at Mersin on the south coast not far from Tarsus, the birthplace of Saint Paul. They travelled by bus along the coast, stopping for a night's rest at Antalya and Mugla before arriving at Izmir where Mehmet Ali's sister Nafia met them. A cold wind blew in from the Aegean Sea but Leyla's heavy cloak kept her warm. It was not yet necessary to hide her pregnancy. A squat, dark-skinned, rather ugly woman, Nafia Ozkara had overcome her physical shortcomings by hard work and study to reach the position of Associate Professor at the new Ege University. She considered herself an emancipated woman. She had a strong will and was determined to advance the rights of women in a male-dominated Muslim world. Since the age of fifteen, Nafia had borne rejection by men because she was not considered attractive. Now, at the age of fifty, she held her pregnant young niece close to her ample bosom.

"My lovely, you are welcome and safe here with your aunt. Together we will face the future, whatever happens." Her voice was strong and reassuring.

"*Anne* will stay with us for a few days then she must go home to my father." Leyla reached out a hand to Gulten.

"Of course. This is a busy time for your father. So much is happening in Cyprus. He needs his wife to look after his needs so that he can do what is possible for his people." She put an arm over her shoulder. In her heart she looked forward to having Leyla all to herself. Gulten was nice and kind, but limited in too many ways.

Nafia's small house stood on its own piece of land, in the suburb of Konak, with a view of the water. The holy season of Ramadan was just beginning but Nafia had long since abandoned any pretence of the fasting or prayers required of a follower of Mohammed. However, in public she was careful not to attract criticism from overzealous colleagues.

Nafia's mother, Jale, had recovered once more and the bent old lady with a face like a pale-brown walnut greeted her granddaughter with joy. She was unaware of the situation. She sat holding Leyla's hand, gazing at this child who looked just as Jale had done all those years ago when she had met her husband on her wedding night. Smiling and nodding, her mind wandered to that stern man who had given her five children before he died from tuberculosis. Three children had died and only her son and daughter had survived to warm her heart as she drifted ever so slowly through the last years.

"My darling, the world is hard for women." Nafia sat close to Leyla. "What men do is okay, but women, we are told to have no feelings, no rights, and no bodies with the same needs as men. Together, you and me, we will see this through."

"Thank you, Aunt." Leyla spoke softly.

"A child will come and we will care for that child. You will see, it's not the end of the world, just the end of the world for some things. Last year I was in Paris, I listened to a woman, Simone de Beauvoir, ah, such a woman."

"But Aunt Nafia, what will I do? No man will want me for a wife, if I have an unwanted child. Isn't that right?" She put a hand to her belly, feeling nauseous.

"No man wanted me for a wife, but I have my own life. I am not a slave to any man who calls me princess for a year and then ignores me, or runs away, like your soldier man."

Leyla heaved a long sigh and thought of the handsome Alexander who had stolen her heart and her precious virginity. Then he'd vanished like a thief in the night.

"You'll like Izmir. Legend has it that the Amazons founded the ancient city of Smyrna that later became Izmir. Its first great period was during the reign of Alexander the Great."

Leyla winced at the name "Alexander".

"Then the Romans came in the first century of the Christian calendar. So it has a long history."

"But I saw nothing of this history on the drive through the town."

"Ah, between them, men and nature have destroyed Smyrna. Each time it has been rebuilt they have destroyed it again."

"When did you come here?"

"Ege is a new university. It began in 1955. With my experience and all my study I was appointed Director of the School of Nursing." Nafia straightened up with a look of satisfaction.

"We were all very proud in Ghazientop." Leyla smiled, eager to please.

"Hmph. Anyway, the city is not very pretty but there are beautiful beaches not far away and when spring comes the hills are covered with sage, thyme and oleander."

"What will I do while you are at work?" Leyla looked around the small room. "Besides looking after grandmother Jale?"

"*Anneanne*, grandmother, is no problem. She stays in bed till noon then sits looking at the garden. The university has a wonderful library. I'll bring home some books for you to read."

"I like reading," Leyla said eagerly

"We'll open up a new world for you. The French Revolution brought enormous change in political thinking but it's the new French revolutionaries who will change the world with their philosophy."

"How?"

"I have the one of the books from the French woman, the one I mentioned. You will see. It's not the end of the world for you, just the beginning of a new world."

Leyla read each book her aunt brought home in a daze of wonderment. When Jale began to prepare the evening meal, she reluctantly put down her book to help her grandmother. "Aunt Nafia told you about the baby, didn't she?" Leyla faced the old woman and spoke slowly.

"Yes, yes. You will soon feel better. Nafia will make sure you get the right medicine."

Leyla blinked, unsure what to say. "You had how many children, Grandmother?"

Jale looked at her with a blank stare.

"My father, Mehmet Ali, is your son. Aunt Nafia is your daughter. Were there other children?" Leyla spoke even more deliberately.

"You look just like me when I was a girl," Jale smiled at the memory, "when I was married. He was a stern man. Nothing was good enough. Five children. But only two lived. Then he died. The chest disease."

"Tuberculosis?" Leyla prompted.

"The lung disease. Is that what you have?" She looked closely at Leyla.

"No, Grandma. A baby. Aunt Nafia told you." She stroked the old woman's face.

"Well, we must feed you. It's the best thing for the lungs. We'll make some *kofte*, kiymali borek and liver. That's good for you. Maybe some rice pudding. I like that. It's easy to eat." She began assembling some pots and pans.

On a cool Saturday in December, Leyla was sitting by the window, reading.

"You can put aside that book. I know it's very interesting but you need some fresh air." Nafia gave her a moment then took the book and placed it on the shelf.

"Did you read the part about Jewish morning prayers, Aunt?"

"Of course. It's no different to how all men are no matter which God they pray to."

"Can you imagine thanking God every day that you are not a woman?"

"And they truly mean that prayer. Not all Jews. Modern Jews are not so stupid."

A mournful Leyla gazed at her aunt with big sad eyes. "I wish I'd been born a man. Then I could do as I please."

"You can. It's up to you. You've read the books. Don't blame others if you haven't the courage to be your own person." Nafia snorted then looked kindly at her niece. "Come along. Get your cloak and let's be off. Reading and thinking is for later."

"Where are we going?" Leyla nodded towards her grandmother's bedroom.

"She'll be fine. She'll sit by the heater when she gets up. Let's head south today. We'll go to Selcuk then Ephesus. But you need to be careful walking on those stone paths. They can be dangerous for one like you," she said patting Leyla on the stomach.

As they drove down the road to Selcuk, Leyla came back to the subject of men and women. "Alexander often used to say that he wanted to look after me," she said wistfully. "I'd be his princess."

"Then you're better off without him. Find a man who wants to share with you. That's a real man."

"But a woman needs a man to look after her, like my father."

"One day, when your father gets over his hurt pride he'll send for you. You are an only child, one day you will have the entire farm. You can choose any man you like, then." Nafia grinned.

Tears formed as Leyla softly said, "I would still choose Alexander."

"Forget all this talk, let's get there and enjoy some good clean air. Izmir gets so polluted."

The dusty brown town of Selcuk lay under a hill topped by the Church of St John where he had written one of the Christian gospels.

"See," Nafia pointed, "it says on this tomb that the Apostle John is buried here. Now we'll go and see where Mary the Mother of Jesus is said to have ended her earthly days."

"Is that the Mary mentioned in the Koran?" Leyla trotted after the plump figure.

"That's the one," Nafia said, puffing as she walked.

A dirt road led up a nearby hill to a small church. "This is where she is supposed to have lived before she ascended to Heaven." Nafia peered into the dark interior.

"Is she buried here too?"

She gave Leyla a quizzical look. "Probably, but the Roman Church says she went body and soul straight to Heaven. So maybe they haven't looked too hard to find a grave. It's all about believing."

"Surely we must have belief in the Holy Word, whether it is Christian, Jewish or Islam?"

"All written by men. Do you believe that you're having a child or do you know? Think about it, my little one. Well, maybe not so little."

Leyla's head dropped.

"Sorry, sweet. I should have just said young one. "She put an arm round Leyla's shoulder.

"How did they know the Mother of Jesus lived here? It was a long time ago."

"A German nun had a dream. A blind nun. She told some people where to find this place. I wonder if she was born blind?"

"Look, Aunt, there's a little spring coming out of that wall over there. Let's have a drink."

Several people were filling bottles with the crystal-clear cold water pouring through a pipe in the moss-covered stonework. One old lady said that it was holy water and would cure any ills.

"Have some, my sweet, but it won't cure being pregnant," Nafia patted Leyla's expanding belly.

"I've had enough of this place. Let's go to that other place. Ephesus?"

Nafia was sorry that she had been so flippant over such a serious matter for her young niece. "Let's go then. And we'll talk no more of religious things."

They strolled among the deserted ruins of the ancient city of Ephesus. Only a few hardy tourists ventured to Turkey during winter. Once capital of Roman Asia, Ephesus had been a vibrant, prosperous port at the mouth of the Meander River. Over hundreds of years the bay had silted up and the river had found a new route to the Aegean Sea, leaving Ephesus stranded miles from the sea. Without the benefit of modern transport, Ephesus had slowly died. Its once magnificent buildings had been plundered to construct new homes in nearby towns. Sand and weeds covered its crumbling ruins like a protective blanket until a new age had come to unveil what remained of its old glory.

"You know, Leyla, what you see here are mainly Roman ruins. But long before that, this place was the centre for the worship of the Greek goddess of chastity. Sorry, that was a little thoughtless of me." She waved her hands in a helpless manner.

"Aunt Nafia, you must not reproach yourself. It is *I* who do that every day." She shrugged, a little helpless shrug that was becoming a habit.

How sad, Nafia thought, that loving someone could lead to so much unhappiness. "Look, see here, the Library of Celsius. Isn't it still magnificent? To think that all those years ago, we had libraries. Ah, how important it is to have the written word, books for anyone to read."

On another day they visited Leyla's favourite place, the port of Cesme, about an hour's drive from Izmir. Cesme means "fountain", the name attributed to the many springs and fountains in the area. Fields of aniseed, sesame and artichokes, bordered by fig and eucalypts, in the peaceful valley, was a balm to her troubled soul. Surrounded by the Aegean Sea with its clear, deep blue water, she loved a day in Cesme with its wondrous landscapes.

"Let's go to the market. See if we can find something nice for you." Nafia wanted to cheer up her lovely but despondent niece. "I like to look at all the old books. They often have foreign ones."

"Look, Aunt Nafia," Leyla picked up a book with a hard cover. "It's about a town like a woman. How strange."

"*A Town Like Alice*," Nafia read out the title. "That's different. Most towns are named after men. It's in English. Do you want to read it? I don't think my English is good enough."

"Yes, please. Let me just see what it says." She opened the book. "It is about a woman. Let's take it."

The winter was unusually mild and Leyla enjoyed sitting in the small garden listening to her grandmother chatter away about her life in Cyprus, how it had been when she first saw her husband, how she lived with her new family and waited years before she was anything more than a servant in the home of her husband's family. The little walnut face bobbed up and down as she told of her first visit to Nicosia, the first time she saw the sea at Kyrenia. "Now," Jale's eyes misted over, "I live far away in a town that is full of people, more than all Cyprus. What a place to live. Oh, how I miss Cyprus, Ghazientop, my olive trees."

Leyla patted her grandmother's hand.

"So big, the trees, but small the olives. I could never grow big olives like the ones from Greece. I had a nice chair, near the door. I could see the trees, the clothes drying in the sun." With a long sigh she closed her eyes and drifted off to when she was young again.

Leyla placed her hands across her swollen body. Only four weeks to go, she thought, and then I will know my fate. If it's a boy child perhaps my father will be pleased and welcome me back to Cyprus. I love Aunt Nafia but Izmir is too big for me. I am lost here. One day my mother will need me, when she is old like Grandmother. Maybe nobody will care that she has a daughter and a child, but no man.

Thanks to Nafia's position, Leyla received the best of care at the Kuren Hospital next to Ege University. Leyla spent a few hours each week at the hospital and learned all about childbirth. Gowned and masked, she was able to witness several women give birth. Sometimes she would tremble with fear as a woman screamed out in pain but seeing the mother's joy as the baby finally appeared would bring a smile to her lips.

Without warning, the labour pains began two weeks early. Grandmother Jale was confused and upset.

"Count the time between the contractions," Nafia implored. Leyla concentrated. "Keep breathing. Pant."

"Oh, Oh, it's coming faster," Leyla gasped.

"Right. It's early but we won't take any chances." Nafia wasted no time and within an hour Leyla was safely in bed in hospital with doctors ready to assist. On 29 March 1959, at 4.30 in the morning, after eight hours of labour, Leyla Ozkara gave birth to a baby girl.

Tired but happy, Leyla gazed at the pale red face that squinted and grimaced as if unhappy to be out in a bright, white world full of the strangest sensations. She lifted back the soft, cotton wrapping and looked in wonder at the little body, perfect except for a left arm that tapered off at the elbow to end in a tiny fist with three fingers and no thumb. Tears welled up and she carefully covered up the baby. I will love her, she thought, even if Allah has punished me for my sin.

Her aunt visited two or three times a day. "Everything is fine. I see that you have time to read?"

"Yes, it's that book about a town called Alice. You'd like it. It's about brave women in war and then a town called Alice Springs in Australia. There, the woman finds a soldier who helped her in Malaya in the war. I cried, it's such a wonderful story."

"Love only happens in stories," Nafia snorted. "Puh, love stories."

"But it's not just that. It's about a woman who overcomes all kinds of troubles, she really is a very special woman," Leyla protested.

"Who wrote it? A woman?" She reached out a hand.

"No." Leyla held up the book. "A man called Neville Shute. I think I'll see if I can find out if he wrote other stories."

"You won't have much time for reading once you leave here. I phoned your father. He says he is pleased that you are safe and well."

"That's all?" Leyla whimpered. "Nothing more? And *Anne*?"

"I didn't speak to her. Look, it's early days. Maybe I can call again and say that his mother, Jale, is dying. If he sees you and the baby, well, who knows? You are his only child."

England, December 1958

Alexander Forbes, Acting Sergeant, Royal Army Medical Corps, marched into the main office at RAMC headquarters.

"At ease." The seated Major waved a hand at the salute. "Here's your discharge papers, train voucher to get you home, and this commendation. Apparently you didn't collect it in Cyprus. It'll be a nice memento of your service in Cyprus."

"Thank you, Sir," Alex took the green book, the voucher and a coloured certificate. "Can I stay in camp until after lunch? My train doesn't leave Kings Cross until seven."

"Leave your gear here and do what you like until you're ready to leave. You've been a credit to the Corps. Best of luck for the future." Alex saluted for the last time.

He boarded the train at Kings Cross Station and whiled away the hours reading and talking to the other people in the carriage. The *Flying Scotsman* rattled away through the night, clickety-clacking its way up north. He dozed off and on. The carriage emptied as all his fellow travellers left the train at Edinburgh. Alex stretched out on the seat and slept so soundly that he awoke to find that he was in Aberdeen, a hundred miles past Dunkeith. The next train to Dunkeith was not for another three hours. A dark, slate sky blanketed the windswept railway station. With just a few shillings in his pocket, it was a cold and hungry Alex who finally arrived home on a cold January day at half-past two in the afternoon. He lugged his case and kitbag up the three flights of windowless stairs where his mother who had been waiting hours by the window greeted Alex with hugs and kisses.

"Ach, son, you're looking fine. My, you look grand. Eh've had some soup and a meal ready since eleven. What happened? Did ye miss the train?"

Alex explained he had slept through the stop at Dunkeith

and had a cold wait at Aberdeen for a train back. "This soup's great, Mum," he said between spoonfuls. "It's delicious."

"It's the same as it's always been. Ye've just forgotten. My, it's grand to see you back again."

"There's nothing like home cooking. You've no idea some of the rubbish the army serves up."

"Weel, you can't have eaten much. Ye're as skinny as a rake. Eh'll get some fish for the morn."

Darkness fell quickly and, with the lights on, Alex felt trapped. The house seemed so small and closed. The bright sun of Cyprus, the gardens and even the sense of space in his tent, made him suddenly feel that he was in the wrong place. This was no longer home. Nothing was familiar. Only his mother was real. After his father had eaten his evening meal, Alex continued with stories of his time in the army in far-off Cyprus. He avoided any mention of Leyla and the shooting. Despite the little heater, his bedroom was cold and depressing. He unpacked a few essentials from his kitbag as he shivered in the small cold room. He was back home. But not for long, he thought.

"This is not where I'm going to live," he told his mother the next day. "I don't think I can stay in Scotland. It's too cold and miserable."

"Where dae ye think ye might go?" his mother asked with a tight little smile.

"I quite like London. There're plenty of places to go and see."

"Ah the places on the Monopoly board. It must be grand." Alice sighed at the thought.

"You'll come and stay with me one day. You'll love it. The Horse Guards Parade, Trafalgar Square. It's...it's, just so big."

"A visit, maybe. Eh could never leave Dunkeith."

"One day I'd like to go back and visit Cyprus. It's a wonderful place despite all its problems. The sun shines just about every day. The sea is warm, you can stay in for ages."

"Not like here," Alice laughed. "It's in and oot efter fev

minutes. Ye've got a grand colour though. You gae wherever ye like. Just get on, that's ah em askin. Tae think ye're daen awright, that's enough fer me." She put up a hand to the cheek of her tall son.

"I'll go and get a bus. See what it's like in Dunkeith after a couple of years."

"Ye'll find it's busy. The jute mills are doin fine. They make a kind o things we it now. Curtains, even dresses." She sounded cheerful.

"It's a bit smelly isn't it?" Alex protested at the thought of a woman wearing jute.

"No, no, they deodorise it. And colour it. It's amazing what they can dae."

"What about Dad? What's he up to these days?"

"He's no sae bad. He's got a jobe at the Cash Register. There's heaps o new factories gone up. American, Timex, National Cash Register, a ball-bearing place. They pay good money." Alice nodded approval.

"What about the shipyard? Still going strong?"

"No. Too many strikes. They've lost a lot o contracts. Always going on strike. Nae wonder the Japanese are building a they new ships."

"I'll go into town first. I'd better get a new suit. Need to look good when I go for a job."

"Eh'll come we ye. It'll be nice tae have my laddie walkin we his mither." Alice hurried off to get a warm coat.

Alex was surprised to see many more cars on the streets as they walked into town.

"See ah they new restaurants?" Alice pointed at some shops. "Mair than just fish and chips now."

"It's hard to believe, in a couple of years. I hope the Palais is still there." Alex was looking forward to escaping to the darkened world of the dance floor.

"Oh aye, but you won't find many o yer pals there. A lot have got married or are goin steady."

That Friday, he caught a tram to the other side of town and

sauntered into the Palais just after 8pm. The crowd was sparse. He knew it wouldn't fill the hall until the pubs closed at 9.30pm. This gave him a chance to check out some of the good dancers and he found that after nearly two years he could still dance. As the evening wore on, the dance floor became more crowded. Alex spotted a slim, attractive and animated woman on the far side. He asked if she would care to dance. She accepted and they slid easily into the throng of dancers for a slow foxtrot.

Her name was Sheila and she talked about herself. "I'm divorced, well, actually separated. My man's looking after the kids. It's his weekend. That's how come I'm here," she explained.

He nodded, unsure how much he should tell.

"So, you see, I'm footloose and fancy free. Just out for the night with a couple of my girlfriends," she said, lightly, pulling him closer. Sheila was quite short but with high heels she came to a few inches below his chin. Alex inhaled her femininity as they moved slowly to Dean Martin's hit "Return to Me" sung by the band singer.

"I've just finished National Service. Just got home."

"You don't speak like a Dunkeith lad." Sheila pulled back to look in his eyes.

"Been in England then overseas. Cyprus."

"My, that must have been exciting. I've read a bit about that in the papers. Are you glad to be home?"

"Yeh," Alex lied as he pulled her in close, her breasts pressing into his chest. His hand pushed against her lower back, thrusting her groin into his bulging erection. Alex was lost in the sensation of a woman so close. A married woman was something new in his experience. He felt a desperate need to relieve his tension. With two kids, he thought, she'd know what it was all about.

Sheila returned the pressure, knowing what was on his mind. More dances followed and Alex asked to take her home. It was still public transport followed by a ten-minute walk past row after row of council houses, all exactly the same. He couldn't believe his luck when Sheila put a key in the front door and said to come in.

"The kids are at their father's," she reminded him.

Inside, Sheila turned and they kissed, their hands running up and down the cold coats.

"C'mon," she pulled him by the hand up the stairs to a room with a large double bed. She turned on a bedside lamp, took off her coat and started to help Alex. Shrugging off her help, he was soon down to his shirt and underpants. Sheila was not so quick and he enjoyed the sight of her taking off her slip, bra and panties.

"I'll be just a minute." She tiptoed out of the room.

Alex began to shiver.

Sheila came back, and laughing, pulled back the covers and slipped under the sheet. "Hurry up, it's freezing in here," she cried as Alex joined her in the cold bed.

It was the first time he had lain fully naked with a woman. Sheila lay on top. She kissed him and rubbed herself up and down his body, Alex stroked her back. Quickly, the rhythmic dance began and ended too soon for Sheila.

"Next time, slow down, slow down."

Alex took a deep breath and paused. Sheila pushed him over on to his back and slid on top again. Pushing up, she looked down at him in the soft light of the bedside lamp. Alex opened his eyes to look at the white breasts hanging down like melons.

"Is it all right? You know?"

"Aye, it's fixed. Now, you're too fast, laddie. Just relax and we'll take our time," she said softly as she undulated and moved slowly up and down.

For a second, Alex thought of Leyla and her golden skin. But then his body took over. "You have no idea how good that was," she whispered in his ear. "You are magic. Where were you years ago when I was twenty-one?"

"Wha—how old are you?"

"Thirty-three," Sheila whispered. "Does it matter?"

"Not to me, it doesn't," Alex replied, thinking the opposite. Hell, a woman over thirty. He soon felt aroused again and ran his hands over Sheila's breasts and stomach. It was quite a sensation to feel the loose skin and stretch marks. She pulled his hands up to her breasts.

"Not very nice, is it? I must do some exercises and get it all tight again."

Alex stopped her with a kiss and began moving again. Gasping for air, neither spoke. Then she moved slowly out of the bed. Alex watched as she tiptoed out of the bedroom door. He heard a toilet flush and then running water in a sink. He lay there for what seemed like ages.

"I just got rid of my Dutch cap." She gave a little shiver. "So no more hanky-panky, okay? Do you want to stay the night?"

"Look, I'd better go. But I'll see you tomorrow. Do you want to go to the pictures?" Alex didn't feel comfortable at the thought of staying the night. It was a long walk home and he was glad to get between the sheets in his little bedroom.

They arranged to meet at the Odeon Cinema in High Street where buses from the outlying suburbs terminated. The weekend went by in an orgy of sexual acrobatics. On Sunday afternoon Sheila said he should leave. "Bob will be bringing the kids back soon. If you want, you can come during the week? After ten. The kids'll be asleep by then. Do you want to?" she asked anxiously.

"Okay." With a hurried kiss he was out the front door. For the next week Alex went to Sheila's house after 10pm and spent two hours in her bed before walking home through the park, sore but physically satisfied. On the long walks in the dark quiet nights his thoughts turned to Leyla. He pictured her in a white shroud. What would she think of him, acting like an animal? He didn't even really care that much about Sheila.

The next Saturday, he went into town to collect his new suit.

"A married woman called while you were out." Alice spoke the words with a grim look.

"Oh!"

"I told her that you were arranging a train ticket to London. You were going there for a job, I said." She looked hard at her stony-faced son.

"Look, son, she telt me who she was. It's no good getting mixed up we a married woman with two bairns. Get yourself out of here and get a better life. There's nowt good here." With clenched fists, she looked up at him.

Alex, lost for words, was slightly shocked at being told off but appreciated his mother's words of wisdom.

"Ye've no done a that study to throw it awa on a married woman we kids."

He stood there ashamed in front of his mother. It had been fantastic shagging in a comfortable bed, but he knew that there was no future in the relationship. A little slip, a mistake, and he would be trapped by a pregnant woman.

"You're right, Mum. Look, I'll go to London. I have a mate, Chas Dow, who served with me. He was the Education Corps sergeant at camp. I'm sure I can stay with him for a couple of weeks until I get a job and a place to live."

Two days later, Alexander Forbes left behind the drab streets of Dunkeith and headed south. He was lucky that Chas Dow's parents were pleased to have him stay with them for a few weeks. It was a short ride on the Tube from central London to Bethnal Green. After a nice meal and a chat about his time in Cyprus with their son, it was time for bed. Next day, happy to be walking the streets of London, Alex made his way to Russell Square and the offices of the Pharmaceutical Society. There, he scoured the positions vacant board. Dozens of jobs were on offer but only one caught his attention. It was an advertisement from a pharmacy in Melbourne, Australia. A Mr Maurice Jacobs was offering a salary that looked better than anything he could hope for in London and there was the offer of accommodation at reasonable cost. He took a copy of the address, caught the Tube to The Strand and walked up to Australia House.

The tall fair-haired young man was enthusiastic. "You'll do well in Oz!" His face glowed with pride. "It's a great country. Lot's of beaches, surf and good-looking sheilas."

Alex cringed at the name "Sheila". "How does the salary sound?"

The clerk's head went up and down when Alex mentioned the amount he'd been promised.

"My word, you'll have a good time on that. Melbourne's all right but you want to think about my home state, Queensland. It's beaut. Summer all year round."

"It's hot in Melbourne though, isn't it?" a concerned Alex leaned on the counter. "The chemist I'm going to work for said it was really hot when I phoned."

"Too right. It gets really hot in summer. Listen mate, you'll love it. Wish I were going home soon. The bloody winter here's enough to freeze the balls off a brass monkey." The clerk gave him picture books and leaflets.

Alex phoned the pharmacist again, at his home in Caulfield, Melbourne, and his flight was arranged. As a sponsored migrant, Alex was committed to stay in Australia for two years. He phoned his mother, who wished him luck and told him to have a better life even if she would not see him again for a few years. It was a long flight, but he enjoyed the meals and free drinks. He chatted to one of the air hostesses, Jenny, and forgot the name of the place he was going.

"It begins with Ca..." he said trying to remember. "I think it's in Melbourne somewhere?"

"Carlton," she whooped. "It's a lovely part of Melbourne." She looked pleased. "Lots of restaurants and nice shops. It's got the university there. Plenty of students."

"Sounds pretty good." A slightly tipsy Alex tried to picture the scene.

"I share a weatherboard with three other hostesses in Richmond. That's not far. I'll write down the address for you."

"Thanks, Jenny. Can I give you a call when I get settled in at work?" He couldn't believe his luck, four air hostesses!

"I may not be there but I'll tell the girls that you might call. We throw a pretty good party," she giggled.

"Sounds great. By the way, what's a weatherboard?"

"A house, you dummy. Lots of houses are made out of thin sheets of timber. Timber boards. You'll find out."

"Sorry. I've never heard of a house made like that. Anyway," he rushed on eager to hide his ignorance, "I'll look forward to catching up with you as soon as I can."

Jenny patted his cheek, thinking this one would be a good catch for someone. After a short doze, Alex took out the Australia House magazines again. They were full of enthusiasm for the vast continent. An article by the Minister of Immigration explained the policy of encouraging people to migrate to Australia. The country, with only eight million in a huge land, felt it had been in danger from the Japanese during the Second World War and needed to boost its population for future defence. The article went on to say how successful migration had been after the war with almost two million migrants from the Netherlands, Germany, Italy, Greece and Yugoslavia. The government had spent millions on renovating ships to bring people from across the world. Alex dozed off and on before arriving at Melbourne Airport, tired but happy to be on firm soil again.

Melbourne, Australia 1959

Maurice Jacobs met Alex at the airport. Although officially autumn, it was a warm day. Alex was pleasantly surprised at the large car, a Holden, that Maurice drove into town. The first stop was the pharmacy in Russell Street, not far from the Police Department. It was a large pharmacy with a narrow frontage but depth. One whole wall held counters with different cosmetic brands and it seemed to sell everything, even cigarettes. He was introduced to all the staff including a middle-aged woman pharmacist who said that she was just a locum. None of the names stuck in his mind, everything was so new and exciting. As it was still early, Maurice said there was time for a little tour before taking Alex to his lodgings in Drummond Street. Maurice was amused as Alex kept remarking on the sights.

"My God, these streets are so wide." Alex looked out as they drove along. "Gee, these buildings are pretty big." Everything was bigger, brighter, and more elegant than anything in Dunkeith. It was like The Strand, Regent Street and Oxford Street in London. Everything looked big.

"What did you expect, Alex?" Maurice turned quickly to look at the bright young face, "dirt roads, kangaroos and wooden houses? We have those too, mind you."

Alex loved the trams, which were just like the ones back home in Dunkeith. It came as a shock when Maurice drove over to the left-hand side of the road and then did a sweeping turn to the right.

"It's because trams cross both ways here."

"How do you know where to turn, Maurice?"

"Look," said Maurice, "up there, see the sign? It shows you that to turn right you first go over to the left." Sure enough, Alex saw the picture high up on overhead wires.

"Boy, what a street," he cried out as they drove down St Kilda Road with its canopy of trees, their leaves just beginning to turn golden-brown. "This is the best street I've ever seen." Although Dunkeith was blessed with many parks thanks to the generosity of the jute barons, Alex gazed in awe at the magnificent gardens alongside St Kilda Rd. Everything was so big including the Shrine of Remembrance built to honour Australia's war dead.

"We don't have many really big international hotels," Maurice sounded apologetic. "There're a few here in Melbourne but outside of the city I can't think of any."

"Jenny, the hostess on the plane, said that there're lots of restaurants, is that right?"

Maurice laughed. "There's a good selection of Chinese and others but once you get away from Melbourne it's mostly steak, chops, chips and eggs. There are a few Italian places in Lygon Street."

"What about Greek and Turkish? I picked up a liking for those in Cyprus."

"Yes, we have a few near the shop. It's a bit of a Greek area. Turkish, I don't think so. Indian, maybe."

"Well, that's more than we have in Dunkeith."

Maurice nodded as if trying to picture the town in far-off Scotland. "This is a great country. But funny in some ways. The hotels, the pubs, close at 6pm. There are no little wine shops like in Europe. If you want a drink after six you go to a restaurant."

"Go on!" An unbelieving Alex shook his head. "We had some nice wines in Cyprus. Commanderie St John. A kind of port. Cheap as dirt."

"Most of the popular wines here are sweet. Sweet and fizzy. Not like champagne, more like lemonade with alcohol. Even the imported wines are sweet. Mateus Rose and the German wines. My friends and I, at home, we drink some good red wines from South Australia."

"That's far away, isn't it?" He pictured the map in one of the brochures.

"Everything in Australia is far away. You'll find out."

"So do people go to places like that on holiday?"

"The older ones do. The young ones, all they dream of is 'going home'. Hah."

"Don't they live here?"

Maurice gave a sarcastic laugh. "Of course. But 'home' to them is England even if they were born here. Everything in the papers is about England." He emphasised the word England disparagingly. "They're full of the Royal family or what the British Government is up to. It's stupid."

"It's a long way for a holiday. Must cost a fortune," a doubting Alex glanced at the elegantly dressed man driving.

"Oh my word. But the dream is to go overseas, for a year. They work and travel around England and Europe when they have saved some money."

"Gee, that must be all right." Australia didn't seem so far away after all, he thought.

"If only they would learn something, yes. But they still like to drink only beer and stick together. They never meet the local people."

"So they like beer?"

"Naturally. But it's not like your beer. Here, it's icy cold with lots of gas. At parties all the men are at one end of the room drinking beer and the ladies all drink sherry or gin and tonic. Just like the English. The men talk about football and the women talk about babies."

"And they don't drink wine?" Alex frowned.

"Hah. They say only Balts and wogs drink wine. And Jews."

"What are Balts? I've heard of wogs, Egyptians, aren't they?"

"Anyone who is from foreign countries and is not Anglo-Saxon. That's wogs. Balts are from near Russia."

"What am I?" Alex's eyebrows shot up.

"Probably a Pom but if you tell them you are Scottish, then you're okay." He gave a cynical laugh.

Finally, Maurice turned left and they drove past some elegant houses then streets with houses cheek by jowl and then into Drummond Street in Carlton where he was to stay at Mrs Elliot's small boarding house. The two-story weatherboard house was made of horizontal white-painted wooden boards.

"It's an old house. Probably sixty or seventy years. That's old here," Maurice explained. "It belonged to Mrs Elliot's parents. She moved in with them when her husband was killed in the Korean War."

"Come away in. Wipe your feet," a cheerful woman said in a twangy accent. "I hope you like it here. I do the cooking and cleaning for my three boarders. There's you and two girl students from Melbourne University, Jessica Butler and Amy Watson. They're from the country. Up near Mildura. That's right at the top of Victoria. Both girls are first-year students studying for science degrees. They—"

Alex broke in, "Maybe I can give them some help?"

"You'll have to ask them. I told them you were a chemist. A bit of help with revision work wouldn't go astray. Might keep them in for once." She sounded disapproving.

The University Hotel was just a short walk away and Alex was able to join the crowd in company with the two girls. Although he was older than most students, he was welcomed as a person from "home". Most students were Anglo-Saxon and eager to hear all about England and London in particular. It was every student's ambition to work in England for a year after finishing his or her degree. Alex pretended to know more about the London scene than he did. He always had a new and eager audience. The Royal Women's Hospital was a stone's throw from the University Hotel and further up Lygon Street was high-rise student nurses' accommodation. With so many healthy, country girls eager to enjoy life in what they called the "big smoke", Alex was never short of invitations to parties at the nurses' residence, with enough bedroom Olympics to keep him satisfied.

Maurice Jacobs, a practising Jew, invited Alex to dinner

with his family once in a while. Alex knew about Jews mainly from newsreels after the war. Jews owned the biggest department store in Dunkeith, or so he believed. He had once played the part of Shylock in a school production of Shakespeare's *The Merchant of Venice*, so his was an ambivalent view of these successful, unfortunate and somewhat exotic people. The happy, cheerful household of mother, father and two married sons with their wives and children seemed at odds with the images in his mind. Alex liked the whole family because it was a real one and despite the often-lively arguments at the dinner table, they always parted with hugs and kisses. Maurice loaned him a book, *Exodus*, by a Jewish writer, Leon Uris. Over three nights, he devoured the story and was moved by the struggle of a people to find a place of peace and safety in a world that had persecuted them throughout history. Late that winter, the film was released in Australia. There was something in the story, perhaps it was the Cyprus connection, or perhaps it was the hero, Ari, but Alex felt a strong bond grow within.

Alex was ready to fall in love again. The nostalgia of his first love, Leyla, was a fading memory. Maurice approved of his interest in Jewish culture and invited him to join the family for *Purim*, a special feast day. It was a hot night and Maurice had opened up the French windows to extend the large family room out to a softly lit patio. Their good friends Tzvi and Lenore Hyams and their daughter Barbara joined the Jacobs family. A senior medical researcher at the Royal Children's Hospital, Barbara Hyams was a willowy, attractive, dark-haired woman of twenty-nine. She wore a black, knee-length silk dress with a deep v-neckline, and to Alex she looked stunning and very desirable. During the meal they made frequent eye contact and he could feel a mutual attraction. A little wine, some party games and some dancing and he was sure that he would see this woman again.

Alex and Barbara sat out on the patio away from the crowd,

enjoying some coffee and *hamentaschen*, a triangular fruit filled biscuit, made especially at *Purim*.

"So, you work for Uncle Maurie? Do you like that?" she asked, her shapely bosom rising from her earlier exertions. Alex was drawn to the deep v-line, adorned by a heavy gold chain with a Star of David pendant.

"Oh, yes, he's very good. I enjoy the work. I wander round the city during my lunch break. I love watching all the different people, hearing strange languages. It's fascinating." He looked up from her bosom to her dark, deep-set eyes.

"Uncle Maurie says that you're from Scotland, but you don't sound like the Scottish people I know. I can hardly understand some of them. But I like your voice, nice and deep." She held his gaze.

"Well, I work with the public all the time. It's no use if they can't understand me. So I gave up my accent and now I just try to speak like they do on the BBC, you know, the British Broadcasting Commission?" Alex said with a smile and shrug of the shoulders

"And you're not married? Never been married?" She cocked an eyebrow.

"No. And you?" he asked, liking the way she kept eye contact.

"No, I'm a great disappointment to my parents. A good Jewish girl should be married by my age, they say. They've tried hard to find someone, but, well, I just never have."

"Are you a good Jewish girl?" he asked in a playful tone, enjoying this little game of show-and-tell.

"Oh, yes, I am. I've resisted all temptations. So far. But you, you must have had lots of girlfriends, it's so easy for a man."

"I had a girlfriend once, but she died." He quickly told the story of Leyla and how she had been killed in Cyprus.

"That's so sad. You must have been devastated. Did you grieve for a long time?" She looked sympathetic and put a hand on his arm.

"I guess so, although it seems like a faraway dream now. It

is faraway, here in Australia," Alex said, hoping to end all references to the past. "So, do you still live at home with your parents?"

"Yes. I suppose I should find a place of my own or share with someone. I have a colleague at work who lives in Hawthorn. Doug's at the University, and we met at a staff function and we've kept in touch."

"Is he an Australian?"

"No, American. He and his wife live in a huge house and they're keen for me to share with them. The rent is pretty high but they wanted a big place. They entertain a lot. I could have my own room and bathroom and share the living costs."

"That sounds pretty good." He thought about Barbara in her own room.

"Except for my parents. But it would help Doug and Andrea. She doesn't work, and the place costs a fortune. Doug is in the archaeology department, a really nice man. Uncle says that you live in a boarding house. Is that okay for you?"

"It's all right, but one of these days I must look for a place of my own. Maybe your friends' place would be a good idea, if they want someone, that is." He looked hopefully at Barbara.

Before they could explore the matter further, Maurice came to say that people were leaving and to come and say goodbye. And so the evening broke up. Alex caught the tram back to Drummond Street. The lights sparkled in the trees along St Kilda Road, a festive touch to what had been a magical evening, a family gathering that made Alex feel warm and safe. Silently, he cursed his lack of a car or he could have offered a ride home to Barbara and continued the enjoyment of her company. Still, he mused, maybe that would be pushing things a bit far, her parents may not have appreciated his offer. The following week, she called in at the shop just before closing time. Hotels were prohibited from selling alcohol after 6pm, so he asked if she would like to go somewhere for a coffee. Knowing that he would be later than usual, he telephoned Mrs Elliott to ask that his meal be kept warm. It was a perfect late spring evening in

Melbourne so they strolled up Burke Street to the Windsor Hotel. Built in 1883, the Windsor was Australia's last remaining grand hotel, a beautifully preserved and renovated example of the period. Despite its grandeur, the coffee lounge was only mildly expensive and its large ornate chairs and sofas made it an ideal place for people to meet and enjoy coffee and biscuits.

"Here we are again," Barbara began.

"I've been wondering how I could get in touch with you." He reached out to touch her hand. "I wasn't sure if your parents would object. When I mentioned how much I had enjoyed meeting you, Maurice just nodded and gave me a kind of vague look so I let it drop."

"Well, you're not Jewish and there are certain kinds of, well, not taboos, but more, not encouraged, you know what I mean. Jewish girl, *goy boy*." She laughed nervously.

"It's only a religion, isn't it?"

"Oh yes, but a very strict one. Not that Maurice or our families are orthodox Jews. I couldn't stand that. No, we are Reform Jews so we don't follow all the laws on food like having two kitchens, one for meat and one for dairy, and we do eat prawns. Or things like questions about the children of a Jew who marries out. We're like Catholics who don't have the Mass in Latin or have to eat fish on Friday, at least I don't think they have to, now. Do they?" She waited for an answer.

"I used to be a Catholic but we ate whatever we could eat, never mind about Friday." Alex threw out his hands.

"My father says it's not what's in the stomach that matters but what's in the heart," she said jokingly.

Alex experienced a strange *déjà vu* feeling. It was like something he'd heard before but he couldn't remember when.

"I've been thinking about those people you work with, the ones with the house in Hawthorn. Would they be interested in meeting me? About the room they have?"

"I did ask, as a matter of fact," Barbara said shyly, her eyes down. "They would like to meet you. What about this weekend?"

"Yes. I must get a car, you need a car here. I've never owned one, though."

"Neither have I! It's funny, but I think I've always felt that my parents would think I was too independent. They're like that. They're very protective in so many ways."

"Right, I'll get a car this weekend, Saturday afternoon, no, wait, I need a driver's licence. Bugger! I'd better get one. I'll check out how with one of the police guys who come regularly into the shop. They're big on cures for hangovers."

"Well, I'd better get off home. What say I meet you at lunchtime, Saturday, you finish then, don't you? We can get a tram out to Hawthorn, then it's not far to Chester Street."

Alex was tempted to kiss her just before her tram arrived. They moved forward, then separated and waved as the tram pulled away from the stop.

Maurice never worked on Saturdays. Barbara watched while Alex locked the shop at one o'clock. To his surprise she put her arm through his, squeezed and marched him along the street. The Number 24 tram took them all the way to Glenferrie Road. Arm-in-arm they strolled, like any loving couple, up to 21 Chester Street. Doug and Andrea Stretton were waiting to greet them. After introductions, Andrea offered coffee and sandwiches. Alex had never been in such a huge two-storey house. It's big enough to be a church or an art gallery, he thought. The ceilings were very high, the rooms were large and filled with bright sunshine. The kitchen was enormous with a timber dining table able to seat twelve people. After lunch, they sat talking and found that they shared many interests.

Doug looked at Andrea. "We're both big readers, aren't we hon?"

"I think Alex can see that from the amount of books." She glanced at a wall of shelves crammed with books.

"I love books," Barbara joined in. "Unfortunately I don't have enough room to keep all the ones I'd like to buy."

Alex was eager to be included. "I spent so much time in digs and even at home my favourite place was the library."

"Is that right?" Doug nodded approval.

"Yeh, it was always warm. It had central heating. I was usually the last to leave on winter's nights." He laughed self-consciously, wishing he'd never made the comment.

"Well, let's have a look at the room. Don't feel obligated if you don't like it."

Alex was pleased at its size. "This is great. I can have a double bed, a wardrobe, and a couple of chairs. It's perfect."

"And just here," Doug walked to a narrow passageway, "is a door to the back. You can come and go without bothering anyone. Not that it'll be a bother, don't get me wrong."

"Even better," Alex agreed, opening the back door to a side garden area and a large tree in the lane.

"You can park your car under the tree in summer. It's terrific shade." Andrea beamed.

"I'm hoping to get a car soon. Look, this is just right. Now it's just a matter of how much?" Alex looked at Doug then Andrea.

"What do you say to three pounds fifty and a share of the food bill? Split three ways?" Andrea posed the question.

"No problems. But Barbara said you like to entertain. How do we work that out?"

"If we have a party, or you, then you buy all the food and drink you need for the night. It's simple. Anything special you cough up on your own. Isn't that right, hon?" Doug said.

"That's it. I think this'll be real neat, don't you, Barb?" Andrea turned to Barbara with raised eyebrows.

"Okay," Alex held up his hands "I'll give Mrs Elliott two weeks' notice, that should be enough."

"Oh yes," Barbara clapped her hands, "and that'll give us time to organise a bed, bookshelves, and some pictures. We'll check today's *Age* and see what's on offer in the second-hand columns."

"Isn't that a bit quick?" Alex shook his head.

"Nah," Doug said, "You can move anything in you like. The room's empty, anyway."

Barbara clapped her hands again. "This will be fun. You have *The Age*?" she asked.

"Sure, it's in the kitchen. Go for it."

The time flew by. Maurice gave Alex some sheets and a doona. "So. It looks like you will be staying in Melbourne. Good." He smiled.

"You know, I've meant to ask you, Maurice. How come you advertised for a pharmacist in the UK? Most of the graduates here prefer to work in Melbourne. So why not take one of them?"

Maurice lowered his head and peered at Alex. "Most young men here want to own their own business. They look for opportunities to open up a new pharmacy as soon as possible. A cousin of mine in Leicester told me that this is not so in England. People work all their lives for Boots and the like."

"That's true. It costs a lot of money to buy a pharmacy, especially a good one," Alex nodded. "You don't have to be a qualified pharmacist to own a pharmacy in Britain. All you need is money."

"So I thought, maybe I should look for an assistant from England. One who would stay for a few years." He shrugged apologetically.

"I see." Alex understood.

Most people on the staff had little odds and ends, a bedside table, an unused easy chair and any number of paperback books to fill his bookstand. Alex's collection grew. He was lucky. One of his policeman friends took him for a drive, said he was okay and arranged for a licence. It was as simple as that. Maurice had several friends in the used-car business and Alex was soon the proud owner of a six-year-old Holden sedan with a bench front seat. He worked till six, so it was almost dark by the time Alex arrived home. On several nights, Barbara joined them for dinner. Afterwards they made changes to his room and sat listening to the radio or playing records on an old player she'd found in a second-hand store. Alex drove her home around 9pm each night. The final move was made on a Sunday and they celebrated with a bottle of Great Western champagne.

With the radio playing soft music, Barbara sat on Alex's lap in his only easy chair. They kissed and caressed like lovers. But when he tried to go further, she pushed away his hands. "No, that's enough, I don't want to. Not yet. Just hold me."

Alex sighed with frustration but knew that he had to be patient. Jewish girls didn't jump into bed unless it would lead to something permanent and he was not Jewish so that was a big problem. During his lunch break, he wandered down to the Victorian State Library with its considerable and eclectic collection of books on every subject imaginable. A recent addition was John Mayer's *Jewish-Gentile Courtships*, a book that totally dismayed him. If the Catholic religion was restrictive and complicated, Judaism was even more so. But he determined that he would try to understand. He secretly attended services at the Reform Synagogue in Toorak Road. He would take a paper yarmulke at the entrance, and sit and listen to the unintelligible prayers followed by an English oration by the rabbi. As he read, he began to understand the richness of the ancient religion and was attracted to the importance placed on family.

They advanced to lying, facing each other on his bed. The closeness and whispered words made it easy for Alex to raise the subject of perhaps becoming a Jew.

"Oh, darling Alex, it's not so easy. My family hopes that one day I will marry a Jewish man, even if I've never shown any interest at all in the men who have been introduced to me. I'm not even sure about marriage myself. It's wonderful being with you, but I'm not sure."

"But you know how I feel," he whispered in her ear. "We're right for each other. I feel it. I'd like to marry and have a family, just like yours and Maurice's."

"Alex, Alex, you're far away from your home, you want to belong. I understand that. But try to be patient. There's so much to think about." She groaned.

He thought of how those words seemed to echo in his mind.

Unattached and earning an excellent salary, Barbara was in the habit of going with one of her girlfriends to the theatre, the ballet or performances of the Melbourne Symphony Orchestra, usually during the week. She explained to Alex that she could not suddenly abandon her friends and did not intend to. He was happy with the arrangement as it gave him the chance to become better acquainted with Doug and Andrea. In no time he acquired a kind of trans-Atlantic accent, much to Barbara's amusement. Autumn gave way to winter. The trees in St Kilda Road and the nearby parks lost their leaves. The months had drifted by, pleasantly, with Alex learning more and more about Australians. He enjoyed working with Maurice who began to drop hints about Alex becoming a partner in the business.

One day Barbara phoned him at work. "Myra, my girlfriend, is sick. Do you want to come to the Town Hall tonight? The Melbourne Symphony concert? I know you're not keen on classical music but I think you might like tonight's programme."

He hesitated. "What is it?"

"It's Mozart. The Horn Concertos. Barry Tuckwell is the soloist. He's brilliant. Say you'll come. I'd like you to learn about classical music. It's something we can share," Barbara pleaded.

She was right. Tuckwell was brilliant and Alex was converted. Classical music never quite replaced his love of Frank Sinatra but he soon began collecting classical records. One of his favourites was *Concerto d''Aranjuez* by the Spanish composer Rodrigo. Although she held back on full intimacy, Barbara would occasionally allow Alex to fondle her firm, rounded body. She avoided any mention of a future permanent relationship. A cool but not unpleasant winter turned to spring. Melbourne in springtime was an explosion of leaves and blossom. Every tree-lined street came alive. The many gracious parks beckoned lovers to stroll arm-in-arm to the sound of trams clacking around the park perimeter. Just east of Melbourne, winding up a road flanked by towering eucalypts, Alex drove slowly so that they could catch glimpses of the abundant wildlife in the Dandenong Ranges. They drove past rich strawberry farms with welcome signs, and arrived at the Golden Cottage in Cockatoo in good time for lunch.

In the sheltered courtyard, he commented on her gloomy expression. "What's up? Is it that time of the month? You seem very down."

"Well, you see, it's like this. Since before I met you, I've been going once a week to a group meeting, you know, where people can talk about their feelings and so on. A Jewish psychologist runs it. It's just a dozen or so people. We do some meditation, breathing exercises and things like foot massage. Then we talk about anything that bothers us. Anyway, I've been thinking for a few years that I want to go and live in Israel. But, well, my parents. They only have me."

Alex was deflated. "Are you still thinking of going to Israel?"

"I know it's hard, but I've been wanting to go for years. I believe it's important that we help Israel. It's just important, that's all. And I have qualifications that would help." She slumped lower in her seat.

"But what about us, I mean, would you leave me and go?"

"I know this isn't the right place to talk about it, but I told the group about you and everything. How bad I felt. Like I've led you on. I mean, I feel guilty that I never told you about my plans." She looked away as she spoke.

He sat, silent, unable to think what to say. Suddenly his whole world seemed to be ending. His shoulders slumped, his body was heavy, and he struggled not to let tears form. He swallowed hard to get rid of the lump in his throat and he stuttered, "What about if I came with you?"

"I'm not sure, Alex, whether you can. Or if you really want to. There's the language, work, you're settled here. I know you like it here. God, I feel awful." Her pale face reddened as she raised both hands to her cheeks.

"Shit, how do you think I feel?" He grimaced.

"Oh, Alex, I'm sorry. Look, I have to go, it's something I promised myself. Maybe I can, well, let's see what happens when I get there. Maybe it'll be possible for you to emigrate there, I don't know. We'll write and, and, see what happens." She shrugged helplessly.

"Well, that's it then." The words came out like an explosion. "Have you decided when to go?" He tried to sound calm, but he knew that it didn't look good. Christ, he thought, bloody Israel.

"I thought maybe in December. That's winter in Israel, so it's easier to acclimatise." Her softly spoken words were like the closing of a door.

"That's only two months. Well, that's it then, isn't it?" Alex couldn't keep the anger out of his voice.

The drive back to Melbourne was miserable and mostly silent. Violent endings come with a bang. Slow death departs with a whimper. Monday to Friday each week dragged along like a lead balloon tied to his heart. Although she spoke optimistically about the future, Alex found it hard to smile.

Only two weekends remained. Barbara told her parents that she would be staying on the Saturday night with a girlfriend. She'd done that often in the past before meeting Alex. Her mother, Lenore Hyams, drifted through each day, a handkerchief ever at the ready to dry the tears that never seemed to stop. Each evening, Barbara's father, Tzvi, sat staring at the new television, the flickering black-and-white images sending him off into a depressed trance.

On Friday, Barbara phoned Alex at work to ask if she could stay at his place the next night. Alex could hardly wait to finish work the next day. They walked down to the Hollow Frog in Glenferrie Road and shared a bottle of Barossa claret with dinner. The restaurant was crowded, and noisy, making conversation difficult. Back at the house, he poured two glasses of port.

"Shall I put on Rodrigo?" he turned to her. "Low?"

She sat on his lap and they listened to the haunting Spanish guitar.

"I've brought some spermicidal cream and condoms." Barbara kissed him on the cheek. "Just leave one light on while I get undressed. Please?" She stood up and turned to face him. In the soft light she slowly removed everything except her panties, black, lacy things. Alex quickly undressed.

"Just lie down and turn your back while I put in this cream," Barbara pleaded.

As she slipped between the sheets, Alex reached out for her. He muttered words of love and lust. His mind said "slowly and gentle" but his body failed. For hours, they rolled and kissed, sucked and rocked. Finally, exhausted, they fell asleep, Next morning they began all over again. Barbara insisted on catching a tram home, and left a happy yet sad Alex at the tram stop. Sensing some kind of closure, he walked slowly back to the house. After a quiet dinner with Doug and Andrea he sat in his room playing Rodrigo again. By the time he'd drunk half a bottle of whisky he barely made it to bed and oblivion. He dragged himself to work the next day, and found it hard to concentrate and had to check every prescription twice, even three times. He heard one of the girls say he looked a wreck. Barbara was no longer working and he was afraid to phone her at home. The week was never-ending and no word came from her. The weekend came and went. Doug and Andrea tried hard to raise his spirits but to no avail. On Monday afternoon the phone rang at work.

"Jacobs the Chemist, Alex speaking."

"Alex, it's Barbara."

"Hi, I've been waiting to hear from you, are you okay?" He spoke quickly.

"Oh, yes, I'm fine. I was so sore after, after, you know, I went to see my doctor. She examined me and said I was all right, just bruised." She laughed, a harsh laugh. "Anyway, I told a lie. I don't want unhappy farewells so I just called to say I'm flying out in a few hours. I'll write, I promise, so keep thinking of me. I'll be thinking of you," she faltered and said in a choked voice, "Goodbye. For now." The phone went dead.

Alex put down the phone and walked out of the shop. Holding back tears he walked quickly up the street, sucking in air, his teeth chattering. "Fuck, fuck, fuck," he repeated over and over. At last he stopped, wiped his eyes and walked back to work.

Barbara did write, a postcard every week for six weeks. The words were meaningless.

"Settling in."

"The weather is cool but nice."

"Found a job on a kibbutz, just temporary."

"Miss your voice, keep well."

Alex had no address to reply to so he grew more and more despondent. Finally, a letter arrived full of enthusiasm about the future of Israel and how well she was settling in to her new life. There was an address and Alex poured out everything he felt. It was another month before he received a reply. Barbara wrote that she was happy in her new land and was sorry that it was unlikely that he would be accepted as a migrant, not being a Jew. A week later, another letter told him that she had met a doctor from Germany, a widower with one daughter. She was seeing the doctor. Alex did not reply. He knew that he would never go to Israel.

Cyprus 1959

Mehmet Ali's heart was heavy. His only child, his lovely Leyla, was far away, bearing a child he would probably never see. He was weary of his work as the local commander of TMT. He longed for the days of coffee with Demetrio, Leyla by his side eager to learn. Aware that he could be the target of a reprisal by *EOKA*, he was forced to leave more and more of his duties to some of the old men in Ghazientop. He was in a gloomy mood at a meeting at the home of Dr Kucuk. Denktash, the burly lawyer, flanked Kucuk at a table. With a large, dome-like head and eyes that could see into a man's soul, Denktash slowly looked at each man in the room, assessing their courage and commitment.

A young man asked the first question. "Fazil Bey, we know that Turkey is looking after our welfare, but the Turks are not here. They do not have to deal with the day-to-day problems."

Mehmet Ali leaned forward. "I have trouble with some of the young men. They sometimes attack and rob people who do them no harm. We need more discipline."

"My good friend," Kucuk looked directly at Mehmet Ali, "you are a wise man, a good leader to your people. We must at this time, while the negotiations are proceeding in London, ensure that trouble is kept to a minimum."

Denktash had been listening intently to the questions. He shook his fist. "Let no-one point a finger at us. We must not lose the respect of the British and Americans. Any renegade Turks must be controlled."

Murmurs of approval came from many in the room. Kucuk held up a hand for silence.

"I will be in London next month to meet with Averoff, Zorlu, Makarios, Clerides and the British. Rauf will be there." Kucuk brought the meeting back to the real business. "We believe that a resolution is near, one that will ensure our continued existence in our homeland. The Turkish and Greek ministers have a solution almost ready. Is this not so, Rauf?"

Denktash rose to his feet. He waited until every face was concentrated on his. "We have, through Turkey, negotiated with the Greeks to save our people. But we are not fooled by promises of being welcomed and cared for in a new Cyprus."

Kucuk nodded approval.

Denktash continued. "Too often in the past we have listened to promises and we all know the result. Expulsion, death and the destruction of our culture. This will not happen in Cyprus. We will not give away our rights. This is the homeland of two communities, theirs and ours. We are not one nation struggling to be independent. We are two peoples and two peoples we will remain. Or we will die fighting. We will not surrender, even if we are abandoned by the world, we will not allow the red priest and his gunmen to drive us from our homes."

"*Inshallah*," came from the mouths of many in the room.

"So what will we achieve in these negotiations?" Mehmet Ali stood as he asked the question.

"With the might of Turkey beside us, we will accept nothing less than a full partnership in a new Cyprus. Not a majority, or a minority, oh no." Denktash let this sink in. "That will expose us to discrimination in every field and we will be squeezed slowly out, one way or another. A partner has equal rights and cannot be dominated by the other partner, even if he has a smaller share. That is how business works and our future is a business, not a dream of some utopian paradise where the father cares for his son and leads him to a bright future." Denktash extended both arms as if to embrace the room.

"But," Mehmet Ali was aware that he might appear negative after these rousing words, "but will Makarios agree to our demands? I think not."

Denktash beamed down a look of sympathy and understanding at this respected leader of his people. "My dear friend, you are wise to be sceptical. But know this. Everyone is sick of this useless, needless wrangling and waste of life. This is not 1918. America, Greece, the British, all want a just solution. Turkey too needs the right solution."

At the mention of Turkey, everyone nodded.

"The great powers wish to keep control in the eastern Mediterranean." Denktash closed one eye. "The British will have their bases and the Americans will keep NATO intact." His stern gaze swept the room, "Greece has enough troubles and they don't need the burden of Cyprus."

"But what of Makarios?" a voice called out.

"Makarios will be happy to be the President of a free Cyprus. He is no fool, that man. His ambition is to lead the Greeks on the first step of *his sacred path*," Denktash said with a mocking laugh.

"So we can rest easy. Fazil Bey? You have everything under control?"

"No!" thundered Denktash, "we only have the present situation under reasonable control. We can win a good result, but that will only be the beginning. Makarios and the Greeks still dream of *Enosis* and forever we will have to be vigilant to ensure that we never lose our rights."

Dr Kucuk rose to his feet. His lugubrious face brightened. "I have had long discussions with Foreign Minister Zorlu. He has made it clear that Cyprus will never become a Greek outpost with the potential to threaten Turkey."

In his relaxed, measured voice he explained the diplomatic manoeuvres that would surely bring about a Republic of Cyprus where Turks could live in complete safety.

"Turkey, Zorlu told me, would demand the right to intervene if there was ever a threat to Turkish Cypriots. This he has promised or there will be no alternative but partition, *taksim*. That threat, he has made clear, will ensure that Makarios and Grivas will accept a compromise, despite their protestations. Zorlu said that there would be no retreat from this position."

The assembled men smiled at each other.

Zurich 1959

"You've had a look at our proposals?" Averoff, the Greek Foreign Minister, was the first to speak.

"Yes, and I think I can say on behalf of Turkey that we are in general agreement." Zorlu flicked over the pages of a typed document.

"Good. Then we should arrange for a meeting next month of our Prime Ministers and advisors. It's time to settle this business once and for all."

"I agree. The format of a presidential regime with the legislature and civil service shared along the lines of 70 per cent Greek to 30 per cent Turk seems reasonable. It guarantees the security of the Turkish Cypriots."

"You're happy with the separate Greek and Turkish municipalities in the five main towns?" Averoff said.

"I think this will work. Of course the new Cyprus Government can review this after five years. It may not be cost-effective."

"Besides the British bases, we are in agreement about having contingents of Greek and Turkish troops deployed near Nicosia?" Averoff looked up from his notes.

"Yes, we will not pursue the matter of us having a full military base. But we need to have a guarantee."

"Guarantee?" Averoff looked quizzical.

Zorlu stared hard at his opposite number. "Yes, you, me and the British must have a Treaty of Guarantee. One that allows each of us, individually or in partnership, to intervene if the Constitution fails to work."

"An alliance?" Averoff frowned at the suggestion.

"Why not? We have already spent so much time on this matter. There will be those who are unhappy with our decisions. A Treaty of Guarantee will deter them from trying to overthrow our arrangements."

Averoff looked uncomfortable. "I'm not sure if Makarios will agree to that."

Zorlu's response was unyielding. "He has no choice. The alternative is partition. I think he will see sense, assuming that he becomes President."

"Oh, he won't have any trouble there. You're right. If we walk away from him he has nowhere to go. We're all sick of this endless, useless campaign. Especially the Greek Cypriots."

"Then we will proceed to get the paperwork done before we meet next month?" Averoff picked up his document and nodded vigorously. "Is Zurich satisfactory?"

Zorlu put out his hand. "Zurich is fine. It has a nice ring to it. I know that we have had our differences but I'm happy to say that all that is now past."

The two men shook hands and left to report back to their respective governments.

At the Dolder Hotel in Zurich, Prime Minister Karamanlis of Greece and the Turkish Prime Minister Menderes reached agreement on the future of Cyprus. Averoff flew to London to give the news to the British Government.

The British Government was pleased that it would soon be able to end its rule in Cyprus and accepted the proposals without delay.

While Alexander Forbes was preparing to fly to Australia, Archbishop Makarios and Dr Kucuk arrived in London.

Makarios met with Averoff immediately. "The proposals, especially the separate municipalities, are not acceptable." His face was inscrutable. His black eyes glinted.

"Why?" Averoff sat stone-faced.

"Because it is a defacto partition. The Turks will control their own affairs."

"Only in a few towns and only for five years. It won't last." Averoff's eyes never left Makarios' face. "Beatitude, it is now time to face the political realities of the situation. You understand?"

"Of course, Minister. But we do not wish to see the Turks gain control of parts of Cyprus. That will lead eventually to what they want, a divided island."

"Then we must look for ways that achieve Greek rule of Cyprus without upsetting Turkey. That Turkish pig Zorlu is not easy to shift."

"Then oppose the separate municipalities," Makarios persisted.

"They are a stubborn people, the Turks. They have the patience to wait and wait until they achieve their demands. The British now see that they can escape with some dignity if they allow independence yet retain their bases on the island." Averoff pressed home his point with a clenched fist. "I have informed General Grivas of these things. His work is over."

"I understand fully, I assure you, Minister. The struggle is beginning to tell on my people." Makarios looked relieved at the mention of an end to the involvement of Grivas.

"Beatitude, we have supported you in this just cause, but now the Americans wish an end. We rely upon loans and funding from America but they do not give it with an open hand. NATO is important to them."

"It's a pity. I have the Russians with me." Makarios smiled enigmatically.

"There are conditions, you understand. The US Administration supports us in our fight against the communists but they wish for more in return. In politics there are secrets and no secrets. There are payments to be made and they also know that we cannot resist their demands. Their main concern is the future stability of NATO, which means they have to consider the views of Turkey. One does not need an army of occupation to determine the fate of a nation."

"Yes, of course. We all know that. The Turks make this clear to me on every occasion. I understand that Queen Frederika has made an appeal to Foster Dulles to maintain a neutral position with regard to our aims. I have no wish to see your government fall. That would not be in anyone's best interests when we have come so far."

Averoff glared at Makarios

"My flock grows weary of the killings, as I do." A wavering Archbishop bowed his head.

"Then we are in agreement. We will sign?" Averoff asked hopefully.

"An end must come. I am prepared to accept independence based on fair and reasonable conditions." He spread out his hands.

Averoff smiled with relief. "So we agree to a Republic of Cyprus with each community having a share. Of course, you will be the dominant party with yourself as President. It will not be perfect but time changes many things. We will get rid of the British and outside involvement and wait for the opportune time. You understand?" He arched one eyebrow.

"Once we have the reins of power, we will be patient like the Turks. But I am determined to make Cyprus a Greek island."

Averoff rose to his feet, and kissed the ring finger of His Beatitude Archbishop Makarios.

"We'll meet again tomorrow then."

Makarios went to his hotel, the Dorchester, where a delegation of Greek Cypriots was waiting to hear the news. They were dismayed at the proposals but over six hours of heated debate he convinced them that the outcome was the best that could be expected. The main problem was the matter of separate municipalities.

"These areas are poor and badly serviced," Clerides sounded pessimistic. "If they are under a Greek-dominated council there will be constant demands from the Turks to improve conditions. I say we let them run their own affairs."

Makarios gave Clerides a look of approval. "Let the Turks look after their own." His lips curled in a cruel smile. "The poor are always with us, but the Muslims can look after their own poor. Now I must contact Grivas and give him the news at once. You have a contact number?"

Grivas was upset that he had not been consulted about the agreement. He made his displeasure known to Makarios.

"This is not what the Greeks of Cyprus fought for. You spit upon their sacrifice by agreeing to abandon *Enosis*. What did we struggle for if not to be part of the Hellenic world?"

"My dear fellow, it is not only you and I who can determine the future. We are but a small island. We are less in number than Thessalonica. Without the support of Greece, and through them the Americans, what can we do? Bomb our way into oblivion? How can we ask the people to keep fighting when no-one cares about us? Do you think the Americans will risk offending Turkey, our enemy at the door?"

"There is only one result we fought for and that is *Enosis!*" Grivas shouted into the phone.

"Be reasonable, be patient. History is not written in a year or ten years. The people tell me that they are sick of living in fear, in fear of losing a loved one." Makarios gesticulated to no-one in particular.

"Well, I shall await your return for the details of this 'Agreement'," Grivas said ominously. "You'll have to make the best of the bed you have made for our Greek Cypriot brethren. I will no longer lead the armed struggle. I will so inform my members. From now on *you* will have to deal with them."

Back in Athens, before a room full of journalists, Makarios drew on his Christian readings and simply said, "It is finished," echoing the words of Jesus Christ as he hung on the cross.

The Turkish Cypriot delegation, composed of Dr Kucuk, Rauf Denktash and many *muktars*, was convinced that they had won a major victory.

Kucuk looked around the smoke-filled room. "First, let me pay tribute to Rauf Bey and our team of legal experts. The final draft is most satisfactory."

Denktash bowed his head in acknowledgement of the compliment.

Kucuk continued, "We have representation far beyond our numbers. The separate municipalities in Nicosia, Limassol, Larnaca, Famagusta and Kyrenia are a major concession won. We have the vice-presidency with the power of veto. We have a contingent of Turkish troops on our soil to safeguard our interests."

A few handclaps greeted this statement.

"Now comes the hard part. We must find sufficient good men to stand for election to the House of Representatives. Even more difficult will be the recruiting of suitably qualified people to take up the 30 per cent of the public service positions that are ours."

Denktash held up his hand. "Without the leadership of Fazil Bey we would not have this happy predicament. I for one hope that Fazil Bey is elected Vice-President and continues to lead our people in what will be difficult but not impossible years ahead."

Dr Kucuk bent forward as everyone in the room clapped hands and murmured words of support. He held up his hand to stop the acclaim.

"Despite our success we must remain vigilant. His Beatitude will not easily give up his dream of delivering *Enosis* to the Greeks. Nothing we do must give him any excuse to bring this about. Now we will sign the papers that guarantee our survival in our home."

At Lancaster House on February 19, 1959, all parties to the dispute signed the documents that ended the Cyprus problem. The lawyers and bureaucrats were given the task of arranging for the transfer of power to an elected Cyprus Parliament. Once again in its history, the people of Cyprus had not been allowed to vote on how their country should be governed. Within weeks the terrorism had ended. Makarios was now free to return to Cyprus and the following month on the first day of March he made a triumphant return to the island.

"We have won," he declared to a jubilant throng of supporters.

The majority of Greek Cypriots knew little of the details of the Agreement. They were overjoyed at the return of their spiritual leader who had, in their eyes, ended the long years of bitter upheaval. Now they wanted nothing more that a return to the happy days before 1955. Apart from the fanatics, most Greek Cypriots had no real stomach to confront the British in a bloody war. A happy, peace-loving people, they admired the English and respected their institutions and sense of fair play. While they might long for the days when Greeks ruled half the known world, most had grave doubts about being part of an impoverished and strife-torn Greece. While agreement had been reached in broad outline the real work of creating the Constitution now began. Archbishop Makarios sent a message to Colonel Grivas asking him to come to Nicosia. He was surprised when Antonnis Georgjiadis, Grivas' faithful companion in arms, turned up at the Archbishopric.

"Where is Colonel Grivas?"

"Beatitude, he prefers that you inform me of any news. I will then report to him." Georgjiadis explained. "Let's just say that he is not happy."

"Pity. I prefer to deal directly with him. However, I wish him to know this." Makarios paused for a minute, wondering how to present the result in the best light. "Say that before he went to Zurich, I agreed with Karamanlis on the general outline of the Agreement. I did not know its precise details until after I signed along with the others. Karamanlis went far beyond what I thought we had agreed upon."

"Why did you not refuse to sign then?"

"I had no choice. The alternative was to lose everything. Turkey would have won. Partition was the only alternative and Greece would have agreed to that."

"My leader will be disappointed. I'll report what you have said. No doubt he will get back to you." Georgjiadis knelt and kissed the ring finger of the Archbishop before leaving a melancholy Makarios.

Grivas was more than unhappy. "You see, Antonnis, we've been sold out. Greece has abandoned us." Grivas glared at those in the room.

"His Beatitude said that he has achieved the best outcome possible. He had no other option." Papadopoulos spoke in a conciliatory tone, hoping to calm the Colonel.

"Maybe I should carry on alone. We have shown that only a hundred or so men is all it takes to force a better result, the only result we have fought five years to win. *Enosis* was what we fought for and what men died for. Now we are walking away with the final victory in sight." Grivas looked at him with disgust.

"What's done is done. Will you now agree to end all hostilities?" Clerides asked. "Under the amnesty the authorities expect you to leave Cyprus and return to Greece at once. I understand the Greek Government intends to honour you."

A tired and shrunken Grivas pulled himself up to his full height. "You can inform the Archbishop that I will give the matter some thought. I'm not ready yet to abandon the fight."

"Then there's nothing more to say. We'll see that His Beatitude gets your response. It's a pity that it's come to this. We should be united."

Papadopoulos and the other important *EOKA* members rose and shuffled out. The disappointed group headed to their cars. Grivas did not hurry to make a decision. He knew that carrying on the war in opposition to Makarios' wishes could lead to civil strife between his supporters and those who preferred to follow the Archbishop. Finally, after convincing the authorities that he would not leave until all prisoners were freed and allowed to remain in Cyprus, he agreed to return to Athens.

The following day, General George Grivas, leader of *EOKA*, issued a statement:

"It is pointless to reject the Agreement and to continue the armed struggle. To do so will only divide the Cypriot people and eventually the whole Greek nation. It is not the outcome we expected but it is better than national discord. In the end we might lose everything."

Not all the men who had served under Grivas were easily convinced. They had been uncontrolled warriors used to having their demands met, and were reluctant to accept the political solution.

After two weeks of nervousness throughout the island, Colonel Grivas was flown by the Royal Hellenic Air Force to Greece. No-one was at Nicosia airport to bid him farewell. Dressed in his guerilla clothes and wearing his familiar beret, he sat exhausted, looking out to the Aegean Sea far below as the jet took him away from his greatest triumph. For five years he had tied up thousand of British troops and never been captured. Landing at Athens airport, he tried to adopt a defiant and valiant pose as he stepped from the plane to a deafening roar from the thousands gathered behind the terminus barriers.

"Welcome home, Colonel Grivas, victorious leader of *EOKA* in the fight against the colonial enemy." The Greek Foreign Minister Averoff kissed Grivas on both cheeks then held up his arm in a salute to the cheering crowd.

The Archbishop of Greece, Theoklitos, embraced Grivas and shouted out above the noisy crowd. "A Greek hero has returned to the bosom of Greece."

Grivas walked slowly to the terminal building, waving to the adoring multitude. He forced a weary smile for the flashing newspaper cameras. The following night, at a reception in his honour, the Greek Government promoted him to the rank of Lieutenant-General. After five years on the run, he could now retire on a full pension.

Cyprus 1960

IN 1960, on 16 August, a hot, oppressive day in Nicosia, the Republic of Cyprus was proclaimed. Few people on the island rejoiced. Five years of guerilla warfare, murder, hatred, suspicion and torture could not be waved away with a new flag. The forced marriage would require goodwill and understanding on everyone's part. Each community had its own Communal Chamber to deal with matters of religion, education and so on. Each community elected its own representatives to the legislature according to the 70:30 basis. As it happened, the marriage was never consummated.

Turkish Cypriots celebrated in an atmosphere of relief that their future survival appeared assured. Greek Cypriots were less enthusiastic. Now they had to share government with a hated minority with more members in the legislature than their numbers warranted. Turkey, Greece and Great Britain signed a Treaty of Agreement guaranteeing the Constitution and reserved the right to intervene should the Constitution be abrogated.

The new vice-president of the Republic of Cyprus, Dr Fazil Kucuk, and the President of the Turkish Cypriot Communal Chamber, Rauf Denktash, sat in Kucuk's residence. Lawyers, businessmen, *muktars* and two officers of the Turkish Army were ushered in and soon the room was smoke-filled and noisy.

"*Effendi*," Kucuk began, "this is a an important landmark in the history of our people. Now we have a new Republic, one in which our voice will be heard. I hope that the fighting and killing is over. Now it is time to use the political process to ensure that the guarantees that we have won are not withered away by time or the chicanery of the Archbishop and his die-hard Greek assassins."

"They won't be," Denktash interjected.

"From this day on we will begin the political struggle to make certain that the advantages we have won in the Zurich and London Agreements are not diminished in any way. Never think that the Agreements are the end of our struggle. They are just the beginning. Makarios will need to keep a tight rein on his side. Many of them will never give up the dream of *Enosis*. Rauf?"

Denktash rose to his feet and waited till the murmuring had stopped. "Grivas has gone to Athens, and is now General Grivas. That's how they reward a man responsible for the loss of so many innocent lives. He is gone but his commanders and henchmen are still here, and will be in the government. Do you think that they will forget?"

"No," came mutterings of support.

"Hatred dies hard in the heart of a Greek. So, we will continue to train our fighters, we will take the opportunity to build up our weapons. A contingent of the Turkish army is to be stationed south of Nicosia, well away from the Turkish quarter of Nicosia. The north is where we must concentrate *our* fighters."

"Yes. And to the west." Mehmet Ali waved a hand high.

"If, and it may be soon, the Greeks wish to get rid of us, then it is to the north that we must bring our people. Our intelligence indicates that Clerides, Georgjiadis, and Sampson when he returns under the amnesty, will all continue with the objective of making us a community subject to Greek control."

"Rauf Bey," an old man interrupted, "if we have the right of veto, how can they do anything?"

Denktash looked at the short, bearded man with a compassionate smile, thinking that the road would be long and hard with so few men of intellect. They had good men, simple and kind-hearted, but not wise in the way of the world outside of their village. "Listen to me and listen carefully. The right of veto is limited and only comes at the end of protracted negotiations. In the meantime the Greeks can control almost every aspect of our lives. So we have the Ministry of Defence, but we have no army and no money to form one. It is in key areas such as the Interior Ministry that the Greeks will slowly extend their power and authority. What the Minister of the Interior and his majority Greek staff do with their budget will be beyond our efforts to control."

Kucuk stood up. His lined, saggy face looked heavier than usual. "In the parliament we can make our voice heard if we see something untoward, but it is those who will run the government departments, the bureaucrats, who will determine where the money is spent. Do we have enough first-class people able to see what is going on in their department? I think not. Not at this stage. So we must encourage our young men, and women if there are any, to study hard, to learn the system and to enter the public service." He sat down wearily.

Still standing, Denktash nodded agreement and supported him saying, "You understand? Time! Time is what we need to bring on these future accountants and policy makers. And before then? Before then we must stay alert, armed, ready to defend our communities, our villages. Because the Greeks will not lay down their arms until they drive us out of Cyprus. Our intelligence tells us that the Greeks are meeting regularly, training, testing explosive devices, waiting for the word to drive us into the sea."

Everyone nodded at this statement. A swarthy village *muktar* stood up. "And what are we doing? Most of us are scattered all over the island. It's all right for Nicosia and Larnaca, they have the numbers. It won't be easy for the Greeks to kill all of you, but Kondera, my village, or Nadir here in Ashira. How do we prepare? We're surrounded." He cast a worried look round the room.

"That's where our preparation comes in." Denktash banged his chest with a clenched fist. "We understand the problem.

You will be busy in your fields all day. So we will allocate two or three fighters to stay in the village, to organise your defences. I know that many of you have been living with Greeks for years. You've had no problems. But it is not the village people we have to fear, it's the different groups, EOKA and others. Every town and village has its commander, and some just follow the local leader. They are not interested in anything except killing Turks. They are like the mafia, a law unto themselves."

"What authority will these fighters have? Am I the *muktar* who tells his people what to do, or does some young fighter tell me what to do?" Mehmet Ali stood and looked directly at Denktash.

Kucuk jumped to his feet. "We are not some uncivilised rabble," he shouted as murmurs of support for Mehmet Ali grew, "the rule of law, of elected leaders, prevails. Of course you are a *muktar* and it is your duty to look after the interests and safety of your people. The fighters are there for a specific purpose. They will do nothing without your authorisation. Is this not so, Rauf?"

His face turned red as he looked at Denktash whom he knew was more inclined to militant action. But Kucuk was prepared to give the new Republic a chance to see if it could work before breaking it apart.

"*Taksim*, partition, is I believe, the only solution." Denktash was adamant.

"You may be right, Rauf, but we must see if Makarios is willing to work with the Constitution." Kucuk turned to him with a pleading look.

The meeting went on for several hours, every man wishing to contribute something to the discussion, everyone with questions. Outside in the courtyard, groups formed and there was general agreement that Kucuk was a fine leader who would see that their interests were protected. There was, however, a growing measure of support for the more aggressive attitude of Denktash.

In spite of the Agreements, they knew from the past five years of anti-Turkish violence by the Greeks that peace between the two communities would not be easily achieved. There were too many Greeks still determined to kill Turks. After Denktash returned from the conference organised to draw up a Constitution, Kucuk called a meeting of the most able people in the Turkish community.

"We may have the Agreements but there is still a great deal of work to do." He looked intently at the group. "Rauf?"

Looking serious, Denktash consulted his notes. "The basis of any free State is its Constitution. I have worked closely with the Greek, Turkish and Swiss lawyers to ensure that our rights as co-inhabitants of this island are protected."

"We're still a minority," Mehmet Ali interjected.

Denktash pulled himself up, chest out. "Not under the Agreement and what we have insisted upon for the Constitution."

"How?" came a question. "We have been given the status of partners in a bi-communal state. That means that we are not a minority but equal under the law. With a better than expected number in the Legislature, the army, the police and the public service, we have guarantees."

Mehmet Ali stood up, again unsure if he should be asking so many questions. "But, Rauf Bey, can we trust Makarios and the Greeks to abide by this Constitution?"

"It is recognised in international law and guaranteed by the Treaties of Alliance and Guarantees. It would take an extremely cunning and devious person to deny us our rights."

"Such a man is Makarios," a man cried out to much laughter.

"Thank you for that comment. That is why we must remain vigilant. We must remain armed and on guard." Denktash's powerful words brought forth murmurs of agreement.

Kucuk stood and held up a hand for silence. "Trust us to make sure that our rights are protected. Now, all of you, give some thought to the upcoming election. We need good men, honest men. Men prepared to work hard. Seek out among your people those suitable for the public service. That will be the battleground."

Izmir 1960

Leyla came home to find her aunt poring over a newspaper. Finally, Nafia noticed her.

"Sorry, my sweet. It's the news from Cyprus."

"Not bad news, I hope?" Leyla feared the worst.

"No, no. It's the elections. Makarios, the priest," she spoke disparagingly "he's the President. Kucuk is Vice-President and Rauf Denktash is President of the Turkish Communal Chamber. And guess what?"

"What?"

"Your father is in the legislature. Imagine that."

"Oh, Aunt Nafia. Please write and see if I can go home. *Baba* will need help to run the family business. I know I can help. Please?"

"Just be patient, child. I sense that your father is thinking about you. He gives little hints."

"What does he say?" Her eyes opened wide in anticipation.

"You know it's not easy for a man like your father. He is kind but stubborn. Maybe when he settles into his new position? No-one will say anything about a member of the legislature with an unmarried daughter with a child. I'll even go there next year. Face-to-face is better."

Leyla knelt down and put her head on her aunt's knees. "Tell him I'm sorry. But tell him he has a beautiful grand-daughter who needs him."

Nafia patted her on the head. "I need you too," she said sadly.

"Aunt Nafia!" Leyla let out a long sigh.

"But your place is with your mother and father. I will have to holiday every year in Cyprus." She laughed. "C'mon, cheer up. It will all work out in the end."

Izmir 1961

LEYLA WATCHED as her daughter Gulten walked, unsteadily, across the room, her disfigured arm out from her side for balance. Now that her grandmother, Jale, had died, Gulten had a room of her own. She was a restless child, active, never sleeping like an ordinary child. Leyla had named her after her mother, determined that, unlike her namesake, she would not be condemned to life just as a housekeeper and bedmate for any man. When she began to talk, Gulten had difficulty with the hard "g" of her name and began to refer to herself as Chulteen and finally it became Julie. Although her grandmother's mind had gone somewhere else in her last year, Leyla missed her physical presence. Now there was only one child to care for. Mehmet Ali had not come to Izmir for the funeral. The journey would have taken too long. According to custom, Jale was buried the day after she died. There had been no communication between Leyla and her father since she had left Cyprus, but Aunt Nafia was a willing go-between.

"Your father is very busy these days, a member of the Legislature, the Communal Board, and so many committees that I don't know how he has time to look after the farm." She always made plausible excuses for her brother's inability to reach out to his only child.

"If I could just visit, I'm sure that he would take Julie into his heart. A child is a child, with no sin," Leyla beseeched.

"I know, but he is a man, a proud man, and it is not easy to bend to the winds of change. Oh, he can do that in the world of politics, but a woman? No, it is difficult for him. Just be patient. Soon, we can find someone to look after Gulten and you can begin your training to be a nurse," she said kindly, hoping some work would keep Leyla too busy to think about Cyprus.

"I know, Aunt, but I'm not sure that is what I want." She held out her arms in resignation.

"My child, few people, especially women, get what they want. But there will always be a need for a nurse. And, you know, many countries are looking for nurses. You can go to England, think of it. A sensible country, if a little cold."

"I suppose so," Leyla sighed, thinking that maybe...no, she had put the thought of Alex out of her mind. But he crept back again.

"Don't look so sad, my little angel. There was a time when I wanted a man to be mine. Any man, even a farmer. But I would have been unhappy."

"Why?" Leyla shook her head in wonder.

"I see women all the time, beaten by a jealous husband. Or a brother who thinks that *his* honour has been insulted. Bah, men. They have their rules and only their rules."

"But the world needs love, Aunt," Leyla protested.

"Remember that the world just goes on, even when a love is over. Just be happy that you have a child. His child. It may not seem much today, but don't shed tears for what might have been. You are you and together we will love the child." Nafia's gaze was full of love and understanding.

Looking at the little girl rocking back and forth, Nafia determined to find a suitable woman to come in each day to care for Julie. It would be best if Leyla began work soon, she decided. In a city the size of Izmir there was no shortage of black draped widows, but finding one who lived nearby was not easy. Fortunately, she was able through her contacts at the hospital to find one, recently widowed, a woman with a young son. Her husband had been killed in an accident on the way to work and she needed some income to help with a small pension. Leyla was unhappy to leave Julie each day, but she understood that to be an independent woman she must train so that she could support herself.

Work on the hospital wards was hard, and nurses were the drones of the system. As one of her fellow students commented, "It's a shitty job but someone has to do it." And it was shitty. However, she enjoyed the lectures at the School of Nursing, and despite the fact that many of the other trainees regarded her as an outsider because of Julie, she managed to accept each day, knowing that she would be able to return home to her beloved daughter. The worst times were when she was on night duty. Then she would arrive home tired and after a few hours' sleep Julie would demand all her attention and energy.

One day, Leyla looked closely at her aunt. "Aunt Nafia, I swear that you are looking younger every day. Is there something I don't know?" She remarked in an approving tone of voice.

"It's the child. That's all. Don't go getting any romantic notions. I'm happy to share our lovely baby Julie." She swayed in a little dance movement.

"I think you like it when I work nights." She smiled at her plump little aunt.

"I do," Nafia laughed, "then I can spoil my little Julie. That way she doesn't miss her mother. She's at the best stage of life, eager to play, and learn new things. I think she shows promise of having both your beauty and your brains."

"I hope she grows up with more sense. Anyway, you are good for her, because I'm so tired these days."

"Well, I'm planning a little holiday for us. We'll go down to a nice little place on the Mediterranean. Julie will be old enough to appreciate it. It's called Kalkan. Maybe we'll go next year."

"The Mediterranean. Oh, that sounds so good. Can we swim? I'd love to learn how to swim. Julie would love to splash in the water."

Nafia held up her hands in horror. "You can swim, women do now. But not me, I'm too old to start."

"Well, Julie and I will. In proper swimsuits too," she said triumphantly.

At the beginning, working at the hospital, Leyla had received little pats on her rear and had the occasional brush against her breasts, but she never responded. A cool, stern glance sufficed to discourage any further advances from the young doctors. She mentioned these incidents to her aunt. Nafia said, "Men have this idea that nurses deal with naked bodies all the time so they must know all about sex. Bah, just ignore these advances. Unless you're ready to look at another man?"

"No, not yet. But who knows? Maybe one day my prince will come." She gave a derisory laugh.

A cosmopolitan city, Izmir was a mixture of old and new Turkey. Leyla was obliged to wear a headscarf at the hospital but not on her days off work. She took Julie for a stroll along the beautiful boulevard, and watched with envy the women wearing high-heeled shoes, make-up and the latest fashions from Europe. One day, she thought, that will be me. I will leave Turkey and go to England where women can wear what pleases them. Then she would feel a sense of guilt. Aunt Nafia would miss her and Julie. It would be unfair to desert her after all she had done for them.

"Aunt Nafia, would you mind if one day I went to live in England?" She put down the magazine she was reading.

"Well," Nafia looked up from her book, glasses perched on her nose, "everyone leaves a loved one at some stage. Maybe it's to live somewhere else, or they die."

"Don't say that! Don't even think it!" Leyla looked shocked.

"I'd be sad, but you have your life to live. You may get married and move away, or go back to Ghazientop. Do what makes you happy."

Leyla changed the subject. "Let's not talk of going away, unless you want to tell me about going to this place Kalkan."

Nafia smiled, thinking, it's best not to contemplate life without Leyla and Julie.

Cyprus 1963

SUPPORTERS OF MAKARIOS, mainly ex-*EOKA* leaders, had been given all the plum positions in the new government. The *EOKA* commanders who had been successful in waging a guerilla war were mainly uneducated criminals totally unsuited to running a country. Despite the fact that Turks were to occupy 30 per cent of the civil service positions, this was not implemented. The boundaries for the separate municipalities had still not been fixed years after the birth of the Republic. Obstruction on both sides became the order of the day. Within three years, Cyprus was a virtual arsenal. All it needed was someone to light the fuse. The Minister of the Interior, former high-ranking *EOKA* member Polycarpos Georgjiadis, met with the President.

"Polycarpos," Makarios began, "I can no longer tolerate these restrictions on our authority. Kucuk uses his veto to thwart my major decisions. We have no National Guard thanks to his refusal to allow integration of the force."

"We don't need one. I have enough men and arms to wipe them out. Just say the word."

"Not yet. Not yet. What I'm telling you, in confidence, is that it is time to end this farce of a Constitution. When the time is opportune, I intend to propose amendments to the Constitution so that majority rule will be implemented. We must get rid of these Turks."

"I'll do it, Mr President," Polycarpos boasted.

"No, I mean get them out of any positions in the government where they can oppose the will of the people."

"Mr President," Georgjiadis smiled. "As you know, I have followed your instructions. Our army is ready to act as soon as you give the command. We have formulated a plan. The Akritas Plan. When you announce the changes, the Turks will start to fight, believe me. Then I wipe them out."

"No doubt you are right," Makarios looked thoughtful. "The Turks have convinced the world that *Enosis* will lead to their enslavement. So we must change that opinion and stress that we are struggling for self-determination as granted to India and Sudan, say."

"Then we govern in our own right? The majority? A Greek state?"

"Yes. That is why we must get rid of the Agreements and the Treaty of Alliance. That is our argument. The Treaty of Guarantee must go. That way no force can interfere in our aim to have a plebiscite of all Cypriots. That is the way we shall win."

"No-one will interfere with what we do. It will be too late," Georgjiadis said.

"I will put forward my proposals to change the Constitution. As you say, the Turks will rise up. World opinion at present is very much against the oppression of minorities so we must act quickly."

"That's the plan, my plan, the Akritas Plan." Georgjiadis squared his shoulders.

"If the Turks do not attack, you must provoke them. We must become masters of the situation in a day or so. Then outside intervention will not be possible, probable or even justifiable. It is our right, based on democratic principles to be masters in our own land."

"We all agree. Everyone one of us."

"We will have the right to put down any insurrection by militant minorities. Can we achieve this quickly?" Makarios looked at Georgjiadis for reassurance.

"When you make the announcement of the changes, the Turks will start fighting, believe me. They too are ready. Then we will move in and finish them off in a day or so. Trust me." Georgjiadis said confidently.

The first move was an attack on the right of Turks to have separate Turkish municipalities. The Greek deputies in the legislature refused to extend the existing municipal law. The Turks ignored this by passing a law in their Communal Chamber setting up their own municipalities. Then the Greeks introduced legislation abolishing all municipalities, both Greek and Turkish. The Supreme Constitutional Court, under its neutral President, Professor E. Forsthoff, declared both actions unconstitutional. In a press release, Archbishop Makarios refused to accept such a finding. Forsthoff resigned at this insult.

Izmir 1963

Nafia was seated at her desk, thinking about her joy in presenting Leyla with her diploma of nursing that evening at the university main auditorium. Then they would have their long-planned holiday. Her assistant entered and slapped a newspaper on the table. "Director, you will want to see this."

Dated December 1, 1963, the headline blazoned the news "*Makarios to End Cyprus Agreement*".

The report stated that Archbishop Makarios had declared that the Constitution was unworkable and he had proposed several changes to eliminate impediments to the functioning of government. The right of veto by the President and Vice-President was to be abandoned. The Turkish Vice-President was to be elected by a majority of the House of Representatives, not the Turkish Cypriot community. The Communal Chambers would be abolished and the public service to be staffed in accord with the percentage of Greeks to Turks, down from 70/30 to 82/18.

The article continued, "Dr Kucuk has declared the proposals as completely unacceptable." The page was filled with every detail of the proposed amendments, which Kucuk claimed could only lead to the Turkish Cypriots becoming a minority in a Greek Cypriot state.

Nafia rushed home after work. Leyla was playing with Julie. "That bloody priest is at it again," she burst out, "sorry, Julie, close your ears when Auntie swears."

"Naughty Auntie." The girl returned to playing with her dolls.

"What is in the newspaper now, Aunt?" Leyla asked.

"Well, it says here that Archbishop Makarios gave a speech at Panayia where he was born. He should have been drowned at birth, no, that's not what it says. He said, and listen to this, 'Unless this small Turkish community, forming part of the Turkish race which has been the terrible enemy of Hellenism, is expelled, the duty of the heroes of *EOKA* can never be considered terminated'."

"No!" Leyla exclaimed.

"I ask you, is this not a crazy man?" Nafia waved her arms in the air.

"Father always said that he could not be trusted."

"*Trusted? Trusted?* We should never have agreed to joining with them. They think we should all go home. But Cyprus is our home, just as much as theirs. You know, your father was right when he wrote that things were getting worse. Kucuk is doing his best but the Greeks put obstacles in the way, all the time. They want to get rid of all Turks from any position of authority." She slammed the paper down on the table.

"It's so sad," Leyla groaned, "it all seemed to start off so well. Now what will happen? Will we have to leave, or be killed? What is wrong with people?"

"Religion, and nationalism, that's what. And the leaders are to blame. They want to go down in history. Bah, who cares about who ruled who a thousand years ago? Nobody except politicians and fanatics." Nafia had raised her voice.

"Sorry, baby," she said to Julie who frowned at this noisy interruption.

"It's all right Julie," Leyla soothed her daughter.

"I hear that people are beginning to leave Cyprus. Some in the village have left for England. Can you imagine, England, where there's no sun? Some are even going to Australia, I ask you, a million miles away and full of black people and kangaroos that hop all over the place," Nafia spoke disapprovingly.

"Poor father, he must be very worried. He always hoped that we could live happily together. Before *EOKA* started all this trouble I had some nice Greek friends. Angela was nice. Some didn't like me but, then, there are some Turks I don't like. You can't like everyone, can you?"

"No, my lovely, just as you can't love everyone. But you can learn to love more than one man, so don't be afraid to open up your heart again. Life is too short. You will see, one day. Don't wear your sorrow like a scarf so that no man will approach you."

Cyprus 1963

Three weeks after Makarios' discussion with Georgjiadis, on a cold, windy December day, the offensive began. Georgjiadis had ensured that all Turkish police had been disarmed the previous day. So the Turkish Cypriots had little defence as former *EOKA* members and Georgjiadis's underground army began a major attack on the Turkish quarter of Nicosia. Hundreds were killed, 700 hostages were taken, homes were burned and looted, shops were destroyed and the first refugees appeared.

Makarios sat with his head in his hands. "I did not expect this savagery," he moaned to his brother. "I said to show them we mean business, not slaughter hundreds. It won't look good in the world press."

"What will happen now?"

"We shall soon find out." Makarios pursed his lips.

In the late afternoon, Mehmet Ali sat in the overcrowded coffee shop in Ghazientop, the wood stove providing much needed warmth. Everyone was talking at once. He stood up, and called for silence. This was not easy to achieve as once a Turk began a conversation with a friend, he was reluctant to interrupt it even for a speech by a leader.

"We will achieve nothing if everyone babbles like women," he shouted, bringing silence to the agitated group. "Keep calm and listen to what I say. This has been a long time coming, but we are ready. We knew this would happen one day so we will now take action to protect our bothers and sisters. Do not do anything on your own. It is essential that we act as a unified force under the area commanders. Everyone must obey the advice of Fazil Bey and not return force with force until we are sure that the Greeks intend all-out war."

"But Mehmet Ali Bey, I have heard that already they are attacking all over the island. Will we be next?"

Jet planes from the west, flying low, heading for the capital, drowned the words out. Everyone rushed outside and shouts went up, "They're Turkish fighters, they have come to save us, Allah be praised".

"They're heading for Nicosia," a man called out.

"A bomb or two will sort out the Greeks," another shouted to cheers from the crowd.

The small Turkish contingent allowed under the Agreements, stationed south of Nicosia, moved north to take up strategic positions near the Turkish quarter of Nicosia. As the planes disappeared into a pale blue wintry sky, the men sauntered back inside the coffee shop, slapping each other on the back, their clenched fists raised in victory.

"Silence," Mehmet Ali called out, "a few planes will not stop the Greeks. Before the telephone line stopped working I was informed that many villages have been destroyed, with who knows how many dead. The Greeks are intent on a swift end. We must now protect our people. Ali, Tanju, get your men ready and set up roadblocks."

"Right away, *effendi*," Ali jumped up.

"Close all roads into the town. Huseyin, you and your men get down to the coast. Set up defensive positions, just in case. The coast road may be important. It connects many villages to the north. They will need our help." He sounded desperate.

"We're on our way." Huseyin signalled to several men.

"Kokina will be important, we may need a place to land supplies later. I will go to headquarters in Nicosia. Dr Kucuk will wish to inform all deputies of the situation." Mehmet Ali began to move.

"Be careful," Tanju muttered. "Wait till dark."

"I'm sure the sight of Turkish warplanes will have dampened the enthusiasm of the Greeks for continuing the killings," he reassured his friend.

"What about Andreas and the other Greek families?" Tanju inquired. "Do we send them on their way to Morphou? Or will we keep them here as hostages if we are attacked?"

"Tanju, my son," Mehmet Ali gave him a withering look. "Have they not lived here with us all these years? We are all just human beings under God. If they wish to leave, they may. It is up to them. No harm will come to them if they stay, be sure that this is so."

The main direct road to Nicosia passed through Morphou. A much longer route was through Xeros to the south. Mehmet Ali chose the shorter route as he was anxious to meet with Fazil Kucuk and the Leader of the Communal Chamber, Denktash. He passed defence barricades on each side of the road into Morphou, and was not surprised at the lack of people on the normally busy main street. The eerie feeling as he drove slowly though, penetrated to his bones. He heard gunfire and struggled with the steering wheel as the car's tyres exploded. The end was quick as a hail of bullets smashed through the windscreen and he slumped forward, a bloody sight. No-one came out on to the street as he lay there dead, a silent monument to centuries of hatred. It was several hours before word of his murder reached Nicosia.

The killing of an unarmed important member of the Legislature was a blow to Dr Kucuk. "I never expected this," he groaned. "I had hoped to stop any reprisals by TMT after the killings and destruction in Nicosia. But now?"

"The Greeks have uncorked the bottle. Killing Mehmet Ali ends any chance of peace. Now we'll show them how to fight!" Denktash stormed out of the room.

Georgjiadis' plan to destroy the Turks in a matter of days had ended in failure. In both camps, undisciplined gangs, unaccountable to the central command, went into action and a bloody Christmas holiday period ensued.

Makarios called an emergency meeting of all his senior advisors. "The Akritas plan has failed. The Turks are resisting everywhere and now Turkey is involved. Tomorrow I will announce that we, the Government of Cyprus, no longer recognise the Treaties of Alliance and the Guarantee. We have wide support in the UN for this action. They understand that no sovereign nation can be subjected to outside interference. By abrogating these Treaties, the right of Turkey to interfere in our affairs will be at an end."

Kucuk sent his personal assistant to Ghazientop with his condolences to Gulten and the town. The house was full of weeping women. He learned that the only child, a daughter, was living in Izmir. It was two more days before Leyla learned of the death of her father.

"I must go home," she said in a low, controlled voice to her aunt. "My mother will need me and it is my duty to be with her. Whatever I must face because of Julie, I will face. An unmarried mother with no husband is nothing to the loss of my father and the problems of our people."

Nafia organised the flight to Ankara then Adana where Leyla and Julie took a bus to Mersin and then a boat trip to Famagusta. An exhausted mother and child arrived in Ghazientop two days later. She entered the house, removed her headscarf and, seeing all the weeping, head-covered women, silently promised herself never to wear it again. Her mother immediately began to wail and clutch Leyla to her breast, as she cursed the Greeks for taking her husband and protector. Then, turning, she clutched young Julie and began to weep once more. It was several hours before Leyla was able to empty the house of everyone. Her daughter was fast asleep and she was able to comfort her mother with the promise that she would be staying forever in Ghazientop. Finally, as the last of the light faded, she lay down beside her little girl and fell into a troubled sleep.

Leyla walked in the town the next day, and was surprised to see tents where only open fields had existed. People were standing around in the pale sunshine, shuffling from tent to tent, chatting and sharing a cigarette. News came through of a massacre at Omorphita to the north of the old city of Nicosia. The story was passed on and on until everyone knew of the terrible actions of a man called Nicos Sampson, the murderer who had been released under the general amnesty. The sick, wounded and those whose homes had been destroyed were crowded into the Turkish quarter of the capital. Turks began leaving their isolated villages, seeking safer places. The call went out for doctors and nurses to come to the aid of the unfortunate victims. Leyla decided that it was best that she stay in Ghazientop. Her mother had never been involved in the farm management and Gulten was too hysterical and unwell to make any decisions.

"You are needed here, Leyla *hanim*," Tanju earnestly implored. "People are coming from everywhere. Soon we will have twice as many people as before this stupid business began. Already we have problems with sick people, a lack of proper facilities. We must set up new toilets, it is getting very bad. You must stay here, please. For your father."

"I know, Tanju. I can't believe all this is happening. In Izmir people read about Cyprus but no-one knows how bad it is. Anyway, we must do our best to help these people. We have enough food?"

"Yes, of course, we can easily feed all of them at present but, if more come, who knows? But medicine, for sick children, we have none. I will organise to get some from Nicosia. We can forget Morphou. It's closed to us now." He shrugged his shoulders.

By general consent, Tanju Sayar had been elected *muktar* until the current situation was resolved. It was not a role he sought, but there were so few to choose from. Mehmet Ali had been the most educated man in Ghazientop. Tanju was a good businessman, but relied mainly on native wit to command respect. Leyla made a list of the basic medicines she would need. Armed men escorted the small van to Nicosia where their request was met with little enthusiasm. Everything was in short supply, they were told. Tanju went to the house of the Vice-President, Fazil Kucuk, and was able to meet Rauf Denktash. He scribbled out a note that authorised the hospital to supply his needs.

"Tell the daughter that we will do our best to help her father's people. Say that I will be visiting many towns and villages in the next few weeks. I will pay my respects to Mehmet Ali's widow and his daughter. What is her name?" he asked.

"Leyla, Excellency," stuttered the driver.

"Ah, a lovely name. Travel safely and do not stop for anyone, even police. No-one is to be trusted, understand?" He closed his eyes as if in prayer.

The list of items was supplied, grudgingly, and it was a relieved Leyla who greeted the men on their return to Ghazientop. As winter faded into spring, the situation became worse. Mixed village after mixed village was emptied of its Turkish Cypriot population. The Turkish Cypriots were squeezed into smaller and smaller areas. While it gave them safe havens, it made it easier for the now all-Greek Cypriot Government to control them. The government placed an embargo on the enclaves. All essential supplies including medicines, building materials and even shoelaces were on the banned list.

Makarios was extremely active in gathering support in the United Nations. He had a valuable ally in Secretary General U Thant who was committed to the Non-Alignment Movement. With the help of U Thant, a resolution was drafted and passed by the UN on 4 March 1964. It asked members not to interfere in the internal affairs of Cyprus. To the dismay of Kucuk and Denktash, the UN asked the Government of Cyprus to do everything possible to maintain law and order.

"How can they call Makarios and his *EOKA* thugs the Government of Cyprus?" Denktash protested.

"He has the numbers in the UN," Kucuk replied with a shrug.

"He, Makarios, has asked for a peace-keeping force to be sent here." Denktash swore under his breath.

"He's won, hasn't he? The bastard has won. He planned this knowing that the UN would back him." Kucuk looked defeated.

"He hasn't won yet. We'll fight to the end. We'll go to Turkey and London, tell them they must intervene. There is no government unless it includes *us*." Denktash tried to encourage his leader.

In his study at the Presidential Palace, dressed only in trousers and a short-sleeved shirt, Archbishop Makarios smiled at Clerides as they discussed the news from the United Nations. "Now we are the political masters in our own land, Clafcos. I have drafted a letter to Prime Minister Papandreou in Athens. See what you think. It is, of course, not to be discussed with anyone."

Clerides read the short note out loud.

"Our aim, Mr Premier, is the abolition of the Zurich and London Agreements, so that it may be possible for the Greek Cypriot people, in agreement with the Motherland, to determine in an unfettered way its future. I am a signatory to these Agreements on behalf of the Greeks of Cyprus. In my personal opinion, in the conditions now prevailing, naught else was to be done. But not for a moment did I believe that the Agreements would constitute a permanent settlement of the Cyprus drama, which was the lesser evil at that time. Since then internationally and locally the conditions have changed and I think the time has come for us to undertake to rid ourselves of the Agreements imposed upon us. The unilateral abrogation of the Agreements without the process of law and without agreement of all the signatories will possibly have serious repercussions. But we shall not proceed to any such action without prior agreement with the Government of Greece."

"Well, it certainly puts our decision clearly," Clerides nodded. "The whole business has been a travesty of justice since day one. Besides, who ever heard of a country gaining independence then having part of the country excised as sovereign bases of a foreign country? And what other independent country has permanently stationed military contingents from two other nations, as we have from Greece and Turkey, Of course we have right on our side and the non-aligned countries recognise this right. Russia is with us too, isn't that so?"

Makarios made a gesture of acknowledgement. "The Great Powers, the Americans and the British, think that they and only they know how to use diplomacy. I am not impressed with some of these leaders. Of course Russia will be with us. Already I have an assurance from them. I put our case clearly to them. They will veto any attempt by the Treaty guarantors to deny that we are the legitimate government. Oh, they fear each other so much it is easy to play one against the other."

"You are so right, Beatitude, Mr President. "Clerides hastily added.

"However, U Thant has made it clear to me in our private discussions that he wishes to have no violence against the Turks. The Akritas Plan has failed. Georgjiadis underestimated Denktash and his TMT fighters."

"Costly mistake," Clerides stammered out.

"So, we will blockade them and starve them out. I want Georgjiadis to limit the amount of food supplies getting through to these Turkish areas. Allow only enough of, what you call, calorific value to sustain them. We are not unmindful that they are our fellow human beings, but they are not welcome here." He looked sternly at Clerides.

"The blockades will present a few problems, we lack effective manpower for one."

"Soldiers will be coming from Greece, it is arranged. They will be part of our National Guard. Already, preparations are underway." His look betrayed his smugness.

"There's also the problem of undisciplined irregulars. People like Sampson, they are difficult to control. There are so many, we need strong leadership to keep them in check. Grivas may be the man to do this. He knows how to manage such people."

"The National Guard will be headed by a Greek General but it may well be that we need to recall *General Grivas*." Makarios stressed the word in a derogatory manner. "He is more likely to appeal to the people, he is after all a Greek Cypriot and a hero to many. How they loved him when he made his return to Greece!" He sounded distinctly unenthusiastic.

"Then we are agreed. We keep U Thant on our side by limiting violence but make life so unpleasant that the Turks leave. I understand that many are already planning to emigrate to Britain," Clerides said with enthusiasm.

"Clafcos, we are on the road to victory. We must act like statesmen. The United Nations is now the one to participate in our future. The British have abdicated their role. All they wish is to keep their bases, and the Americans their surveillance devices. It is only a matter of time and we will achieve true self-determination and majority rule. As it should be."

"It will take time for this United Nations Peacekeeping Force, UNICYP, to arrive and assume their duties. Georgjiadis recommends that we attack strategic positions and control vital areas before UNICYP arrives. It will be swift. Shall I advise him to proceed?"

"Of course, we must take advantage of any opportunity to consolidate our territorial gains. The Turkish troops have moved out from their camp in our controlled area and have taken up positions on the Kyrenia pass. We must limit them to only this point of entry by sea. Have Georgjiadis take whatever action he deems necessary. Let's hope this will be over soon." Makarios let out a heavy sigh.

Denktash arrived in Ghazientop just before the UN Resolution was passed. He stood before a packed room at the primary school, while his horrified audience was informed of the disasters that had befallen Turkish Cypriots all over the island.

"We have sustained more than a hundred dead and many more wounded. So far." He let the words sink in. "But for Turkey's threat to invade, all of Nicosia would be under Greek control. Many are dead in Nicosia, Larnaca, Mathlati, Ayos Vasilios and Kyrenia. We have arranged the exchange of hostages. The Greeks we captured were for insurance only. They were not harmed. Communications are poor, the telephone lines are often disrupted. It is my sad duty to tell you that a mass grave has been uncovered near Ayos Vasilios. Twenty-one bodies have been found, some obviously tortured, some with hands tied, all shot. It is a terrible thing. The foreign press has seen this massacre. Soon the world will know of the bestiality of the Greeks."

"Not before time," a voice called out.

Denktash ignored the comment. "Cease-fire lines are in place. The British from their bases are patrolling these lines in Nicosia and Larnaca. It is all as we feared. I am proud that our fighters have resisted everywhere. I will be going to London soon. Makarios has been warned not to abrogate the Treaties that protect us."

"He already has," another man called out.

Denktash squinted as a ray of sunshine came through a window and temporarily blinded him. He held a hand up to shield his eyes in order to see who had spoken. "Now Makarios says he intends to achieve this by appropriate means. Whatever that means! I will attend the conference called by the British and insist that *taksim*, partition, is the only answer on Cyprus. We can never live with these people. We must have our own state. Nothing else will do unless we divide Cyprus between Turkey and Greece. The north should go to Turkey since it is her guarantee of safety from attack from the island. The central committee urges all Turkish Cypriots to move to safe areas."

"Are we safe here?" a bearded man called out.

"You, here at Ghazientop, you will have to take many more refugees from the outlying villages of Greek-controlled towns. It is the only way to prevent their elimination. I am sure that you will rise to the task you must face. These are your fellow Turks. Never forget that. I will send extra fighters to protect your boundaries and your work in the fields and orange groves. This will be a long struggle and we will need every bit of food that you can grow."

Many men rose to ask questions when Denktash sat down. The noise was unbearable. People asked about a brother, a cousin or an uncle. Denktash answered calmly on the understanding that he was not able to confirm news of every individual. "It has been a long day, my friends. My voice is disappearing, with so many meetings. Now you must excuse me. All further information will be sent to you, by telephone or by messenger. Do not be alarmed at bad news. There will be bad news but we must be strong. We will win through, *inshallah*." He held two arms high above his head and, kissing on both cheeks as many as could crowd near, he left the school.

As a show of respect to Mehmet Ali, Denktash agreed to have dinner at the house of Gulten and Leyla Ozkara. At the dinner table were Denktash, Tanju Sayar, Leyla and a young man who was introduced as Hasan Mehmet. Gulten brought in each dish until the table was covered, and then she retired to the kitchen to eat with her granddaughter Julie.

"Hasan here will be in charge of defence," Denktash paused between stuffing his mouth with *kofte*, Turkish bread and various vegetable dishes. A large man, he enjoyed eating. Now that the holy month of Ramadan had passed, he particularly enjoyed eating in the evening. "There is no disrespect to you,

Tanju Bey. You, of course, are *muktar*, but the defence of Ghazientop must be under the control of a trained fighter and Hasan is one of the best. I assure you."

Hasan Mehmet, a young man with closely cropped hair and a tight serious face, nodded his agreement. From time to time he cast his eyes at the woman seated opposite. At twenty-four, he was unmarried but had tasted the pleasure of a woman on more than one occasion at a brothel in Nicosia. It was expensive, drinking champagne that was lemonade until enough was consumed to pay for a night with his hostess. Hardened by his training, his body ached to lie with a woman and this was a woman who smiled at him with deep brown eyes. He knew that she was the daughter of the famous Mehmet Ali, a martyr. And he knew that her family was under the patronage of his commander-in-chief Rauf Denktash.

Leyla, despite her lack of years, did not feel intimidated in the company of men. She had read enough books and seen enough of men's bodies to know that they could not bear pain like women, their bravado was a front to impress. Smiling inwardly, she looked at Hasan then at Denktash. Here was a man, a real man, and a leader, like her father.

"So the situation is this," Denktash stopped eating, "our future security is *taksim*, and we can achieve this by setting up all-Turkish areas, to run our own communities, and eventually the powers that be will see the wisdom of this. With goodwill, we can secure a large part of the north as a Turkish federal state. It's the only way to live together on this small island."

"But what about the farms, all over Cyprus? Will we have to give those up? What will the people do who lose their farms? If they cut the phone, will they also cut the electricity?" Leyla's questions bubbled out like lava from a volcano.

"Yes, Miss Ozkara, there will indeed be many problems. But they will be solved and it is better to be safe in Nicosia or Kyrenia than dead on some isolated farm. Preserving the lives of our people is the first priority."

"*Inshallah*," Tanju muttered.

"The Greeks have failed to get rid of us with a single blow. So we are here and here we will stay until a solution is found." Denktash emphasised his point with a wave of a spoon.

"How will we feed and house the people who are forced to leave their homes and move to these safe areas?" Leyla persisted.

"It's good to see that you understand the difficulties. The Red Crescent is aware of our needs and is well advanced with its preparations to assist when needed. We hope to have control of Kyrenia so it can ship in food and medicines under the protection of the Turkish navy. I understand that you were educated at the Greek Gymnasium and that you trained as a nurse in Izmir?"

"I was educated by my father." Her cheeks coloured as she looked angrily at Denktash. "The rest only added to what he taught me."

Denktash laughed.

Hasan jumped in at once, eager to show that he was an important part of the meeting. "And now we will educate the Greeks. They will learn that we are not easy to destroy. With guns from Turkey, we will protect every town and village and clean out the Greek spies."

"Dead women and children are all dead whether they are Turk or Greek." Leyla sighed and looked at Denktash for approval.

"Hasan is right, we will protect our people. But if we retaliate we will lose face in the international community. And it is they who will decide our future, not the Archbishop." He leaned back and placed his hands on his ample stomach. The next hour passed with questions and plans for the security of Ghazientop, the control of roads, the need for rationing of food and the conservation of water.

Denktash left, followed by his bodyguards, saying that he would go to Ankara before heading to the United Nations in New York. "When I return to see you again soon, I hope to have good news. The Security Council will hear our pleas. We need the Turkish army and the Greeks to act under the Treaty of Guarantee to restore order and the legal Constitution. This is as much our island as it is the Greeks'." He pounded a clenched fist into his hand.

After a stopover in Ankara for consultations with the Prime Minister, Denktash flew on to New York and addressed the members of the Security Council. He stood at a podium and looked at the President of the Security Council.

"Your Excellency, Greek Cypriot insistence on the recognition of the integrity and sovereignty of Cyprus by the Security Council is nothing but a trick. The Republic signed a Treaty of Guarantee. Now they say this is no longer valid. They wish you to recognise them as the legitimate government of all Cyprus. Then they ask you to stop anyone interfering in their plans to rid Cyprus of my people. You will then be responsible for Turkish Cypriots being treated like dogs. The Treaty they signed obliges them to respect the law, the Constitution and to treat their fellow human beings with equality and justice. For three years they have refused to do this. They have taken away our rights by brute force and inhuman acts of violence. An illegal and unconstitutional Greek Cypriot army is being formed with arms of all types being imported to arm twenty or thirty thousand Greeks. They claim that this is necessary in case of the threat of a Turkish invasion. But the real aim is to annihilate the Turkish community when they obtain a free licence from the Security Council. Today, in Cyprus, all human rights have been trampled on by the Greek authorities. The people responsible for this state of affairs are here, claiming that they are the victims of a situation of their making. They invite the world to look on and do nothing because they say that this is an internal matter for Cyprus alone. You cannot allow the Greek Cypriots to conduct genocide against us by supporting a resolution that gives them the power to do so. The Greek Cypriot delegation claims the need for an international peacekeeping force. The Treaty of Guarantee already provides for such a force. Greece, Turkey and Britain are obliged under the Treaty to secure peace in the island and to restore the Constitution. Why continue this debate when more and more Turkish lives are being lost in Cyprus?"

The following day, the Security Council passed Resolution 186 that recognised the Greek Cypriot administration with the authority to act as the government of the Republic of Cyprus. It issued instructions for this government to restore law and order. It was like giving the cat permission to look after the mice. Denktash left the Chamber in tears. He then flew to the capital of Turkey for consultations with the government.

Within a few days, Makarios instructed the Greek Cypriot House of Representatives to pass a law that Denktash was not to be allowed to return to the island. If he tried to return he was to be arrested and face serious charges, including leading a rebellion against the lawful government of the State of Cyprus as recognised by the UN. A week later there was a buzz in the crowded village square of Ghazientop. Everyone pushed in to listen to Tanju.

"What's going on?" Leyla asked the *muktar* when he called at her home.

"It's Denktash. He's been arrested. He landed at Ayios Amvorossi early this morning. He didn't make it to Nicosia."

"What'll happen now?"

"I have Sinet with his ear glued to the Greek Cypriot News. I'll go back there now. As soon as there's news I'll let you know."

Every day the news was different. One day Denktash was to be tried for alleged offences in 1963, the next day Turkey threatened action if he was not released. A day later the United Nations urged Makarios to send Denktash back to Turkey. Clafcos Clerides, his old adversary, visited Denktash in jail.

"Rauf. We're not boys any more. Let's stop all this posturing, shall we?"

"And it's nice to see you too, Clafcos." A sarcastic Denktash offered a handshake.

"Sorry, my friend. I shouldn't forget my manners. But I still stand by what I said. Why not make a statement? Something less provocative than usual? Give the President a way out?"

"What President? That puffed-up little fart of a priest?"

"There you go, you see. You object to him but the world recognises him as President of the Republic."

"There is *no* Republic. He destroyed it and you helped. You signed the Agreements. Then after three years you say that you didn't really want to sign. Talk about the Trojan Horse." Denktash showed his anger with a rude gesture.

"It was a gift though, wasn't it? Letting a minority share the government."

"And you can't get it into your collective heads that we are not a minority but a separate and equal partner in this country of ours." He waved his arms in protest.

Clerides put his hands over his ears and looked down at the seated Denktash. "We've had many battles in court, Rauf, and watched some unfortunate go off to jail. I don't want you to go to jail. Especially a Greek jail. What I'm saying is this. Make a statement that you will not engage in any subversive activities and I'm sure I can persuade the Pre—Makarios to grant you amnesty."

Denktash looked up. "Any other conditions?"

"What if I make a statement to the media saying that you are happy to support the work of the UN negotiator in securing peace on Cyprus? It's a gesture."

"Well. I don't see any benefit for my people if I spend years in jail so I agree. But add nothing more." He jabbed a finger at his adversary.

"Good. I think the Archbishop will take that as a sign of goodwill. I'll advise him to send you back to Turkey. Is that agreeable to you?"

"Can I come back?" he asked hopefully.

"Only through legal channels. If you are granted permission by our government." Clerides looked anxiously at his legal colleague.

"So be it." He acknowledged the compromise with a shrug.

Two days later, the Archbishop granted Denktash an official pardon for alleged crimes against the State in 1963 on condition that he return to Turkey. Addressing a packed media room, Makarios read a statement. "This gesture of conciliation by me on behalf of the people of Cyprus will, I hope, lead to a cessation of violence and a return to the negotiating table. With the valuable assistance of the United Nations, we will solve our difficulties and live together in peace."

As the daughter of the largest landholder and the former *muktar*, Leyla assumed many of his responsibilities. Despite the desperate times, she was not welcome to attend to business at the coffee shop like her father. Mehmet Ali's house became the centre for transactions of a financial nature. Notwithstanding the difficulties, she was determined to continue to care for the future welfare of her mother and her daughter Julie. One day, this madness will end, she thought. Crops must be planted, seed bought, money lent and the harvest sold. Records must be kept for, one day, compensation would have to be paid.

Tanju sat in the coffee shop, complaining. "It's not right, a woman in charge of so many things," he looked around the tables for approval. "The proper place for a woman is in the home."

Hasan agreed but was quietly pleased that he could visit Leyla in her home to discuss matters of security. It was much better, he decided, than sitting in a crowded coffee shop with old men. A woman, especially a rich one, needed protection and he was the right man for the job. With his sten gun slung over his shoulder, and a handgun stuck in his belt, he called on Leyla at any time of the day or evening.

"Your daughter, Gulten, a beautiful child. Pity about her arm. Is your husband not here with you?" He knew the story of her disgrace.

Leyla smiled at his arrogant posture and obvious approach, but was nevertheless aware of his masculinity. She knew that that he had been a minor clerk in the Ministry of Foreign

Affairs office. Now he was a fighter and someone important, at least in his eyes.

"There is no husband, as I'm sure you have been told. Let's not play games, Hasan. We have enough problems without all this circling around. I have a daughter and that is enough for me."

"I don't mind that you have a child but no husband. It's okay with me. I wouldn't object to a woman with a child, especially one as beautiful as you. You see, I am quite modern." He stood up to his full height. He was shorter than Leyla. "The old ways are dying. War changes everything. No?"

"It does, it has, and we must support each other and everyone."

"Then you can count on me for anything you need. Just say the word and I am here." He braced his shoulders as he spoke.

Leyla understood his meaning and graciously did not try to stop his frequent visits to the house. At least he was young and full of energy.

By now there were 50,000 displaced Turkish Cypriots living in increasingly squalid conditions in ghettos throughout the island. Sanitation was a major health problem as summer followed spring. From her training, Leyla understood that proper hygiene was more important than medicines. Prevention was better than trying to cure such things as diarrhoea and infected sores. The port at Kyrenia was closed. The Greek authorities at the port of Famagusta checked all the Red Crescent supplies. What they allowed through were not always the things most needed. As the number of people in Ghazientop grew and grew, the toilet facilities were stretched beyond their capacity.

"Tanju. Organise some men to dig trenches on the edges of the nearest fields. The men can use those as toilets," Leyla issued the instruction.

"What about the women? They can't go there." He sulked at the command.

"Every house must allow the women living in tents to use their toilet."

No houses had Western-style toilets, a typical one being a hole in the floor with two footprints marked out for standing on the right spot. A small tap on the wall or a bucket provided water to wash the anal area. The left hand was used for washing and so the right hand was always used for eating. The bucket of water was used to flush any material down the hole. When an epidemic of diarrhoea occurred, the stench became unbearable. As summer passed into autumn and then winter the living conditions became appalling. The Greek Cypriot administration had no control over the many gangs of irregulars who attacked and looted any Turkish Cypriot village with inadequate defences. More and more left their homes and farms until 200,000 Turks were crowded into only 3 per cent of the island.

"At least the enclaves are under our control and protected by our fighters," Kucuk said to a crowded meeting in Nicosia.

"Yes, but we have vast acres of land lying idle. No-one dares work in the open for fear of passing gangs opening fire with rifles and shotguns," a farmer countered.

"There's nothing we can do," Kucuk shrugged. "Without some real help from the United Nations Peacekeeping Force."

Another man spoke up. "They're useless. We get attacked and they say they can't fire on the Greeks to protect us."

"Why do they carry guns if they're not allowed to use them?" a gnarled little man asked.

"To protect themselves. That's all. Only if they are attacked can they respond with bullets. That's their mandate," a despondent Kucuk replied.

Another year of misery rolled on. Julie had grown into a boisterous young girl. Leyla encouraged her to be inquisitive and outgoing. Everything in Ghazientop was shared, but young Julie was spared much of the harsh conditions thanks to a nice home and a reasonable supply of food. *Anneanne* Gulten had become more and more of a recluse, never venturing outside the house. She continued to cook and clean but her conversations with Leyla and young Julie were concerned only with household matters. Thanks to the intervention of UNICYP, some of the blockades were opened up from time to time, allowing limited travel between the major towns.

"Thank God for the radio." Leyla switched on a small portable battery-operated radio. "Even if they cut the electricity we can still get some news."

"None of it's good," Julie grumbled.

The poverty-stricken ghettos were struggling under the harsh embargo imposed by Makarios despite the fact that the United Nations had requested that improved food and essential supplies be increased. Old tents, home to the British Army before 1960, gave shelter. In winter with no heating oil available, families huddled together soon after dark. Only the radio gave any comfort. Besides the marauding gangs and undisciplined army under Georgjiadis, Turkish Cypriot gangs took advantage of the situation. Abandoned villages were looted and Greek Cypriots who ventured anywhere near Turkish Cypriot strongholds were attacked, beaten and robbed. Hostage-taking became a way of life.

The following spring, mosquitoes flourished in the damp, unsanitary conditions and Leyla became exhausted trying to cope with hundreds of people with festering sores. The heavy rains caused contamination of the soil from the toilet pits. Vegetables were polluted and diarrhoea was endemic. Despite her exhaustion, Leyla decided to make the journey to Nicosia in the hope of obtaining supplies of kaolin and codeine.

Hasan was against the idea and offered to go in her place. "I will go. It's a job for a man," he boasted.

"You know nothing about medicines, Hasan. If there is no codeine or kaolin there may be something else. You won't know what to choose from the stockroom. Just give me a driver and we'll leave as soon as it's dusk. The road is open and anyway, most people will be indoors eating their evening meal. Even *Greeks* have to eat."

"I'll get Kazim. He looks like a Greek. No guns, so if you do get stopped, they won't shoot unarmed civilians. Draw a Red Cross sign and put it on the windscreen. Don't stop for anyone. Understood?" He barked out the order.

"As you say, Sir! "she snapped back, anxious to get organised.

Just on 5pm Kazim arrived at her house with a battered old Mercedes. He smiled, opened the passenger door and Leyla slipped into the torn seat.

"Look after her," Hasan shouted as the car slowly drove off.

A short, slim young man, Kazim sported a moustache in the Greek manner. Hunched forward in the driver's seat, looking far ahead in case of any trouble, he said nothing as they drove slowly towards Morphou, They passed through the town with no sign of a blockade. At Peristerona, the Byzantine church dedicated to the Saints Barnabas and Hillarion stood dark next to the mosque with its single minaret.

"If only we could live side by side with the Greeks like that," Leyla whispered.

"Fuck all Greeks, I say," he muttered.

"Don't say things like that," she admonished him. "Just because a few are bad, we must not condemn them all."

Kazim decided to remain silent for the rest of the journey. He was uncomfortable in the company of this knowledgeable young woman. It was a blow to his manly pride that a woman was undertaking this dangerous journey. A man would have been better. The road narrowed as it approached the little Greek village of Akraki. Suddenly without warning, several oil drums rolled out across the road and Kazim was forced to brake sharply. Before he had time to put his foot on the clutch, the engine stalled. Ten, maybe more, men in uniform rushed out. Later, under questioning, he couldn't remember how many men had emerged from the shadows.

"Get out of the car," a voice commanded.

Leyla wound down the window and called out, "We're on our way to Nicosia to get some medical supplies, please let us through." Her Greek was good, but not good enough.

"Get out of the car, Turkish bitch, and you, too," a man screamed. Kazim stepped out, put his hands high in the air and was felled by a blow from a rifle butt. Leyla's door was wrenched open and several hands pulled her out. A torch was flashed on her face and on the dress she'd borrowed from one of the Greek women in Ghazientop.

"She's a Turk all right," a soldier cried out as he threw her to the ground. Several hands pinned her to the ground as a heavily built soldier pulled up her dress and with one jerk ripped off her cotton panties. The torchlight lit up her exposed lower body, the stretch marks and soft fleshy rolls from childbirth clearly visible. Writhing and bucking, Leyla tried to free herself, but four men held on firmly to each arm and leg.

"Hold her down, this one knows what it's all about. She's had it before. She'll enjoy this," a soldier exulted as he pulled down his khaki trousers. "Pull her legs out, more, more," he cried out as he lowered himself over her squirming body. With a savage thrust he rammed his swollen penis into her. Leyla screamed as the pain shot through to her tortured brain. The soldier pounded in with as much force as he could manage before finally ejaculating with a triumphant cry.

"Who's next with this Turkish whore?" he cried out. There was no need to ask as the next man quickly unzipped his pants and fell upon Leyla like a ton weight. Despite her pain, Leyla was even more sickened as the second man tried to kiss her mouth, his foul breath and bristly moustache only adding to her nausea. Twisting her head from side to side, screaming, moaning and trying to break free, her movements merely stimulated the man to shouts of encouragement from his fellow soldiers. By the time the fifth or sixth man had forced himself on her, Leyla had lost consciousness. When she came to, she was sprawled inside the car, her dress ripped from top to bottom, her breasts exposed. The pain seared through her brain and she reached down to touch her bloody, sore, torn, sticky, vagina. Shuddering with horror at her condition, she turned and fell out of the car door on to the ground. The car lights were still switched on and crawling round, she found Kazim. His head was caved in on one side but he was still alive. The wound was serious and with nothing in the car, Leyla lifted him into the passenger seat as carefully as she could. Barely able to stand the pain, she forced herself to sit in the driver's seat. Starting the engine, she put it into first gear and moved off. Putting it into second gear increased the pain so she left it there and drove slowly the fifteen miles to Nicosia hospital. Pulling together her torn dress with one hand, she entered the hospital, cried out for help and then collapsed.

She woke later to find herself in a clean bed with white sheets. The Matron, a Turkish Cypriot, was called at once.

"Oh, my dear, what a terrible thing they have done to you," she said, arms wide in supplication. "We've cleaned you up, it was best while you were oblivious to anything."

Leyla did not respond.

"Your friend has been attended to and will make a good recovery. He will need to stay in hospital for some time." The Matron nodded sympathetically.

"I want to go home," Leyla murmured, "I am a trained nurse. I'll be better at home. Can you give me some clothes?"

"Of course, my dear. To think that men, beasts, would do this to a young nurse. I am ashamed. The police have been informed. They will wish to speak to you, to find the men responsible. To punish them."

"I don't want the police, there is nothing they can do. It's over. How will it help? Soldiers did this to Kazim and me. No-one will do anything. Just give me some clothes and I'll leave. Someone in the Turkish quarter will take me home."

"Is there anything I can do?" Matron asked in a gentle voice. "Anything?"

"We came to get some medicines, we are desperate for antiseptics, codeine, kaolin. We need everything."

"I'll see what I can do, even if I have to steal it. I'll get you some clothes and whatever I can find or take. Try to have something to eat while I'm away. You must try," she implored.

Lying in bed, eyes closed, Leyla re-lived the terror of the night. Revulsion came up like bile and it took all her strength to drink some water. As soon as Matron returned with clothes and a bag of medicines, the best she could do, she said sorrowfully, Leyla dressed with the Matron's help

"I'll drive you to the Communal Chamber headquarters. Someone there will be able to arrange to take you home. Ghazientop, isn't it?"

Leyla responded with a wan smile, her only thought to get back to Julie and the safety of home. Dr Kucuk was in New York, Denktash in London but the name Ozkara was known to everyone and by late afternoon she was back home in the arms of her weeping mother. While Julie played with her dolls, in the kitchen, Leyla explained briefly what had happened.

"Julie is not to know or hear anything. Maybe when she is older, but not now." She embraced her mother.

"No-one will say a word to her, the shame we will keep to ourselves," Gulten began wringing her hands, unable to understand what was happening to her world.

"Well, it will soon become known to everyone, but not the child. She's too young to know such things. Bastards!" She couldn't stop her anger pouring out.

Hasan demanded to see her.

"Tell him I don't want to see anyone." She looked blankly at her distraught mother.

Hasan burst into the room. Gulten moved to stop him.

"Where is Kazim? What happened? Did you get the medical supplies? Where is the car?" Hasan pumped out questions like a sten gun.

"Yes, I am safe." Leyla interrupted in a sarcastic voice.

He bowed in apology. "Sorry, I mean no offence. I am just so concerned as Kazim is not with you. Did you have trouble? Tell me. Were you stopped by the police?"

"No, not the police. Soldiers, Greek army, I think. It was dark, I can't be sure but they rolled out some drums and we had to stop. One of them hit Kazim with his rifle and then, then, they took me." Her words ended in a whisper.

"Took you? Did they harm you?" He stared at the pale vision propped up by pillows on the divan.

Leyla looked down, ashamed to look at him. "If you call being raped over and over by Greek soldiers *harmed*, then I was *harmed*." She looked up, her face showing no emotion.

"Fucking Greek bastards!" Hasan screamed and stormed out of the house. He raced into the square, and shouted for every man to come out. When the number reached forty or so he raised his arms high above his head for silence.

"Our dead *muktar*'s daughter has been defiled by Greek pigs!" he shouted above the noisy mob. "Now we will have no more Greeks in Ghazientop. Get your shotguns and any weapons, axes, knives, anything. We'll drive out these Greeks who hate us so much they rape innocent women."

"Are you sure?" a voice asked timidly. "Mehmet Ali..." he began.

"Mehmet Ali, praised be his name, said not to harm our Greek neighbours but they are no longer our neighbours. Get back here quickly and we'll drive them out," Hasan screamed. "Hurry!"

The mob went to every house in the Greek streets, kicking in doors and shouting at the people to leave or be killed.

"But what have we done? How can we leave? This is our home," a voice behind a closed door called out.

"Not any more it's not. Get your carts and trucks and take what you can. You will be out of here in two hours. Go and stay with your Greek friends who rape women and treat us like cattle!" Hasan waved his revolver. "You can go without harm, in memory of Mehmet Ali Ozkara. But others will not be so lucky."

By nightfall the Greeks of Ghazientop were strung out along the road to Morphou, a sad caravan of helpless victims, casualties of things they knew nothing of. Arguments broke out in the crowded coffee shop. The Greek houses had been looted and some had taken more than others.

Hasan struggled to bring them back to his plans for the next day. "Stop this squabbling like Armenian thieves," he called out above the noisy din, "tomorrow we will pay a visit to Parsito and show those Greeks that we are not taking this abuse of our women like curs. We will pay them back for every insult."

"But Hasan Bey," a voice interrupted.

"Shut up! They call us barbaric. They are the ones who starve us, who force us to live like animals in filth. Now we will show them that we are men. Men who protect their women and children." He threw out his arm defiantly.

"What will we do? How will we show them?" Tanju asked nervously.

"We'll leave after morning prayers and show these Greek bastards that we are not to be taken lightly. Get off home, sleep and be here at daybreak," Hasan raised his revolver and waved at the crowd to disperse.

Tanju shook his head, bewildered. The next day a hundred men descended on the village of Parsito, eight miles away. Despite Hasan warning them to destroy only property including machinery, several took the opportunity to beat up Greeks they held a grudge against from some long-ago business dispute. Leyla was angry at the raid on Parsito but said nothing, as it would mean listening to the bravado of Hasan. She remained at home, nursing her grief, only rousing herself to play with young Julie who had heard the tears and wailing on her mother's return from Nicosia. But like children everywhere Julie quickly forgot all about it as life went on as usual.

When Leyla finally ventured outdoors, she was aware of the downcast eyes of the women and the resentful look from the men. Damn them, she thought, no more would she put herself at risk for such men who in their hearts held her partly at fault. To these men, a woman should stay at home, bear children and cover her head like a nun.

It was a month before Dr Kucuk returned to Cyprus from Turkey where he'd held talks with the exiled Denktash. On hearing the news about Leyla, he sent two cars, heavily armed, to bring her to Nicosia where he assured her that investigations would be made to find those who had perpetrated that cowardly crime.

"We have many contacts and it should be easy to find which contingent of the Greek Military was in the area at the time of your attack. If they are still on the island, my men will find them and they will pay dearly." His voice was full of anger.

"Dr Kucuk." She closed her eyes and shook her head sorrowfully, "I appreciate your concern, but killing, I mean dealing, with these men will only lead to more reprisals. And then some other woman will suffer the same fate or take to wearing black. Is it worth it?"

"I understand your thoughts, Leyla, but we cannot let such incidents pass."

"Incidents? That's a very political way of describing rape."

"Yes, I'm sorry for that unfortunate word. Of course rape is a very serious offence against a woman. However, I insist. These men, if traced, will be dealt with according to our law. Our women depend on us to avenge such atrocities if we can." His heavy jowls quivered.

"Since the murder of my father, whose killers have never been brought to justice, I depend on no man. Do what you have to do, but it's not going to change what happened. That's something I'll have to live with." A sad-faced Leyla averted her eyes from his look.

"But we need to show them. For your father."

"When this is over, I may move to Turkey or England. Perhaps there I can walk with my daughter without having to endure the looks of pity or disgust from ignorant people." She was unable to disguise her annoyance.

Kucuk looked tired and weary, his deeply pouched eyes

closing as if in pain. "It is such a burden for one so young. God willing we will have our own safe country one day. A place where we can live without fear of molestation from those who hate us. Come and see me any time. Your father was a good man, the welfare of his family is always close to my heart."

Leyla returned to Ghazientop determined to hold her head high in the hope that the looks would one day vanish. Day by day the situation became more intolerable. Four women arrived with two children from the mixed village of Amberlou. Heavily armed Greek Cypriots and soldiers had attacked the village.

"They overpowered us. The men had no chance. They were herded into the barn of Erhan Maz. The Greeks set fire to the barn, it was horrible. Some of the men escaped but the Greeks took them away. Lala here was molested. Pigs! Our husbands were not in the barn, we don't know where they are. The Greeks took them, I think?" The words of hate and despair poured out. Leyla's heart went out to the four women. Like her, there was no man to look after them, to protect them.

"So, you are six," she said, lips pursed, "then we must offer you a place to stay until we can find someone to build you a shelter. You can all share my father's, I mean, my mother's room. She will sleep with Julie and I will sleep here in the sitting room. This is the biggest room but I need it when people come to see me."

"Oh, you are a blessed one, thank you. Everyone knows the name of Ozkara. If you can get some men to help us, we will be grateful," a diminutive young woman, Jema, kissed Leyla on both cheeks. Only seventeen and married for barely a year, she looked in wonder at this tall, elegant woman who commanded so much respect, even from the men.

Leyla spent more time with Jema than the other women. She felt that they had something in common, a brief time with a man then he disappeared. Oh, Alexander, she thought, where are you? In her mind she pictured him married, to an English girl, with children. His wife would be happy in a nice home, taking the children shopping, cooking a meal for when he returned home from work. And then, lying in his arms at night, making love. Stop it, she scolded, what good does it to be thinking of such things? He left and never tried to make contact. If only Father were here. No, she decided, a woman should not need a man to make decisions, that's the old way. One day I will meet a man who respects me as an equal, who loves me not like a mother but with respect for me as a human being. I have no wish to be a prisoner in love but a partner in love. Sighing, she tidied up the room and lay down to re-read one of her favourite books.

The women worked hard, moving as much furniture as possible out of the rooms to make room for the extra bedding. Julie was fascinated by all the activity and was soon bossing around the two children, who stood wide-eyed and silent. Before long they were all playing happily in the garden mixing water and dirt to make little mounds with a stream passing through. Leyla watched from the kitchen window, a grim smile on her face. How lucky they are, she thought, the world is falling apart and they just go on playing.

"How many have we now in the village?" she greeted Tanju when he arrived.

"It must be more than eight thousand now. Double what we had," a despondent Tanju replied. "Some new men have been sent by Headquarters. Zeki Askan is to be in charge of security. Dr Kucuk's orders."

Leyla made a face. "What about Hasan?"

"He's not happy. But Zeki is a former policeman in the Turkish auxiliary. He's been training with the Turkish Army contingent. It's now north of Nicosia, as you know."

"So he's a good man to command the defences?"

"Oh yes. I think even Hasan accepts that. I don't think there will be any trouble. His pride is hurt but it's for the best that Zeki is in charge." He nodded with authority.

"Pride. Is that all men think about? We don't have time for pride. There's so much to do. How many Red Crescent parcels came through yesterday?"

He shrugged his shoulders. "Headquarters sent us twenty boxes. Most of it's useless. The driver said that the Greeks take most of the good stuff, food and tools, out at Famagusta before they release the shipment."

"I can't believe that these so-called Christians behave like this. Why don't we complain to the international Red Cross? They're good people. Can't they help?"

Tanju shook his head. "Nobody cares about us. We don't exist in the eyes of the world. Tourists come to Cyprus but they never see us."

"I'm going to write a letter to a newspaper in England. Maybe they'll send someone to see how we live like farm animals." She accepted a kiss on each cheek before he left.

Sanitary conditions deteriorated even further despite the use of toilet ditches. Leyla was overwhelmed with relief when she began menstruating three weeks after her rape ordeal. If there is a God, she thought, I thank you for sparing me from an even greater shame. The news on the radio was full of fighting in many parts of the island. Those who understood would listen to the Greek radio station. The reports were of life returning to normal, hotels being built at Paphos, Famagusta and Larnaca. Reports of violence were reported as TMT guerillas disrupted communications, robbed travellers and made life difficult in mixed Greek and Turkish villages by preventing normal trade.

"My God," an exasperated Leyla said, "doesn't anyone know how things really are?" No-one answered. They were too busy worrying about survival.

A timid Jema finally looked up at the agitated Leyla. "Even if the United Nations know, what can they do now? They've given power over us to the all-Greek Government in Nicosia."

That night, lying on the divan, Julie asleep on the floor on a pile of rugs, she listened again to the Greek radio station. In a breathless voice, the announcer stated that General Grivas, the glorious leader of the *EOKA* uprising, had returned to Cyprus to take control of the National

Guard. She listened with horror as the voice of Grivas came over the airwaves.

"It is time to disarm all people except the National Guard of the Republic of Cyprus. No exceptions will be made. All civilians will hand in their weapons to the authorities. Anyone found in possession of guns will be shot on sight."

Without approval from Makarios, Grivas launched an all-out offensive against the Turkish villages along the coast about twenty miles southwest of Ghazientop. His plan was to capture the one beachhead where arms from Turkey could safely be landed. All through the night, Leyla and the villagers could hear gunfire, mortar shells and see flares in the night sky. As dawn broke the roar of planes was heard and everyone rushed out of doors to see a dozen Turkish planes fly over Ghazientop, heading west. Within minutes, huge explosions could be heard as people stood in huddles, arms clasped to their chests.

Zeki Askan sent a party of twenty men, including Hasan, by truck to find out the situation. In the late afternoon two men returned on foot to say that Grivas had captured several villages but not the coastal landing area at Kokina.

"His advance was stopped thanks to air attack by the Turkish planes," one man said.

"We saw huge craters and fires caused by napalm bombs. It's impossible to say how many have been killed and injured," added the other.

"What about the injured? Any of ours?" Zeki turned to the first man.

"I don't think so. I'm not sure. I saw trucks taking the worst cases to Nicosia. There're blockades everywhere. Hasan and the others will stay in Kokina until it's safe to return."

"But you managed to get through?" Zeki looked at each man in turn.

"We came through fields and tracks. The others are staying with the truck."

Zeki passed a long night checking on his sentries at regular intervals. Dawn arrived and fires for cooking were lit all over the rough and ready encampment in the adjoining fields. Women busied themselves with heating water and cooking soup. The baker was hard at work making as much bread as he could with the little flour available. Shouts brought Zeki to the western perimeter. Four men were carrying a rough-and-ready stretcher made out of long jackets. Eager hands rushed to help as they brought a bloodied body to the coffee shop.

"Get Leyla Ozkara," someone shouted as the stretcher was lowered to the ground. A white-faced Hasan lay there, his chest a mass of congealing blood.

"What happened?" A tired Zeki took hold of the jacket of one of the men.

"Hasan said that Kokina was okay after the planes bombed shit out of the Greeks. He said we should get back in case we were needed." The exhausted man shook his head. "We were just about back, a mile away no more, when we were ambushed. The truck's useless. Its tyres blown to pieces. We didn't stand a chance."

As Zeki knelt down to check on the wound, Leyla rushed up with her canvas bag of emergency equipment.

"Get back, everyone." She waved them away.

Everyone stepped back. After a quick glance, she told Zeki to put some tables together in the coffee shop. "Get him up on the table and everyone out." She signalled to several men in the shop.

She carefully cut open his wet shirt and removed it as gently as she could. It was obvious that he'd lost a great deal of blood. Her main concern was that it was arterial blood. She slipped her hand behind Hasan's back and discovered that there was no exit wound.

"The bullet must still be inside," she called out to the stunned group outside. She wiped the area with some weak disinfectant and could see where the bullet had entered the front left shoulder just bellow the clavicle. Blood oozed from the wound but as there was no spurting she guessed that it was not arterial blood.

"This is serious," she said to no-one in particular, "we should get him to hospital. Nicosia."

"Don't think so," Zeki said, "after the bombing there'll be roadblocks everywhere. Can't you fix it up, you're a nurse?"

"I'm a nurse, not a surgeon. I can't do it."

"Do what you can while I send out a patrol to see what the Nicosia road is like," Zeki said.

"All right. I'll see what I can do with what I have." She took a deep breath. "Give him something to bite on, a cloth soaked in brandy."

She cleaned a sharp knife with some alcohol, and began to cut away some of the macerated flesh. She decided to enlarge the wound by cutting through the skin and subcutaneous tissue and with difficulty she held the flaps apart. Leyla saw some white fascia and assumed that she was over the pectoral major muscle.

"Get some clean cotton sheets if you can," she called to the small crowd gathered outside. Leyla cut through the fascia and opened up the muscle as best she could. She could see some bone fragments that must have come from the coracoid process of the scapula. She carefully removed the fragments, and snatched a handful of pieces of cotton sheet from a man. She mopped up the blood and found a vein seeping blood. With only some rough cotton thread, she tied off the vein and was able to see more clearly. She probed carefully as Hasan moaned and grunted, and felt the bullet. Without forceps, she was forced to use long scissors. It was a miracle that she was able to grasp it and pull it out.

"I'll need some fine thread and a piece of tubing, hurry," she again turned to the crowd by the door of the coffee shop. In no time a cotton reel and needle arrived and old Ozer, who liked to make his own wine, produced a piece of rubber tubing. Leyla used up the last of the antiseptic, and roughly stitched the wound, leaving the tubing to drain any possible infection.

"That will have to do. I can't do any more." She stood back

and straightened up. She was about to fall down when a chair was placed at her back and she sat down, exhausted and trembling.

Makarios had been alarmed at the response of the Turkish military and immediately went on radio to announce a cease-fire together with an appeal for all Cypriots to stop acts of aggression. All roadblocks would be lifted. Leyla was told the news as she dozed in a chair at Hasan's improvised bed.

"Thank God," she said, "get Hasan to Nicosia Hospital straight away. He needs blood or everything we've done will be a waste."

Zeki looked doubtful. "I still think it's dangerous. I don't trust every Greek to listen to Makarios."

"Just get a van and get him to hospital," she insisted.

The hospital was overflowing with Greek wounded. When a request was made to take in Hasan and give him some blood, his escort was met with a tirade of abuse.

"There's no blood available. Take him away, there's no place here for a Turk," a doctor barked.

The escort was made up of simple men, used to obeying orders from doctors. So they returned to Ghazientop. Leyla was furious and demanded that she return with them to Nicosia.

"Wait till morning." Zeki was not willing to let her go again in the dark.

She sat with Hasan all night, but the loss of blood and possibly some infection due to her lack of asepsis took its toll and, at four in the morning, Hasan Mehmet died. He was only twenty-five years old. Leyla could find no tears. Slowly she walked back home and lay down beside Julie. Sleep came quickly and her daughter, just a child, oblivious to all the horror that was Cyprus, awakened her as another dawn heralded a new day in Ghazientop.

Life became a never-ending cycle of uneasy calm with more savage outbreaks of senseless violence, much of which was directed by Greeks against Greeks and Greeks against

Turks. Long forgotten feuds were re-visited and revenge exacted. The Greek-run government imposed harsh bans on all kinds of essential materials. Then the bans would be lifted and frantic efforts were made to bring in much needed supplies. No sooner had men ventured out into the fields to plant crops than the blockade would return. Nothing was being produced and only the money and foodstuffs smuggled into the island saved the Turks from starvation.

Melbourne, Australia 1964

After Barbara had left for Israel, Doug and Andrea rallied round and organised parties so that Alex would meet new people. He was constantly surprised at how easily the Americans attracted friends. It was something about their easygoing manner, he decided, and the interest that most people had in the richest country in the world. Doug was popular among his colleagues, especially the head of the drama department, Jason McArthur. They shared a love of theatre and what they called "gress". Jason came from a well-known family and supplemented his income by writing for *The Age* newspaper as a theatre critic. One of the perks of this job was an ample supply of free tickets to opening nights of less popular plays.

"Actors can't make a living from regular theatre work. I guess the population's too small," Doug said to Alex.

"Maybe there are too many people wanting to be actors. It was like when I was in the army. There were too many chemists chasing too few postings." He thought about his past experience.

"It's just as well they can pick up some money doing television advertisements," Doug concurred. "Anyway, they all seem to be happy enough. It's a precarious living, though. That's probably why they love to party. Any excuse, opening night, closing night, a good revue. Boy, do they like to celebrate." He laughed. "They sure love to drink and smoke pot."

"I suppose it's a chance to meet other people in the profession, find out what's coming up?" Alex wondered out loud.

"You've just got to come along to the next party. You'll meet some really interesting people."

"I'm not the artistic type." He held up his hands in mock surrender.

"Listen Alex, any extra man is always welcome. Half the guys are homosexuals, so the ladies always welcome a straight guy. You'll have fun and besides, what have you got to lose? Just don't take it too seriously. These guys move faster than you know. Here today, Sydney tomorrow." Doug laughed and punched him gently on the arm. "Relax, buddy."

Alex smiled, a resigned smile. He had yet to tell Doug and Andrea the news. Maurice had hinted on more than one occasion that he was looking to slow down, get out of life.

"The way things are going," Maurice had said, "I can see you as a partner in the business. A junior partner. It's a step in the right direction."

Maurice began to go home from work early, leaving Alex to lock up. He was surprised to find Maurice still at work just after six one evening. A sombre Maurice looked at him as he stood up after locking the heavy floor safe with the day's takings.

"Alex, my boy. You know I like you like family?" He concentrated on a spot on the floor.

"Yeah, I know. You're really something, you know that." Alex dropped into his USA speak.

"But something's come up. I didn't expect it. You see, my cousin, Chaim that calls himself Harry now. Anyway, Harry has a son, Ruben, he's still Ruben. Anyway, he tells me that Ruben has just started study at the Pharmacy College in Royal Parade. He wants him to work here some hours each week. I said okay."

Alex knew what was coming but stood there po-faced.

"Then he says to me, when I retire, maybe Ruben could buy the business, you know?"

Alex's chest felt tight. Show nothing, he told himself. Show nothing. Show nothing. The words were repeated over and over in his head. It kept his emotions under control.

"So you see," Maurice continued, "it's difficult for me, you understand. He's family, real family and, and well, you understand?"

Alex stood, jaw locked tight, tense. He nodded, slowly, eyes uncontrolled, filling, moist. Swallowing hard, a lump in his throat, he evaded Maurice's apologetic look. "Sure, Maurice, it's okay. You have to do what you think best. Look, you lock up all right, I'll see you tomorrow."

He walked quickly to the door, opened it with his key and hurried off down the street. Fuck, fuck, fuck, he said to no-one, words discharged staccato-like. Four and a half years of working for Maurice with the dream that he would become a business owner, or at least part of one. With luck I'd be well on the way to security with enough money to forget the past. The worn-out shoes and the sleeve covered with snot because he had no handkerchief. Now he would have to re-think the future. Shit, he thought, here we go again, another goal almost reached and then bam, sorry, Alex, you don't deserve it. Okay, stop feeling sorry for yourself, you're not yet thirty so look around, there has to be an opening somewhere in this bloody country. The atmosphere at work was gloomy.

From time to time Maurice glanced at Alex working on a prescription, his face solemn, looking every inch the worried Jew. "Alex, I've been thinking," he began hesitatingly, "I have a bit of money invested, shares and debentures, you know. Maybe we could look around for a business for sale. I could put down the deposit and you could pay me back in time? DHA, Drug Houses of Australia, would be the people to check out what's on the market. Anyway, think about it. I know you would like to be your own boss. It's what everyone should aim for."

Still depressed at the turn of events, the seemingly easy way to owning his own business gone, Alex nodded, head down, trying hard to concentrate on the job in hand.

"Why don't you go and see them? Eh? DHA are the biggest buyer and seller of chemist shops. If anyone can get you a business, they can. Get something small that you can build up. You have a way with customers. They like you, what do you think? Want to give it a try?"

"Yeah, well, I'll give it some thought. I could go up there in my lunch break, it's just a block away," he muttered into the workbench, not willing to look at Maurice.

"You don't have to go in your lunch break, I'll be all right here. Go any time. Make an appointment. See, see what's his name, Gerry Allen, he's the man who handles buying and selling. Give him a call now and fix up a time."

"Maybe later," Alex wavered.

"He's often out, in fact, he goes bush, to the country, quite a lot. You know, that's not a bad idea. Most owners in the country can't sell their business, nobody wants to go bush. But, hey, you can get something cheap and then sell after a few years. Come back to the city and get something here with a bigger deposit." He rattled on, keen to boost Alex's spirits.

Alex tried to take all this information in. The thought of leaving Melbourne was not appealing. Shit, the bush, he thought. It was all right to visit, it was a great big country. But outside the state capital it was a cultural desert. Sure, most little towns had tennis courts, a pool, and a pub or two, but they died at 6pm and didn't wake up till the next morning. It was okay for a family man with kids, but not for him, he decided. Decisions, decisions. Why can't I get a bit of luck like other people? If only I had been born to parents with money. Money makes money, that's for sure. But, his brain kept interrupting, what is the alternative? If I don't get started now with something, anything, I'll still be an employee when I'm forty and it'll be too late. Bugger it, I'll go see this Gerry guy.

"Okay, Maurice, I'll take your advice. It's not your fault. I guess it makes me appreciate the value of a close family. Your nephew is lucky. It's handy having someone to give you a leg up. *C'est la guerre, c'est la vie*," he finished with a smile on a grim, wooden face.

He made an appointment with Gerry Allen for the next

Friday. He was still feeling angry at the world, his poor background, Maurice and his Jewish cousin. He went out on Saturday to a party with an acquaintance he'd met at drinks after an Australian Rules football game. The pain of rejection was eased with copious glasses of beer and a few joints. He woke next day to find himself in bed with two girls, obviously twins, side by side, snoring, still asleep. His head was going boom, boom, and his mouth tasted like the inside of a parrot cage. He crept to where his clothes lay scattered on the floor. Taking them, he stumbled out into the lounge room and, with some difficulty managed to get dressed. He wondered if he had driven to the house. The street was lined with cars. All the houses were jammed cheek to jowl. He vaguely recognised that he was in St Kilda. Finding the car, Alex wondered how he had managed to drive it there. Fumbling in his pockets, he was happy to find the keys and easing into the driver's seat, he slowly took off for the drive back to Hawthorn. Crossing every tramline was a jolt to his brain. After a few painkillers to lessen the pain in his head, he drank several glasses of tepid water and crawled under the sheets hoping to still the pressure inside his head. After what seemed like hours he drifted off into a nightmare and woke to find he was soaked with sweat. I have to get out of here. Maybe the country will be good. Away from all this drinking and smoking pot.

A nervous Alex waited to see Gerry Allen.

Gerry Allen soon put him at ease. "So, Alex, you'd like to get into your own business?"

"Yes, but I've not much money." He felt ashamed at the admission.

"Well, that's not a big problem really. We look at a business, see what it's worth and then we guarantee a bank loan to you, or anybody, on the basis that the business can afford the repayments. Okay?" The words were spoken casually.

"What about a deposit?" Alex tried to sound businesslike.

"Obviously that's good, but it's not insurmountable. Especially if you're prepared to go outside the metropolitan area. Some of the sellers are even happy to leave some capital in as a deposit, separate-like. That's an arrangement between you and the seller." Gerry made it all sound easy.

"So, what is there around?"

"Depending on where you'd be happy to go, there's plenty on offer. For example, you don't have to jump at this one, but it's a good little business and it has potential. It's on the coast, the west coast, about 70 miles west. It's a little place called Pointsea. Ever been there?"

"No, never heard of it." Alex hunched despondently into his seat.

"Not to worry. It's more of a holiday town, about twelve hundred people but bound to grow. Great part of the country. Beaches, surf, bush, you name it, it's there." Gerry was enthusiastic. "The old guy, Charlie Anderson, opened the business twenty years ago, and now he wants to quit and move to Queensland. Got a daughter there. But it's not easy to get you young fellows to move out of the city. But Pointsea has most things a young family needs."

"Not married," Alex interjected in a flat voice.

"Well, like I say, there's a school, golf course, library, no cinema, but it's not that far, so it may be what you're looking for. You can get in on no deposit, Charlie will leave five thousand for four years at no interest. It's a pretty good offer. He owns the premises."

"So the lease will be secure?" Alex began to relax.

"Oh, and it has a small flat above it. All up, you'd be in debt for about twenty-five thousand dollars. I calculate that you can improve the business, put in more hours than Charlie and pay it off in ten years. How does that sound?" he looked with raised eyebrows.

Alex sat for a few minutes. "How much would I get out of it?"

"I can give you all the details, Maurice can look at them if you like. I estimate that, opening every weekend, Charlie doesn't now, you should net, after expenses about eight or nine thou. What do you make now?"

"Just over a over five." He was happy at the thought of more money.

"There you are, it's more than you make now and in ten years you'll have a business worth probably double what you'll be paying. Plus you can save on all kinds of things, through the business. But it's not up to me to tell you how to run the show." Gerry winked. "Want to check it out? Arrange a visit? It's up to you. It won't last long on the market."

The thought of going into debt did not appeal to Alex. Thoughts of his mother paying the credit man every Friday night sprang to mind. But Maurice was enthusiastic and told him to take a day off the following week to visit Pointsea and meet Charlie Anderson. The deal was done and three months later, on the first of September he was the owner of a pharmacy in Pointsea with a staff of one.

Alex was nervous about telling Doug and Andrea that he would be leaving Melbourne. "Sorry to leave. I know it's not easy to get someone who'll fit in."

"Oh, Alex," Andrea laughed, "we were wondering how to tell you. Doug has been offered a position at Nebraska University starting October. We've been trying to get the agent to find someone to take over the lease, someone who wants to share. This is cool, now we can all relax, it's worked out real neat."

Alex breathed a sigh of relief.

He opened the shop every day, including weekends, and drove up the turnover. With a bit of luck, he knew that he would pay off his debts in fewer than seven years. The business would be worth more than double what he'd paid. He never tired of counting the takings, banking the money and writing cheques for goods purchased. Each week he took two hundred dollars cash from the takings and sent fifty dollars each month home to his mother. "Get your hair done once a week," he phoned his mother. Everyone soon got to know everyone else in a small town. As the local chemist, in a very short time, he was a respected member of the community.

The one doctor in town, an older man, Adrian Jones, worked only the hours that suited him. He was from the old school. Dr Jones rarely contacted Alex and never invited him to dinner. Locals relied on Alex to keep them supplied with medicines until they could see Dr Jones. It was an easy step to keep fishermen happy in exchange for lobster and snapper while the newsagent next door bartered cigarettes, books and magazines in exchange for perfume for his wife. In winter, when business was quiet, he closed at 1pm on Wednesdays and took his growing cash collection to Colac where he had opened a private bank account under a different name. It was four years before he could afford to pay a locum so that he could enjoy a two-week cruise to Fiji.

Pointsea was famous throughout Australia for its magnificent surf. In summer the population swelled to ten thousand and many well-known Melbourne people came to the coast for January. Although it was his busiest period of the year, Alex always managed to find time for a party on Saturdays. The birth-control pill had brought in a new attitude to sex. Wife-swapping parties had become fashionable. Most middle-management men went back to work in Melbourne after the weekend, leaving a wife and children to lap up the sunshine and surf. A Saturday party sometimes led to a dinner invitation during the week from a wife bored after a day looking after children on the beach. Alex was always happy to respond to any advances. Life became a settled routine of work, money and the occasional chance to bed down an unhappy wife or a recent divorcee looking to escape the past. As the only chemist in town, he knew as much as Dr Jones about the physical and mental problems of most of the residents. He was a good listener with a sympathetic ear, and also he was a confidant to lots of people, mostly women, but he was always careful to offer sexual comfort where there was no possibility of emotional entanglement.

After four years, the town had grown considerably as people had retired and left the big city of Melbourne for a more leisurely life on the coast. Alex now had two girls working for him, Jacqui who'd been with him for years and new, sixteen-year-old, Alicia, who thought it glamorous to work in a pharmacy with cosmetics. He sat in the little storeroom eating a sandwich for lunch, and sighed when Alicia popped her head through the door. "There's a young couple want to speak to the chemist," she hunched her shoulders apologetically.

Alex heaved himself out of the beach chair, hoping that one of these days he would get enough time to eat his lunch without being interrupted.

A tall man of about thirty offered his hand. "Hi, I'm John Stone and this is my wife Vivienne."

"Viv," the slim, attractive blonde added.

"G'day. How can I help?" He shook her by the hand.

"Well, I'm a doctor, and Viv here is a pharmacist. We're looking around for a place to set up a practice for me."

Alex's heart jumped at the words. It was like manna from heaven. A new doctor in town would be good for business. "Great! You've come to the right place. Dr Stone is working less and less and you'll soon build up a good practice in Pointsea. It's really coming on. Are you from Melbourne?"

"Actually I'm from Shepparton, well, outside, my father farms up there. I've been working in Melbourne, and so has Viv. That's where we met, at uni. But we'd like to get away from the big smoke. We're not city people, are we, Viv?" He smiled at his wife. "Viv's from the LaTrobe Valley but we're not keen to go down there."

"We thought that you might be able to tell us a bit about the place. Ask your chemist, right? Of course, we've been here before on the way to Lorne, but that's different. Can it support John? Is there any chance of me getting some work here? Not that I want to set up in opposition or anything," she smiled coyly.

Alex was surprised at the friendliness of this couple. Most

doctors he'd come across tended to be a bit aloof. "I don't know what kind of income you expect to make, but you'd certainly be welcome in town. Doctor Jones wouldn't mind, that's for sure."

"Do you have a suggestion where I might open a surgery?" John glanced out of the shop door. "I couldn't pay much in the way of rent, well, not to start."

Alex ushered them outside. "See that house there, "he pointed to a weatherboard house next to the shopping strip, "that's available. The people are sick of all the traffic. They're getting on a bit and they'd be happy with a decent offer."

John looked at the house and shook his head. "We've only been married a year and I couldn't afford to buy a surgery and a house to live in. We don't fancy living on the premises. Viv wouldn't have much of a life, people calling at every hour just because we're there."

Alex wasn't about to let an opportunity like this slip by so he jumped in, "Look, I have a bit put by. I'll see my accountant. I reckon I could buy the place and pay it off. I'd let you have it at a very reasonable rent. Let's face it, you being here would be good for me. Not that I expect anything. You can tell your patients to go to Colac. That's up to you."

John grinned. "I don't think that's likely but I get your drift."

Alex liked the honesty of the man, so he made a quick decision. "If I buy the place, and spend a bit fixing it up as your consulting rooms, would that help with your decision where to set up practice?"

"Would there be any chance of me doing some locum work for you?" Viv asked.

"Not a problem," he said happily. "I wouldn't mind every Wednesday off, and holidays, that would be great."

Later that day, he phoned his accountant, Andrew Clissold, and gave him the news.

"This must be your lucky day, Alex," Andrew sounded happy.

"I know, it's fantastic, isn't it," Alex agreed.

"Not just the doctor. You know those spec shares you bought a couple of years ago? The one the bank guy told you about?"

"Poseidon? Those?" Alex asked.

"That's the one. They're taking off. Big time."

"I only bought 500. Just to keep him happy." Alex tried to remember what the bank manager had told him. "Oil, was it? What was it again? Forty-six cents each?"

"Nickel! Well, they're over three dollars and going up. I rang Mark, my stockbroker, and he said it was worth a punt so I bought a thousand at three dollars."

"Shit. What do they expect them to go to?" Alex couldn't hide his surprise at the good news.

"At least ten, maybe twenty, they reckon. Do you want any more?"

"Shit no," he stammered, "I have enough on my plate. I'm going to make an offer on the Abbotts' place. I'll borrow the money from the bank and rent it out to the new doctor."

"Well, don't say I didn't warn you. This could be as big as West Central Mining."

"I'll keep what I've got. They only cost a few hundred. I'll see how far they go."

"Fair enough. Let me have the details when you settle up on the house. It's all tax deductible."

"Good on you, mate." Alex hung up and went whistling into the front shop.

In no time it was all settled. Dr and Mrs Stone found a weatherboard cottage to live in. The Abbotts accepted the offer on their house. The bank was happy to lend the money and Poseidon continued to rise. With a new, enthusiastic doctor, the prescription side of the business boomed.

John Stone's grandfather, an Englishman, had migrated to Australia in search of gold. After serving in the Great War in Egypt and the Western Front, he'd been granted a piece of land on the Murray River under the soldier settler scheme. Like many others he had never made a go of it and struggled to make a decent living from the farm. John's father had taken over the farm and with rising prices for milk managed to make a living. John had won a scholarship to Melbourne University to study medicine. He met a young psychology student, Vivienne Fletcher, from a middle-class family that owned a shoe store in Leongatha. Vivienne was a sensible, no-nonsense kind of person. After two years of psychology, she had switched to pharmacy and worked at weekends to gain experience and help out with the cost of sharing a flat with John.

When Poseidon shares reached sixteen dollars, Alex sold half. Seven weeks later they reached one hundred and twenty dollars and he pocketed thirty thousand dollars. Three months later, in December, the shares reached two hundred and eighty dollars. The following year they were worth 50 cents each. Only in Australia, Alex thought. With this windfall and the increase in turnover and profit, Alex took the advice of the only real estate man in town, Josh Brady, and bought three adjacent fibro-cement-sheet cottages on large parcels of land with wonderful views out to the point.

Josh stared out to the craggy point with the surf crashing into shore. "Look, Alex. They don't make any more views like this. Not here, anyway. I guarantee that in ten years these will be worth a small fortune."

"It's beautiful, isn't it?" Alex agreed, seeing the future potential of land with such views. He looked out to sea and thought that one day he might build a house here.

"Let them out to some young surfers. It won't matter if they wreck the houses. It's the land that's valuable. Three or four to a house, they'll pay a decent rent."

Viv came into work for a couple of hours twice a week to learn the layout of the pharmacy and to get to know the customers. As soon as they were settled in their weatherboard cottage with its native bush garden, the Stones entertained Alex to dinner most Saturday nights. He enjoyed the evenings where discussion ranged far and wide. As their friendship grew, Viv began to question him about his background and life.

"You know, Alex," she introduced a serious note into a conversation on surfing, "you have such a lot to offer. I see that with the way you speak to customers. Why is it that you've never married and settled down? That was always your dream as a kid, and a young man, wasn't it?"

"Wow," Alex leaned back in his chair, "how did we get on to this? You're really laying it on the line."

"C'mon, be honest." Viv put her hand over his.

"I just never seemed to have any luck with women. They're either intelligent like you and not really interested in a poor chemist or they're young and good-looking, and great in bed, but that's it. We have nothing in common, you know."

"You see what I mean," Viv cut in, "you put yourself down all the time. If you'd had the chance, financially, that is, you could have done medicine or the law, you have the gift of the gab," she smiled. "There's nothing wrong with being a pharmacist, you know. It's not as if you don't make a good living. Besides your other investments."

"Well, that the way the cookie crumbles," he shrugged his shoulders.

"The way I see it, I hope you don't mind me saying this, I think you're looking for some idealised version of your mother. She doesn't exist, believe me. I think you should take a trip home and maybe realise that?" Viv gave him a quizzical look.

"Maybe you're right. It's been a long time." He sat for a moment, a faraway look in his eyes. "Of course, we write once a week, or did. She's not so good at writing now."

"All I'm trying to say is that you should, maybe, read about what modern women are thinking. Not everyone wants to stay at home and be looked after by *their man.*"

"Okay, okay, I know you mean well. You suggest a few books and I'll read all about the new modern woman. Not that I seem to have met many, stuck in the shop, it's not easy, is it?" He forced a mocking smile.

John frowned at his wife, changed the subject to the latest government policy on health and they finished the evening talking about business and money matters.

The following Monday, Viv dropped off half a dozen books at the shop with the request that Alex read them and think about a trip home to Scotland.

"I can look after things for a couple of months. You can afford it and we need a new fridge, the old one is at death's door." She smiled. "Now, I don't want you to think that these books are about you. They're just some books written in plain English, easy to read. A bit of a mix, but just to get you started, think about what it is you really want out of life. A couple are novels but I think you may relate to them."

After she left to do some shopping, Alex glanced at the book titles. Okay, he thought, these two are pretty small, *The Great Gatsby*, *The Outsider*, no problem. *Games People Play*, that's not big, then there was *I'm OK–You're OK*, and an interesting title, The Art of Loving, nice and thin, but I don't need a book on sex, and a great thick book called *The Second Sex*. Well, that'll keep me busy at nights.

He read the short books first, and enjoyed *The Great Gatsby*. He read *Games People Play* and began to think about the way he'd seen himself and some of the things he'd done.

A letter arrived from America. Usually Doug and Andrea sent a Christmas card from wherever they were living. This time, Doug wrote at length about a new position at Vassar College in a place called Pougkeepsie in upstate New York. It was one of the best known colleges in America, he wrote and he'd been invited to set up a new course in archaeology. The letter ended with the usual plea that Alex visit.

"That's it," he told Viv when she arrived for work on Wednesday. "I'll go home, see Mum, then go on to America, and see Doug and Andrea."

"Good on you." She patted him on the back then gave him an unexpected hug.

Suddenly he felt enthusiastic and began making inquiries

about a round-the-world flight that would fit in with his plans. Winter was busy but still much quieter than the hectic summer season and it would be summer in the northern hemisphere. So he asked Viv if she would cover for him for seven weeks and she readily agreed.

Lynn in the local travel agency organised everything. He caught the bus to Melbourne, then the airport bus to Tullamarine. Flying QANTAS, he sat back and relaxed with a drink as the 747 headed for Singapore, then Rome. A swarthy Italian met him at the airport and drove him to the Hotel Alephi where he was to stay for three nights. After a few hours' sleep, he wandered down to St Peter's Square. After the cool, coastal winds of Pointsea, the heat was too much for Alex and he was glad to spend a few hours inside the Basilica of St Peter. Like every other tourist, he walked around head up, gazing at the overpowering wonder of the great church with its art and history. For a Catholic-educated boy, it was a moving experience that made him feel proud. Then it was on to the Vatican for another round of gazing up at the ceiling of the Sistine Chapel with its Michelangelo masterpiece. On the third day he went on a bus tour of some of the sights of Rome. The afternoon he spent writing postcards and then wandered off to find a place to eat that night. Sitting in his room watching television in a foreign language, he felt lonely with nothing to do and no-one to speak to. At least, they'll speak a language I can understand in Scotland and America, he thought as he curled up in the large bed, light still showing through the drawn blinds.

The next stop was London, and then he spent just over three weeks in Dunkeith. His mother was very pleased to see him, taking him shopping in the town centre where she stopped everyone she knew. She introduced her son from Australia, her son who had done so well, his own business, no less. Big Eck, or Alec as he was now more commonly known, had slowed down considerably. Now over sixty, he was happy to go for a few drinks on a Friday night and then take his wife to one of the new clubs that had opened up thanks to the increasing prosperity in the town. In a strange way Alex felt sorry for the old man. He could have done so much more with his life. Now he was a gatekeeper at the battery factory. After his evening meal he sat in his chair reading a newspaper or book, hardly ever bothering to ask a question about Australia or Alex's success. Alex hired a car, and took his parents on day drives up into the heather-covered hills, parking beside a burn or stream for a picnic lunch. On these occasions, he had his father's full attention and tried to mend some of the bridges that had been destroyed in their turbulent past. His efforts met with no success but he saw sympathy and understanding on his mother's face. Because of her, Alex was pleased he'd come back to Dunkeith. Then the visit was over and he caught a flight to New York.

There was Doug, smiling and waving. He still looked like Doug except that he had lost his hair and was quite a deal heavier. After hugs and explanations that Andrea had stayed home because of the kids, Doug hurried him out to the massive car park and his Jeep.

"Man, it's so good to see you after all these years. Are you married, divorced or still playing the field like always?" Doug had so many questions that Alex was glad when they reached Poughkeepsie.

By now it was after eight but Andrea had kept Joshua and Miriam up to see "Uncle Alex" from Australia. The steamy heat in Poughkeepsie was overpowering. The college owned the house so only the bedrooms had air conditioners, poking out of each window. The large sitting room had two fans but he was glad when Doug showed him to his bedroom where he was able to change into shorts and a T-shirt. Finally, they all sat down together and began to talk. In no time at all he was back in the easy American twang and using words such as cool, neat, unreal, man that was really scary. Doug and Alex did most of the talking while Andrea sat back, listening and watching Alex.

Andrea spoke. "You know, you sound different. The things you're talking about don't sound like the old Alex. What's changed? Found a new love?"

"No, nothing like that. I guess I just have a new slant on life. I'm not getting any younger and maybe, maybe, I'm just a slow learner. To tell you the truth, I have a lady, a great lady, the wife of the local GP. She's looking after the business for me. She's a qualified pharmacist and a bit of a psychologist on the side." He laughed. "Anyway, to cut a long story short, she kind of analysed me and got me to read some books. Pop psychology, I suppose you might call it. Anyway, I finally got it into my head that I was okay. Know what I mean?"

"But you've always been okay, Alex," Andrea gave him a funny look.

"No I haven't. I've been playing a role. You know, 'please like me' kind of thing. I know I'm no good, but please like me. That's been me." He uttered the words with a little difficulty.

"I never knew that." Doug murmured. "Still, we know what you mean, don't we, hon? We had a couple of rocky years, remember, Andy? I guess sometimes we get so bound up in our own life, we don't ask how our partner is doing. Right?"

"So what are your plans?" Andrea asked. "Have you thought of going into therapy? Lots of people do. It can be painful, but sometimes you need to suffer a little to come out the other end a better person. I know that Doug and I found it difficult when we saw a counsellor years ago. We thought that having kids would make things right, but it didn't."

"Yeah," Doug yawned, "Sorry, yeah, Andy's right. I was so wrapped up in my work and myself that I didn't realise Andy was slipping away. We almost came to the stage of splitting up."

"I was kinda scared about the whole idea of leaving Doug, but I was just unhappy. Couldn't see the point of going on like we were for the rest of our lives. Then I read about some courses and before you know it, I'd enrolled for a semester in human relations at Nebraska. I guess that changed my life."

"Best thing that coulda happened." Doug gave a loving glance at his wife.

"Well, maybe you're right. It's something to think about. You know, like Andrea, I sometimes wonder what the hell I'm doing, just drifting along. Okay, I'm making money and I've got a couple of blocks of land to build a house on one day. But there's no-one to share it with, know what I mean?"

Andrea gave him a hug that went on and on. "Alex, honey, you've just taken the first step. You know something's not quite right and you're going to do something about it. Cool."

He slept well that night. The long talk with his friends had left his mind calm, with a kind of peace, and he drifted off into a dreamless sleep. The two weeks flew by. On the final night they had a cookout.

"You know," Alex said in a happy, tired voice, "I'm going to miss all this when I get home."

"Did you ever get back to Cyprus?" Doug asked. "I remember you wanted to. I'd sure like to visit there one day. Lot's of interesting sites on that little island."

"No. I thought about it but it's a long time ago. Probably best just to let those memories stay in the past. Sometimes I hear something on the news and I think about it. But forget it. After a few drinks I'll get maudlin thinking about what might have been."

Andrea changed the subject back to the present. "Honolulu next, isn't it?" She drawled. "You'll soon forget all this when you hit Waikiki beach and all those gorgeous girls,"

With a sinking heart, he took his leave of the family. This had been the best part of the trip so far, he thought. Honolulu was everything he had imagined it would be. Golden sand, nice waves and a beautiful old hotel right on the oceanfront. The Royal Hawaiian, resembling something out of Moorish Spain with its dusty pink stucco walls, was the ideal place to stay. After breakfast and a clean up, he strolled out on to the beach, soaked up the sun and enjoyed a body surf in the even breaking waves. There were lots of pretty girls on the beach but Alex felt like an outsider reduced to just looking. After the dry, dirty green of the Australian bush, the lush greenery was stunning as were the beaches on the north shore. Huge waves crashed in unendingly. A few drinks in the bar followed a lonely dinner at the hotel. With no-one to speak to, he went to bed and watched television. To fill in time on the last day, he went on a tour to Pearl Harbor. The bus was full of Americans except for an older Australian woman. Alex guessed her to be about sixty. She explained that she was a widow. For her age, she was not unattractive, a little wrinkled and down at the mouth, but she'd obviously been good-looking in her younger days.

Elsie Thomson was from Perth in Western Australia. "I'm staying at the Pacific Beach Hotel, it's just a block away from The Royal Hawaiian. Tonight it's their Hawaiian Tropical Night. Why don't you join me for dinner there? It's better than eating alone." Elsie looked wistful.

"Yeh, that sounds like a good idea. You get a bit tired of sitting at a table for one." She's a nice lady, he thought. Anyway, I'd like to hear something about the West.

He found Elsie waiting for him in the bar at the Pacific Beach Hotel. "You're looking special tonight." His admiring glance took in the silky, coloured Hawaiian dress. Hair piled up, Elsie had a bright pink flower over her left ear.

"It means you're available." She looked embarrassed.

"Well, you look lovely." He made a mock bow. "Shall we go in for dinner, m'lady?" he held out his arm.

Alex listened as she spoke about her life. "Jim was a good man. Hard-working and a good father. I'm not sure what happened but the last ten years he became depressed. Lost interest in everything. I mean everything," she lowered her eyes, "Even so, I do miss his company."

"How long since he died?" Alex sensed her loneliness and longing.

"Just over two years. He just made sixty." She hesitated.

"That's young," he sympathised.

"Nice of you to think so. It's been a lovely evening, Alex. Come up and help me empty the mini-fridge. I'm not going to leave a thing behind. You can help me give it a shake. Please?" a flushed Elsie reached out a hand.

The room on the sixth floor was immense. Besides the queen-size bed there was a sofa, easy chairs, table, writing table and a refrigerator. Elsie opened the mini-bar, and asked what he would like to drink.

"Might as well stick to the wine," he said after checking out the contents.

"Right, well, I'm going to have a gin and tonic, mother's ruin." She laughed.

Then Elsie persuaded him to have a whisky. "You Scotsmen like whisky, don't you?" She touched her hair in a flirtatious manner.

"Och aye." He responded with his best Scottish accent.

"The light's too bright." Elsie rose to get them both another refill. In the low light Alex looked at her, smiled and taking his glass, he put it on the table. Elsie bent over and kissed him lightly on the lips. He could taste wine, rum and gin. "Just hold me for a minute."

She put her arms round his neck. He breathed in her perfume. Elsie pushed against him, kissing him with a desperate urgency. Alex felt aroused. She leaned back and pulled him over. The kissing became desperate.

She pulled back, breathing hard. "Come and lie with me. Just for a minute," she begged, taking him by the hand and leading him to the bed.

After some fumbling and moaning from Elsie, she pulled off his tie and unbuttoned his shirt. Alex felt light-headed after the whisky. Standing up quickly, Elsie pulled the zipper at the back of her dress and let it fall to the floor. Without thinking Alex stood up and held her. She unbuckled his belt and after some more fumbling they were both undressed. They lay naked on the bed. Grasping Alex, she quickly moved on top and then rolled over so that he was on top. Elsie was slack and he felt no pressure. Over her flaccid, slim body, with Elsie bucking and grunting out obscenities, he responded until she rolled on to her back, gasping for air.

"Oh, that was beautiful. Thank you, Alex. That was so good. It's been a long time. I feel like a woman again. You don't know what it's like. Oh, it feels so good."

He put the back of his hand to her cheek. "Ah, you're fine, Elsie. Just remember, you can do anything you want. It's up to you. There's plenty of people in the same boat out there. All you have to do is step out and meet them. Anyway, I hope you've been happy tonight. I know I have. You're a very nice lady." He squeezed the flaccid skin of her upper arm.

"What a pity you don't live in Perth," she whispered, "still, I suppose you've no shortage of younger women where you are?"

"Lie still and don't say anything." He didn't want to have a conversation. After what he thought was a reasonable time, he rolled off the bed.

"I'd better get going. Early flight tomorrow." He looked down at the older woman.

"Yes, I suppose so." She heaved a sigh of disappointment. "Thanks for being so good to me. I'll never forget it. And Honolulu."

He leaned over, kissed her on the cheek then walked out of the room. There was a mirror in the elevator and a red, slightly blotched face looked back at him. Now I'm having it off with old women.

Viv hugged him like a long-lost friend. "Alex. It's great to see you back. It took me a while to get used to standing on my feet for a whole day. My back ached for days. It's better now. But I'm looking forward to sitting down and relaxing."

"Everything else all right?"

"Most of the mail has been dealt with. The invoices have all been checked and the monthly accounts paid. There're just a few, personal letters. I didn't open them."

He sat alone in the flat above the shop, and opened the rest of the mail. Charlie Anderson wrote that he wanted to sell the freehold of the shop and flat, was Alex interested? Naturally, he jumped at the chance. Next day he put the transaction in the hands of his solicitor, David Bell.

"Looks like you've struck it rich again. Maybe I should have done pharmacy," David joked.

"Then you wouldn't be playing golf twice a week. Now all I have to do is pay this off and I'll be set for life." He wondered why he wasn't feeling over the moon.

"You might even get married. You need someone to spend all that money you're making," David chuckled. "I'm serious."

"One of these days, one of these days," the words came out with little enthusiasm.

Cyprus 1968

LEYLA MADE A TRIP to Morphou. Demetrio Katos was no longer Mayor. Despite his humiliation at the hands of *EOKA*, he was still engaged in farming and trading with overseas customers. She bowed and pleaded with her father's old friend. "Mr Katos. We are desperate. What little we are able to grow we need to sell. We can't live on oranges and lemons."

"My dear, how I miss your father. A wise and kind man. How did we ever get to this?"

"Mr Katos, we all miss him. But can you help us? Can you buy our fruit and sell it for us?"

"Oh, my dear, you're asking me to put my family at risk. If I help you, the secret police will know and then I will be in danger again."

"You can't believe that's it's right that we should starve?" Leyla's appealing look was heartbreaking.

"Of course not, but that appears to be the policy of the government. I can't stand up against the government. They have police and soldiers everywhere. So many gangs, it's not possible to do business with Turks." He gave a helpless shrug of his shoulders.

"We'll sell our produce for less than it's worth. We need the money to survive." She made a great effort to convince him. "Please, if you're not able to help, is there someone you know? Someone the police don't watch day and night?"

"Now you are frightening me. But out of respect for your father I will see what can be done. There will be some prepared to take the risk. If they can make a good profit!"

"It's impossible for us to move anything. The blockade. But

if we can transport the produce to the Turkish quarter in Nicosia, can we smuggle it across the line to a Greek buyer or Lebanese? The UN Peacekeeping Forces may be able to assist? In letting us bring in some trucks?"

"The Greeks won't let them."

"Probably not but it's worth a try. We're desperate," she begged.

"Let me think about it. I will go to Nicosia and drink some coffee. There may be a way but it will cost you. No-one will take the risk unless the rewards are great."

"My father trusted you as a friend. For his memory I'm sure that you will do what you can. My greetings to your family. Is Georgio still in Cyprus?" she asked politely.

Demetrio Katos gave a cynical laugh. "Georgio went to England. He doesn't want to have anything to do with Cyprus. He says that Greeks and Turks from Cyprus in London are sick of everything here. He's a doctor. Still studying. He wants to be a specialist. A surgeon. He says he wants to save lives not take them."

She smiled at the thought of Georgio living a good life in London thanks to his father's courage in staying in Morphou after his humiliation at the hands of *EOKA*. "Well, I won't take any more of your time. Please do what you can to help us." Leyla shook his hand and left.

Demetrio looked at the young woman, departing, thinking how proud Mehmet Ali would be to have such a daughter who could cope with everything a crazy world had thrown at her.

She arrived back in Ghazientop depressed and fearful about how the swollen population would cope with the approaching winter. She found Gulten being comforted by several women, all in black.

"Is it Julie? Has something happened to Julie?" she looked around, terrified that she would find a dead child. The women sat back and allowed Leyla to hold her mother.

"Tell me it's not Julie?" she whimpered.

"Oh, Leyla, child. It's not Julie, it's my brother Mustafa."

"What's happened? Is he dead?"

"No, the Greeks have taken him. No-one knows where he is." Gulten burst into tears again.

"When did this happen. Today?" She struggled to get a coherent response from her distraught *Anne*.

"No. He's been missing for two weeks. Father phoned to say that Mustafa was on a bus with some other men and two women, young women. They were on their way to the British base. Greek soldiers stopped the bus and that's the last he's heard."

"Maybe they'll be all right. Maybe they've been taken as hostages. Be brave." She tried to reassure her mother but in her heart she knew that too often Turks just disappeared, never to be found. After five days of worry, the phone rang. As usual, Leyla was relieved that the phone line was still operating.

"*Effendi*," she said, hoping that it might be Mr Katos. After some gasping sobs a man's voice began to speak.

"Is that you, Gulten?"

"No, it 's Leyla, Gulten's daughter." Her heart thumped but she tried to stay calm.

"Oh, Leyla," the grief stricken voice tore at her heart. "It's your uncle Mustafa."

"Mustafa, you're safe. Thank God. *Anne* has been so worried. Are you all right?"

"I *am*. But it's been a terrible time."

"What happened? Were you held hostage?"

"They, the Greek soldiers, took us to Papilino jail. I thought they would kill us. We men were put in a cell. The two girls, Emine and Turkan, were in another cell."

"Where are they now? Have they all been released?" she asked hopefully. The voice sobbed once more.

"All night we could hear the girls screaming. They were being raped. Not just once but time after time. We could hear it all," he stammered.

"Oh, Mustafa." Her voice was filled with compassion.

"We could do nothing. Nothing. Just hear the terrible cries." His voice broke again.

She thought of her own ordeal at the hands of Greek soldiers. "Are Emine and Turkan safe now? Are they free?" Leyla could picture them in their shame.

"They kept us for over two weeks. Almost nothing to eat. That's okay. But Emine, she was only seventeen. She hanged herself on the third day after she'd been raped again." Mustafa's voice faded and she waited patiently as he struggled to speak over his sobbing.

"I'll tell Mother that you're safe. I can't tell you how I grieve for Emine. It's a terrible way to end a young life. Please look after Turkan. Be understanding. Her shame is not her doing. Can you hear me?"

"Yes," the tortured voice came through and the phone connection ended.

She sat for a moment. How much should I say, she wondered. If I tell the whole story it will only put fear into the women.

"*Anne*," she looked at her watching mother, "Mustafa is safe, they let him go."

Gulten burst into tears as she clutched her daughter's hands.

The following week a noisy crowd was gathered in the square as Leyla was on her way to see what was available in the shops.

"What's going on, Tanju?"

"Rauf Denktash is back in Cyprus." An exultant Tanju punched the air with his fist.

"Well," the word came out in a long breath. "So maybe we will get something done. Surely he's bringing some news from Turkey?"

"That's what I think," he agreed. "It's been what? Four years since Makarios banned him from Cyprus?"

"Perhaps something big is going to happen?"

"He wouldn't take the risk otherwise. It'll be something big. I'm sure," Tanju enthused.

"Are the United Nations troops covering the road to Nicosia today? We should go and see what Mr Denktash has to say."

"The road is open. At the moment. But what if it's closed after we reach Nicosia?" He frowned, always she wants to be involved, he thought.

"That's a chance we'll have to take. We can't go on here much longer. We're only a small place. The big towns can cope but we can't."

"I'll go and phone Nicosia, see what the story is. All right?"

"Fine, Tanju Bey. I'll let *Anne* know that I may have to go to Nicosia. She'll worry anyway but everyone worries every day now."

Gulten held Leyla's two hands, afraid to let go. She asked why some of the men couldn't go without her. "Because I am my father's daughter. Keep Julie with you. I'll see what Tanju has to say. We'll see if we'll go."

"We can't get through. Denktash will be making a statement. We'll wait." Tanju didn't sound entirely disappointed.

George Grivas had accepted the appointment as Supreme Commander of the Greek and Greek Cypriot Armed Forces. With over 20,000 troops under his command he was impatient with President Makarios and the slow progress towards *Enosis*. He decided to show the Turks that it was finally time they left Cyprus. With tanks, artillery and a thousand armed infantry, the Turkish village of Kophinou was bombarded. By day's end, thirty Turks lay dead including six women who had been doused with petrol and set alight. Hundreds of wounded were scattered in the burned-out dwellings.

Leyla learned the news of the latest disaster from the Turkish Cypriot radio. She hurried down to the coffee shop and saw Tanju sitting outside, head in hands hunched over an empty coffee cup.

"Tanju Bey?"

A weary face looked up. Poor Tanju, she thought, with all our troubles he just can't cope.

"Leyla. The bad news just keeps coming."

"I know, but we have to keep going. What's the situation with the Red Crescent food supplies?" She knew that it was important to attend to ordinary matters.

"Nothing. They are still at Famagusta dock. For checking."

"For what? Do they seriously think the Red Crescent will be sending us guns?" an exasperated Leyla cried out.

"No, of course not. It's just another way to show that they control us."

"Well we only have enough food for one or maybe two more days. We need more medical supplies. More babies are being born every day. We need antiseptics, sutures, and needles. I can't help without some new supplies."

"I don't know what to do, Leyla *hanim*. Perhaps you can contact our people in Famagusta?" The lights in the coffee shop went out.

"That's it," Leyla's hand flew to her mouth, "the bastards have cut off the electricity. Now we're totally cut off again."

"I don't know how much longer we can go on like this. My wife says we should leave. Go to England. Or Australia. She has a cousin there."

"No, no, Tanju Bey. If you go, the people will lose heart. Don't even think it or talk about it. If they hear you say such things everyone will start to think the same."

"But it's true. I'm beginning to think so too." He bent over, rocking from side to side.

"Then the Greeks will win. Is that what you want? Is that what the past five years have been for?" She couldn't keep the scorn out of her voice.

"I don't have the strength of your father, Leyla *hanim*. A hundred villages have been destroyed all over the island. Mass graves are being found. Slowly but surely they are squeezing the life out of us. Better to be alive in England than dead in my burned-out house."

She looked at him with sympathy knowing that he was right. At a time like this, Ghazientop needed a Mehmet Ali.

"Tanju Bey. Remember Kokina? It was nearly destroyed. But it's still there. The people have survived. The dead cannot be forgotten by running away."

"Now I am ashamed. To think a young woman has to make me face up to my duty. I will tell my wife that we are not going anywhere. This is our home and we will stay here and die if we have to."

The lights came back on. "Ah, the power is back. I'll see if I can get through to Famagusta." He scurried to the phone. She followed.

"Leyla?" a woman's voice came from the doorway. "Come quickly. Nur is having trouble. The baby is not coming. You will need to do something."

Leyla put her hands on top of her head. "I'll come." Turning to Tanju she threw up her hands. "I have nothing left. No materials. It's now in Allah's hands."

She worked feverishly to help Nur with her first child, she was dismayed to find it was a complete breech presentation. With no chance of performing a caesarean, Leyla worked to bring out the baby. Unfortunately, the head refused to come through. After a few minutes of struggle she brought out the head but the baby was dead. She knew that the spinal cord had been too damaged in the attempt to twist the body to release the head.

"Another disaster that could have been averted. Why do these people treat us so?" No-one answered. Only weeping filled the air.

Cyprus 1970

THE GREEK military Junta deposed the elected government of Papandreou. A victory in Cyprus would boost their popularity in a Greece that was bleeding a hundred thousand emigrants a year since 1963. The Junta saw Makarios as an obstacle to the final solution of ridding Cyprus of the Turks. They gave support to a new National Front whose sole objective was renewed violence to achieve *Enosis*.

Archbishop Makarios, President of the Republic of Cyprus, hitched up his cassock to climb into a helicopter. He was due to attend a service at Makheras Monastery. It was a memorial service for *EOKA*.

"What the hell!" the pilot, Constantine, cried out as gunfire came from the roof of a nearby school.

Makarios ducked as he saw Constantine slump forward, blood spreading over his shirt. More gunshots rang out as several people ran towards the helicopter.

"Get Constantine out." Makarios spoke in a calm voice. He followed them back to a small shed where his Mercedes was still standing. "Put him in the back seat, Andreas, and then head straight for the hospital."

With horn blaring, Andreas drove to the hospital in ten minutes. As soon as Constantine was safely inside, Makarios returned to his car. "Andreas, drive to Makheras. As fast as you can but with care."

He spoke at the *EOKA* memorial service calmly, telling the packed congregation, "*Either Cyprus will be returned to Mother Greece or Cyprus will become a holocaust.*"

His words were given rapturous applause by the

predominantly *EOKA* congregation. The report of his words in the *Cyprus Daily* next day proved less popular with the masses who were not keen to be part of any holocaust.

After reading the newspaper, Makarios called for the police chief and his senior supporters. "I want those responsible for the assassination attempt apprehended and brought to justice. Although I must say that I see a hand stretching from far-off Athens seeking to end my existence here on Earth."

Two days later, the former Minister of the Interior, Polycarpos Georgjiadis, was stopped from boarding a flight to Beirut. Makarios had sacked him the previous year. His private army and his influence had become a threat to the President's power. A week later the bullet-riddled body of the once high-ranking Georgjiadis, creator of the Akritas Plan, was found in a field five kilometres east of Nicosia. The unravelling of Greek unity on Cyprus was under way.

At the insistence of Makarios, Grivas lost command of the armed forces. He then formed *EOKA* B, a follow-up to *EOKA*. Its aims were the same, *Enosis* through violence. Now it was Greek against Greek.

Once again Grivas became a guerrilla leader. At a meeting in Nicosia he outlined his plans. "The Greeks in Athens are in disarray. Makarios has lost control of large sections of his community. We, *EOKA* B, Sampson's mob and the military Junta are all against him."

"What about the communists, AKEL?"

"Russia has made sure that they support him. With Makarios in power they know that NATO will be disadvantaged. The man is cunning. He plays one side off against the other." Grivas snarled, his face twisted with loathing.

"If he falls, will it be better or worse for us?"

"It can hardly be worse. Besides, we have enough arms to repel any serious attempt to dislodge us from our safe enclaves." Grivas looked grim. "Short of Greece declaring all-out war. And that won't happen. I can assure all of you of that.

Turkey is at this moment preparing for such an eventuality."

"That will be a disaster for us."

"We'll keep up the pressure on the priest. This land will be part of Greece or I will die in the attempt." Grivas stubbed out his cigarette and looked around at his men.

"Even the Turks won't stop you, Dighenis," a bold voice answered.

Australia 1970

Alex had never forgotten Cyprus. Occasionally as he slept he dreamt of the moment he had pulled the trigger and shot the young Greek Cypriot. Without a photograph, the memory of Leyla's face faded as the years passed. One night after locking up, he sat watching the ABC seven o'clock News on television. And there on the screen was a picture of Archbishop Makarios. In rapt attention, he listened to the newsreader: "The President of Cyprus, Archbishop Makarios has survived an assassination attempt on his life. The President was on board a helicopter about to leave the capital Nicosia when shots were fired from the roof of a nearby school. Reports say the pilot was seriously injured. It is understood that the President drove the pilot to Nicosia hospital before continuing by car to Methera Monastery where he conducted a memorial service for *EOKA* heroes. No-one has claimed responsibility for the attack but the former Minister of the Interior, Polycarpos Georgjiadis, has been detained at Nicosia Airport pending inquiries. Further reports in our late bulletin at 9.30."

Old Makarios was still at it. The bastard should have been shot long ago. I wonder what happened to old Mehmet Ali? Probably still there. One of these days I must go back and look him up. I'd love to see the place again. I could visit Leyla's grave. Then the night bell rang. He struggled into his shoes and went downstairs to see who needed something urgent at this late hour. The later news was much the same and next day Alex was so busy that it was several days before he thought to check on the situation. It was no longer news.

Cyprus 1972

"RAUF BEY," a young fighter by the name of Hakki spoke up. "Makarios has lost the support of more than the fanatics. He's now being opposed by the most respected Greeks in Cyprus."

"Correct. Now, they have formed a new committee to work towards *Enosis*. They support Grivas. God, that man should die and let sanity prevail."

"Should we go on the offensive?"

"No. We will let them kill each other. There are so many different groups that they are fully occupied fighting each other. Respond if you are attacked. Otherwise, we keep our ammunition ready for the real fight as it won't be far away."

"How soon will that be?"

"Already, there have been several unsuccessful attempts to ambush and kill Makarios. One may succeed. He is the only unifying force among the Greeks."

"Is it true that Makarios is importing guns from Czechoslovakia?"

"That is true, although he says it's the Greek Government. How the international aid agencies allow him to spend the money like that I can't understand." A mixture of disbelief and disgust crossed his face.

"Because the Americans are behind him," a young man interjected.

"The Americans are behind every disaster in the world. Not just Greece and Cyprus," a scornful voice called out. "Their fear of communism is stupid. Now they are supporting the new military regime in Greece." Denktash shook his head in wonder at the foolishness of the USA."

What do you hear from Clerides at the never-ending discussions?"

"He's a worried man. They would like to get rid of Grivas. He's making them uncomfortable. But they're afraid to lock him up. Too many Greeks still think he's a hero. A jailed hero becomes a martyr."

"Is it possible that we can make life easier for Clerides? Can *we* take out Grivas?"

"Don't even think that. Besides I believe that he is sick, very sick. Let nature take him."

"But we owe it to all those he's had killed. To be given that task would be an honour." The young man made a shooting gesture with his finger.

Denktash waved the man down. "Forget it. I will be going to Turkey next week. Another change there. I hope to have more news then. In the meantime, keep up the training. After two or three years in the Security Forces we must have some excellent leaders by now."

"If the Greeks want a fight we'll be better prepared this time. We may be trapped in our enclaves but the bastards can't knock us all out. We'll show them how Turks fight."

Denktash smiled. "You are right, my son, *this* time we will show them."

Julie was at the age when a child, especially a girl with no father, begins to question everything. The Ghazientop school functioned as best it could but, with shortages of everything from pencils and papers to new books, the teachers worked under great difficulty. Leyla's mother was a tower of strength. With the stoicism common to Turkish nature, she did the best she could given the restricted food situation. She was always there with a meal and a comforting bosom for Julie when she was hungry, tired or upset at her mother. With her father gone, Leyla turned to her mother and found that the silence she had maintained when Mehmet Ali was alive was not due to a lack of intelligence, knowledge or a sense of humour.

"*Anne*, I've been thinking about Julie and the future. There's nothing for me to do here now. There's a doctor and two nurses now. I think about England sometimes but so many are going that I feel I must stay in Cyprus." Gulten was distressed.

Leyla began again. "I understand that the school in Nicosia is doing well and maybe I should send Julie there. She is getting bored here and quarrelsome. I think a new school with more challenges would be good for her. Mr Denktash has often said that he could find work for me if I wanted to, in Nicosia. Would you like to come with us?" she asked in a caring voice.

"Ah, Leyla, it's not easy for you, a woman. But I don't think I could leave my home, my kitchen, my oven, and the garden your father made. You can go, but I'll stay here. Nicosia is not so far. I can have another woman and a child share the house. It's only right to help those who have less." A resigned smile disappeared quickly.

She gave her mother a kiss on both cheeks and a hug. "*Anne*, you are so strong. You just accept things so well."

"It's God's will. We do what we can and hope that something good will happen. One day."

"Well, I *have* to do something. I have to make a decision about Julie's future, *Baba* would wish me to do that."

"I agree, your father was a wise man, always looking to the future. Will you work in a shop or something in Nicosia?"

Leyla laughed and hugged her mother again. "Of course not. Mr Denktash said that he would find work for me in his office, translating, reading news reports. There is so much to do, he said, and not enough of the right people to do it."

"Oh, that's good then. You will be like your father, helping the people. Maybe there are some possibilities that you will meet a husband?" Gulten looked shyly at her daughter.

"That's not on my mind, but it would be nice to meet different people. Even for me, Ghazientop is a little boring. All we ever talk about is food and how to fit in more people. The years just go by. I'm now over thirty, there has to be something more than this life." She let her feelings show.

"Have you talked to Julie?" Gulten inclined her head.

"No, it's not her decision and even if she knows it's the right thing to do, she will say that she doesn't want to leave you, her *Anneanne*, and friends. She will do as I say. I can't have any argument." She stamped her foot.

Leyla travelled to Nicosia in a truck full of oranges and vegetables to be sold for less than they were worth to a Greek wholesaler. Denktash, relishing his position as the new leader of the Turkish Cypriots, controlled the allocation of posts in his administration, that was funded by the Turkish Government. He was pleased to have a bright, lovely young woman on his staff. Obtaining a small apartment for them was no problem for him and he assured her that Julie would be enrolled at the Turkish High School as soon as they had moved to Nicosia. Leyla had always liked Denktash's ability to act with authority and knew that she would have an unfailing mentor in this man. The work was not difficult and soon she was given more and more responsibility. She was flattered the first time Denktash requested that she accompany his small delegation to Ankara. Gulten was happy to stay with Julie in the apartment while Leyla flew with Denktash, Fatih Ozgun and two others to Ankara for discussions with Nihat Erim, the new Prime Minister.

On the flight, she sat next to Denktash. He leant over and patted her knee. "Every time we think that Turkey is settled and fully supporting us with funds, something happens. As you know, the military coup has seen the end of Demirel and now we have to negotiate once gain, this time with Nihat Erim."

"But surely they will continue with the same policies towards Cyprus?"

"I would like to think so, but in politics one never knows. The military is never far away from government. They have their own agenda. It may be that we are not on that agenda. To them we may be an embarrassment, better off left to fend for ourselves. I can never understand the military mind." He glanced at her with an affectionate look, and patted her knee again.

As he approached fifty, Denktash was an imposing figure. Leyla gave him a serious look to indicate that she preferred not to be touched like an innocent young girl.

The meetings in Ankara were a great success. With all the internal problems facing the new government it would have been political suicide to abandon the Turks of Cyprus. Leyla enjoyed the luxury of the hotel in Ataturk Cadessi, the beautiful meals and the attention she received from a number of young graduates employed in the public service. It was, she realised, a long time since she'd been made to feel like a desirable woman.

Julie settled in well at school, relishing the challenge of competing with students who were slightly more advanced in their education. She missed her *Anneanne* who always cooked better meals than her mother. Leyla was forced to work late when cables and faxes came through requiring translation, and had to cook simple, easy-to-prepare meals. Late-evening discussions with various administration heads, many of whom had come to rely on her opinion, meant she was usually still at her office at 8pm. But there was no shortage of women ready to have Julie at their home until Leyla collected her after the evening meal or even later. Most Turkish Cypriots, particularly in the overcrowded Turkish quarter of Nicosia, led a bleak existence. But the inner coterie of the administration lived and ate well. Trips to outlying areas were common. Always the accommodation was good and the food the best available in the town or village. A thriving black market flourished and those with money faced relatively little hardship. Leyla's circle of friends had grown in the various departments. They regularly dined out at restaurants and although she felt guilty at her good fortune, she accepted invitations to dinner with people who could afford such luxuries.

By the time she was fourteen, Julie had taken to calling her mother Leyla. Once again, she raised the question of her father.

"It's a long time since you asked me that," Leyla look hard at her adolescent child, "why are you interested now? I told you, there is no father, just us two."

Julie was determined to keep asking questions. "We're doing reproduction at school so there must be a father. No?"

"Yes, of course. He was a soldier," she said blandly.

"So you had a boyfriend, a soldier, and you became pregnant?" Julie persisted.

"Yes, it happened just one time and that's how you came to be." Leyla tried to keep the explanation simple.

Julie kept on. "But how is it that he never knew?"

"It was a long time ago, just as bad as now. Your father was doing some work for the British army, and your grandfather helped. His name was Alexander, and he often came to our home. And, well, *Baba*, my father, seemed to like him and there was a long time when there was no fighting. We used to go and see lots of places." She shrugged.

"But did grandfather let him touch you?" Julie asked the question with a look of surprise and horror.

"Well, it wasn't quite like that. My father wanted to help the British and Alexander was part of them. *Baba* thought that we should be hospitable as they were our hope for the future." Leyla hoped the questioning would end.

"But how could it happen?" She tried to picture her mother in bed with her father.

For a moment, Leyla was lost for words. She understood the difficulty her daughter, felt, just emerging as a young woman, becoming aware of her sexuality and the attraction of boys.

"Oh, Julie, do you expect me to tell you? These things happen sometimes when a girl is not careful. Things were much different then. You study all about these things at school now. Not everything, but reproduction, well, it was only when you came along that I learned so much."

"How old were you?" a wide-eyed Julie gazed at her mother.

"I was young, not much older than you. One day we went too far and that was it. So you see, it is important that you remain innocent until you meet the man you are to marry." Her voice was tinged with a little sadness. She knew that the world was a far, far different place to when she had been a young girl of thirteen.

"And you never saw him again from that day when, when, I was conceived?" Julie's eyes opened wide again.

"Oh yes, we saw each other, but not for long. That was when I was shot. You've seen the scars. The army took him away. Then my father sent me away, to Aunt Nafia, and that was it. I never heard and we never tried to find out what happened. He didn't know about you so maybe he just forgot about me and married an English girl." She suddenly felt a cold shiver.

"Bastard!" Julie spat out.

"No, my little one, you mustn't say that," Leyla frowned at her outburst, "how can we know anything? It was a bad time, just before the end of the *EOKA* war too. I sometimes think about him, you know. I wonder where he is, what he's doing, whether he has other children? All useless, of course. We must just forget all about it and go on with life." She wished that Julie would tire of the whole thing. Her head began to ache.

"Well, one day I am going to find him. I'll let him see his daughter that he doesn't care about." Julie stamped her foot and waved her little hand.

"Maybe one day you will, but until then you must work hard at school. Besides, Mr Denktash says there are disturbing signs coming out of Athens. Who knows if we will ever be able to do the things we want? In the meantime, we must look after each other. Will you do that for me?" She put her arm round Julie and kissed the top of her head.

"You're the best mother in the world. Everyone says that," Julie mumbled into her mother's bosom.

Leyla was glad when she went off to the kitchen to find something to eat. She sat there a long time. I'm over thirty now and where am I going? In a few years Julie will be thinking of going to university. That means Turkey or England. Then what? Apart from one man, the rape was something else, I've never known another man. Never been held and loved. Ah, she sighed, if only *Baba* was still alive he would have made the decision for me. Maybe it's time for me to think about myself.

Denktash held regular meetings with members of UNICYP, the United Nations Peacekeeping Force. Leyla had never attended one of their meetings. This time he asked if she would like to assist that afternoon. "You may have to deal with these people in the future. It's time you stepped up. We need to have women in our administration. I think you're ready."

"You mean a position of authority? Like public relations, maybe?" Her face lit up.

"Why not? You can speak Turkish, Greek and English. These are all needed for a responsible position." He gave her an encouraging look.

"Well, I must say that I've been thinking about the future," a pensive Leyla replied.

"Good. Then we will meet with the UNICYP people at their headquarters later this afternoon. Listen, learn and be open to suggestions."

"How long has UNICYP been operating here?" She wasn't sure.

"Since 1964. Not that they've been much of a peace force. They haven't exactly been a deterrent on the actions of the Greek militia or the Cyprus National Guard."

"Why is that?" She needed to know as much as possible before the meeting.

"Because they operate with the approval of the only government recognised by the UN, the Greek one." His frustration was obvious.

"In other words, we exist only as a rebellious minority?" She stared at him.

"That's how the Greeks portray us. They control the flow of information. We have to get better at it."

After making the introductions, Denktash began by attacking the lack of cooperation of UNICYP forces with the Turkish communities trapped in the scattered enclaves. "General Johansen, our main concern is of course the lack of protection being given to Turkish villages which are under constant attack by Greek militia."

"Excellency, as you know, I have only been here two months. It is regrettable that UNICYP forces are rotated every few months. This means that we work on a day-to-day basis dealing with outbreaks of violence as they happen."

Denktash showed his annoyance by waving a hand back and forth. "Yes, yes, I know that. But you have detailed reports from your predecessors, have you not?"

A blond-haired Major raised his hand. "Major Henk Van de Lei, Netherlands unit. Excellency, we are guided by the mandate proclaimed by the United Nations. We are a peacekeeping force. It is not within our mandate to fight your opponents. We can only try to prevent outbreaks of violence."

"Major. When a village is attacked by vastly superior forces it is your duty to stop that attack." Denktash glared at the Major.

"Excellency, I refer you again to our mandate. We are not permitted to fire upon any combatants. We have to use persuasion to stop such violence, but we cannot attack Greek or Turkish militia."

Leyla smiled at the composed Dutchman who appeared unruffled by Denktash's accusations. He looked to be about her age. "Then Major—" she began.

"Henk, please," he interrupted, happy to make eye contact with a good-looking young woman.

Smiling again, she leaned forward, "then what is the point of UNICYP being here in Cyprus?"

"Miss...?"

"Ozkara. Leyla Ozkara, assistant to Mr Denktash," she answered confidently.

"Ah, Ms Ozkara, that is something I can't answer. We are soldiers. We do our duty. Our orders are to be part of the United Nation peacekeeping force. In my case, I have been here only one week and after another three months I will return to duties in Holland."

"That's hardly long enough to get to know us and our difficulties," an exasperated Leyla shot back with a deprecatory wave of her hand.

Major Van de Lei noticed that she wore no rings. "Perhaps, if you are free this evening for dinner, I may be able to learn more?" he responded with a bow of his head.

Denktash looked at Leyla with raised eyebrows then turned to Henk Van de Lei. "Miss Ozkara has a young daughter. I doubt if she can spare the time."

She gave Denktash a sharp glance then smiled at Henk Van de Lei. "Thank you. I'm sure that I can arrange for my daughter to stay with a friend. If you only have three months then we must ensure that we educate you as quickly as possible."

"Wonderful. I'm staying here at the hotel. Shall we say seven?" He asked, lowering his head in a bow. Before Leyla could answer Denktash began to speak so she merely nodded acceptance.

"Can we get back to our complaints? Is it not within your power to provide escorts for food shipments from Turkey? We have many villages that have been cut off for a long time. The people are starving."

General Johansen placed his hands flat on the table. "Unfortunately we don't have sufficient personnel to do everything you would like. I'm hoping that troops from the British base at Dhekelia will be seconded to my command. If that happens then we may be in a better position to undertake escort duties."

"What about Kokina?" Denktash glowered at Henk Van de Lei. "It's been cut off now for four years. Four years of hell for the eight hundred or so inhabitants. Can you imagine? And you do nothing."

"Excellency. You must understand our dilemma. There is a government here in Cyprus. That government is responsible for what goes on. The UN says that this government is legitimate. We are here merely to try to keep the peace between the Greek Cypriots and Turkish Cypriots. What the government does is not for us to interfere in."

"So you are all happy to see people starve to death?" Denktash looked at everyone around the table.

"Excellency. We are not an occupying army. Our instructions are clear. A legitimate government elected by the citizens is in power. We are here at their pleasure."

"What about our lives?" Denktash pounded the table.

"You must take up any complaints such as you describe with the relevant authorities. That is not UNICYP." General Johansen made a gesture of resignation.

"Then I will contact the United Nations. Again. Probably with the usual result. They do nothing to save my people. So. If you will not stop the Greeks from attacking us, then how can you expect us not to use force to help the victims of this oppression?"

"You must do what you think is best. If you send in armed men with the intention of shooting your way in then I must send in my forces to intervene." The General looked evasive.

"Will your troops fire at us?" Denktash was determined to get a definite answer.

"No. Unless you shoot at us. We can return fire only to protect ourselves. No-one else."

"Good. At least we have agreement on something." Denktash banged the table with his hand.

"Mr Denktash, it's now four-thirty. You have an appointment at five." Leyla glanced at him then at Henk Van de Lei who made a slight bow.

"Thank you, gentlemen." Denktash stood up and shook hands all round. "Major, I'm sure that Miss Ozkara will give you some important background information on the difficulties we have faced for the past ten years. You will learn much."

"Look forward to that, Excellency." Henk Van de Lei stood up, a tall, slightly overweight man, his face flushed as he once again bowed in Leyla's direction.

Walking back to the car, Denktash held Leyla by the elbow. "He seems a nice young man, the Major. I'm sure you will have a nice dinner. Tell him our problems but nothing else."

Patting the hand on her elbow, she looked up and smiled. "You can rely on me to be careful. About political matters, that is." Then she laughed at his obvious discomfort.

At the home of Julie's friend, Lala, she explained that she was going out for dinner with a Major from UNICYP.

"Can I sleep over here then?" an eager Julie asked.

"If that's all right. Or I can pick you up about ten." She was not keen on the idea of Julie staying over again.

"No, no. It's okay isn't it, Lala? Your mother won't mind?" Julie appealed to her friend.

"No, that's fine. We can study together." She put a protective arm round Julie.

"Are you sure? Your mother isn't here. Maybe she would rather I picked Julie up?"

"She'll be back soon but don't worry. It'll be all right," an impatient Lala pulled Julie back by the hand.

A laughing Julie smirked. "Well? You have a date? Wow. Finally, my mother is going out on a date."

"It's not a date, as you call it. It's part of my job." She scowled at her daughter.

"Well, it's a date to me. So there. Wear something nice and—"

"Stop right there, young lady. This officer has only been here a week and I'm going to tell him all about our troubles for the last ten years." She tried to sound cross. Julie held up her hands in mock surrender.

"Just look your best and have a nice dinner. Hah," she looked sideways at her mother.

"Lala, tell your mother I'll phone later to see if everything's all right."

"Off you go, Leyla," Julie urged. "We're fine. Just have a good time. Is he handsome by the way? Or is he married?" A dismayed Julie put her hands to her cheeks.

"I don't know and yes, he is good looking. Now I'm off before there're any more questions." She kissed them both and left them smiling and happy.

Leyla decided to wear the dress that she'd bought in Ankara on her last visit there with Denktash. It was below the knee, a navy blue crepe de chine slim-fitting dress, with a v-neck that showed off her figure to perfection. She stood in front of a mirror and ran her hands down to smooth out any wrinkles. I look like a schoolgirl, she thought, except that I've put on a little weight since moving to Nicosia. For jewellery, she chose a gold chain with a pendant, a gift from her Aunt Nafia on the birth of Julie. At seven sharp she walked into the foyer of the Ledra Palace hotel.

Henk van de Lei was waiting and moved forward quickly to greet her. He put her hand to his lips and said, "Ms Ozkara. You look even more beautiful than this afternoon."

"It's Leyla, and I thank you for the compliment. It's seldom that I get the chance to wear this dress. Only since I began to work for Mr Denktash."

"Then I'm a lucky man. Would you care to have a drink in the bar before we go in for dinner?"

"No, thank you. I can't be too late. My daughter." She hesitated.

"And your husband? If I may ask? Is he in Nicosia?"

"Let's sit down before we ask so many questions, shall we?" She turned in the direction of the dining room.

"I'm sorry, forgive me. I'll try to slow down." He offered Leyla his arm.

Several heads turned to watch them walk slowly towards the hotel dining room. Henk studied the wine list while she looked round the room. As it was still early, most diners had yet to arrive. He ordered a bottle of Chateau Neuf de Pap, and turned his attention to Leyla. "So," he opened his hands, "you were telling me about your husband?"

"Was I?" her eyes opened wide. Then smiling, she said, "Sorry, I'm being disingenuous. I was not talking about my husband because there is no husband."

"So, you are maybe divorced?" he looked uneasy, afraid that her husband had been killed in the fighting.

"No, not divorced and to get this out of the way, I am not and never have been married. I have a daughter. It happened a long time ago. He was a soldier from England, from Scotland. And you, Major?" She tilted her head to the side.

"Please, we're off-duty. Just Henk."

"Well?"

"No, I'm not married. I once was but it didn't work out. So now I am married to the army," his full-blooded laugh echoed round the room.

"And you travel the world with your wife, 'the army'?" Leyla tilted her head as she smiled at the man who looked as if he enjoyed life. "Have you been married to 'your wife' for long?"

"Since I am eighteen. Then, when I am an officer I married my childhood girlfriend. She is an accountant. Her work is good and after five years she has the chance to go with Shell, it's a Dutch company, to work in America. I could have gone too but then I would not have a job."

Leyla watched his face as he struggled to find the words, his native tongue tempering his excellent English.

"So. A decision was to be made and Hennie, my wife, said that she could not be an army wife and took the job in America." He looked dejected.

"And then you divorced her?" She spoke softly, aware that he was a little distressed.

"Oh no. I still loved her. But in America she meets a man and then she divorces me."

"How terrible. And now? You still love her?" She watched his face intently.

"What can I say? Life must go on. Yes, naturally I miss her, but now I think maybe it's for the best." Henk shrugged.

"I assume there are no children?"

"No. That is good. Well, maybe not so good. With a child we may have been together still. Now, that's enough about me. I want to know all about you."

"Let's forget the past, shall we? It's in the past. What would you like to know about my country? That's the reason I'm here." She was determined to enjoy the present.

He grinned from ear to ear. "And I was thinking that maybe it's my charm that you accept the invitation?"

"Oh it is," a laughing Leyla replied thinking that it was fun, this repartee with a man.

"So. I'm learning so much about Cyprus before coming here. They gave us long lectures and books too. But I didn't see any mention of people in ghettos."

"Ah, well, you see, that is a major problem for the Turks of Cyprus. No-one hears our voice. The Greeks are very strong in making propaganda against us. They have many influential people all over the world."

"It's a nice country, Greece. Like the Netherlands, it is part of NATO so I have met some of their military. Our headquarters is in Brussels. Just over the border from my country. But I'm thinking that it is not very rich, Greece. So people go to other countries to make a prosperous outcome."

"My people too," Leyla sighed.

A waiter covered the table with a variety of dishes, *mezes*. Between mouthfuls of Turkish bread, savoury dips, olives, dolmades and cooked beans she told Henk about the breakdown of the original Republic of Cyprus and the ensuing fate of the Turkish Cypriots. Complimenting him on his choice of wine, she nodded as the wine waiter offered to pour her a second glass. The evening wore on. They were served a small dish of deep fried calamari then a steak. She thought of the people in the enclaves. No, she told herself, I can't worry about such things. By the time coffee was served it was almost ten o'clock.

"So," Henk said again "would you like to try a drink from

my homeland? I have some Dutch Jenever in my room. I brought it specially from home."

"Major Van de Lei?" Leyla pretended alarm, "I do believe you are asking me to your room. Just for a drink?" She felt a little flushed and relaxed, and raised an eyebrow as she tilted her head to the side.

"It is an innocent offer." Henk's lips curled ever so slightly.

"If you excuse me, I'll just telephone my daughter. She will have been wondering where I am. I said I would call and I've forgotten. It must be your charm," she said provocatively, enjoying the feeling.

After phoning, Leyla went to the ladies' room. She looked in the mirror and was surprised at how glowing she looked. Bother, she thought. I'm over thirty and a man has not held me for such a long time. I'll stay just a little while. A few kisses won't make me a loose woman. Feeling bubbly, she returned to tell Henk that she could accept one drink. "Then," she lied, "I must collect my daughter soon. She worries if I am late."

The rooms at the Ledra Palace had that colonial air, large with high ceilings and an overhead fan. Besides the two single beds there was a writing table and chair, and a small two-seat divan with a minute coffee table. Henk took a stone bottle from the refrigerator. He poured two small glasses of the pale liquor.

She took a sip, and gasped. "My God, this is pure alcohol. What are you trying to do, Major?"

"Sorry, I should have warned you. This is our national drink. But it is *sterk*, strong. Please don't drink it if you don't like it," he apologised.

"I think it's like our coffee. It needs a glass of water," a teary-eyed, breathless Leyla wheezed. In a single movement, Henk put the glass to his mouth, threw back his head, and swallowed the contents.

A startled Leyla put down her glass. "I think I'll pass, Major, Henk. But now that I've tasted your native drink I think I must go."

He bent down and kissed her on the lips, a gentle kiss that developed into a tongue-search kiss. He pulled back and looked into her eyes. "So. I don't know. When you came into that room this afternoon I sensed something. I, maybe a sense of loss, a needing. I'm not so good with words like this. I hope we can see each other again?"

She tilted her head and gave the slightest of nods. "You're a nice man. A soldier far away from home. We'll see. It's been a very special night for me. Now, I really must go." She stepped back, afraid that he would kiss her again and weaken her resolve.

A look of disappointment crossed his face. "So. Shall I arrange a car to take you home?"

"No, no, don't bother. There're lots of taxis out front. Turkish ones."

Lying in bed that night, Leyla thought of what she'd said 'a soldier far away from home'. Just like *Baba* had said to Alexander. How strange. Her mind struggled to think but the wine carried her off into a dreamless sleep. Next morning she awoke, slightly heavy-headed, but after some coffee and a wash she was cheerful and ready to collect her daughter for school.

"So how was your date?" was the first question from a bouncy Julie.

"It was not a date, as you call it. But it was very pleasant to go out in nice surroundings. The food and wine were excellent. And the Major was charming. Is that all?" She glared at her grinning daughter.

"You had wine? Did he try to get you drunk?"

"Quiet. You've been reading too many wrong books. I must speak to your teacher."

"Oh, *Anne*, Leyla, I'm too old to be told what to read," Julie pouted.

"Well, life is not like books," she admonished her precocious daughter.

"Did he kiss you? Was he strong and masculine?"

"Child! Where do you get these ideas? Come, call Lala and I'll take you as far as school. I have a busy day ahead."

"I'll still have more questions when I get home tonight." Julie grinned, happy to be teasing her mother.

"And you will get no more answers. Now hurry up or we'll be late." Sighing, she watched Julie and her friend walk through the school gates. They grow up so much more quickly today. How would *Baba* cope?

Australia 1973

IT WAS a Saturday night, just after eight. Alex had finally closed up shop. Too tired to watch television, he sat drinking a glass of wine. Gazing out the window at distant waves pounding into shore, he felt lost. Business was good. The previous week his accountant had called him into his office to sign his tax return.

"Alex." The usually serious Andrew's face broke out in an expansive smile, "It's looking really good."

"How good is really good?" He looked across the leather-covered antique desk..

"Well, allowing for this year's tax plus provisional, I'd say you'd be up for just over fifteen thousand. That's you, personally. The company is even better."

"Shit," he groaned.

"No, really, that's an excellent result. With all the deductions for the interest on the properties, the rents on the five properties you have rented out, the payments to the company superannuation and the deductions for depreciation on the shop, we've come out well."

"I suppose if you make it you have to pay the tax."

"Yes. It seems a lot, but your assets, all told, are over five hundred thousand and they'll keep growing."

A tired Alex nodded. "I just wish I had time to enjoy it. You know, I've had two holidays in what? Twelve years? I'll be forty next year. Christ, I promised myself when I was a kid that I'd never be poor, and I'm not. But what's it all about?"

"What you could do is pay off all your debts and put in a manager. You can afford it. If you pay a manager a good salary, get a good man, then you'll be up for very little tax."

"What are you saying?" Alex leaned forward, feeling a little less depressed.

"Look at it this way. With the rent from the houses plus your take from the shop, you are able to afford to take as much time off as you like. Especially in the winter when things are quiet.

"What if I sold up everything? How much would I have to live on?" he asked.

"Why would you want to do that?" Andrew waved his hands in the air.

"I'm sick of pharmacy, Andy. Eating lunch on the run. Tied down every day for ten hours. If I sold the lot what could I expect as income?"

Andrew punched away on his electric calculator then looked up. "If, I say if, you did that, I calculate about 40 to 50 thousand. But think about it. With a manager you'd probably get more and still have assets that are growing. It's the best return on capital you'll ever get."

"Fifty or sixty, then, Andy? Let me see if I can find a young fellow, not long qualified. Maybe just married. If I can, then I'll do it. Shit, it's time to do something besides dishing out pills every day."

"Good decision. Once the guy's settled in, take a year off. I know you've been pushing it hard, but you've done it. Financially, you're well-off. Why not enjoy it?"

"Too bloody right."

"You've no ties. No kids at school. That's one expense you don't have. Look, mate, if I was in your shoes I'd do it."

"Okay, Andy. There'll be a new batch of graduates after Christmas. I'll put out some feelers. Anything else?"

"No. Just sign here, and here and here." He flipped over the pages of Alex's personal and company tax returns.

Alex began to dream of a less restricted life. An old saying from his Catholic schooling crept into his mind. He couldn't remember the words but it was about gaining the world and its possessions but losing his soul. That's me, he thought. I've got money but I'm not happy. Not happy like I should be with all this money. By the time he arrived back at the shop, he was keyed up.

Viv could see that he was excited about something and after he explained, she invited him for dinner. "John and I would love to talk about it," she said, "you know we've often said to each other that you need to slow down, get something else out of life. So we'll see you about seven-thirty. Is that okay?"

He told them his plans. "I'm going to do something I've always wanted to do. I'm going to open a restaurant."

"A restaurant?" John and Viv both echoed.

Alex smiled like a Cheshire cat. "It's not as stupid as you think. Ever since I was a kid helping my mother cook, I've wanted to be a chef."

"That's something you've never mentioned before." John looked doubtful.

"I know. I probably thought I'd never make much money as a chef. Anyway, what I'd like to do is this. Take a year off and see what the trends are in restaurants overseas. Then I'll open a restaurant here in Pointsea for, say, four or five months of the year. It'd be hopeless after Easter."

"But Alex, a restaurant. Who'd do the cooking?" Viv shook her head in disbelief.

"Think about it, Viv. Chefs go up to the snow in winter and I could get one here for the spring and summer months. I know how to cook and anyway, it's just like being a chemist. You mix the ingredients and out comes the result." He held out his hands.

"Well, you're certainly a good cook, Alex. But cooking for a whole load of people? I'm not sure." John began uncorking a bottle of wine.

"It's a bit of a pipe dream, I know. But after twenty years in pharmacy I'm going to see what else I'm good at. What do people like to eat here on the coast? Fish, scallops, calamari, crayfish. I'll keep it simple." He bowed like a headwaiter.

Over a typical Pointsea dinner of fresh lobster, roast potatoes, salad and a fine dry Riesling wine, he laid out his plans. "You know I told you about my time in the army? And the Turkish girl I met in Cyprus. How she died and all that? Well, that's one of the places I want to visit. The food is terrific. Nothing like it here."

"There're lots of Turks in Melbourne now, you know," Viv waved a fork at Alex.

"Are there? I don't remember any." He frowned. "Are you sure?"

"Definitely. I remember reading it in *The Age*. Plane-loads coming in. Caused a bit of a controversy."

"Why?"

"For a start they're Muslims and second, we have a huge Greek population in Melbourne. Apparently, they don't get on too well."

"Well, there you are. That is very interesting. Anyway, apart from Cyprus, I thought Greece, Turkey and France. What do you think?"

"Listen, Alex." John filled Alex's glass. "We've only been to Surfers, and that was for our honeymoon. No, I tell a lie. We went to Adelaide, remember, darl?"

"How could I forget? The rotten car broke down. I think we lived on hamburgers that week." Viv laughed at the memory.

"Wasn't my fault," he protested.

"Old cars need oil, sweetheart. You may be a good doctor but you're hopeless when it comes to motor cars." She made a face at him.

"All right, you two." Alex pretended that he was separating two boxers. "I'll see the Pharmacy College on my next day off. Now, raise your glasses and drink to my new adventure."

Before the evening was over the glasses were clinked several times.

Cyprus 1974

IN 1973 the Greek Cypriot population had once more elected Archbishop Makarios President of the Republic of Cyprus. No-one dared to stand against him. But by the end of that year things began to change. Besides Grivas and the *EOKA* B terrorist organisation, other groups began to act, independently, against Makarios. Nicos Sampson, who had been supportive of the Archbishop, now switched his allegiance to *EOKA* B. Irregular bands operated in various parts of the island. UNICYP Forces were undermanned and constantly on the move. Major Henk Van de Lei had been out of Nicosia for a month. It had been an anxious month as he had been eager to return and meet once more with Leyla Ozkara.

In the Presidential palace, the Archbishop sat at his table, head in hands. Clerides and the Police Minister, Pandapas, sat waiting. The President's secretary, Thea, stood waiting with notepad in hand. Finally Makarios looked up. "It's all unravelling, isn't it?" he said to no-one in particular.

"There're too many of them," Pandapas spoke softly, afraid to deepen the President's gloom.

"Yes. I am aware of that. First *EOKA* B kills some members of the socialist left. Then some of our people, I assume they are ours, kill a Grivas man in Limassol. Now, the Minister of Justice has been taken captive."

"What is Grivas trying to achieve this way? Why take hostages?" Clerides hesitated as he spoke.

"He wants an amnesty for all the political prisoners we hold. That's his first demand." A weary Makarios slumped forward in his chair.

"Impossible," Pandapas burst out. "That would be a signal to the people that he is controlling the agenda."

"Grivas and Greece," Clerides added.

"Grivas is spreading rumours that these prisoners are being ill-treated. Just like in Greece. It's time you, Clafcos, and people like Tassos began a campaign in the press to discredit him. It's ironic that he's proving as difficult for me as he was for the British."

"I can't understand it. He has maybe a hundred or so men yet he creates havoc everywhere." Pandapas shook his head.

"That's all it takes, Minister. That, and the anarchy that infects our people. The few take advantage of the situation to line their own pockets. These people are not patriotic Greeks but a rabble." A gloomy Makarios looked at his colleagues.

Clerides sought to raise his spirits. "Beatitude, you are the only one the people truly trust."

"I grow weary of all this discord among the faithful. But I accept my duty to bring a peaceful Cyprus to Greece and one day that will come about." His voice was barely audible.

"You will, Mr President." Pandapas did not sound confident.

"Well, we must try to find out where our Justice Minister is being held. Probably Limassol, Grivas appears to have many friends there. See if we can find him. Make that a priority."

"It already is." Pandapas objected to the suggestion that he was lax in his duty.

Makarios ignored the protest. "I will make a public statement denouncing the actions of Grivas. I'll say that the hero of the struggle for independence is now destroying that independence. Perhaps I will suggest that he should return to Greece and live out the rest of his days in peace. I understand that he has not been well for some time."

Clerides stood up, believing that he could contribute nothing more. Makarios waved him to leave.

"Minister, how many have been killed so far this year?" Makarios tugged at his greying beard.

"Sixteen, Mr President."

"How many by the Turks?"

"One. Unconfirmed. He may also have been killed by EOKA B."

"So many and the year has just begun. And yet the economy is strong, tourists still come. At least they leave the tourists alone."

"The hotels and resorts are well policed, Beatitude. Even Grivas knows that the death of a tourist would horrify even his supporters."

"We can thank God for some small mercies. Now, you find me the Justice Minister while I send a strong letter of protest to Athens. Sorry, Thea, I'll dictate that letter now."

He waited until Pandapas kissed his ring then shuffled out of the room. "Thea, let's begin. To President Ghizikis say this:

'As President of an independent Cypriot State I protest most strongly at the support coming from Athens in encouraging the return of General Grivas to Cyprus. His presence here endangers the stability of my government and the peace and tranquillity of the lives of the people. The National Guard under Greek officers is supplying the General with men, arms and materials to threaten me in particular and the people in general. I request that you withdraw these Greek officers and send instructors to assist in the creation of a solely Greek Cypriot army. I demand an end to the financial support Greece gives to those newspapers and radio in Cyprus that oppose my government. If I do not have a positive response to my demands I will inform the people of Cyprus of the duplicity of your government. My words will resonate not just here in Cyprus but throughout the entire Hellenic world. Several attempts have been made to end my earthly existence. Rumours abound that attempts may be made to depose me. As the only person deemed worthy of the support of the vast majority of Greek Cypriots, the consequences of such an attempt would lead to civil war. The Soviet Union would not hesitate to move to secure the continuance of the elected government under my leadership.'

Add the usual 'yours faithfully' and so on. Have it ready as soon as possible and I will see that it reaches Greece tomorrow."

Thea walked quickly out of the room, leaving the President of the Republic of Cyprus to ponder his future. He understood the chances he was taking. The Junta under Ghizikis would not take kindly to a rebuke. He knew that they were impatient for a resolution to the problem as it affected their standing with the people of Greece. They were determined that the island would become part of the new Greek empire. Under extreme pressure at home, they needed a victory in the Cyprus. Enlarging the Hellenic empire would ensure continued American support. Failure would mean the end of their military rule. A dispirited Archbishop decided to spend the night at the Archbishopric. I always find comfort there, he thought.

The first thing Henk Van de Lei did when he arrived back at the Ledra Palace Hotel was to phone the office of Rauf Denktash. "Can I speak to Ms Leyla Ozkara, please?"

"Speaking."

"So sorry, I didn't recognise your voice."

"That's hardly surprising since you only heard my voice for one day and that was some time ago." Her response was abrupt but not cold.

"I've been all over this island. You've no idea how many trouble spots there are," a contrite Henk tried to excuse the fact that he had not been in touch.

"Well, Major, what can I do for you?" Her tone was businesslike.

"I was hoping that we might have dinner. There's still a lot I have to learn about your country. Or maybe we could go for a drive? Would your daughter like that?" He thought that inviting Leyla's daughter would allay her fears that he was insincere.

"I'm sure that Julie would love to meet you. But she's at a

very impressionable age. I think not. But dinner one night would be fine."

"Shall we say the day after tomorrow? Friday? Would that be suitable?" He was concerned to meet as soon as possible.

"Just a moment," Leyla held a hand over the mouthpiece and waited, not wishing to appear too eager, "Yes, Friday will be fine. Would you like to eat at a Turkish restaurant? It's simple but the food is good."

"Of course. Whatever you wish," a relieved Henk answered back.

"I'll meet you at the hotel. Then it's not far to walk. The restaurant is in the Turkish quarter. It's quite safe to walk."

"Shall we say seven? Shall I wear a suit and tie?"

"Major," she exclaimed, "this place is not the Ledra Palace. Just slacks and a shirt open at the neck. Turkish restaurants are for eating, not showing off."

"Then slacks and shirt it is. And you?" his voice rose.

"You'll have to wait and see." She laughed.

The Kibris Kebab restaurant looked most uninviting to Henk as they entered the run-down dimly lit shop with a television high up on the wall near the kitchen. It had Formica-topped tables on thin metal legs and plastic chairs, and the place looked more like a workman's café than a restaurant.

"I told you it wasn't the Ledra Palace." She grinned at a disheartened Henk.

"So. This is a Turkish restaurant? Not quite the place I would choose to bring a beautiful woman," he said gallantly, looking at Leyla in a white blouse with short sleeves and a pale brown skirt that let him see her shapely legs. She carried a jacket over her arm in case the late evening turned cool.

She delighted in his compliment and admiring glance. "Ah, but wait till you taste the food."

"It's quite warm in here, isn't it? I would have been out of place and too hot in a suit."

"That's the oven there. See." Leyla pointed to a large brick, dome-shaped oven with glowing coals. "They bake the bread, lovely Turkish bread and cook chicken and lamb in that."

"I've seen those everywhere. Mostly behind houses. Shall I order some wine? You can choose the food." He looked around for a waiter.

Leyla swallowed before telling him that there was no alcohol served in this restaurant.

"That's okay. Water is fine. Perhaps we can have a drink at the hotel later?"

"Let's eat and this time you must learn something more about my people and their suffering for the past eleven years." She spoke rapidly in Turkish to a woman wearing a full headscarf. She ordered Turkish bread, hummus, yoghurt and cucumber-and-garlic dips.

Henk began dipping chunks of bread into the dishes. "This is good."

"Wait till you taste what's to come. String beans, cooked in oil, tomato and garlic until they melt in the mouth."

"Then?" he asked.

"I've ordered *borek*, that's a flaky pastry stuffed with minced lamb. The main dish will be kebabs on a bed of rice with pickled vegetables. Then if you are still hungry we can have a plate of figs, candied aubergines and baklava, with Turkish coffee to complete the meal. How does that sound?" She smiled at an open-mouthed Henk.

"Well, it's certainly different to Dutch cooking." He tore off another piece of Turkish bread and used it to scoop up more dip.

"What is Dutch food?"

"Ah, Dutch food, well," he paused, thinking how he could describe it, "we have cold winters so the food is quite heavy. Many meat and potato dishes. We eat a lot of fish and cheese, eggs, and Indonesian food is very popular."

"Indonesian? That's strange." Her brow furrowed.

"So. Holland was a large empire at one time. We ruled what is called today Indonesia. Then, after independence, many

Indonesians came to live in Holland. Surinamers too, from the Indies."

"Then you have many different races in your country. Do they fight each other?"

"Of course not. Nederland has a long history of tolerance. People have come there from many countries, usually if they have been persecuted for religion. I think now there are many people from Turkey in Holland." He nodded to reinforce his statement.

"Goodness! And they all live together with no trouble?" A doubtful Leyla leaned forward.

"*Natuurlijk*" He shrugged as if it was the most natural thing in the world. "That's why we can't understand why you and the Greeks can't live together on such a small island. Holland is small so we must get on together. Didn't Turks and Greeks live happily side by side before all this happened?"

"Yes and no. Understand this, although we have lived together in Nicosia and in mixed villages, we have always been separate."

"How so? Separate?" He frowned. "You mean like it is now?"

"No! It's difficult to explain to a foreigner. We don't share a common faith. Our customs are different. Greeks and Turks live separate lives, spiritually, culturally and in every way."

"But you did live in peace?" a perplexed Henk tried to remember what he'd learned about the island before leaving Holland.

"Only because of first the Ottomans and then the British. But when we became independent after *EOKA*, things went very bad." Leyla shook her head from side to side.

He rubbed a hand across his chin. "You became a republic? With everyone sharing in the government and the country? That's right, yes?"

"That was what was meant to be. But the President, the Archbishop, wanted to change the rules. He never wanted us. He once said that it was the duty of the heroes of *EOKA* to expel the Turkish community. He said that we are part of the

Turkish race that is the terrible enemy of Hellenism, of Greece, that is." Her face froze as she said the words.

"So he did not keep his word? When he agreed to the Constitution? Is that right?"

"Mr Denktash says that the man is a pathological liar. He agrees with everyone. He sucks up to anyone who can help him," she said disparagingly.

"That's politics, surely." He shrugged.

"But his duty as President was to look after everyone in Cyprus. I remember Mr Denktash spoke at a meeting of Greeks in Nicosia. He told them that Turks are part of Cyprus. We cannot be thrown out. He said that we, Turkish Cypriots, don't want much, but we don't want to be 'not wanted'. You understand?"

He nodded in agreement. "And the Greeks don't want you?"

"You see," Leyla's eyes were bright with passion, "this is our land too. We've been here for hundreds of years. We have a right to be here. Now we have been excluded from everything. No say in government, no jobs in the public service, no food, no trade." She sat back in her chair and raised her hands in dumb despair, then put her hands together on the table.

Henk put his hands over hers. "I wish there was something I, the United Nations, could do. Something worthwhile."

"The United Nations!" She spat out the words. "Makarios has them in the palm of his hand. He is a master of persuading people to listen to his pleading, his claims that Greeks should be masters of Cyprus."

"So? What is the future? Will he succeed?"

"Mr Denktash says that it will be over his dead body. Please don't say I told you, but Mr Denktash meets very often with Ministers in Turkey. He says that Turkey will never, never let Cyprus be a Greek state, be part of the Hellenic dream."

"Turkey is a big country. I think they have a very large army. If it came to it, I think that Greece would not wish to fight Turkey. That is the feeling in NATO. As they showed in Korea, Turks can be counted on in a fight." Henk raised a clenched fist.

She gave a helpless shrug and looked angrily at the fist. "That's not the kind of reputation I like. I prefer that they be famous as a progressive, tolerant country. The Greeks are always saying that Turks are barbaric." A downcast Leyla spoke softly.

"If we have finished," he pushed his coffee cup away, "perhaps we can go back to the hotel and relax with a nice drink. No Jenever, I promise." He roared with laughter.

He tucked her arm under his and they walked slowly back to the Ledra Palace, a happy couple out for an after-dinner walk. The bar at the hotel was crowded with noisy members of the UN peacekeeping force in Cyprus. Beautifully dressed Greek and Turkish women were enjoying the company of soldiers with money. All the tables and chairs were taken. Henk grimaced and turned to her. "I have a lovely bottle of wine, Commanderie St John. The man told me it was a nice sweet wine. Would you prefer that we enjoyed a glass in my room?"

Leyla tilted her head to one side and decided that this was no time to be modest. All around, people were enjoying the company of the opposite sex. Why not, she thought. It's time to open up to whatever life might bring. "I think that would be much better than competing with all these people." She nodded towards the noisy crowd of revellers. He smiled with relief.

Once inside his room, she removed her jacket, her white scalloped blouse showing off her pale olive skin. She sat on the divan and accepted a glass of the golden liqueur. "That's so much nicer than your Dutch poison." She took a small sip. "This I can drink with pleasure."

"Good. Now we just relax and forget all the problems and take pleasure in each other's company."

After a second glass of the sweet wine, Henk reached out and pulled her in close. He kissed her softly, then harder as her arms went round his neck and she strained towards him. Leaning back, the bedside table lamp casting delicate shadows on the wall, Leyla looked into his eyes. "Henk? You're a good man, I think. You've probably done this kind of thing before. A soldier. But I'm afraid," she began nervously.

"Leyla. You're a beautiful woman. I want to be close to you, *natuurlijk*. But I don't want to do anything that would upset you." He kissed the palm of her hand.

"It's not that. I, well, I haven't, not for a long time. Please, I don't want, I'm not sure if I can?" She hesitated. "But you're a very attractive man."

"If you want, I have protection. The army always thinks it's best. Would you like to? It's been some time for me too. I would like to touch you. May I?"

"Oh my God. I want to and I don't." She could feel a warm glow from the wine.

She trembled as he ran a hand over her breasts. The kissing deepened, mouths open, exploring, tasting the sweetness of the wine. Leyla pulled back, breathing deeply, unsure if she wanted to go on or stop before it was too late.

He stood up. "Come, this is not comfortable. The bed, we just lie down? I'll be very gentle. Don't be afraid. Tell me to stop if you want me to." A serious Henk pulled Leyla to her feet. He took her by the hand, and standing by the bed, he unbuttoned her blouse. He kissed her above her breast, and undid her brassiere. He kissed her neck and moved down.

"Oh, oh," she cried as he moved back to pull off his shirt. She closed her eyes as the cool air swept over her nearly naked body. Leyla groaned with pleasure. Holding his head so that he would continue with the beautiful sensation. She moaned, "So good, so good. So good."

He lifted his head and looked up the length of her body. "Shall I go on? You are okay?"

She moaned and whispered a breathless yes. It's too nice to stop she thought. Lying side by side they stroked and touched.

"It's okay," he said as he continued to run his hands over her tense body. Leyla's mind flicked from the pleasurable sensation to the thought that she barely knew the man giving her such ecstasy. He moved away. Reaching over, he pulled open the drawer of the bedside table. Leyla lay uncertain but still tingling with pleasure. Finally, he lay on top of her.

"Is it okay? Does it feel good?" he panted.

"It's all right." She breathed out. "You can keep going." She tensed, aware of his weight. For a fleeting moment she thought of the Greek rapists, the pressing weight. "Not so hard," she hissed and bit his ear lobe.

"Ouch, that hurt," he reacted loudly. "Oh, you're beautiful. Beautiful." He breathed in deeply.

Leyla found his heavy body not unpleasant but she needed more air in her lungs. Pushing gently, she eased him on to his back. Then she lay her head on his chest.

A feeling of relief swept over her as she realised that she'd made love with a man. She could hear the sound of the band in the bar downstairs. I managed it, the thought came into her mind. Maybe next time it will be better.

He stroked her bare arm then pushed his hand through her hair. "I hope I wasn't too quick. It's been a while. Are you all right?" he asked, hoping that she had enjoyed it as much as he had.

"I'm just fine," she whispered. "But I must go now. I must go home. Stay there while I get dressed. No, stay there. No need for you to dress. I'll slip away." Leyla dressed quickly. Henk watched through half-closed eyes feeling a little disappointed that she was leaving so soon.

"Thank you for tonight. You're a very nice man." She bent over and kissed him lightly on the cheek. Henk tried to get up but she pushed him back on to the bed. "Goodnight. Stay there. I'll leave now. Goodnight."

The following morning she was still half asleep when Julie arrived home from Lala's at nine.

"Well, my *Anne* still in bed," she said with a cheeky grin. "Must have been a late night?"

"Go make some coffee while I get dressed," Leyla commanded.

Getting out of bed, she ran her hands over her stomach. A little bit tender, she thought. Then an ache and she cursed. It was that time of the month again. She looked in the mirror and smiled at her lovely figure marred only by a few stretch marks and the two old scars. Funny, Henk never mentioned them. Did I tell him about the shooting? She couldn't remember. Well I did it, she thought. Singing softly, she went through to the kitchen where Julie was grinding some coffee beans.

"You sound happy. Had a good time with your Dutchman? What are we doing today? I've done all my homework." She put down the grinder with a thump to attract her mother's attention.

Leyla stared blankly, lost in space for a moment, wavering. She jerked back to the moment. "Oh! It's been ages since we've been to Ghazientop. My *Anne* will think we've forgotten her. It's time we paid her a visit. We'll go today. Okay?"

"I suppose," came the bored answer, "another exciting Saturday."

"It will be for your grandmother. She always likes to see you," she scolded.

"I bet." Julie pouted.

"I don't know where you get that kind of language. We're all she has. Family is important." A stern Leyla wondered about the future of her family.

"Do we catch a bus or will you get a car?"

"A car, I think." She was sure that a word from Mr Denktash would be enough to give her one of the office cars for the day. A phone call was all that was needed and just after midday they were sitting holding hands with Gulten, who had a thousand questions.

"Mother has a boyfriend, *Anneanne*," Julie wasted no time in saying.

"That's good," Gulten nodded approval, "is he working with you and Mr Denktash? Is he old?"

Before Leyla could answer, Julie popped in. "He's with the UN, a Major. A Dutch Major."

Gulten looked disbelievingly at her daughter. "A soldier, a foreigner. Is that good?" She clasped her hands together.

Leyla made a dismissive wave of her hand. "It's nothing, *Anne*, Julie likes to make out something that's not true. The Major works for the UN and I met him at a meeting with Mr Denktash. So we've had dinner. Twice. He'll be finishing his tour of duty in, I don't know, less than two months."

"But dinner? With a soldier?" A worried Gulten looked first at one then the other.

"He wanted to know all about our struggles. Our side of the story. People only know the Greek side. Now he knows!" An exasperated Leyla began to wish she had never met Henk.

"Did you tell him about, about, what happened?" Gulten asked with clenched fists.

"No, *Anne*. I don't tell strangers things like that." She paused for a moment. He is a stranger, she thought. A very nice stranger, but one who will be leaving soon. Yet despite the thought that the previous night had not been entirely fulfilling, she couldn't help feeling a sense of loss at the thought of him leaving.

"Enough of all this talking about men in front of Julie." Gulten said. "We'll go and see what there is to eat. Are you staying here tonight? I don't like you driving at night," she shuddered.

"No, we'll get back to Nicosia before dark. I think Julie would like to go to the picture house." She looked at Julie hoping that the offer would make up for the visit home.

Julie nodded happily like a donkey. "Yes, please. I think this week they have *Saturday Night Fever*. It has John Travolta. He's cute." She did some twisting dancing movements.

Leyla nodded approval. "I think I've heard of it. Yes, that should be a good one."

"Maybe you can ask your boyfriend although he's probably seen it, it's old." Julie chirped.

"If I hear the word boyfriend again from you, young lady, you'll be reading a book tonight." She glared at Julie.

Gulten looked at the mother and child and shook her head. How the world is changing, she thought. Nothing is the same any more.

Australia 1974

Alex found a good manager, Gareth Evans, and his wife, Jenny. After seeing the happy couple on their way, Alex felt his heart pumping at his good luck. Right, he thought, I'll get out the atlas tonight and start planning. Greece, France, Germany, Spain, maybe even Cyprus. Why not? I could see if Mehmet Ali is still there. I never did get to say sorry about Leyla. The rest of the day dragged by despite a late surge of customers with mild cases of sunburn.

Cyprus 1974

Denktash called out from his office. "Leyla, can you come in?" His fingers were drumming on the table.

"Yes, Mr Denktash?" She appeared in the doorway.

"We need to go to Ankara again. Can you make arrangements for your daughter?"

"How long for, a day or two?" she asked with a puckered brow. She was not keen to have Julie stay at Lala's home too often.

"It may be longer than that. I have a number of proposals to put to the government and you know as well as I do that they will be passed around before a decision is made. Best say five days. Is that all right?" He looked up at his willowy assistant.

"Five days? I'll have to see if I can get my mother to look after Julie for that long. I did have some things planned," she lied, thinking that she might be seeing Henk again soon.

"Well, one of the proposals I have is to set up a public relations department. I thought you were interested?" He peered hard at Leyla.

She blushed with shame at her lack of appreciation of his offer. "Of course I can make arrangements. Some kind." She apologised. "When will we be going?"

"The day after tomorrow. Is that enough notice?"

"I suppose it'll have to be. Can I have the rest of the day off then to organise something?" she asked with a sinking heart. Poor Henk would be disappointed. Then she remembered that she still had her period for another few days.

Denktash nodded approval. "Then you're happy to be part of this new initiative? I think you will impress them." He beamed at her.

"Of course. You can count on me. As always, you are right." A happy Leyla looked with admiration at the man who never stopped thinking about the welfare of his community. With four members of his staff, including Leyla, Denktash flew to Ankara. While he held private meetings with the Prime Minister and senior ministers, she met with staff members in the Department of Foreign Affairs and Public Relations. With growing confidence at these meetings, she offered her opinions and bargained for funding. No promises were forthcoming. Discussions continued at dinner when the Cypriot team joined Ministers and senior bureaucrats.

Leyla marvelled at the skill of Denktash in arguing for more funding. "I appreciate, all my people appreciate, the sacrifice made by Turkey in providing what? A few million? But it's not enough. Much of that has gone in defence expenditure, armaments and the increased Security Forces." He looked slowly around the table.

"And it keeps on growing." Feyyaz Hayam, the head of the Department of Finance pointed a finger. "And what are we achieving with all this money?"

Denktash glowered at the public servant. Bean counter, he muttered under his breath. "What we are achieving, Mr Hayam, is the survival of your Turkish brethren in Cyprus. We are also maintaining a Turkish presence in Cyprus. Or would you rather we crawled away and left it to the Greeks?"

"I didn't mean—" Hayam began.

"I know what you meant!" Denktash thundered. "You have your problems balancing the books. But if we are forced out of

Cyprus then Turkey will spend ten, a hundred, times what we receive in protecting the mainland from an enemy at the doorstep."

"Do you have a concrete proposal? Costs, outcomes?" Hayam tried to calm the situation.

Denktash looked at Leyla with a slight frown of warning. "Ms Ozkara, the daughter of Mehmet Ali, member of the 1960 Legislature, murdered by the Greeks, has been studying the matter. Leyla?"

She looked slowly around the table and was pleased that every face looked at her with a new respect. "The situation is this. Since his election as President of the Republic in 1960, Makarios has travelled the world. He has been greeted and honoured by President Kennedy, Tito, Nasser, Brandt, Nehru, and every non-aligned world leader. He is recognised."

"That is only natural, surely," Hayam interrupted. "That's hardly new?"

Leyla paused, and then gave Hayam a stony stare. Then she lifted her head. "Please allow me to continue. After 1963, thanks to his prestige abroad, he is still recognised as President of all Cyprus. As Head of State he meets with the Queen and other Commonwealth leaders, and he has a special relationship with U Thant. He has made State visits to Tanzania, Zambia, the USA with Nixon, Kenya and the Kremlin."

"What is the point of this history lesson?" a dark-skinned man at the far end of the table interrupted.

"The point is this," she raised her voice. "We are forgotten, nothing. No-one sees or hears us. The Vice-President is invisible."

"That is his nature." Hayam grunted. "He is not the most charismatic man I have met."

She ignored the comment. "What we need to do is to lift our profile world-wide. And that will cost money. We need the world media to see our plight, to recognise the injustice of our situation. It is time to use similar propaganda tactics to the

Greeks. They have the money, the machinery, of Government. We need the same resources."

"I sympathise with your dilemma," Hayam shrugged, "but money won't buy you invitations to meet world leaders."

"Wrong, Mr Hayam." She looked to Denktash for support.

He glowered at Hayam. "Every time Makarios goes overseas his meetings with world leaders are reported in the world press, their press. He spews out the same message everywhere. We, the Turks of Cyprus, are rebels. He is the peacemaker. The only way to counteract this blatant propaganda is to set up our own propaganda department, a public relations office under Ms Ozkara. We need to get our story out to the world. Through journalists, film-makers, radio broadcasters."

"Yes, yes. I understand your, in fact our, difficulties. We are not very good at promoting ourselves. Never have been. We have and always will be the barbaric Turk, the enemy of Christianity. Nothing, no amount of money will change that." Hayam looked around for support.

"It won't if we continue to adopt that attitude," an angry, frustrated Leyla came back with. "As my father used to say, we have to forget this will of Allah business and start making our own destiny."

Several people around the table shook their heads, muttering incoherent words. She looked slowly round the table making eye contact with each man. "Look at the mass graves holding the bodies of innocent women, children, a four-month old baby? I'm talking about Atilar, Murataga, Sandallar and other places. The discovery of these atrocities barely makes a ripple outside Cyprus. Why no world condemnation of Makarios and his gang of ex-*EOKA* killers?"

"It was mentioned in the British *Guardian*," another voice jumped in.

"Mentioned? Mentioned? Is that all you have to say? Mentioned? My God, if we kill one Greek attacking us we are branded by Makarios all over the world as fanatical Turkish brutes. Here we have a mass grave of women and children. Their hands were tied behind their back before they were stabbed and shot." Leyla's face flushed with passion.

"It's always been that way," another man shrugged as he spoke. "What can we do?"

"You can choose to suffer the slings and arrows of outrageous fortune or get off your backside and fight." She was surprised by her boldness. "Give us the means to show the world what we have endured and are still facing, even if the last few months have not been so bad."

Denktash stepped in. "One day, our turn will come, and it may come sooner than we think. Opposition to Makarios is coming from several quarters. The Junta in Greece grows impatient. They see Makarios as losing his enthusiasm for *Enosis*. But they need it to show Greeks all over the world how good they are. If they succeed next time in eliminating Makarios then all hell will break loose. At least with Makarios we have one enemy. Without him we will have every small thug and his gang out to kill as many Turks as possible and take our land. Is that what you want?"

"Please, Mr Denktash. There is no need to berate us. Without Turkey Makarios would have, well...?" Hayam stopped.

"Let me put it this way," Denktash began again, "if the time comes that Makarios is killed or deposed, Turkey will need to act. Militarily. If that happens we need to have world opinion sympathetic to such an action. That is why we must begin work immediately to bring our forgotten plight to the eyes and ears of the world."

"I understand. I will speak with the Minister. I will put your application before him. You have made some very telling arguments. Give me your proposal, Ms Ozkara. Now, I think we should stop here. Perhaps coffee and some informal talking? Do you agree?"

Denktash looked at Leyla and nodded.

"Thank you, gentlemen, for the opportunity to put our

case." She looked at each man individually and was pleased at their admiring glances.

Drinking coffee and chatting with Hayam, Denktash watched most of the other officials gather round Leyla. There's nothing like a beautiful, articulate and educated woman to attract attention, he smiled to himself. I've made a good choice. She will win support where I might not be so lucky. It was well known in Ankara circles that Leyla was a widow, or at least without a husband. The men clustered round and vied with each other to engage her in conversation.

"How long will you be with us?" a small man who barely came up to her shoulder asked. "Will you be free to see some of Ankara? Perhaps you would do me the honour to show you some interesting places. We have some excellent restaurants. Maybe dinner if you are free?"

Leyla enjoyed all this attention. She surprised herself by openly flirting with the group. "I would love to continue with these discussions, if that would help us," she smiled coquettishly. Several offers were immediately forthcoming. "I will have to check with Mr Denktash. I'm not sure what our program is. I will have to let you know."

Every man assumed that she was referring to his offer. She went to bed that night feeling full of confidence. The next two days were busy with meetings. Leyla met the State television director, and several journalists with friendly contacts in the UK and America. The Director of Public Relations, Fatih Ethem, was very supportive but admitted that his department was under-funded to the extent that he had insufficient translators, antiquated printing presses and only two professional photographers.

"Even with whatever funding you receive, Ms Ozkara, you will find it difficult to find the right people to help you. For too long we've failed to recognise the importance of good public relations. It's not our way. The Greeks have a long history of working in this field. They have many, many, trained people. Not just in Greece but especially in America."

"You are so right. It is frustrating, but we have to make a beginning. I hope that I may call on you for any advice and support."

With a bow, the Director took her hands in his. "I am at your service. If my duties permit, I will try to visit you in Nicosia. Perhaps there I can get a better picture of your facilities and staff."

"But of course. I hope that I can telephone you from time to time." Leyla was not sure about the need for the Director to visit the island where she would be expected to entertain him. I mustn't allow this work to take up too much of my spare time. The thought of Julie popped into her mind. Then she realised that she had not thought of Henk and of spending time with him.

Australia and Cyprus, March 1974

Alex's mother had become vague and forgetful over the past two years so he phoned his brother, who was now back in Dunkeith.

"Mum's no good," Frank said. "She sometimes doesn't recognise me. After the old man died she seemed to get worse."

"Shit. When did the old man die? Nobody told me." Alex rocked back at the news.

"I thought Mum said she'd told you." Frank was apologetic. "So I assumed you knew. Sorry about that. It was a year last December. A heart attack. Quick."

Alex wasn't sure how he felt at the news.

"Come and see for yourself. But don't be disappointed. Mum's in a home for people with dementia. It's a right circus. Everyone thinks I'm there to see them," Frank chuckled.

"I got your Christmas card. As usual, three words."

"I never was any good at writing. Anyway, he was no great loss."

"I'll be in touch again when I get my flights organised." He heard his voice echo back down the phone line. "Should I come to Scotland first? The way things are with Mum?"

"It's up to you. Mum could go on for years. But, then, you never know." Frank sounded unsure.

The weeks flew by with too many farewell dinners and the usual offers to carry his bag on the trip. It was a stinking hot day, with Melbourne suffering under a high temperature from a northerly wind. Alex Forbes set off for Athens, Greece. He was excited and apprehensive at the same time. The airport was a shambles with seemingly no-one in charge. He was surprised at the number of armed soldiers everywhere in the terminal. "What's the big deal with the army?" he asked a stewardess walking past.

"The military runs Greece. Didn't you know? You'll see plenty around. But they won't bother you, a tourist. Out of Athens it's not so bad." She gave him a thumbs-up sign.

He nodded thanks, thinking that Greeks seemed to have a penchant for guns. The taxi driver spoke only a few words of English so Alex was not able to ask about the various buildings and monuments they passed on the drive into Athens. Two armed soldiers stood, one on either side of the entrance to the hotel. While signing the register, he questioned the desk clerk. "Why so many soldiers with guns? I saw dozens at the airport and now a couple outside."

"So sorry, Sir. You are from Australia? Your first time in Greece?" He looked closely at Alex.

"Yes. I spent some time in Cyprus years ago but this is my first time here in Athens."

"Ah, Cyprus. Lovely place. But like Greece, there are some problems." The desk clerk shrugged and held out his hands in a gesture of failure.

"What kinds of problems?" Alex wanted as much information as possible.

"For years now we have a military government in Greece. Many problems. Always trouble. You will see. But be careful not to ask questions. Just enjoy the lovely places to visit. I can't say more." He put a finger to the side of his nose.

"And Cyprus. I'm going there too. Do they have the same problems?"

"No, no. Just the Turks. Always fighting. Bad people. But you have been there in Cyprus so you know." The clerk winked with one eye.

Alex made no comment and merely nodded as if he understood. Sounds like nothing's changed, he thought. What a pity they couldn't bottle people like old Mehmet Ali. Bad people, indeed. Better not mention again that I've been to Cyprus before, he decided. From now on I'll just be an Australian. I'll say my parents were Scottish in case anyone queries my accent. Not that it's very Scottish. After two weeks he decided to fly to Cyprus where he could hire a car and drive around at his leisure. The flight to Larnaca Airport in Cyprus took just under two hours. Stepping out on to the tarmac, Alex breathed in the air, a mixture of diesel, kerosene and decaying vegetation that said he was back in Cyprus. A little Morris was ready for him but he decided to opt for a bigger car, remembering the drive with Leyla from Kykko to Paphos. He decided to head first for Famagusta. How long had it been since Leyla and he had sat on that beach? Well, more than he cared to remember. He would never forget that time with her. To think that he could have been living here all these years if, if that little Greek bastard hadn't taken a shot at him. The road hugged the coast, past dirty salt flats, then round the bay on the way to Dhekelia, the British Army base. On an impulse he pulled off the main road and drove up to the boom-gate entrance to the base.

A Military Policeman moved forward, "Yes Sir?" He gave a half salute. "This is a military base. No admission without authority."

"G'day. I'm on holiday. I used to be in the army here. I've been to Dhekelia many times. Thought I'd have a look on my way to Famagusta."

"Sorry, Sir. Unless you have official business I can't let you enter the base."

"Any chance of you checking with a senior officer? I was here during the *EOKA* trouble. It's kind of a trip down memory lane." He looked hopefully at the sentry.

"Will you be in Cyprus long, Sir?" The reply was polite and measured.

"Don't really know. Couple of weeks maybe. Why?" Seated in the car, he was forced to look up at the MP.

"You can phone and make an appointment to inspect the base. You probably won't recognise it, mind. Been a lot of changes. In the meantime, turn round and return to the main road." The sentry saluted.

"Maybe see you later, then. Cheers mate," he gave a hearty call as he drove off back to the main road.

Just past Dhekelia he was surprised to see two tanks and three trucks full of soldiers. Not British soldiers, he thought. Unless they've been here a while. They all looked dark and swarthy. Nodding as he passed, he realised they were probably part of the Cypriot army. That's right, he thought, Makarios, they're still at it, fighting each other. With the sun now behind him, Famagusta loomed up ahead, a fortress city, the minaret of Lala Mustafa Pasa Mosque standing clear above the city. A roadblock not far into the city forced him to stop.

"What's up, mate?" he asked in his best Aussie accent.

The soldier unslung his sten gun and moved towards the car, its barrel pointed at Alex. Two other unshaven soldiers walked round inspecting the car. One called out something in what Alex presumed was Greek. An officer stepped out of a little box-like hut.

"English?"

"Aussie, mate. Australian," Alex shouted confidently as if the man was deaf.

"Ah, Austraalyeean," the officer smiled. "Many Greeks in Austraayeea. Good on ye, mate." He mimicked.

"That's right. Can I get through? I'm on holiday. Go see Famagusta." He smiled, thinking how like a tourist he sounded with his pidgin English.

"No possible old city. Turks they have it closed." The officer shrugged.

"Can I get to the beach? Want to see beach. Famous beach."

"Ah, beach. Go down this way until past city walls then you can go. Maybe checkpoint today?" The Greek officer pointed Alex to turn right and head for Palm Beach.

The beach was deserted. He stood on the promenade and looked all the way down the coast. Nostalgia filled his throat as his mind went back to that day with Leyla. He stood there for several minutes, then, shaking his head, he walked back to the car. Might as well head for Nicosia, he thought, check into a hotel and pay the tourist office a visit. He drove through the villages of Kouklia and Kondea. Soldiers seemed to be everywhere. He thought it was strange that no-one had mentioned that Cyprus, like Greece, appeared to be under military rule. Nicosia appeared to be a city under siege. Oil drums blocked side streets. Soldiers and men in trousers and shirts stood at several corners. Finally, he found himself in Homer Avenue and pulled up at the Regina Hotel.

"Yes?" the desk clerk looked suspiciously at Alex.

"Got a room, mate? Two, three, maybe more nights?" He reached inside his bag.

"You British? Newspaper man?" the desk clerk continued to look warily at him.

"No. Just a tourist from Australia."

"Ah, Austraalyea. Good country. Many Greek Cypriots in Austraalyea."

Alex shook his head at this mantra. It's a wonder there're any Greeks left in Greece and Cyprus, he thought.

"Good room for you, Sir. Own bathroom. Okay?" the clerk pulled a key from a set of pigeonholes behind the desk.

"Too right," Alex said. "Make it three nights to start with."

After the usual formality of showing his passport and signing the register, he carried his suitcase up a flight of stairs to a room with the most basic of furniture. He decided to unpack later. The tourist information office in Metaxas Square welcomed him to Cyprus, and then issued a series of warnings about places to visit. "Sorry. Ghazientop is not suitable. Orta Keuy? Why do you wish to go there?" The tourism officer gave him a puzzled look. Alex decided to cut short the conversation after being told that many places were "rebel" controlled towns and villages. He realised that any further requests might be viewed with suspicion. Thanking the tourism officer, he went for a walk. At the Ledra Palace he found Canadian soldiers with United Nations helmets and insignia manning a checkpoint. He waved a hand at the corporal standing on duty.

"G'day, mate."

"Yes, Sir?" The corporal moved forward.

"What's with the checkpoint? I'm an Australian on holiday. I wanted to drive north to Kyrenia." He waved a hand towards the north.

"That's fine, Sir. We have a buffer zone here to separate the Greek part of Nicosia from the Turkish quarter. But you can go through if you like. Just be careful. We've had very little trouble recently but you never know. One gunfire and they'll all start."

"So I can go through now? I can walk through? No problems?"

"It's up to you. You can walk or drive. If you're after buying some souvenirs or the like, best to do it this side. Not much over there." He inclined his head north.

"Well, I'll have a look, anyway. Might as well while I'm here." He decided to check out the so-called Turkish quarter. Maybe they have their own tourist office, he thought. The guard raised the boom and Alex sauntered through just like any tourist out for a stroll. After about twenty minutes he reached a run-down little house with a small sign that said "Public Relations Office".

"Is this where I get tourist information?" he asked a young woman with close-cropped hair, seated at a desk.

"No English." She smiled apologetically.

"Anyone speak English?" He smiled back

"English? Miss Ozkara. No here."

"When?" Then he paused. Ozkara. Coincidence. Could be a relative, he thought. "When come?" he said the two words slowly.

The girl shrugged, obviously not understanding. Alex pointed to his watch and repeated the words "when come". The girls smiled shyly and moved her finger in two revolutions. "Ah, two days?" He said the words slowly. The girl shrugged again. He looked around the room. There was no sign of any maps or tourist brochures. Mainly files. He went out. Not much joy there. he thought, but it might be worth a visit in a couple of days. This Ozkara woman might know Mehmet Ali.

For the next two days he wandered round Nicosia, on the Greek side, enjoying seeing some familiar places. He decided to drive north to Kyrenia and stop at the Public Relations office on the way. "It's me again," he said to the uncomprehending girl in the front room. "English-speak lady?"

The girl shrugged.

"Ozkara lady?"

The girl smiled at the name and walked over to the door of a room off to the side. He watched as she tapped on the door. Alex heard a voice say something, obviously Turkish. The door opened and his mouth dropped open at the sight of a very attractive woman who looked a bit like Leyla, only older and more mature. She stared at him for seconds then put a hand to her mouth and gave a cry.

"Alexander! Not you." She began to cry.

"Christ," the word came out strangled, painful. "Leyla? My God. Leyla? You're alive?"

He moved forward and took her hands in his. She staggered back and collapsed in a chair in front of a desk. Alex knelt down, still holding her hands. He buried his head in her lap then looked up at the tear-stained face. "I—ah—I—ah, I thought you were dead. They said you had died. Christ, this is unreal." Leyla was trembling, unable to control her body.

He lifted up her hands and kissed each one. No ring, he noticed. Miss Ozkara. Not married, he realised and his heart jumped. "They told me you died. They sent me back to England. I can't understand." His voice began to crack. Finding Leyla was overwhelming, like an incredible, overwhelming nightmarish dream. But she was real.

Leyla sucked in deep breaths, her breasts heaving. She brushed at her tear-filled eyes. "You. It is you. You look only a bit different." Her voice choked again as she looked down at the young man who had grown older, more full in the face, but was still Alexander.

"You still look beautiful. You are beautiful. Christ, I can't believe this is happening." He kept his eyes fixed on her face. His heart was going thump, thump and he wasn't quite sure what his mind was doing.

Leyla shook her head from side to side. "I don't know what to say. What to do." She began crying again and Alex kissed her tears, then gave her a gentle kiss on her lips.

She pulled back. "No. No. Please, it's all too much. I can't believe you're here. Why are you here? Where have you been all these years?" She jerked back, agitated.

He grabbed a chair from behind the desk and sat it down next to Leyla's. He shook his head from side to side. "I can't understand it. They told me you were dead and that your father was being moved to Famagusta. I just thought it was the end. I'm so sorry. I should have tried to contact your father but...but after two weeks at sea and then, then, all the interviews, I thought it was over."

Leyla fumbled for a handkerchief and blew her nose. Then she patted her hair. "But how are you here? In Cyprus? After all this time?" She made a gesture of hopelessness.

"Can we go somewhere? Not here. I need to explain. Not here." He put a hand under her chin and looked deeply into her eyes.

"Oh, Alexander. You don't understand." She sighed deeply.

"You're married?" He felt his heart sink.

"No. No." She put both hands to her head. "I have to think. I have to think. You'll have to give me time to think."

"Tell me what it is," he persisted.

"No." Leyla coughed and sat up straight. "Please. Let me think. Take all this in. I can't talk now. I have to think." She pushed his hands away.

"Later, then. When you finish work? I'll pick you up. I have a car. Please."

"Oh, Alexander. If only it was that easy. No. Go away now and I'll, I'll see you tonight. About eight? Are you alone?" Her voice wavered.

"Yes. Just me. I'm on an extended holiday. From Australia. That's where I live."

"Australia? What happened?"

"It's a long story. It's not important. I don't want to leave but if you promise we can meet tonight?" He took hold of her hands again. "I'm just as shocked and shattered as you are." Alex could see the colour return to her cheeks. Christ, he thought. I feel so weak.

"Oh, Alexander. I need you to go. Now! I can't stop shaking and feeling awful. My body is collapsing. Let me go now. We'll meet tonight." She pushed his chest to make him leave.

"Where? Where will we meet?" He had to have an answer.

Leyla was about to say Ledra Palace then checked herself. "Where are you staying?"

"The Regina Hotel. Do you know it?" His eyes were fixed on her face.

"Of course. It's on the Greek side. Maybe we'd better make it the Ledra Palace after all."

Alex wasn't sure what she meant but hurriedly agreed. "Much better than the Regina. You're sure you'll be there at eight?" He couldn't tear his eyes away.

"I'll be there. I can't believe this is happening." She shook her head again. "Now, please go before I start to cry again. I must look a mess."

Carefully kissing her on the cheek, Alex stood up. His legs were shaky. He saw an older but very beautiful, mature Leyla.

Her tear-stained face looked up and she smiled, a bewildered, childlike smile.

"Eight o'clock then, the Ledra Palace?"

Leyla nodded, unable to speak. When she was sure that he'd left the office, her mind jumped from Alexander to Julie. How would she tell her? How would she react? Her stomach felt heavy as if she'd been punched. Keep calm. Get through the day. Then face Julie. Closing her eyes, she thought of the man who had just turned her life upside down once again. She finished work early and met Julie at the school gate.

"What's up? You look a bit pale, *Anne*? Leyla? Is everything all right? Is it *Anneanne*? Has something happened?" The questions gushed out.

Leyla's head was aching and the torrent of questions didn't help. "No. She is fine. It's something else. I want to talk to you about it. Wait till we get home." She began to feel weak again.

"But tell me on the way."

"Just be patient. Wait. We won't be long." How like Alexander she looks now that I've seen him again. As soon as they were inside the house Julie demanded to know what the big secret was.

"Sit down and listen. Without interrupting for once." Leyla pushed her down on the divan. Julie frowned and then pouted.

"I met your father today." She let the words hang in the air.

"My father? Is he here? In Nicosia? Is he married? Does he have a family?"

Leyla waited until Julie had stopped firing questions. She took a deep breath. "He came into the office. I nearly died. No, he's not married as far as I know. Maybe he was. He didn't mention a family." Her eyes filled with tears. Julie took hold of her hand and held it to her cheek.

"What made him come back? After all these years? Can I meet him? When?"

Leyla held up her hands to stop the deluge of questions. "I'm meeting him, Alexander, tonight. I didn't tell him about you. He doesn't know. I thought I'd speak to you first. How do you feel?" She couldn't stop shaking.

"Fantastic. I'm going to see my father. I knew I would one day. I told you I would. Can't we go and see him now? Please? I can't wait." Julie pulled away.

"Slow down. He doesn't know you exist. I think I should tell him first, talk to him. Then we'll see." Leyla put her hands to her cheeks. She felt hot.

"What time are you meeting my father?" Julie persevered.

"At eight. At the Ledra Palace." She took out a handkerchief and blew her nose.

"Can't you make it earlier, then bring him home?"

Leyla put a hand to her forehead. It was throbbing. She looked at her excited daughter who seemed to have no idea of how incredible the whole thing was. "I need to lie down for a while. I suppose I could phone him and make it earlier. I'm not sure if I should bring him here. Are you sure that you want to see him tonight? It might be upsetting." She looked anxiously at her animated daughter.

"Just meet him and bring him round. Or can I come with you?" She seemed oblivious to the strangeness of the situation.

"No. Not to the Ledra Palace. Let me lie down then we'll decide." On shaky legs Leyla went to her bedroom. She fumbled in her handbag and found a painkiller. Lying on her bed, she could hear Julie singing in the sitting room. Sleep wouldn't come but she felt rested and calm after an hour.

"I'll phone and see what I can do," she said. Julie clapped her hands.

The clerk at the Regina Hotel was put out that he had to go upstairs to inform Alex that he had a phone call. She explained that she would prefer to meet at six and then maybe go on somewhere else. He agreed to the change of plans, happy to meet Leyla sooner rather than later. He was waiting impatiently when she walked in through the entrance. "You look even more beautiful," he said as he put out a hand to touch her arm.

"No tears and a little make-up." She smiled even though she felt very nervous.

The lounge bar was almost empty so they sat down and Alex ordered a wine for himself and a soda for Leyla.

"Do you have a family?" she began.

"No family. Never married. And you?"

"Well," Leyla wondered how to tell him. "I have never married but I have a daughter. She's fifteen." The words hung in the air for seconds.

"Fifteen?" Alex stared hard at his first real love. "Fifteen? Then, then she was born in sixty-nine?" he leaned forward, thinking of sixty-eight when the girl might have been conceived. "Is she my daughter?"

"Yes. Julie is your daughter. How do you feel about that?" Leyla's eyes never left his face.

He brushed back his hair with both hands and stared at her. "My daughter? Julie? She's fifteen? I can't believe I have a daughter. I like the name. Does she know about me?" he asked breathlessly.

"Only that I met a soldier and we made...we ended up with a child. She knows your name is Alexander. She has no idea what you look like. I never had a photo. She looks a lot like you. The same skin, the nose, the eyes. She has a malformed left hand. It's not too bad." She shrugged. She put a small handkerchief to her nose.

"Oh. Uh. Have you told her you're meeting me?"

"She knows." Leyla tried to keep any emotion out of her voice.

"What did she say? Does she want to see me? Would she like to?" he asked hopefully.

"That's why I'm early. She wants me to take you home. Now. She's waiting."

He put down his half-full glass. "Let's go, then. I can't wait. My daughter. All these years and I never knew."

"What will we say? About us, I mean? She's at a difficult age. Fifteen." She patted her hair.

"The truth. We were in love and it happened. We made a mistake. They told me you had died. Let Julie decide. She can ask the questions." He reached out and touched her hand.

The walk to Leyla's home was sombre. He wanted to hold her hand but sensed reluctance on Leyla's part. He kept glancing at the beautiful woman. She looked the same but there was a difference. What do you expect, he thought, it's been sixteen years. She tried not to look but her eyes wandered to the man striding along beside her. He's still Alexander, she thought. He's still good-looking in an older way. Leyla's emotions were a confused tangle. She had a feeling of relief mixed with an uneasy awareness that this night could be a closure or a turning point in her life. Her hand shook a little as she pushed a large key into the lock and opened the door. Julie was seated on the lilac-covered divan, hair brushed back, tied with a ribbon, and a hint of lipstick on her lips. She had on a knee-length pale blue denim dress, and sat with hands in her lap. Leyla and Alex stood side by side in the doorway. Julie stood up.

Leyla moved to her side and put out a hand, "Julie. This is your father, Alexander. Julie," the words straggled out as she looked at Alex.

He held out his hands like a priest about to give a blessing. His eyes filled up and he moved towards Julie, seeing her through crystals of tears. She flung herself into his open arms and held on so tight that he could do nothing but breathe in the perfume behind her ears. Leyla watched as they remained locked together, his head bent, resting on Julie's shoulder. Now her eyes began to glaze over with tears as she felt a sense of love and loss. Eyes glistening, she smiled a happy, contented smile that Julie had found her father. Then her smile faded as she felt a sense of dread that someone else would be sharing Julie's love. She began to feel uncomfortable as they continued to cling to each other. Finally, they parted and Julie looked up at her father. "I knew one day I'd find you. I told *Anne*, Leyla, that I would find you. Now you've found me. I feel all funny inside. Just seeing you. You know, a man. My father."

"I'm sorry. I never even knew that you existed. Did your mother tell you I thought she'd died? After she'd been shot? I didn't know about you." He looked down in wonder at his young daughter.

"Come and sit down. Beside me. My legs are like jelly. You too." She pulled Leyla down on the divan beside her with her father on her other side. She held each one by the hand. He held the small hand. He made no mention of its slight deformity. Julie thought nothing of it.

"Well," she broke the silence, "I have a mother and a father now. You've found each other." She sounded happy.

"Julie!" Leyla wanted to dampen this obvious enthusiasm about them "finding each other". "Maybe I should make a little something to eat. You can talk to Al—your father?"

Julie turned to face him. "What should I call you? *Baba*? Or father? What?" Her eyes lit up as she beamed a smile at Alex.

"Most kids call their father Dad in Australia. But it's up to you. Just so long as you're happy to have a dad."

"Dad." She said the word and wriggled. "I like that. It's like they say at the pictures."

Leyla kissed Julie on the cheek. Raising an eyebrow, she looked questioningly at Alex and went to the small kitchen to prepare some food.

"Tell me about yourself." He took both Julie's hands. "There's so much I don't know and fifteen years is a long, long time."

"Well, we live in Nicosia now. Before that we lived with Grandma in Ghazientop and before that we were in Izmir with Aunt Nafia. That's where I was born. My real name is Gulten, after Grandma." The words spilled out.

"You've certainly been around. All those places. And Turkey, far away." Alex couldn't think of anything else to say.

"Not as far as Australia. Is it a good place? We've seen a little on television. Is it like Cyprus, only bigger?" Her eyes took in every inch of his face.

"Oh, it's a big place, all right. I haven't seen much of it but I'd like to." He shrugged.

Leyla stood in the kitchen, unwilling to interrupt the flow of questions and answers. She could sense Julie's interest in that far-off country. She thought of the book about a town called Alice.

Julie was telling him all about the struggles of Turkish Cypriots. "But you must know how it's been for eleven years," she insisted.

"You have to understand," he tried to think how to explain, "Australia has been more concerned with the war in Vietnam. All the newspapers ever talk about is Vietnam. I did hear about an attempt on the life of Makarios. But that was back in what, 1970?"

"So you don't know that for eleven years we have been prisoners in our own country?" Julie was incredulous. "How can that be?"

Leyla called from the kitchen. "Because the Greeks control the government and the world media. They're very clever. We Turks are just an ungrateful rebel minority."

He looked at Julie. "Did you know I have a year, almost, before I go back to Australia? Would you mind if I change my plans and stay here for...I don't know, maybe until the end of summer? Would you like that?"

"That would be fantastic. It won't be long and I'll be on holiday. And I can see you after school until then. Can't I, Leyla?" she called out to her mother.

Bringing in some dishes of bread, pickles, olives and cheese, Leyla gave her a stern look. "Don't start making too many plans. Yet. We'll see how things go for a week or two first."

"*Anne*," Julie protested loudly, "Ba..., Dad wants to stay and so do I."

"Is it a problem, Leyla?" He wondered why she was so cautious.

"Leyla has a boyfriend." Julie looked daggers at her mother.

"He's not a boyfriend. He's a man, a soldier, I've been out with a few times." She glared back.

Alex felt deflated. He knew that he had no right to expect

that Leyla would not be married or in a relationship but the news still made him feel like an intruder. "A Turkish soldier?" he asked, uncertain.

"He's a Major in the United Nations lot. He's from Holland. A Dutchman," Julie scoffed.

"He's a Major with UNICYP actually and he's due to return to Holland very soon. Two weeks, I think?" Leyla spoke softly. "I'm not sure."

"Oh," a relieved Alex muttered, "so what happens then?"

"Nothing. Nothing. I don't know why Julie brought it up. Look, have something to eat. I don't have any beer or wine. Would water be all right?" She was eager to change the subject.

Leyla hadn't told Julie anything about the night at the Ledra Palace Hotel. She'd lied when she had told Julie that she had had to go to the Turkish enclave near Akrotiri and would stay overnight. But she and Henk had gone to Kyrenia to the Dome Hotel. Poor Henk. Her period had arrived that same day. Henk had spoken about returning to Holland. Although she liked him, she couldn't see herself and Julie leaving Cyprus. He'd been disappointed but accepted her decision with little argument. By ten o'clock she decided that it was time for Julie to go to bed. Alex made no move to leave so she said that she had an early start to make up for leaving work early. Julie kissed Alex on both cheeks and gave him a hug as he was leaving. Leyla accepted a kiss on the cheeks before he gave a small wave and promised to take them out for dinner the following evening.

Julie looked up with a cheeky grin as she lay in bed. "Leyla, he's very nice. I can see why you fell in love with him."

Leyla kissed her goodnight with a warning. "Don't get your expectations up too high, little one. You know very little about your father. And neither do I. It's all been a bit of a shock for him too. Let him get to know you slowly. You have the whole summer. Who knows? Don't press too hard. All right?"

Julie smiled up at the concerned face. "I love you, *Anne*. I'll never leave you," she murmured sleepily.

"Yes, you will. But that's all in the future. Go to sleep now."

Sitting quietly on the divan, Leyla thought about Henk leaving, Alex turning up and her daughter. Julie now had a father in the flesh and she wasn't about to let him go. She knew her Julie. It was a long time before she finally fell asleep, her mind going over and over all of the possibilities.

The next day she introduced Alex to Mr Denktash, who took an immediate liking to the man from Australia. He listened as Alex explained his previous work for the army in Cyprus, his friendship with Mehmet Ali and his concern on learning the plight of the Turkish Cypriots. Denktash described to him the negotiations that had led to the formation of the Republic of Cyprus and the untrustworthiness of Makarios and the Greek Junta.

"So how do you see it all panning out, Sir?" Alex asked.

"Since 1970 and the failed attempt to assassinate Makarios, there have been other attempts. The forces against him will succeed one day." He spoke with authority.

"What then?"

"All hell will break loose. There will be a civil war among the Greeks. Each side hates the other. Those who follow Makarios and the supporters of *EOKA* B. Then whoever wins will turn their attention to us. The Akritas plan I told you about failed but they will try again."

"What will you do? If there's a civil war?"

"We are ready. There's no way they will exterminate us. This is our land as much as theirs. If need be, Turkey will send in its army. They too are ready. Everyone knows that. This is much more than Makarios will accept. He is cunning but also blind to the consequences of his actions."

"I can't get over how much has happened here. I know that I've been busy but I don't recall seeing any of this in our newspapers. Maybe I missed it?" Alex looked puzzled.

"That's one of our problems. With so much going on in the world we are forgotten. We are just a small people. That's why I wished for Leyla to become involved in trying to get our message out to the world." Denktash smiled at her.

"I didn't know." Alex shook his head. "I only know what Julie has told me and now you."

"I'll give you some books to read. You have the time? You'll learn about our side of the story." He moved to some bookshelves crammed with books.

During the day, while he waited impatiently to see Leyla and Julie, Alex read everything about the incredible struggle of the Turkish Cypriots to survive. Now I'll have something to talk about with them, he thought. The evening hours flew by as Leyla told him some of the horror stories of the past eleven years. She left a message at the Ledra Palace Hotel. Henk arrived at her office the next day. She explained that Alex had come to Cyprus on holiday and had accidentally found her. She told him about the meetings with Julie and Alex's plans to stay until the end of summer.

"Then I won't ask to see you again. It's best that way. It's been a great pleasure for me to meet you. What a pity I am here for such a short a time. Still, I must be honest. I know that I am not the man for you. I'll always think of Cyprus and you with good memories. Maybe this man Alexander is for you? You deserve the best from life. Remember me as a man who cared very much for you."

She looked at his glum face. She felt a sadness that this good man had listened to her story. He'd graciously accepted the past. But she knew in her heart that nothing could ever have come of their brief affair.

"I wish, I'd hoped, that this might last, but it's not to be." A downcast Henk lifted her hand, kissed it and left an apprehensive Leyla to her thoughts.

Makarios summoned Clerides, Papadopoulos, Kyprianou and other senior members of the government to the Presidential Palace.

"Gentlemen. After the death of Grivas at the end of January I accepted *EOKA* B's offer of a cessation of their operations. In return I gave amnesty to all those who had been attempting to overthrow me, and—"

"A premature move in my opinion," Clerides interrupted.

"In hindsight, yes, of course." Makarios offered a grim smile of acknowledgement of the obvious.

"It has proved useless, Mr President." Papadopoulos tried to share the criticism.

"Yes. Unfortunately, they have continued to disrupt and attack innocent people, including a village priest. An unforgivable sin. So I now propose to ban *EOKA* B as an illegal organisation."

"Will that make any difference?" a doubtful Clerides frowned.

"They have forsaken us. I will give them forty-eight hours to surrender. Otherwise they will be hunted down, arrested and punished in such a way that all will see the folly of opposing me, the government."

"It's not just *EOKA* B but the Greek officers who stir up hatred of us. We need to get rid of them. For our own good and safety. Do you agree?" Clerides looked uneasily at Makarios.

"I will see the Greek Ambassador again shortly. I will insist that these disruptive Greek officers be recalled immediately to Greece. I know that they are part of the plan from Athens to remove me, alive or dead."

"It was perhaps a mistake to invite these officers and the Greek militia at the beginning." Clerides nodded.

"If only we had been able to rid the island of Turks when we had the chance. However, it was unfortunate that I was forced to form a ministry with so many ex-*EOKA* men. Useless tacticians. One is sometimes saddled with incompetents and traitors. Like Georgjiadis. He has paid the price for his treachery." A thin smile creased the face of the Archbishop.

"You did well to dispose of him, did you not, Beatitude?" Kyprianou said approvingly.

Makarios frowned but made no reply to the accusation, however well meant.

"Now we have the matter of the bishops, those who wish me to step down as Archbishop of all Cyprus. Fools. They have no hope of success. But their attempts to de-frock me cause distress among my flock."

"Surely they and the dictatorship in Athens know the dangers involved. This hell-bent desire to affect *Enosis* at this stage is madness. I understand from my contacts in Turkey that plans are already in place to send troops if such provocation continues." Clerides nodded forcefully.

. "I have informed President Ghizikis through the Greek Ambassador of my fears that I see his hand behind my demise. That is why we must remove these officers from our National Guard. They are the real threat." Makarios slapped a fist into his other palm.

"Was that wise? To confront him? He and the rest of them may act sooner rather than later. I am in favour of sending Clafcos to Athens to plead for time. Persuade them that we will bring Cyprus to the bosom of Mother Greece. That is what they want, what they need to stay in power." Papadopoulos glanced at the others round the table.

Clerides held up a hand. "They may not last much longer. The people of Greece are sick of military rule. I say we wait. Ignore them. Let them be the creators of their own downfall."

"I think Clafcos is right." Makarios leaned in his direction. "Even these generals have some brains. They know that unless they kill me, God be with us, they will never have Cyprus."

"I agree," Clerides said. "Despite these different groups, *EOKA* B, Sampson and Yanitis, all agitating for more direct action to bring about *Enosis*, the Junta knows that our loyal fighters will never let them win."

"Well, I want any dissidents weeded out. Make arrests. Show strength. Get rid of these Greek officers and re-organise the forces under our command." Makarios leaned back in his chair, indicating that enough had been said.

"I hope that we are not underestimating these people. The Americans, the Russians are very concerned at the unpredictable nature of the Junta," Clerides warned.

"Leave the Junta to me." Makarios smiled. "I can handle them. They will not dare to act against the chosen leader. I am the one leader the people will obey."

"That's not what the newspapers are reporting." Kyprianou snorted.

"The people know who controls the press. They will not be fooled." Makarios stood up, as did the others. All looked worried as they left the meeting.

The weeks went by with Alex spending the days driving out from Nicosia to visit non-Turkish places he'd known during his army days. Despite the tension and occasional outbreak of violence, he was able to move around unhindered. Nowhere was very far from Nicosia. The only time he stayed away overnight was on a trip to Paphos. He found about a dozen enclaves where Turkish Cypriots were crowded into abominable conditions. How a country led by a Christian Archbishop could allow such suffering was beyond him. Every Turkish enclave told the same story. No employment, primitive living conditions and harassment any time the farmers went out to their fields. As the noose had tightened on the ghettos, many told him that they had left everything behind after being attacked by Greek and Cypriot militia. Some had not seen their farms in over six years. The Greek-controlled part of the island was booming. New hotels were springing up.

"They are destroying our island," one old man said with a sad shake of the head. "I sold my land for a tenth of its value. I need money to eat."

Alex agreed. "They're certainly changing the island."

He phoned Gareth and his accountant every two weeks and was happy that everything was going well. Despite his spending, his bank account continued to grow. Living on Cyprus was cheap and a strong Australian dollar made things even better. Food was plentiful in Greek Nicosia and Leyla had given in to Julie's plea that she and Alex be allowed to cook dinner.

"It's like being a real family, isn't it, Dad?" Julie gave him a mischievous look as she prepared rice to go with the spicy meat dish he was cooking.

"Not sure if your mother sees it quite like that." He was pleased to have her support.

"Oh, I think she does. I notice that she's singing more now. I think she's happy that you've come back." She watched his face to see his reaction.

Alex stopped stirring the rich, fragrant dish. "I see a little scheming going on here. You'd like to think that your mother and I could get together." He closed one eye to look conspiratorially at Julie.

"It would be nice, though. Wouldn't it? What a romantic end it would be. Don't you think?" Julie's hands came together as if praying.

"I'm not sure that your mother is ready to think along those lines. Let's just be patient. We're going along just fine. If you try matchmaking you might just make her back off."

She frowned and pursed her lips at this reprimand.

"But," he smiled, "don't stop altogether. I need a little help."

"So you would like to get married?" Julie whooped. "I knew it. I can see the way you look at *Anne*."

"Well," Alex drawled, "I wouldn't want you to say this to Leyla, but this has been just about the best time of my life. Finding your mother alive and a beautiful daughter as a bonus. What more could I ask for?"

"Then stay longer. You don't have to go back to Australia yet. Till April." She pleaded. "By then she'll be in love with you all over again. I know she will."

"Just play it cool, you beautiful little schemer. We have to get to know each other again. Might not be easy. I may just rent a little place until the end of the year." The decision came out unexpectedly. He nodded to make the declaration definite.

"Hooray. Is that the right word?" Julie beamed. "Shall we tell Leyla when she gets home?"

"Don't jump in with it. Let it come up in conversation. Now, concentrate on what you're doing. She'll be home soon." He pointed her in the direction of the baking dish.

Leyla opened the door to find two happy people humming and singing a song about the sunshine of my life. It sounded good, it made her feel good. Alex was singing "I'll always want to be around you". That could be nice, if...if...she thought, enjoying the homely scene and the nice smell of cooking.

"Leyla. You're just in time. I'm just going to open this bottle of wine. It's not very cold. I meant to get some ice but I forgot. We've been too busy, haven't we, Julie?" He pulled Leyla inside and closed the door. Without thinking, he kissed her cheeks, hugged her and kissed her on her lips. They looked at each other for a second then laughed.

Julie watched with delight. "We're going to have a wonderful dinner. Just the three of us," she announced to her parents.

Sitting on the divan, sipping wine, he asked Leyla for the latest news.

"Mr Denktash is concerned at the number of Turks leaving the enclaves and going to work for the Greeks. He thinks it undermines our resolve. He proposes to punish anyone who cooperates with the illegal Greek Government." She shook her head sadly.

"But you can't blame them. People need to work to feed their families. It's always those at the bottom who suffer the most." Alex felt quite emotional and ached to put his arm around her. She sensed his feeling and leaned against his shoulder for a moment. Julie stood quiet as a mouse, afraid to speak.

"After so many years," Leyla sighed, "we can't give in now. I know it's hard but Mr Denktash knows what's best."

During dinner, Julie decided not to wait any longer. "Dad? Are you comfortable at that awful hotel?" She looked at Alex, then at Leyla who tensed, wondering what Julie was trying to do.

"Not really." He answered between mouthfuls of food. "I thought I might find a place to rent. Something small."

"But I thought you intended to leave at the end of summer?" Leyla's heart gave a little jump. "Is it worth it for a couple of months?" She noticed the look shared between them. The singing, Julie's remark about the three of us, obviously something was going on. With a tilt of her head she looked squarely at Alex. "Is there something I don't know?"

"Well," the word came out slowly, "actually I've decided to stay longer. At least till the end of the year. I've nothing special to do anywhere. And the weather's perfect." He turned to Julie for back-up.

"I see." Leyla looked from one to the other. "What about the visit to see your mother? Isn't that important?"

"Yeh, I didn't mean that. To sound like that. I can always fly there for a week. Or maybe I could go to Scotland on my way back." He waved his hands apologetically.

"There's nothing to rent on this side. We're lucky to have our own little place. So it would have to be on the Greek side." Leyla sounded thoughtful. "A place of your own would be good, I suppose." She blushed as she thought of being alone with him in his apartment.

"I think it's a great idea." Julie enthused. "If it has two bedrooms I could maybe stay there overnight. On a Saturday?"

"Let's not get too far ahead." Alex held up his hands to stop her going on. "First, let me find a place. And see if I can get a six-month lease."

"That would take you up to the end of December?" Leyla couldn't help sounding pleased.

"I can't wait," the words exploded from Julie, "can I help find a place?"

"Better not," Leyla made a face, "if they see you, the owners may not want to rent it out."

"But it's okay for you to visit, isn't it?" He glanced sharply at her.

"That shouldn't be a problem. Depends on where it is. You check out what's available then we'll see." A cautious Leyla nodded.

It was one of the best nights Alex had spent since arriving in Cyprus.

Cyprus, June 1974

Denktash faced a crowded meeting in Nicosia. Everyone was talking and he stood for several minutes before the crowd finally fell silent. "We are receiving so many reports it's difficult to know where to start," he said, shaking his head. "Our information suggests that the Greek Militia and the Cyprus National Guard are up to something."

"Tell us something new," a voice called out from the rear.

"The next person who interrupts with a stupid statement like that will be ejected and fined. Understood? Now listen. They appear to be mobilising for some kind of offensive. A major offensive. Tanks and armoured cars are being camouflaged. Reservists are being called up for duty. A training exercise, they've been told. However, we've been expecting something for the past month." Denktash's eyes swept the room.

"Make that years," the same man called out.

Denktash ignored him. "The Archbishop, Makarios, is under a great deal of pressure. He has no control over the Greek forces and only a few faithful bands of supporters. AKEL still appears to be on his side. I want a message sent out to every village. Keep inside your safe area until we see what develops. If you know someone working illegally for the Greeks, warn them that they will be in great danger if our suspicions are proved correct. We know that something is afoot. We must take no chances. Understood?"

Everyone muttered agreement. As they shuffled out, Leyla asked Denktash if it would be wise to go to Kyrenia for a holiday.

"A holiday? When?"

"The first week in July. Alexander is getting a little house on the eighth. He's offered to take Julie and me for a holiday in the first week." She avoided looking him in the eye.

"I see. You are now having a holiday with this man. Is this what you want?" He looked mystified.

"It's for Julie, really. She's enjoying finding her father." Leyla shrugged.

"And you?" He sounded protective.

"Well, it's been better than I expected. About Kyrenia?" She hesitated, unwilling to divulge any more.

"I think not. Can he afford Turkey? There you will be safe!"

"I'll have to ask. Anyway, if he is able to afford it, can I have the first week in July off?"

"If you wish. I don't think anything will happen in the next few weeks. But who knows?"

Leyla explained the situation to Alex as they relaxed on the divan. "We can fly to Antalya then catch a bus to Kalkan. I've always wanted to go there. My Aunt Nafia wanted to take me there but then my father was killed and we never had the chance." She felt emotional as she remembered her father's death.

The next day, at the travel agency, Alex discovered that a new hotel had just been built in Kalkan. Julie was excited. Leyla seemed happy. He put her reticence down to the fact that they would be together every day for a week. Although they had become closer and closer, something seemed to hold her back from any intimate contact other than an occasional brief kiss on the cheeks.

He gazed in wonder at the size of the bus station or *otogar* in Antalya. Fortunately, Leyla was able to organise the right bus out of the thirty or so buses parked in a huge square. The journey hugged the most magnificent coastline he'd ever seen. "This is even better than where I live on the Great Ocean Road in Victoria," he told Julie as he looked out at the blue Mediterranean on one side and the steep hills on the other. When the bus pulled into the tiny *otogar* at Kalkan, all three stood and admired the view at the end of a narrow street that sloped steeply down to the harbour.

"I love it," Leyla exclaimed. "It looks like something out of a dream. Oh, Alexander, I think Aunt Nafia was right. This is a special place."

He put an arm round Julie's shoulder and looked at his first love. She looked beautiful in a flowery cotton dress that hugged her upper body and flared out to just below her knees. "Let's go."

While Leyla and Alex unpacked in their separate rooms, Julie went down to inspect the hotel. Within minutes she was back upstairs. "There's even a swimming pool. But we have no bathing costumes," she wailed in a pleading voice.

Alex joined them. On hearing the news, he waved his hand in surrender. "We'll buy some tomorrow."

He couldn't take his eyes off Leyla in a pale blue one-piece bathing suit. She kept glancing at his firm body, especially when he stepped out of the pool, water dripping down as he adjusted his bathing trunks. The water was warm and despite a warning, Julie would not rest in the shade. By one o'clock they were ready for lunch and a siesta in their rooms. Julie went back to the pool at three while Alex and Leyla went for a stroll round the picturesque little harbour. When they returned, Julie was quite pink and feeling unwell.

"I should have made sure that she used lots of sun lotion," Alex said. I see this all the time at home. It's my fault."

"It's no-one's fault. She's just so excited. She forgot. I'll put her in a cool bath and make sure she has lots to drink. She'd better stay in the room this evening. Can you get some cream?"

There was no chemist. Leyla cooled down Julie's burning skin. He and Leyla sat by the pool after dinner. An hour passed as he told her about his work and success. They checked on Julie who had not moved.

"She's asleep. Shall we go for a walk until bedtime? Or do you want to sit by the pool again?" She was happy to prolong the evening.

"Come into my room and we'll talk. There're some things I'd like to tell you." He led her by the hand and opened the door to his room.

They sat on the end of the bed. "I've been thinking a lot about you, and Julie." He held both her hands. "I feel, I don't know, I sense that we could…"

She put a finger to his lips. "Don't."

"No. I don't expect you to say anything. What I want to do is for you and Julie. I…whatever happens after this, nothing will be the same for me again. I have plenty of money so I want to give half to you and Julie. It's no good to me. It doesn't make me happy. I can always make more and…"

Leyla looked at him with glistening eyes. She felt an overwhelming emotion, a release. Putting her arms round his neck, she kissed him with a feeling of gratitude. Then as their mouths opened and the kiss deepened she fell back and allowed him to caress her body. For a long time they lay there, close together. In whispers they talked about Famagusta and how they had felt about each other. She told Alex about the birth of Julie and the years of worry and heartache of life in Ghazientop. Alex told her of his desperate need not to be poor and the years of work. She kissed the palm of his hand. He rolled on to his back, relieved that they had cleared some of the baggage of the past. Leyla turned and lay on top, hands in his hair, pushing and pulling. His hands moved up and down her back, pressing her buttocks, squeezing and arching to press harder into her groin.

"Just a minute," Leyla gasped, breaking away and standing up. She slipped her summer dress over her head and unclipped her bra. Then she lay down on him again.

"Are you sure? It's not just because—"

She put a finger to his lips to stop him finishing the sentence. "Shush. Somehow I knew this would happen when I saw you again, that time."

"Oh God. I can't believe this is happening." His voice cracked with passion mixed with relief.

Tears of joy trickled from her eyes. Alex stroked her firm body. She moaned with pleasure.

"I have to," he panted as he pushed Leyla on to her back.

Pulling off his shirt, he shucked off his slacks and lay on top.

She pushed him away. "We might as well take everything off." She laughed nervously.

In seconds they were both completely naked. Side by side they explored each other's body.

"I like the way you touch me," she whispered. She had a brief vision of that day on the beach at Famagusta.

"I like doing it." Alex tried to sound calm and relaxed. He forced himself not to rush.

"Oh, that feels so good. Keep going," she whispered between sucking kisses.

"God. I want you. Is it all right? Can I?" Alex pulled back, afraid he wouldn't be able to stop.

Leyla sucked in a lungful of air. She knew he couldn't stop. "It's as safe a time as any." Breathlessly. "This time of the month. Anyway I don't care. I need you. Lie still for a minute." Leyla pleaded between little kisses. "Let me feel you for as long as you can. Don't hurry. You feel so good." The words came out one at a time.

Pushing up, he looked down at Leyla, feeling an overwhelming sense of satisfaction at being with her. "I love looking at you."

He moved again. Sensual relief spilled over to every part of her body. Lying, kissing her neck, Alex slowly subsided as she stroked his cheek and whispered something in Turkish.

"What?" he said into her ear.

"I said it was beautiful. So beautiful."

Quietly, wrapped in each other's arms, they continued touching, stroking breasts and shoulders.

"I can't believe I'm lying here next to you, making love. It's just incredible that somebody I thought was dead is here with me now." He touched her hair, looking at her soft cheeks, the perspiration on her upper lip, a glazed, empty look in her dark brown eyes.

"And I can't believe that I'm finding lovemaking so nice, so satisfying." Leyla whispered as she softly nibbled his ear lobe.

"I won't leave you again, I promise." A serious Alex looked into her eyes.

"Don't make any promises, Alexander. Just be here now. We have a week. I'm not sure what I'm feeling. For a long time I never thought I'd feel this way. It's all new."

Alex didn't understand what she meant. "You must have—" he began and she put a finger to his lips.

"Shush. I'd better explain."

Slowly, between little kisses, she told Alex about the terrible time in Ghazientop and her rape by Greek soldiers. Her eyes misted over at the memory. Alex pulled her close and held her. Nothing was said. Then she spoke about Henk and how she'd wanted to see if lying with him would show how she felt about him.

"He sounds like a nice man."

"He was, is, but there was no real ecstasy like now. Does it bother you? So soon?"

"No way! I'm just the luckiest man I know. Whatever happened is past. Now there's just us."

As they began to cool down, he sat up and took Leyla by the hand to the shower. Soaping each other, hands running over each other's body, they kissed and washed each other down. It was a happy and tired Alex who kissed her goodnight as she quietly opened the door to her room.

"Goodnight," she whispered," and thank you for bringing us to Kalkan."

Julie's sunburn had settled down by morning but, taking no chances, they went on a short bus trip to Fethiye, an ancient Lycean city with the nearby ruins of Telmessos. Strolling up a winding street, hand in hand, they visited the ruins of a Roman theatre. The cobblestone streets and views of the Fethiye Gulf made for a leisurely, happy day. Julie kept glancing at her mother and father, sensing some change in their attitude to each other. The next day a bus journey took them to Dalyan where they marvelled at the Lycean rock tombs on the way to Turtle Beach. The weather was perfect as they sat outside the Pirat Hotel that evening.

"I think we make a very nice-looking family." Julie knew something had happened, she saw the loving glances. Alex saw her little smile and felt total contentment. Leyla glanced at him and smiled. The week passed in a blur of eating, drinking, nights of lovemaking and an ever more confident Julie.

"I'm going to stay with Grandma Gulten in Ghazientop for a week or maybe even two," a mischievous Julie said on their arrival back in Nicosia. Alex knew what was in the mind of his clever young daughter.

Although communications between Cyprus and Australia were poor, he managed to get through on the phone to John, in Pointsea. He quickly explained the situation. "Can you send me six months of the latest pill? I think there's a new one out. Fewer side-effects." His mouth pressed into the mouthpiece of the phone.

"Sounds like things are going all right there," the fading voice of his doctor friend came through.

"I'll write soon. I promise. Just keep your fingers crossed. Say hi to Viv. And thanks."

It took over three weeks for the small parcel to arrive.

"How kind of Julie to visit her grandmother. Little vixen."

"It's nice not to have to sneak into your room. I love it like this," a relaxed Leyla snuggled up in his arms.

Archbishop Makarios, President of Cyprus, increasingly used a helicopter to visit different parts of the island in order to limit the chances of being ambushed by his enemies, including *EOKA* B and the Greek militia. However, he was forced to go by car to the President's country house in the Troodos Mountains for a weekend away from the heat of Nicosia. With a heavy contingent of his Tactical Reserve Force, his most loyal guards, he looked forward to a weekend of isolation to consider his future tactics. Early on Monday morning, seated in the shade on the south side of the house, he was deep in thought when his faithful brother approached, distraught.

"Can't I have a few last minutes before returning to the Palace?" He grimaced. "Whatever it is, it can wait!"

"Mihail! News has come through that tanks are moving into Nicosia. Thousands of troops are on the move this morning." He stood wringing his hands.

"So it's begun? It's come to this," Makarios groaned under his breath, face inscrutable. "Get the car ready. We will leave now."

"Is that wise?" One of his guards had joined them.

"We will go and see how bad the situation is. I'm sure we will be safe inside the Palace. There we will see what unfolds." He beckoned them to follow as he made his way back into the house.

Meanwhile in Nicosia, Leyla reported for work as usual only to find a message from Rauf Denktash. Hurrying to his office, she could sense that something terrible was happening.

"Leyla." Denktash made no effort to greet her in the usual way. "Your daughter. Is she still in Ghazientop?"

"Yes." She was surprised that he remembered such small details. "She's still at her grandmother's."

"Then I suggest that you get her back here at once. Reports are coming in of tanks in Greek Nicosia and of our villages in the south being surrounded by militia. Water has been cut off at Lefka, and phone lines are cut. Something big is about to happen. We think there will be massive attacks. Well, this may be the beginning of the end. The bastards want to finish us off this time. I've informed Turkey." He looked bleak.

She raced round to Alex's house. Luckily, he was still eating breakfast. It took a few minutes for him to calm her down and find out the reason for her agitated state. "Then I'll drive to Ghazientop and collect Julie. Your mother, too."

"I'm coming with you," she insisted.

"No way." He pushed her down into a chair. "You stay here. If it's surrounded I can get through. I'll wave my Australian passport."

"I want to go and get my daughter," she protested, looking up at a determined Alex.

"She's my daughter too and you're not going anywhere. So let me get on with it." He reached for the car keys.

She stood up and clung to him. "Be careful. And bring Julie back. We both love you. Don't let anything happen."

He kissed her hard. "I'll be back as soon as I can. Just remember what you said, 'I love you'."

Driving as fast as he could, Alex was held up twice, once at Kokinamethro and again at Morphou. Each time, he said that his Australian wife was on a visit to Vouni and he wanted to make sure that she was safe. The Australian passport was a godsend. Ghazientop was surrounded by hundreds of armed soldiers and two tanks. But they let him through. Barricades were everywhere in the village and the Turks checked his passport as he entered. With an armed man standing in the open car door, he made his way to Gulten's house. Inside, he found Julie and her grandmother with several other women and children huddled together in the main room.

Julie threw herself into his arms. "Dad! How did you get here? Where's Leyla? They say we're trapped. The Greeks are going to kill us all." She was not able to stop trembling. "What will they do to us?" she wailed, thinking of her mother's past nightmare experience.

Alex looked at his lovely young daughter and the same thought went through his mind. If I have to fucking die, I'll take a few with me before they get to my daughter. "There's not much time. The bastards are just waiting for someone to give them the signal. I can take three, maybe four, in the car." He looked at Gulten. She shook her head and spoke.

"Grandma says that she will stay here. It's her home. The others too. It may be safer than trying to get back to Nicosia."

"Right. That suits me. Grab a rug. I'll put you in the boot. I don't know what I'll say if we're stopped but I'll shout and raise hell that they can't harm an Australian tourist. Grab it and let's go." He pulled Julie from her grandmother's embrace.

On the return journey he was stopped only once. He was told to go to Dhekelia. "That's where tourists must go. British army base." The Greek soldier pointed towards the south.

Alex merely nodded and drove on. Driving through the Greek part of Nicosia, he could hear the sound of gunfire and the occasional loud explosion of a large gun. He assumed it must be tanks. His face was familiar to most of the Canadian UNICYP guards at the Green Line Checkpoint. Normally, they just waved him through. This time he was stopped. "We suggest that you stay on this side, Sir," a tall, red-faced corporal said. "We understand that the Presidential Palace is being attacked and Greek troops are massed north of the Turkish quarter. The balloon might be going up."

"It's okay. I just need to collect a few things then I'll be back," he lied. The boom gate was opened and he sped through. He headed straight for Leyla's house. Opening the boot of the car, he helped a stiff and bruised Julie to get out. Leyla opened her front door and dashed out. Crying tears of joy, she hugged Julie as if she would never let go. He watched with feelings of satisfaction and envy. Letting go of Julie but still holding her hand, Leyla put an arm round his neck and kissed him ferociously. Julie joined in and all three stood there, their arms around each other.

Finally, Leyla broke free. "Makarios is dead. The Palace has been destroyed. The National Guard has taken over. It's incredible."

He'd never seen her hysterical before. "The Canadians said that the Greeks are massing to the north. What is Mr Denktash saying we do? Can we defend ourselves?" An uneasy Alex touched her face.

"The tanks can only go in big streets," she said. "The lanes are no good. We'll fight whatever comes. He, Mr Denktash, has been contacting Turkey. They must help. It's our only chance. Enclaves are already being attacked in the south. We're losing hundreds. Women and children. It's awful."

"I'd better get a gun. Can you get me a gun?"

"We'll go to Mr Denktash's place. He'll know what to do. He'll have guns. Oh Julie, this is the worst we have ever faced.

Cover yourself up. Put dirt on your face."

"We'll leave the car here. It's a big target. Let's go." Alex pulled her by the hand.

They locked the car and Leyla's door and hurried to the Turkish leader's headquarters. Alex noted with relief that heavily armed Turkish Security Forces were stationed behind barricades at every street corner. Whatever the Greeks had planned they would not find the Turks wanting in resistance.

Denktash was in shirtsleeves. All around was confusion yet he seemed to stand like a rock, calm and impassive. "Leyla, Julie. So you made it? Good." He nodded approval to Alex. "Start answering the phones. We can't seem to get hold of Prime Minister Ecevit. He's not in Ankara. What a time to be out of the capital."

"What's the latest news?" Leyla enquired.

"That bloody little murderer Nicos Sampson has been sworn in as President. Even the Greeks can't be that stupid. What's that?" he called out to a man with his ear glued to a radio. "Quiet, everyone." Denktash's loud shout brought an immediate silence. Everyone stopped as the radio was turned up.

A voice, it sounded like Makarios, hushed the room, "Greek people of Cyprus, the voice you hear is familiar. You know who is addressing you. I am Makarios. I am not dead, as the Athens Junta would have you believe. I am alive and with you. The Junta's coup has failed and while I am alive the Junta will not have Cyprus. They have used tanks and armour but the resistance of the brave men of the Presidential Guard stopped the armour, stopped the tanks. Do not be afraid. Show that you will fight. Join the loyal forces of our State and victory will be ours. Long live freedom. Long live the Greek people of Cyprus."

The radio crackled followed by martial music.

Everyone turned to Denktash. "So the priest has escaped. Did it say where he was speaking from?"

"Paphos, I think," a voice answered.

"That's one place he'll be safe," Leyla said derisively. "It's one place he has friends."

"There's something coming on television," someone shouted.

They all stood and stared at a picture of Nicos Sampson declaring that he was the new President. He promised to restore law and order, to seek discussions with the Turkish Cypriots to end the Cyprus problem and to hold early elections for every Cypriot Greek.

"*Effendi*," a man called to Denktash. "The first attacks have begun. Not just against us but Greeks are killing each other everywhere."

"Good riddance," Julie spat out the words. Leyla put a hand over her mouth to stop any further words of hate.

"Sampson will want to get rid of any Makarios supporters." Denktash nodded.

News kept coming through in fits and starts. Makarios had broadcast to the United States appealing for help. Greek militia were killing Makarios' supporters by the hundreds. The British had taken Makarios to their sovereign base at Akrotiri by helicopter. Leyla explained to a silent Alex what was being said.

Later that night Denktash was called to the phone. After listening for several minutes he put down the phone. "That was Prime Minister Ecevit. He has met with the General Staff. They are making preparations to come to our aid. Let's hope it's soon before too many more of our people are killed." The tension in the tired people in the room evaporated. "Go to your homes," Denktash ordered. "It's late. The Greeks will wait till morning. They'd sustain too many casualties if they try to attack us tonight."

The walk back to Leyla's house was subdued and eerie. They walked close to buildings with small waves of recognition to the armed guards at each corner. Inside, Leyla put her arms round Alex and leaned against him, exhausted from fear and nervous tension. Julie rummaged around to find something to eat. It was impossible for Alex to return to the Greek side so Leyla fetched some blankets to make a bed on the divan.

"*Anne*," Julie muttered with a mouthful of food. "You can sleep in the same bed. I know you have anyway."

Leyla and Alex looked at each other then burst out laughing as Julie's words broke the intensity of the moment. Unlike Julie, neither could face food so Leyla produced some brandy and after a toast to his success in bringing Julie back to Nicosia, they all went to bed. It was a fitful sleep with first Leyla then Alex waking up and touching to make sure that the other was still there. They woke early and turned on the Greek radio station. The main report stated that Archbishop Makarios was on his way to New York to address the United Nations. Further stories claimed that Makarios had tortured prisoners and had brought Cyprus to the edge of disaster. Fierce fighting had broken out between the forces of the new President, Sampson, and the reactionary supporters of the ousted Makarios, the news continued. President Sampson had declared a curfew and martial law had been imposed, the announcer continued. Clafcos Clerides, Speaker of the House of Representatives, had been arrested the voice intoned. At each announcement, Leyla and Alex looked at each other in amazement.

"They seem to be against Makarios." He shook his head in wonder at the turn of events.

"We'd better have something to eat and then get round to headquarters," she spoke softly, looking at him with tenderness.

"I can't understand what they're saying at HQ. Should I just stay here with Julie?"

"No. Come. I don't want either of you out of my sight." Leyla flinched, afraid to be apart.

A busy, difficult day followed. Alex found it hard to keep up with all the news in Turkish. Leyla brought him a little radio so that he could listen to the British Forces Network. The news came through that Makarios was preparing to address the Security Council the next day. Britain had decided against any military action at the request of Makarios. The British press was up in arms at the appointment of the murderer, Nicos Sampson, as President. Much as the British press hated Makarios, Sampson's appointment was an insult to the memory of innocent British women and children slain by that "monster". The station reported that thousands of Turkish Cypriots were seeking refuge in the British bases at Dhekelia and Akrotiri.

Leyla brought Alex some coffee and small cakes. "Have something to eat." She kissed him on the cheek.

"God, the news just seems to get worse. Is there no-one out there who really understands what's going on here?" He shook his head in disgust.

"What are they saying?" she asked in a weary voice.

"The radio's quoting various newspapers. The *Daily Express* seems to think that the Americans support Sampson. Can you believe that? They mentioned Kissinger."

"Why not? The Americans think he's getting rid of the communists. We believe that he's already killed hundreds in AKEL villages, the communist party strongholds."

Another sleepless night followed. The next day, everyone was depressed. The bad news kept coming. It seemed as if there was a Greek plot to destroy as many Turkish villages as possible and drive the inhabitants into the sea. Alex busied himself at Denktash's headquarters making coffee and preparing some food. Leyla was fully occupied checking overseas newspapers, and radio and television reports. Word came through that Makarios was before the Security Council of the United Nations. The Turkish Ambassador and his staff were sending out reports from New York.

Denktash was glued to the telephone, listening to these reports coming through. "He's accusing the military regime in Athens of violating the independence of Cyprus. He means Greek Cypriot independence, of course. Now he's saying that he knew it was coming. He claims that *EOKA* B has its roots in Athens. He's said that he asked the Junta to remove all Greek officers and militia."

"He invited them," a bitter Leyla interrupted.

"Shush," said Denktash. "He's explained how he escaped. Through a secret door in the Palace. It's an invasion he claims, not a revolution by the people. He's called Sampson a gunman."

"Yes. A member of his Legislature, bah," someone shouted.

"Wait." Denktash held up a hand. "He said that it's his fault for inviting the Greek army to Cyprus. He thought he could trust them."

"Has he mentioned us?" a stocky Turk called out.

"Wait. He said he's sorry that talks between Greek and Turkish Cypriots have failed to solve the problems between the two communities. He said the Greek invasion will cause all of us, Greeks and Turks, problems."

"What is he asking the UN to do?" Leyla asked.

Denktash laughed, a braying sound. "He's saying he wants them to put an end to the invasion. Always he looks to the UN to solve his problems. That's it." Denktash stretched his arms above his head and yawned.

"Mr Denktash?" Leyla looked him in the eye. "What's going to happen? Do you know?"

"Unless Turkey takes some action, then Cyprus will be a Greek island and we will be massacred or maybe allowed to leave. With nothing but our shirts!" He shrugged. "But I won't let that happen. Either Turkey acts or we stay and fight until there are none left."

Alex could see all the faces drop and he pulled Leyla aside. "What did he say?"

"Unless Turkey helps us we will fight until we are all dead." A solemn Leyla ran a hand through her hair.

"I can take you and Julie to the British base at Dhekelia. I have a British passport as well as an Australian one."

"No, Alexander. They killed my father. They shot me, they

raped me, I will stay and fight. You decide what you must do."
She looked disappointed.

He was hurt by the suggestion that he wanted to run away. His only thought was for Leyla and Julie. Taking hold of her hands he said, "This is your country. If you stay and fight for it, then I'll stay. I only wanted to make sure my girls were safe."

She looked ashamed and kissed him lightly on the lips, not caring who saw her open display of affection. "No-one is safe while murderers and madmen are in charge. If we don't survive, we'll know we left this world together. Just don't let anyone touch Julie. Promise? Not that."

"I can't believe we're talking this way. It's 1974, for God's sake," he grumbled.

"For the Greeks it's 1453. Constantinople. They never forget. I think we can go home now. Nothing will happen tonight."

Next morning, July 19, they were all at the office in Denktash's home, it was the residence of the Vice-President of Cyprus although the Greek Cypriot Government refused to recognise his right to the title. Leyla spent the morning checking tapes of British, American and Greek radio programs. One Greek radio station reported that Greek Cypriots were joining with Turkish Cypriots to fight Sampson's government. When she told Denktash, he laughed, "They're not joining *us* to fight Sampson. Our people say that hundreds, thousands, of Makarios supporters have taken refuge in our enclaves. They feel safer with us. Sampson and his Greek killers want to eliminate all opposition." A stern Denktash threw up his hands.

"Are we taking in these people who want to kill us?" an incredulous Julie asked.

"What would you have us do? They are just as much victims as we are. Just foolish people who followed their priest. Fools. That's what they are."

"*Effendi*," a uniformed Turk approached Denktash. "There is a man here, just arrived in Nicosia, who says he saw a massacre at Pallouista."

"Where the coffee factory is?"

"Yes, Excellency. Here he is." He pulled a man forward.

A swarthy middle-aged man bowed. "I saw the factory walls covered in blood. Bodies everywhere. I think it was the workers. They are all union members. AKEL. I didn't stop. I was afraid."

"You see," Denktash glowered, "They are getting rid of anyone who supports Makarios. Sampson will turn to us next. His election motto was 'Death to Turks'."

At that moment the sound of aircraft was clearly heard above the noise in the room. Leyla and Alex went outside, peering up into the cobalt blue sky. Far off to the north they could just make out six jet planes.

"Are they Greek or Turkish?" Alex squinted, a hopeless effort.

"They must be Turkish. It's too far for Greek planes to come." She put her arm though his as they gazed into the distance.

After an hour, word came through that Turkey had sent reconnaissance planes over the Famagusta and Kyrenia areas before sweeping out over the Lefka and Xeros area to the West. The room became a buzz of excitement. The question on everyone's lips was about the purpose of the flights.

"Morphou Bay would be the ideal place to land troops if they are coming," Nail Atalay, who was in charge of foreign affairs, commented.

"They would have the support of our enclaves at both places," Leyla agreed.

"That would give them a clear run into Nicosia, wouldn't it?" Alex looked at her.

Atalay joined in. "In a way, yes. But the Greeks have fortifications in the Troodos Mountains. Heavy artillery. They could easily bombard them from the safety of the high country."

Leyla gave a worried look to Alex. She was thinking about her mother. Ghazientop would be in the firing line if the Greeks opened up with heavy artillery.

"Then where could they land safely?" Alex shook his head, bewildered.

"Probably Famagusta. Capture the port so that they could bring in tanks and trucks. But that's a long way round. The Greeks would spot them early. It would be no surprise." Atalay shook his head.

"Shit, is there anywhere they could land safely?" a frustrated Alex demanded.

"Perhaps north of Lefkoniko. There are not many Greek militia there. We have a very big enclave there. The road through the ranges is not good so I don't know." He gave a helpless shrug.

"What about Larnaca Bay? There's a good stretch of beach there."

"Too close to the British base at Dhekelia. The British might be called on to resist. Too risky." A despondent Atalay screwed up his face.

Denktash strode over and put a hand on of Atalay's shoulder. "Forget this talk of troop landings. It will only raise the hopes of the people. Word gets out. I want you to send a letter by telex to the UN saying that the new Greek Cypriot Government's appointment represents only Greeks not us. He does not speak for us in that assembly. Do that now."

"Can I do anything?" Alex asked.

"You can monitor the BBC and the British Forces Network from Dhekelia. That would be a big help." He patted Alex on the back.

By evening, they were all exhausted. It was difficult to sort out the truth from rumours. One thing Alex felt for certain was that this was a civil war and that meant no-one was safe, Greeks or Turks.

After a miserable meal of scraps left over from the day before they went to bed about ten. Julie was fast asleep.

Lying close in bed, he whispered, "I have a gut feeling that the next couple of days will be crucial."

"Then let's make love tonight. I can't sleep. Not with all this going on."

He checked again on Julie and returned to bed. It was a night of languorous lovemaking, gentle and comforting. Loud explosions woke them at six the next morning. Julie was awake and looking out the window. Dressing quickly, they hurried to headquarters.

Denktash and several senior members were already present. He looked flushed and happy. "Leyla. They landed at four-thirty this morning. Five-Mile Beach. They told me at midnight. There's still a little whisky left. Have a drink, Alex. We're finally going to be saved." He whirled round twice and clapped his hands.

Leyla looked in amazement at her Mr Denktash acting like a schoolboy. He stopped his little dance and called out in a loud voice. "Until we have some news of the battle, no-one is to leave. I want nothing to cause alarm among our people. I have sent out messages that everyone is to stay in their safe areas. Only our Security Forces will go to assist. We don't want the Greeks to turn their guns on civilians."

"It's July 20, will we ever forget this day?" Leyla hugged Alex and Julie.

Denktash pushed people to the radios. "Keep listening to all the radio stations. There may be foreign correspondents up there phoning in news. Get as much information as you can. I'm standing by to hear from Ankara."

After the initial cheering at the news of Turkish troops landing, the atmosphere became more serious as reports came in of fierce resistance by the vastly superior Greek forces. With tanks, artillery and landmines they had pinned down the Turkish force of 2000 commandos, the Turkish military contingent on the island as part of the Agreements, and a small band of Turkish Cypriot Fighters.

"Losses are heavy on both sides," the voice of a man, ear

close to a phone, called out. "We seem to have miscalculated the strength of the Greeks."

"There's worse news from Larnaca. Greek militia have surrounded several safe areas and shelling has commenced. This is a disaster. Those people are defenceless," a man shouted above the noisy confusion.

Alex wrote down the news from the BBC and passed it to Leyla. She held up a hand and reported the news. "Prime Minister Wilson has issued a statement in London. He wants an immediate cease-fire. Turkish troops already in Cyprus can be dispersed to our cantons to protect Turkish Cypriots against Greek attacks, he said. He wants a meeting in London of Greece, Turkey and Britain."

"It's too late for meetings. Ten years ago the English abandoned us. Their efforts now are useless." Denktash spat out the words.

"There's more," Leyla gripped the piece of paper, "Kissinger, he's the American? He has told Turkey and Greece to pull back from the brink of war."

"It's his Junta in Athens. But he can't control them. If they want war, Turkey will oblige." Denktash shouted out confidently.

"The Americans won't allow that," Alex whispered to Leyla. "Then the Russians will move in. Shit. That's all we need."

As evening fell they went outside to see a lot of smoke on the hills to the north. "It's getting dark. Let's go home. Julie, hold my hand."

He held them each by a hand. Smoke began to drift over Nicosia. Explosions burst through the air continuously until well after midnight when sleep finally overtook them. Alex and Leyla were awake after a few hours to find the bombing and explosions still in progress. Tired and weary, they were back at headquarters by six to learn that Greek transport planes with reinforcements had landed at Nicosia Airport in the dark before dawn.

"Several planes have been fired upon by the Greek National

Guard," Denktash said scornfully. "They assumed that they were Turkish planes. Let's hope they lost a few."

"Here's news from England," Alex held out a piece of paper.

Leyla read it out. "The British have complained that the Greeks have used the British air corridor illegally. The British High Commissioner in Nicosia has issued a statement that Britain has not given permission. Britain," she continued, "does not wish to be involved with the Greek or Turkish side in the dispute."

On Monday the Prime Minister of Turkey, Bulent Ecevit, agreed to a çease-fire. He spoke to a packed press conference:

"We have achieved our objective. Turkish troops are now firmly in Cyprus. This balances the British troops and the Greek troops already there. Sampson appears to have lost all support and the Greeks are fighting among each other. We still have concerns about many Turkish villages that are even now surrounded. Some people have surrendered and others have been massacred. Since we are not in a military position to protect them, the UN must stop the killings. Finally, I understand that the Junta in Athens has, or is about to, collapse."

"What do you think, Alexander?" a worn-out Leyla asked as they shared a cup of coffee.

"It may just be a tactic to gain time, the cease-fire." He pushed back the damp hair from her face.

"But if they stop now, how many of us will be killed?"

"Let's wait and see. I'm sure that Turkey didn't start this without being sure that they would finish it. Once and for all." He tried to sound positive.

"Let's hope so." She sighed.

By Wednesday the Turks had brought in reinforcements. The military Junta in Athens had collapsed and democracy had been restored. Sampson had resigned in favour of Clafcos Clerides.

"So," Denktash bellowed. "Turkey's efforts have returned democracy to Greece. I hope they appreciate what we've done for them." Laughter followed his derisive comment.

"What about Makarios? Is he coming back? He seems to have gone very quiet," a man asked.

Denktash gave him a severe look. "Never underestimate that man. He's shuttling back and forth between New York and London. Like Sampson, he's out there somewhere urging the Greeks to resist. But he's not part of the negotiations in Geneva so that's a positive. Now. Everyone. Go home. Get some rest. Eat a little. Drink some wine. We can do nothing more here until the talks come to a conclusion."

Alex, Leyla and Julie were happy to be back home in some kind of normality.

"I don't want to hear any news for at least a day," Leyla plunked herself on the divan, "for one day we'll forget the war."

"What do...?" Julie began then decided not to ask any more questions. "Let's make a nice big salad and have beans and pilaf. It's too hot for anything else. Want to help, Dad?" She smiled, head tilted to the side. Just like your mother he thought.

The next few days were full of tension but at least all the news was of diplomatic manoeuvrings at Geneva. No-one seemed to realise that the Greeks had mined the outskirts of Kyrenia and the area to the north of Nicosia, except the thousands of Turkish troops on the ground.

Makarios in London called Clerides and the new Greek Prime Minister Karamanlis traitors. "Whatever you agree between you and the Turks," he told them by phone, "will not have my signature of approval. The Greek Cypriots will not accept any deal unless it is signed by me."

The first Geneva conference signed by Britain, Turkey and Greece allowed for separate, autonomous administrations on Cyprus. The details would be hammered out at the next conference in Geneva on 8 August.

Cyprus, August 1974

Denktash flew to Geneva for the second round of talks designed to end the deadlock. He immediately refused to sit beside Clerides as the representatives of a united Cyprus.

"There is no Cyprus. Makarios tore the Constitution into pieces. Now there is the Greek community and the Turkish community."

Clerides went on the attack. "I am prepared to form a government within the framework of the 1960 Constitution. But not while we are threatened by Turkey."

"You mean a Constitution that has led to eleven years of suffering for my community?" Denktash objected. "You talk about a framework. What you mean is an amended Constitution where we lose our rights."

The British Foreign Secretary James Callaghan broke in. "Surely a compromise can be discussed, at least?"

"Mr Callaghan," Denktash spoke slowly. "I have known all the people at this table for years. Since I was a young man. Their word cannot be trusted. Didn't they, in 1963, destroy 104 Turkish villages and make refugees of 24,000 Turkish Cypriots? That is why we fear *Enosis*. No. We want to live in peace. The only answer is a separate region of the island for Turks to be secure. We want to look after ourselves."

"Why don't you, Rauf, and you, Clafcos, get together, alone? Thrash out a plan that is acceptable to you both and then bring it back to the conference?"

They retired to a side room.

Denktash was first to speak. "My friend. You know that there are ten thousand Turkish Cypriots under siege in Famagusta. Starving and short of water. Five thousand more are living in appalling conditions in Konedra. The sooner we get this settled the better. There will be loss of life. Your people will oppose the Turkish forces no doubt, but it will be over quickly. Then we will have two separate regions and live side by side in peace. No?"

Clerides was aware that another coup was imminent in Cyprus. "I can't make that kind of decision. You know that. I'll have to contact Nicosia. I can ask them to lift the siege. Famagusta will be all right but some places, well, *EOKA* B never takes any notice of the government." He looked defeated.

"I propose that we have two separate regions. We have 34 per cent."

"I can't go back to Cyprus saying that I have cut it in half," Clerides protested. "Greece won't accept it either. I need to contact Nicosia."

"Act now before that priest returns to Cyprus and upsets everything. He's your problem." Denktash said doggedly.

"Makarios is against any division of the island. You know that. He'd rather go to war than accept such a plan."

There was silence for a few minutes.

"Don't you understand?" Denktash flourished a paper. "Enough blood has already been spilt. For years we have tried to get you to accept a regime that would inspire mutual confidence. No. You were in too much of a hurry to get rid of us. You should have waited for ten, twenty years of peace and prosperity before changing the Constitution. If you had shown good will we would have had trust between us. Now it's too late."

"Are you saying that all this talk is a waste of time? Has Turkey already decided to force partition?" He looked questioningly at Denktash.

"Turkey does not tell me everything. Just be careful. Accept our proposals and save many lives." He held out his open hands.

"You know I can't. I'd be dead in a day if I returned to Cyprus with such a proposal."

"Well, my friend. We shall have to wait and see what the Great Powers decide. It's out of our hands."

"Kissinger is working hard. He's in constant touch with Ankara. They'll have to listen to him." Clerides was in no doubt.

At dawn on 14 August Turkish armed forces advanced from their beachhead at Kyrenia. Leyla and Alex stood silent as the news flash came over the radio. "Holy shit," he roared, "it's on for young and old."

"My mother. What will happen?" Leyla's hands flew to her face.

"I don't know. We'd better get round to—Christ, what was that?" he ducked as he spoke.

"They're bombing Nicosia," Leyla shouted as an explosion went off in the distance. She pulled Julie close. "We'd better stay here."

"Who's bombing? Is it us or the Greeks?" Julie's muffled voice was barely audible.

"Must be Turkish planes. I don't think bombers can make it here from Greece. Unless they've refuelled at Crete." She comforted Julie.

"The phone's dead." An exasperated Alex put down the handset.

"Mr Denktash must still be in Geneva. Why do these things have to happen when our leader is away?" She couldn't hide her anger.

"You stay here and I'll go to headquarters and see if there's any news."

"No. We'll all stay together. There goes another one." Leyla covered her ears. "At least let's wait until the bombing stops. Can you see anything?"

He stood on a chair and looked out the window. "Too many buildings in the way. I can see smoke rising up. It's definitely the Greek side that's being hit so it must be Turkish planes."

"Now they'll get a taste of what it's like." Julie looked at her father.

"Let's hope it's over quickly," he said, taking her hand. "The best laid schemes and all that."

She didn't understand what he meant. For another hour they sat close together listening to the Turkish Cypriot radio station. Leyla explained. The news was good and bad. The

Turkish troops were advancing rapidly. Commandos had landed south of the Kyrenia Ranges. Jet fighters had wiped out many Greek positions in the mountain ranges and the outskirts of Nicosia. News came through of fierce fighting in other parts of Cyprus where Greek forces had opened fire on Turkish enclaves. Famagusta reported Turkish ships were coming into the bay. Kyrenia was proving difficult with fierce resistance, said the voice on the radio. Thousands had been killed or wounded.

"This is incredible," Alex shouted above the continuous noise of explosions.

"It's the end of Cyprus as I knew it." Leyla bowed her head as Julie stroked the back of her neck.

"It'll be all right, *Anne*," Julie whispered, "It'll be over soon. I think."

"Don't be too sure," Alex retorted, "The Greeks have too many troops. I can't see Turkey getting enough men in to get a quick result. Paratroopers are okay but you need at least ten thousand to come in by sea. They've been stuck at Five Mile Beach for weeks. It's too small an area."

The voice on the radio continued with reports of Greek militia attacking Turkish villages in various parts of the island using tanks and mortar. Lightly armed villagers had no defence against such armour, the report continued. The latest report stated that the Turkish Cypriot male population of the village of Toknihi north of Limassol and men from a nearby village had been massacred. More news was coming in of similar incidents. Leyla looked shocked as she translated the spoken words:

"One man who escaped injured at Toknihi has claimed that over a hundred men were killed in shallow trenches. He managed to escape when the Greek soldiers left to fetch a bulldozer to cover the bodies. The man is on his way to Nicosia. We will bring you an eyewitness report as soon as possible."

"Oh God," Leyla cried, clinging to Alex, "how long will this go on?"

"The only good thing I can say is that the Greeks have so many men scattered all over the island that they may not have enough to stop the Turkish offensive. Let's just hope it's over soon."

By late afternoon the bombing had stopped. Leyla agreed reluctantly that Alex should make his way to Denktash's headquarters to find out how long before the bombing would end. There was little food left in the house, just dried chickpeas, some rice and canned fish.

"Try to find somewhere that's selling food. We may need it."

"I'll do what I can. If for some reason I can't get back, stay here," Alex commanded.

"Don't say things like that. Maybe we should come with you?" A frantic Leyla embraced him.

"No. Just wait. I'll be back." He kissed her cheek and left.

At Denktash's headquarters, it was chaotic. Atalay, who spoke good English, told him that the whole island was a slaughterhouse. "Unless the liberating army takes control, we may find there are no Turks left. Sampson and Makarios will have achieved their goal. No Turks in Cyprus."

"Turkey hasn't begun this to walk away now. They must have expected something like this. They must know what's going on. They'll have to attack in strength. Stop this killing." Alex tried to sound optimistic.

"Let's hope so. Now you'd better go home before dark. People will shoot at anything that moves. Everyone is trigger-happy."

"Any news from Ghazientop?" Alex asked nervously.

"Only that there has been fierce fighting. The last I heard, Ghazientop was being shelled. The Greeks are superior in numbers there. They must have been expecting a landing in Morphou Bay."

"See if you can get some up-to-date news. Leyla's worried about her mother."

Alex found a small shop, its metal shutter just open at the bottom. The frightened Turkish Cypriot owner was crouched inside. Alex managed to buy some tins of fruit and some kind of tinned meat. Leyla threw herself into his arms when she opened the door to let him into the house. "What's happening? Will we be saved?" she asked between kisses to his cheeks.

"It's too early to tell. Some bad news, though. Ghazientop is under heavy artillery fire."

"*Anne* should have come with you. It's too far away. Now it's too late to go and bring her here. Isn't it?" Leyla shivered with fear.

"Just be patient. Wait till we get some more news."

Next day, Makarios in London agreed to the autonomous areas but said, "While I accept the Agreement, I do not necessarily agree with all its contents."

On hearing this news, Denktash, in Geneva, reacted and made a statement on Bayrak, the Turkish Cypriot radio station: "This is just another example of the deviousness of this feral priest. With one hand he accepts the agreement and with the other he rejects it. He will agree with anything to achieve his goal, the elimination of Turkish Cypriots."

Atalay cursed as he listened to the radio. "He's right, you know."

Alex looked at Leyla.

"I know," she said, "the man is like a snake. He can shed one skin after the other so that you have no idea who you are dealing with. Mr Denktash is right. We can never live with this man and the people who love him."

"When is Denktash due back?" Alex frowned.

"After the conference ends. Probably the thirteenth."

"I can't believe it's almost the middle of August. I feel as if I've lived a dozen lifetimes since May."

Leyla's smile didn't show. It's been a good twelve lifetimes in many ways, she thought. Calling to Julie, she said, "I have a feeling that this cease-fire won't last long It's a good time to go out and see what food we can buy."

The Geneva conference failed to reach a satisfactory result

and Ecevit instructed his minister to issue an ultimatum. If the Greeks would not agree to some form of territorial division then Turkey reserved the right to ensure the safety of its troops on the island. Greece refused. Alex and Julie cooked a meal of meatballs, potatoes and some beans. Another long night followed with all three sitting close together on the divan listening to the radio. It was almost one in the morning before they finally went to bed. At dawn, Turkey began its second assault. Again, massive explosions awakened them. Looking out the window, they could see smoke rising up in huge clouds from downtown Nicosia.

"This is the biggest yet."

"This time they mean business. I knew it." Alex nodded. "If they can get Nicosia then it might end. Turn on the radio, Julie."

They munched on some dry bread and a dip made from chickpeas and garlic as they listened to the latest news from the British Forces radio station:

"The Turkish forces have captured Kyrenia and are advancing down the road to the capital. Reports suggest that the Greek troops are in retreat, hampered by thousands of fleeing Greek Cypriot civilians." The newsreader spoke as if reporting the weather conditions.

"Looks like they'll be here soon." He took hold of Julie's hand.

"Those poor people." Leyla heaved a sigh. "This is what their leaders have brought to them. If only they had agreed to Mr Denktash's offer none of this would be happening."

"Well, they voted for Makarios all the time. He said that Cyprus would become a holocaust. It looks like his prediction's coming true. He meant for the Turks but now it may be for the Greeks. Stupid bugger. It's the old Greek *hubris* again."

"What do you mean, Dad?" Julie asked.

"It means he thought he was bigger than he really was. It's all about pride. Too much pride! It leads to tragedy. He was going to deliver Cyprus to Greece. *Hubris* is a Greek word. How appropriate."

Leyla screwed up her face in disgust. "It's a typical Greek state of mind. Because they had a brief glorious period in history two thousand years ago, they still think they're number one. And we Turks are, and never have been anything."

"Shit," Alex hunched down as the biggest explosion yet shook the walls.

"God, I wish this would end." Julie crouched down beside her father.

Leyla joined them. "We'll just sit tight and wait."

By evening the radio announced that the Turkish forces had taken control of more than 30 per cent of the island, all of it north of Nicosia.

"I hope my mother and Ghazientop are safely in the hands of the Turkish army." Leyla spoke softly.

"Switch to the BBC."

A modulated voice read a report in a flat, calm voice:

"Here is the latest news from the troubled island of Cyprus. Our correspondents report that Turkish forces have advanced to the outskirts of the capital Nicosia. Thousands of Greek Cypriot refugees are on the move south fearing reprisals by the Turkish soldiers. The Cypriot National Guard is putting up some resistance but reports suggest that the mainland Greek officers and troops under their command have fled. Heavy casualties have been sustained on both sides but there are no reports of civilian deaths. The acting Cypriot President, Clafcos Clerides, and the Turkish Cypriot Vice-President, Rauf Denktash, have both returned to Cyprus from Geneva. President Makarios who is in London has condemned the latest attack as an affront to the United Nations. He has called for support to end the Turkish occupation of his homeland. British tourists and residents who failed to leave after the first assault on July 20 have been taken on board the aircraft carrier *Hermes*. No injuries have been reported. There will be further bulletins as they come to hand. Now for news from Devon where flash-flooding..."

Alex switched off the radio. "Well, we can expect them at any time. Should we go round to headquarters?"

"I think that's a good idea. At least we'll be with Mr Denktash when the Turkish soldiers arrive. Julie. Put on a headscarf. Just in case." Her voice faltered.

An angry, desperate Alex patted his gun. "I have the gun Denktash gave me. I'll shoot any bastard, Greek or Turk, who tries anything."

"For God's sake, keep the gun out of sight," Leyla pleaded.

The solid figure of Denktash was a welcome sight. He was busy issuing commands, reading sheets of paper handed to him and then moving to look at a large map pinned on the wall. He nodded in Leyla's direction but didn't speak. As the day drew to a close, he summed up the situation. "We are now in control of the north, including Famagusta." A cheer went up at his words. He held up his hand for silence. "Nicosia airport is under the control of the British. If we try to take it then RAF bombers will bomb our troops surrounding the airport. Then Turkey would be at war with Britain. So we will wait. Prime Minister Ecevit has agreed to a cease-fire now that our objective has been reached. There are continuing attacks on our villages in the south but we have sent fighters to assist. No Turkish troops will cross the Attila line. We must now be strong. I know there is a desire among some to avenge the deaths of loved ones," he glanced at Leyla who shook her head and muttered a no, "but we are not Christian Greeks so I appeal to everyone here, as I will soon on the radio, that we want no revenge killings."

Several men muttered disapproval.

"Enough is enough. Anyone found committing atrocities against civilians will be dealt with at some time in the future. The world is watching. Do not let them call us barbaric Turks."

A sound of assent went up in the crowded room. But despite Denktash's appeal for calm and peace on the radio, some Turkish Cypriots, too distraught and angry, ignored his plea.

Later that night, Alex and Leyla listened to a BBC broadcast that claimed Turkish troops had looted Greek houses and women had been raped. Leyla lowered her head in shame.

"Don't, sweetheart," he said softly, "it's not you, and who knows, these may just be stories put out by the Greeks to gain sympathy. It's standard tactics when a war has been lost."

"I know. But it's probably true." She shuddered. "That's what happens in war. Men become animals and women are the ones to suffer."

They lay silent for a long time in bed that night, each with their own thoughts. Earlier, Julie had broken the tension by asking if school would begin soon now that the fighting was over.

"Can we see if we can get to Ghazientop tomorrow?" Leyla whispered. "Please?"

"If I can get some petrol, we'll try," he reassured her.

He drove slowly through the burned-out village of Peristerona on the way to Ghazientop.

"Look, Alexander. The mosque and the church have both been destroyed. If this has happened here, what...?" Her voice broke and she covered her face with her hands.

She shouted at some Turkish soldiers blocking the road into Ghazientop, and waved to them to get out of the way. Alex couldn't understand what she said but he had to admire the effect. Leyla began to whimper as Alex drove into the village square. It looked like something out of a war movie, a gutted bombed-out jumble of smashed shops, craters with rocks and huge stones scattered everywhere. The minaret was gone from the mosque, which was a burned-out shell with wisps of smoke still drifting in the air. The acrid smell made Alex cough. A Turkish officer came towards the car. "Where are you going?" he demanded.

"To my mother's house, up there." Leyla pointed to the road leading to Gulten's house.

"You will have to walk. The road is full of holes. Too big for your car."

"What's happened here?" She was close to tears.

"The Greek militia rounded up as many as they could find. Some men were taken as hostages. The women hid in the mosque. Someone said the Greek soldiers set fire to it. They say they heard a Greek say, 'Let them all burn'. I don't know. Maybe it's true or it may have been hit by mortar. Anyway, only a few escaped."

Leyla was shrieking like a banshee. "The house, get to the house," she started running and Alex stumbled after her.

Inside, she found three women sitting in the main room. One looked up and ran to her screaming, then clasped her to her bosom. Leyla looked for Gulten.

"What? What is it?" Alex cursed his lack of Turkish.

Leyla turned an ashen face to him. "*Anne*'s dead. Somewhere in the mosque. She didn't get out." Then she began a wailing that tore out his heart.

He pulled her out of the woman's embrace, and held her, unable to say anything that would ease her pain. The sobbing went on and on. All he could do was hold her. He could think of nothing to say. The other two women rose up from the divan and silently indicated that Alex sit down. He gently lowered Leyla to the seat. The women left and he held Leyla close. One woman returned with a fluted glass of tea. Leyla waved it away. Alex held it in one hand, keeping hold of Leyla with one arm. At long last she looked up. "My poor *Anne*. Don't ever ask me to live with Greeks again. Never. Never."

"We won't, I promise." He put down the glass and kissed her wet cheeks.

"Now they have killed all my family." Her voice was calm, almost deadly in its intensity.

"Are you ready to leave? Or shall I go to the mosque? See if I...I...?" He was unable to finish.

Sniffing, Leyla drew back her shoulders. "I'll go. You too. We'll see..." and she broke out again in sobs.

She was able to recognise Gulten's body. Her face had been badly burned but her long dress had given some protection to her body.

"I think she died from smoke." Alex hoped that would lessen Leyla's pain.

"I know," she said in a low voice, "it's still a terrible way to die. We'll have to bury *Anne* today. Right now. I don't want her left like this. I'll see if I can get some men to help. Stay here with her." She let go his hand and shuffled like an old woman through a hole where the door had been.

Alex stood looking down at the old woman who had never harmed anyone, a gentle unassuming woman of her time. You never had a chance, he thought, from one village under the rule of a father to another as the reliable faithful wife of a man you met on your wedding night. The only world you knew was your family and your village. Then you die like this. What a fucking country. It was beautiful, but dangerous.

Leyla returned with two old men she'd known since childhood, farm workers, peasants whose stoic faces betrayed no sign of emotion. They held a kind of stretcher. Leyla had a sheet. Gulten's body was rolled up in the sheet and placed on the makeshift stretcher. Clutching Alex's arm, they followed the two men to the small burial area on the north side of town. A mortar shell had carved a deep hole in one corner. Leyla indicated to the men that this would be the final resting place of her mother.

As the men filled in the hole with soil, she turned to Alex. "I'll miss her even though I've moved on to a world she could never imagine. Poor *Anne*, poor women who suffer at the hands of men. Don't tell Julie about her face."

Alex swallowed a lump in his throat. He said nothing. There was nothing to say. They drove back to Nicosia as dusk fell on the dusty mudstone houses, the setting sun turning them into an Arabian landscape complete with palm trees and a minaret glowing high above the mosque of Halam Mustapha. After picking up Julie from the home of her friend they sat for hours, silent, staring into space.

At nine o'clock, Alex stood up. "I'll make us something to eat. Not much. Just a little something."

Julie slept with Leyla that night. Alex finished the last of the brandy and fell asleep on the divan. Leyla stayed home for two days, mourning the loss of her mother. Julie stayed in her room, subdued. A sense of guilt pervaded the house. Alex stayed at headquarters until late in the afternoon. He managed to buy a new bottle of brandy. After a simple meal of cheese, olives, bread and tomatoes they began to talk.

"I don't know if I can stay here now." Leyla's voice was composed. "It will never be the same again."

"What will happen to the farm?" Julie asked.

"I don't know. And I really don't care." She turned a sad, resigned face to her daughter.

"Don't make any decisions now," Alex pleaded. "Wait a while. This is your home. You can't let the fu...bloody Greeks win by driving you out. Do you want them to win? To get rid of all Turks?"

"I can't think about it now. Do you still intend to go back to Australia? Will you take us with you? Is that what you want?" An unsmiling Leyla looked at him.

"I don't want you to think about what we might do, where we might live. You're in shock. Wait a few more days. See what Denktash has planned. He'll need every bit of help he can get. I know he relies on you. Wait."

"Give me another brandy. Not so much water." Leyla's wan face looked at him. "I don't want my Julie to suffer like my mother."

"Don't say things like that." Julie was close to tears. "We're all together. Whatever happens we're all together, aren't we, Dad?"

"Come here. Give me a hug." Alex held out his arms. "Things will get better now, I'm sure. Let's just keep our chins up. I have my two lovely girls. I don't mind where we stay. Right?"

Leyla finished her drink in one long swallow. "Here's to us

and a better future. Do I look as old as I feel?" She forced a tentative smile.

Alex pulled her closer and all three sat, a family brought closer together by the events of the past few weeks. That night as Leyla lay in his arms, she whispered, "It'll be all right, Alexander. Whatever we do, we'll do it together."

"Can I ask you something?" he murmured.

"Of course." Leyla's brow furrowed as she turned her face to him.

"Will you marry me? Tomorrow. Or the next day?"

She squirmed in his embrace. "I've been wondering when you would ask. And the answer is yes. After all these years, it's unbelievable." Her eyes glistened with tears. They began kissing for comfort then the loving was slow and gentle.

The exodus of Greek Cypriots began in earnest as soon as news came through of the success of the Turkish forces. The radio reports caused panic among the 200,000 likely to be trapped by the advancing army. Greek education had ensured that they believed that the "barbaric" Turks would show no mercy to Greeks. Within three days the majority of Greek Cypriots had fled south of the Green Line, the Attila line, taking only money and valuables. Their departure was watched unhindered by the Turkish Cypriots. Looting and destruction of homes was widespread. After eleven years of deprivation the Turkish Cypriots took the opportunity to take television sets, furniture and electrical goods as well as furniture and farm machinery.

Denktash went on radio. "I appeal to all Turkish Cypriots. You are now safe. Do not tarnish the image of our people by engaging in looting or the destruction of Greek property."

His words fell on deaf ears.

Leyla and Alex worked long hours preparing releases for the world press. The worldwide Greek lobby went into action to condemn the capture of 37 per cent of the island and the plight of the refugees.

"We're not doing very well, are we?" Alex brought some newspaper reports over to her.

"We never do. It's just the way things are. The West is Christian. We are Muslims. So we must be in the wrong. Don't give up. See if you can write something for the British press. Makarios is unpopular there."

"Do we have any news of Turkish Cypriots in the south? Anything there we can use to show the dangers they're facing?" Alex asked.

"Some have begun to move north but it's not easy. The Greeks prefer to keep them there. The Greek militia has roadblocks everywhere. Those in the far south will have to stay in their enclaves until we can get some kind of agreement on letting them go."

"Has Denktash made any contact with Clerides?"

"He hasn't said, but I'm sure he has. They go back a long way." She looked over to where he was on the telephone.

Calling for silence Denktash raised his voice. "Clerides has made a statement here in Nicosia. He says:

'Greek thinking has been based on false assumptions, terrible mistakes and illusions, the main one of which was that we could treat the Turkish Cypriot community as a simple minority without taking into account that it was backed by Turkey with a population of 33 million. I have to acknowledge that it will be necessary to accept a system of federation with the Turkish Cypriot community'."

"What a pity he's waited till now to realise what we have been asking all along." Leyla snapped.

"He is a reasonable man. Of course, Makarios when he returns will say no to any such proposal," a pensive Denktash pulled down his lower lip. "The Turkish troops now have control of the north but there is still great danger to our people in the south. I will arrange to meet Clerides and work out an exchange of population. It has to happen."

Once again, Cyprus became a land of tents, more so in the south where the abandoned homes of Turkish Cypriots were insufficient to meet the needs of 200,000 Greek Cypriot refugees. Greek Cypriots took to the streets shouting, 'Down with America' as fires still raged in Greek Nicosia. The American Ambassador tried to calm the crowd. A shot rang out and he fell to the ground dead. Cheers went up and then the mob dispersed in minutes.

The mood in Denktash's office was sombre but tinged with a feeling of relief. "This will help our cause." Leyla looked to Alex for confirmation.

"The Americans will definitely react badly, that's for sure. But Kissinger is used to losing some key men. In the long run it won't affect their policy. Have you made contact with Akrotiri?"

"Yes. That's good news. The Commanding Officer says that any of our people who wish to move to the north can go through the base. They have agreed that they can fly to Turkey."

"Turkey?" a disbelieving Alex exclaimed.

"I had to agree. It was that or nothing. Once they're safely out of the south we can bring them back here."

"Shit, that's going to cost a fortune." He wondered who was paying for all these evacuations.

"It can't be helped. There's still fighting going on. Now we have to start work to make sure that the UN and the world understands why all this had to happen."

"What's that, Ahmet?" She turned to a breathless young man.

"There are Greeks protesting outside the office of the British High Commissioner. They're throwing stones and windows have been smashed."

"What is it now?" Leyla frowned. "They're shouting that Britain is against them by allowing the Akrotiri base to fly out our brothers and sisters." A wild-eyed Ahmet was happy to be the centre of attention.

"Tough titty," Alex said then realised it was not quite the appropriate response.

Denktash sat at a large table interviewing one man after another. Each was given specific instructions. One was dispatched to Famgusta to liaise with the authorities for imports of food from Turkey, another the allocation of housing and finally the director of education left to begin organising the opening of a new school year. "Let's get things back to normal." Denktash's voice travelled round the room. "We are beginning a new life, safe from the Greeks. If we show the world that we are capable of running our own affairs in a short time it will go well for us. Let's get to work."

Not far from Akrotiri, in Limassol, over 50,000 Greek Cypriots demonstrated, demanding that the Archbishop be allowed to return to Cyprus from London where he was a guest of the British Government. At the start of October, Makarios flew to New York to address the United Nations Assembly. He was introduced as the President of the Republic of Cyprus even though Clerides had not relinquished the position.

"It is my sad duty to be here once again to plead for justice for the people of Cyprus. Members are aware of the unprovoked and brutal attack by Turkey on the independent state of Cyprus, a member of this august body. A sovereign nation has been attacked and 37 per cent of its land occupied by a foreign power in breach of the Charter of the United Nations. The people of Cyprus are in mourning. Hundreds of thousands have been forced from their homes and now live in squalid conditions, refugees in their own land. I bring to the Assembly the agony of the Cypriot people. They look to you to restore the sovereignty and freedom that all peace-loving people desire. I ask the Assembly to condemn the actions of Turkey and demand that it withdraws its army of occupation and allows the two communities who have lived so long in harmony to begin negotiations to end the current situation on the island. I hope that my return to Cyprus in the near future will assist in bringing a new understanding between the Greek and Turkish people of Cyprus whose only desire is to live side by side in a prosperous and united Cyprus."

"There's no doubt he's a master orator." Alex said to Leyla who was concentrating on taping the Archbishop's speech. "Don't worry about the past eleven years!"

"If Mr Denktash was allowed to address the General Assembly they would get an entirely different story. That's our biggest problem. How do we get our story across?"

"Well, speeches won't change the way things are. The Attila line is in place and the only thing to come out of talks between Denktash and Clerides will be where the line is re-drawn." He put his arm round her shoulders.

Cyprus, December 1974

Two hundred thousand Greek Cypriots met Archbishop Makarios when he returned to Cyprus on December 7, 1974.

"I am alive," he called out to the cheering crowd, "I hope that my return to you will bring about peace. I forgive all those who have sinned against me. Passions and divisions have no place if we are to save Cyprus."

A voice called out from the cheering masses. "Long live our President. Now you are here we will soon be back in our homes."

Later that day he called together Clerides, Kyprianou and other members of the Legislative Assembly and high-ranking public servants. "I know that's it's been a difficult time without me. But I have been working hard in London, New York and Athens to ensure that our just and legal rights will be restored."

A sad and tired looking Clerides shook his head. "Beatitude. Do you really believe that what is done can be undone? This disaster is of our making."

"No, dear Clafcos. It is the fault of the Greek Junta. Now they are gone. Karamanlis has promised his support in every sphere. The damage that has been done can be repaired. Greece has left NATO whose members will insist that Turkey withdraw its army and allow us, Greek and Turkish Cypriots, to determine our future."

"Who's going to deal with Denktash? He now has the might of Turkey at his back?"

"You will offer to meet Denktash and say that we need to begin talks between our two communities. With only 125,000 Turks in the north, they will starve. They will be frozen out. No-one will deal with them. With that small number they cannot survive. Is this not true?"

Clerides shook his head in despair. "Turkey will never leave. Even if it costs them millions. It's not Denktash we have to worry about, it's Turkey."

"You underestimate the power of the United Nations. It is there that we will win the real battle. We have so many friends among the non-aligned nations that Turkey will have to withdraw."

Kyprianou broke in. "We are but a pimple on the elephant's back of world problems. Soon some other crisis will arise and the world will forget us. Greece, through the Junta, let us down. How can we ever trust them again?"

"Under Karamanlis, democracy has been restored in Greece, the very birthplace of democracy. The world recognises this as a great event. Greece is once more showing the world that it is part of the civilised democratic world. Greeks all over the world are celebrating this moment in history." Makarios held out his hands in blessing.

"I think that you exaggerate, sorry, Mr President. You're talking about a country that relies on handouts from America and the money that the Greek diaspora collects to help the Motherland." Clerides looked round the table for support.

"Greece has been a beacon of light for the world for over 2000 years. Are you saying that we are not worthy of our past heritage?" Makarios gazed at him with calm, cold, black eyes.

"I am a Cypriot. A Greek Cypriot. I do not blind myself to the real history of Greece. Since Ancient Greece, the Motherland has been captive of the Romans and Ottomans. The people have left in their millions. Now Greece is poor and who knows, Karamlanis might fall next week and we will find ourselves under another military regime. Like the Turks."

"Ah, the Turks. They too are poor. Can they sustain an army in Cyprus indefinitely? Already, the Americans have cut off funds. The Greek lobby in America is working hard. You will see."

"My immediate concern," Kyprianou cut short the confident Makarios, "is to get our people settled. It will be a long haul. Make no mistake. All this talk of political solutions and world opinion means nothing to them. They only wish to be housed, clothed and fed. When that is achieved, we can look at future possibilities. Agreed?"

"Perhaps I should establish my office in a tent among the ruins of the Presidential Palace. Let my flock see that I share their plight?" Makarios squared his shoulders and sat up straight in his chair as if ready to pose for the camera.

Murmurs of "no" came from all at the meeting. "It is not suitable for the President to make such a gesture. What about visiting ambassadors, UN officials?" Clerides opposed the suggestion.

"It would make for some very interesting photographs, don't you think? Imagine the effect on the Greeks of the world?" he replied with an enigmatic smile.

Kypriainou shook his head from side to side in disagreement. "We have enough tents to show the newspapers. Besides, they may think that it's a stunt to get world sympathy. It could backfire."

"Perhaps you're right. Oh, it's such a pity. So many things have gone wrong." Makarios leant forward as if in pain then sat upright and smiled at his colleagues. "Clafcos. Get on to that man Denktash. Speak to him. I can't bring myself to see him and the smug look on his face. You must persuade him that we mean no retaliation but we need to discuss the return of our people to their homes."

"What about the Turkish army? Can we get them to withdraw to, say, the Karpas Peninsula? That way, the Turkish Cypriots will still feel safe."

"We must be realistic. No? Tell him that we will negotiate. But insist that we will not surrender our land to the Turks. Always give a little but not enough to make them think that we will accept a Turkish state in our land."

"Rauf, uh, Denktash has always been in favour of partition. You know that he's a stubborn man and a born lawyer. He's no fool." Clerides grimaced.

"Then you must use your lawyer skills, dear Clafcos, to make him see that one day the United Nations will force Turkey to remove its troops. This is 1974 and Cyprus is not some backward African country. We are Greece. We do not bow to force." Makarios rubbed his hands together.

Leyla was the first to raise the subject. "Alexander? Have you decided what you will do now?"

"I still have Gareth looking after the business until April and I daresay he'd be happy to stay on longer. He seems to have fitted in well and he's making more money than he would anywhere else. What do you want me to do?"

"Years ago I thought of going to England. I wanted Julie to have a better, a freer life. It's still not easy for a woman here or in Turkey. I know things are changing, but...?"

"They are. Look at the number of women you see out on the streets now. And the number of headscarves, there're not so many. But the decision has to be yours."

"I know. But I can't bring myself to see a bright future here. We've had eleven years with almost nothing. What if Makarios gets the UN on his side again and we have to face more years of embargoes?" She screwed up her face at the thought.

"What about Famagusta? Now that it's in our hands, Turkey can ship in anything that's needed."

"Turkey is just about bankrupt. You've no idea how difficult it was for Mr Denktash to get enough money for us. Do you know what the inflation rate in Turkey is?"

"Pretty high from all accounts."

"Pretty high! Alexander, it's well over 50 per cent. That's the problem. Just keeping its troops here will be an incredible financial burden for a country that's already in dire straits."

"I still have my Australian dollars coming in. We'll manage. And what about the farm? Could you sell it? Who'd buy anything now?" He shrugged helplessly.

"I'll talk to Mr Denktash. The title to the farm will be mine now. Maybe he can find someone to rent it. Help me, Alexander, I can't decide what's best." Leyla's dark brown eyes pleaded.

"Let's wait and see. Give it till the end of summer. If it's no good we head for Australia. You'll like it. Not Pointsea, it's too cold in winter but up north, Queensland, that's the future in Australia."

"Is that where they have sharks?"

"Don't worry about sharks," he laughed, "the chances of seeing a shark are about ten million to one."

"What about the town called Alice? In the book I read, the girl meets her sergeant after the war and she goes to Australia. Somewhere north of Alice Springs?"

"That's some coincidence. Two sergeants. But Alice Springs is not for us. It's out in woop-woop."

"Where's woop-woop?" Leyla laughed as she said the two words.

"It's far away from anywhere and there's nothing, I mean nothing, anywhere near it. You'll see. Australia is huge."

"Forget Alice Springs then. Let's make plans for our wedding. I think Mr Denktash can do civil weddings."

"You're happy with that?" He wanted to be sure.

"Definitely."

Looking intently at her, Denktash measured his words. "We need you and everyone else to stay here. We'll also need people from Turkey to boost our numbers. If you and others leave, what will we have? A province of Turkey. The real Turks of Cyprus will disappear. I don't want that to happen."

Leyla stood, head down like a schoolgirl reprimanded for failing to support the hockey team.

Denktash continued, "I'll be making an announcement soon. It's time we made our position clear. We will declare ourselves to be The Turkish Federated State of Cyprus."

"What difference will that make?" She looked sceptical.

"It means that the Greeks will learn once and for all that this land, here in the north, is Turkish Cyprus. The old French airfield at Timbou will soon be open for flights to Turkey. Ercan will be our gateway to Turkey and hopefully Europe."

Shaking her head, a pessimistic Leyla grumbled, "Makarios will still block us. You and I know that the world continues to see him as President of all Cyprus. He'll keep us pinned down, one way or another."

"Maybe so, but we'll still be here long after he's dead. What does Alexander think? He's been a good help to us. Does he want to stay?" He peered hard at Leyla.

"He's left the decision to me. All he wants is to be with me and Julie, his family."

"And family is important. All of us Turks here in Cyprus are family. We too must stick together." He puffed out his ample chest.

"We've agreed to wait until the end of next summer. Spring will soon be here and that's when we'll get married. Can you do that for us? Marry us, I mean?"

"Of course. You won't have a traditional Turkish wedding? Your father and mother would have liked that."

"No. Alexander is not Muslim and although I was born Muslim I don't believe in all the ritual any more. Allah is God and that's enough for me. So a civil wedding will be fine." She gave him an unwavering look. "You understand?"

"So be it. Now see if you can organise some press releases that show us in a good light."

Cyprus 1975

"ALEXANDER?" Leyla looked over at Alex who was reading an old *Time* magazine.

"Yes, sweetheart?"

"The latest meeting between Mr Denktash and Clerides was a waste of time. As usual. Nobody will give an inch, especially Makarios."

"Well, you can't blame him. Makarios could never agree to a separate Turkish Cypriot state. That's why he won't meet Denktash. He knows he'd go down in history as a failure. Even Napoleon didn't lose France despite his hubris." He laughed.

"I know, but how long will this thing drag on? What about Julie's future and ours?"

"We'll decide soon, I promise. Seeing my mother last week, a body with no-one left inside, I still feel depressed. I can't get over it."

"Alexander, you loved your mother and did the best you could for her. I'm sure she knew that." She gave him a look of compassion.

"Well, there's nothing there for me any more. At least, while I spent the day in London, I was able to organise for you and Julie to come with me to Australia. If that's the decision we make."

Leyla reached out and took his hand. "Only a few weeks till the wedding and Julie's birthday. It's like a dream, isn't it?"

"The best dream I ever had. And it's just beginning." Alex kissed her softly on both cheeks.

Istanbul 1975

Alex held Julie's hand while Leyla searched the waiting crowd at Ataturk Istanbul Airport.

"There she is," an excited Leyla cried out.

A plump elderly lady stumbled forward and wrapped her arms around Leyla, kissing her repeatedly on both cheeks. Tears streamed down her face as she stepped back and took in the picture of her beautiful niece. "You...you look just wonderful," she wept. "Never in my wildest dreams could I have imagined this."

Julie went forward, tentatively, and was hugged so hard she protested. "Enough, Aunt Nafia. You'll squeeze me to death."

"Such a beauty. Like your mother, no, the eyes are different." She held both Julie's hands as she looked at her with brimming tears. "Are you happy?"

Julie turned her head and looked at Alex, smiling. "This is my father."

He took a step forward and was enveloped in the arms of Nafia, her head just reaching his chest. She pulled his head down and kissed him on his cheeks again and again.

"This is my husband." Leyla took hold of his hand.

Nafia began crying again. "I can't help it. After all these years."

Leyla put an arm around her aunt. "Come, we only have two hours. Let's sit down and have a coffee. There's so much to say before we leave."

"I'm sorry I couldn't come to the wedding. I wanted to be there. Even a simple ceremony. It's no good getting old." Her tear-stained face looked up at Leyla. Alex followed on as Leyla and Julie took an arm each and helped Nafia to the nearest coffee lounge.

The announcement was in Turkish and English.

"Turkish Airlines flight THY 84 is now boarding for Singapore with connecting flights to Melbourne, Australia, Seoul, Korea and Hong Kong. Passengers should proceed immediately to Gate 12."

HARRY BLACKLEY grew up in Scotland and graduated as a pharmacist in 1956. He served in the British Army, and in 1958 was awarded a commendation for outstandingly good service rendered in Cyprus.

Harry migrated to Australia in 1965 and worked in a number of pharmacies in Geelong, Victoria. The Mayor of the City of South Barwon 1986–1987, Harry gained a Bachelor of Arts degree at Deakin University, Geelong in 1981.

Together with his wife, Gina, Harry has travelled extensively in Australia and overseas.

Harry Blackley is currently president of the Australia Turkey Friendship Forum.